Leader Scott

The Life of William Barnes

Poet and Philologist

Leader Scott

The Life of William Barnes
Poet and Philologist

ISBN/EAN: 9783337055097

Printed in Europe, USA, Canada, Australia, Japan

Cover: Foto ©Raphael Reischuk / pixelio.de

More available books at **www.hansebooks.com**

THE LIFE OF

WILLIAM ·BARNES

POET AND PHILOLOGIST

BY HIS DAUGHTER

LUCY BAXTER

("LEADER SCOTT")

Hon. Member of the Academy of Fine Arts, Florence;
Author of " A Nook in the Apennines," " Renaissance in Italy," etc.

London

MACMILLAN AND CO.

AND NEW YORK

1887

RICHARD CLAY AND SONS,
LONDON AND BUNGAY.

PREFACE.

SOME men live before their age, others behind it. My father did both. In action he was behind the world, or rather apart from it; in thought he was far before his time—a thinker who may probably lead the next generations even more than his own. A great and deep student of the past, he drew from it inferences and teaching for the future.

The reading world know him chiefly for his poems —but the making of poems was but a small part of his intellectual life. His most earnest studies and greatest aims were in philology; but he was also a keen thinker in social science and political economy. For one hand to do justice to all the phases of a many-sided mind is not an easy task, and no one can feel more than I do my own inadequacy to it. Although perfectly aware that there are many others who would have made a worthier book in its literary aspect, yet when the work of biographer was given to me I gladly undertook it, knowing my father's wishes as to the spirit in which it should be done. He always had a great repugnance to be " written about," and though he so far recognised the possibility of a future necessity for his life to be given to the public as to collect and arrange notes, memoranda, letters, etc., as data for the writer, yet he always refused to commit this material into other hands. On my last visit to England I was one day walking with him in the garden at Came, and begged to be allowed to take his note-books back with me to begin writing his life, but he shrank from it, saying, " If it must be done, I would rather one of my own children should do it, but not now—leave me to my quietude while I live." Again, in his last illness, when speaking with his son, the Rev. W. Miles Barnes, he requested that if his life were written the facts should be simply and plainly adhered to, and not obscured or glossed over by " fine writing."

It is this wish that I have tried to fulfil, and have merely given the true events of a pure and simple life, in as plain and unglossed a manner as possible. No criticism of works has been attempted; indeed what has been done so fully and appreciatively by abler hands would be out of place, from a daughter —there is only a slight description of them, and as much of their inner story as I knew.

I regret that the Life could not have been written in a more joyous spirit whilst he was still with us, but as far as possible it has been my aim not to allow the writer's personality to overshadow the subject.

That the poet may, as far as possible, be his own interpreter, I have selected as illustrations those poems which seem to have expressed his feelings at the different epochs of his life. They are chosen entirely for their fitness, not their literary rank.

I must not neglect to render hearty thanks for assistance in sending " memories " and letters, to the Hon. Mrs. Williams, of Herringston ; Mrs. Tennant, Mrs. Colfox, and Miss Bayley ; to Prof. Palgrave, F.R.S.; Edmund Gosse, Esq. ; Thomas Hardy, Esq.; Charles Holland Warne, Esq.; J. S. Udal, Esq.; Daniel Ricketson, Esq., of New Bedford, Mass., U.S.A.; and the members of my own family.

" LEADER SCOTT."

(LUCY E. BAXTER.)

FLORENCE, 1887.

N.B.—Although I have been otherwise advised, I have decided to retain my signature " Leader Scott," which is better known than my own name to English readers, and was moreover chosen for me from family names by my father himself.

CONTENTS.

xii

CHAPTER V.

CHAPTER VI.

CHAPTER VII.

CHAPTER VIII.

CHAPTER IX.

CHAPTER X.

CHAPTER XI.

CHAPTER XII.

CHAPTER XIII.

CHAPTER XIV.

THE LIFE OF

WILLIAM BARNES

POET AND PHILOLOGIST

CHAPTER I.

RUSTIC CHILDHOOD.

No city primness trained my feet
To strut in childhood through the street;
But freedom let them loose to tread
The yellow cowslip's downcast head;
Or climb, above the twining hop
And ivy, to the elm-tree's top;
Where southern airs of blue-sky'd day
Breath'd o'er the daisy and the may.
      I knew you young, and love you now,
      O shining grass and shady bough !

Far off from town where splendour tries
To draw the looks of gather'd eyes,
And clocks, unheeded, fail to warn
The loud-tongued party of the morn,

B

I spent in woodland shades my day
In cheerful work or happy play,
And slept at night where rustling leaves
Threw moonlight shadows o'er my eaves.
     I knew you young, and love you now,
     O shining grass and shady bough!

Or in the grassy drove by ranks
Of white-stemmed ashes, or by banks
Of narrow lanes, in winding round
The hedgy sides of shelving ground;
Where low-shot light struck in to end
Again at some cool-shaded bend,
Where we might see through dark-leaved boughs
The evening light on green hill brows.
     I knew you young, and love you now,
     O shining grass and shady bough!

Or on the hillock where I lay
At rest on some bright holiday;
When short noon-shadows lay below,
The thorn in blossom white as snow;
And warm air bent the glist'ning tops
Of bushes in the lowland copse,
Before the blue hills swelling high
And far against the southern sky.
     I knew you young, and love you now,
     O shining grass and shady bough!

YOUTH AND FRIENDSHIP.

1801—1826.

THOUGH from henceforth the names of Barnes and Dorset will never more be divided, their connection is by no means a new one. It is supposed that Barnes in Surrey was the original home of the family, though there have been Barneses in Dorset for so many a long century, that it is said the first of the name came down in the train of king John when he visited his hunting lodge at Gillingham.

Gillingham still retains some sign of this royal occupation, for the king's manor and forest keep the old title of a " liberty," and the town has in its quaint Saxon bye-laws the remains of the ancient *sac* and *soc*. In old times its court, which was under the reeve seneschal of the lord of the manor (who in this case was the king), consisted of this seneschal and twelve men called the homage; its business was to hear causes of *sac* and *soc*, and to witness any deeds of the transfer of lands, and its rolls have been preserved intact from

the time of Henry VIII., from whom a certain William
Barnes, for service rendered to the king, had a grant of
land in 1540.[1]

The family must have taken root and flourished at
Gillingham, for in Elizabeth's reign they had also lands
at Bourton and Shearstock, where George, the grandson of William above mentioned, settled.   Three John
Barneses next follow in hereditary succession at
Gillingham, the first of whom was "head borough"
of the town in 1604.   After these comes Jerome (son
of the last John), who was the wealthiest man of the
line, for he owned three other estates, one in Hampshire, one at Todber, and a third at East Stower.   This
latter property fell to the share of his eldest son, John,
through whom in the third generation we reach John
Barnes, the grandfather of the subject of this memoir,
in whose time the last of the lands seem to have
passed out of the possession of the family.

The poet has told the story in "Gwain to Brookwell,"[2]
where, in describing a morning's drive, he says—

> "At Harwood Farm we pass'd the land
> That father's father had in hand,
> An' there in oben light did spread,
> The very grown's his cows did tread,
> An' there above the stwonen tun
> Avore the dazzlen mornen zun,
> Wer still the rollen smoke, the breath
> A' breath'd vrom his wold house's he'th ;

---

[1] The parchment of particulars for the grant of lands and
tenements in the parish of Gillingham to William Barnes is still
preserved in the Record Office.

[2] *Dorset Poems.*   Collected edition, p. 273.

An' there did lie below the door,
The drashol' that his vootsteps wore ;
But there his meate and he both died,
Wi' hand in hand, an zide by zide ;
Between the seame two peals a-rung,
Two Zundays, though they wer but young,
An' laid in sleep, their worksome hands,
At rest vrom tweil wi' house or lands.
Then vower children laid their heads
At night upon their little beds,
An' never rose agean below
A mother's love, or father's ho':
Dree little maidens, small in feàce,
An woone small bwoy, the fourth in pleäce.
Zoo when their heedvul father died,
He called his brother to his zide,
To meäke en stand in his own stead,
His children's guide when he wer dead ;
But still avore zix years brought round
The woodland goo-coo's zummer sound,
He weästed all their little store,
An' hardship drove em out o' door,
To tweil till tweilsome life should end
T'thout a single e'thly friend."

Thus John Barnes, who was left an orphan with
three small sisters, the eldest only sixteen years of
age, was no longer a landowner, but became a tenant
farmer. It is true he had the franchise on the title of
a freehold house and land which he possessed, but he
certainly did not live in it. The birthplace of his son,
our William Barnes, was "Rushay," a farm not far
from Pentridge; the family afterwards removed to the
"Golden Gate," a house which has since been pulled
down, and then John Barnes bought a small lifehold
house at Bagber.

The vale of Blackmore, in which all these houses of

his forbears were situated, is a kind of Tempé—a happy valley—so shut in by its sheltering hills, that up to quite modern times the outer world had sent few echoes to disturb its serene and rustic quiet. Life in Blackmore was practically the life of the seventeenth and eighteenth centuries, until the nineteenth was actually far advanced. The farmer helped to till his own land, his wife did not disdain to churn her butter and curd her cheeses, and the days passed in homely and rustic duties, which to our mind have a sweet old-world charm. The family meals were eaten in the oak-beamed old kitchen, where was the " settle and the girt wood vire," with the hams and bacon hanging overhead, and thus the ears of the boy would have been from infancy accustomed to the sound of that dialect, the love of which clung to him throughout life and was the basis of his fame, being the speech which most easily clothed his poetic thoughts.

Nothing can give so true an idea of the easy rustic life of goodwill and fellowship in this "old-world-vale of Blackmore" than the following description of "Harvest home," which was one of William Barnes's first contributions to Hone's *Year-book* not long after he had left Bagber, and was certainly a page out of his youthful life :—

" When the last load was ricked, the labourers, male and female, the swarthy reaper and the sunburnt haymaker, the saucy boy who had not seen twelve summers, and the stiff horny-handed old mower, who had borne the toil of fifty, all made a happy group; and went with singing and loud laughter to the " harvest home " supper at the farm-house, where they were expected by the good mistress, dressed in a quilted petticoat and a

linsey-wolsey apron, with shoes fastened by large silver
buckles, which extended over her foot like a pack-
saddle on a donkey. The dame and her husband
welcomed them to a supper of wholesome food, a round
of beef and a piece of bacon, and perhaps the host and
hostess had gone so far as to kill a fowl or two or even
a turkey which had fattened in the wheat-yard. This
pure English fare was eaten from wooden trenchers, by
the side of which were put cups of horn filled with beer
or cider. When the cloth was removed, one of the men,
putting forth his large hand, like the gauntlet of an
armed knight, would grasp his horn of beer and, standing on a pair of legs which had long outgrown the
largest holes in the village stocks, and with a voice
which, if he had not been speaking a dialect of the
English language, you might have thought came from
the deep-seated lungs of a lion, he would propose the
health of the farmer in the following lines :—

> " ' Here's a health unto our meäster,
>   The founder of the feäst ;
>   And I hope to God, wi' all my heart,
>   His soul in heaven mid rest.
>   That everything mid prosper
>   That ever he teäke in hand.
>   Vor we be all his sarvants,
>   And all at his command.'

" After this would follow a course of jokes, anecdotes, and songs, in some of which the whole company
joined, without attention to the technicalities of counter-
point, bass, tenor, and treble, common chords and major
thirds ; but each singing the air, and pitching in at the
key that best suited his voice, making a medley of big

and little sounds, like the lowing of oxen and the bleating of old ewes mixed with the shrill pipings of lambs at a fair."

It has been said that the minds of great men are influenced by their mothers; this was evidently the fact as regards William Barnes's earliest development of taste.

His mother, Grace Scott, of Fifehead Neville, was a woman of refined tastes and with an inherent love of art and poetry. She only lived long enough to give her son the very first leanings towards art, which the boy showed in drawings on wall and floor, with chalk or anything which would mark, but the seed planted in the infantile mind grew after her death, as his memories of her strengthened.

These memories showed her to him as a slight, graceful figure with delicate features, they recalled her voice as she recited to him passages of poems which she had learned, and they pictured to him a young mother leading him by the hand through the pleasant country lanes to where some figures in molten lead, representing the seasons, stood on the parapet of an old bridge near her old home at Fifehead. These rustic sculptures, from which he probably got his first idea of the inner meaning of art, disappeared when he was quite young.

Another recollection was of her holding him up in her arms to see a statue on the pillared gate of an old disused manor-house. This was possibly the original of " The stwonen boy upon the pillar "—

" 'ithin a geät a-hung
But fastened up and never swung.

Upon the pillar, all alwone
Do stan' the little buoy o' stwone,
'S a poppy bud mid linger on
Vorseäken when the wheat's a-gone,
An' there, then, wi' his bow let slack,
An' little quiver at his back,
Drough het and wet the little chile
Vrom day to day do stan' and smile.
And there his little sheäpe do bide,
Drough day an' night, an' time an' tide,
An' never change his size or dress
Nor overgrow his prettiness."

The young mother's taste for poetry no doubt threw
a poetic halo on all the scenes in the idyllic vale of
Blackmore, and gave the boy that key to the inter-
pretation of nature which never failed him. We can
imagine him dreaming along the banks of the Stour,
watching the water-lilies floating on its breast, where—

"The grey-boughed withy's a-leaning lowly
    Above the water thy leaves do hide ;
The bending bulrush, a-swayen' slowly,
    Do skirt in zummer thy river's side.
        And perch in shoals, O,
        Do vill the holes, O,
Where thou dost float, goolden summer clote."

Or else we see him as he sings—

" Wi' happy buoyish heart I vound
The twitterin' birds a builded round
    Your high-boughed hedges, zunny woodlands.
You gie'd me life, you gie'd me jay
    Lwonesome woodlands, zunny woodlands,
You gie'd me health, as in my play
    I rambled through ye, zunny woodlands."

Whether in fields or woodlands, the poet was in these early years imbibing at every glance the impressions which later found utterance in poesy. The boy sees and hears only the outward things, and vaguely feels that there is in them some mysterious meaning; the man whose soul is fully grown understands where the boy has wondered, and speaks, where the boy has been dumb.

Some of his memories show that in spite of incipient genius he was very boyish after all. He used to tell his children of a day when their father was a naughty boy, and steered his fleet down the river Stour. The fleet consisted of little William himself in a large tub, and the cat towed behind in a wooden bowl. The boy fearless in the spirit of adventure, and the poor cat with her back arched and her tail extended in the agonies of terror.

William Barnes's young mother used to grieve over him when a child, for he was small and delicate, and when she took his little tapering fingers into hers—he had the psychic hand—she would sigh, "Poor child, how will he ever gain his living?" for the hands were quite unfitted for the manual labour of a farm. To her ideas, which were bounded by ˌrustic life, this seemed the only thing possible. The village oracles in the shape of wise old women comforted her, for one said, "The boy is born with a silver spoon in his mouth," and another, more prophetic but less oracular, quoth, "Never you mind what he looks like, he'll get his living by learning-books and such like."

After his mother's death the boy remembered seeing in the house a pair of embroidered high-heeled satin shoes which had belonged to her, and which lingering in his memory gave rise to one of his most charming poems, *Grammer's Shoes*.[1]

And now a word of the father of William Barnes. It was from him he inherited the stern good sense and keen judgment which marked his dealings with men, and from him he took the ever unsullied good name of his forefathers. John Barnes was an upright old man with an honest, rugged face,[2] yet of the same character as that of his son.

We have little record of William Barnes's early education. He learnt his letters at a village dame's school, and afterwards went daily to Sturminster to attend a kind of endowed school for both boys and girls there. The master was a clever little man named Mullett,— usually known as Tommy Mullett. An old lady of ninety who went to the same school remembers that "little Willie Barnes," as his schoolfellows dubbed him, "excelled all the others and outstripped them by far. He was a general favourite, all the scholars, both boys and girls, would willingly, if necessary, have fought for

---

[1] In after years he tried to obtain these shoes as a relic, but in vain. The following letter was found among his papers after death :—

"Dear Barnes,

"I am very sorry I have never seen your mother's satin shoes since I have been in the house. Your Aunt Jane says there were such shoes, but cannot tell what became of them."

To his last day there hung upon the wall of the poet's room at the head of his bed two little old-fashioned samplers in needlework with the Lord's Prayer and some texts worked in faded silk. The memory of her whose hands had workèd them never faded.

[2] One of the poet's treasures was a portrait of his father by the Sturminster artist Thorne, which the rector, Mr. Lane Fox, once sent him as a present.

and protected him." From thence he was taken into the office of Mr. Dashwood, a local solicitor at Sturminster. The promotion (in the eyes of the school) was so great that it was the "general talk and wonderment of the pupils." Probably in those days writing was more considered than classics, for some remarkable specimens of his youthful skill in penmanship remain to us.

"It was a proud day for the young William Barnes when some time in the year 1814 or 1815 a local solicitor, the late Mr. Dashwood, entered the school and inquired if there were a boy clever enough with his pen to come and copy deeds in his office in a clerkly hand. The only lad who at all approximated to such a high description was Barnes, and the scene of testing him with the long quill pen and paper, and his selection by the lawyer, must have been one to which Mulready alone could have done justice."[1]

Being placed at the office desk so early in life proves that his school education could have been nothing but elementary, but this was of little importance, for the learning which made his name was no grammar-school knowledge, it was the result of a receptive mind which imbibed knowledge in any possible way it was presented to him. No school teaching gave him his faculty of penetrating to the root of every study which came in his way, it was the natural instinct of a keen and penetrative mind. If no schools existed such a mind would educate itself.

The office work at Mr. Dashwood's was on the whole more congenial to him than the labour of the farm, for

[1] Mr. Thomas Hardy, *Athenæum*, Oct. 16, 1886.

much as he loved the country and country-folk he did
not see in it the proper sphere of his life's labour.
His mind craved for intellectual development, and his
passion for books was insatiable. Out of office hours he
was always learning something, either classics from the
good clergyman, Mr. Lane Fox, who lent him books and
helped him in his difficulties, or music from the organist,
Mr. Spinney, who soon found out his talents in that
direction. He dreamed of a wider life, but his means
were limited, and the great world on the other side
of the sheltering hills of Blackmore was as yet unknown to him. However, he soon took his flight over
them, for in 1818 he left Mr. Dashwood and came
to the office of Mr. Coombs of Dorchester. Such was
his loveworthy character, that to the end of their
lives these two estimable lawyers were his firm
friends.

Thus at eighteen years of age began his connection
with the town, into the very heart of which he grew so
deeply, that when he passed away all wished to preserve
his memory in the streets where his loved presence had
been so familiar.

While fulfilling his clerkly duties, he and a friend,
William Carey (afterwards a lawyer at Calne), lodged
together in apartments above Mr. Hazard's pastrycook's
shop, and the spare time of the two young men was
passed in reading and studying. The rector of St. Peter's,
Mr. Richman, soon found out his new parishioner's passion for learning and kindly gave him evening lessons in
the classics, placing his library at Barnes's disposal, thus
laying the foundation of that classical knowledge which
underlies all his philological studies.

One day, not many months after young Barnes
arrived in Dorchester, he was walking up the High
Street, when the stage-coach drew up with a great dash
and clatter of the hoofs of steaming horses. William
Barnes paused to see the passengers alight. From the
seat behind the driver a family party descended ; first
a portly, matronly lady, and then the lithe figures of
two young girls, one of whom, a slight, elegant child of
about sixteen, sprang easily down with a bright smile.
She had blue eyes and wavy brown hair, and wore a
sky-blue " spencer," (which was the name our grand-
mothers gave to a jacket,) and at sight of her the incipient
poet felt his heart suddenly awakened to poesy. He
has often told his children that the unbidden thought
came into his mind " that shall be my wife." I do not
know how long it was before he discovered that her
name was Julia Miles, and that her father, an excise
officer, was to be quartered at Dorchester, but that the
first bright vision grew into a reality in his life is shown
by its stirring the water of the spring of poesy to its
first flow in some lines, " To Julia," published in the
Weekly Entertainer of the year 1820, p. 159, which we
give, not because they are in any way adequate to his
more mature genius, but because they are the very first
expression of his soul in verse.

"To Julia.

" When the moonlight is spread on those meadows so green,
  Which the Frome's limpid current glides by,
  To mark its calm progress, to gaze on the scene,
  May delight the poetical eye.

"To one who in some remote climate has pass'd
A long absence from all he loved here,
How sweet the first glance of the land, as at last
To his own native isle he draws near.

"But by far more delightful and sweet 'tis to gaze
On thy bright azure eyes as they dart
From under those tremulous lids their bright rays
And glances for glances impart.

"The smile of the Muse may the poet beguile,
Or the smile of gay Nature in spring ;
To others Dame Fortune's precarious smile
Its many enjoyments may bring.

"I would envy no poet with thy smile if blest,
Nor at Fortune's dire frown e'er repine,
For Muse's nor Fortune's smile ne'er yet possess'd
Aught to rival the sweetness of thine.

"Dorchester, 1820."

Several poems appeared from time to time in the
Weekly Entertainer, one of which, "Lines suggested by a
Barrow on a Dorchester Down," shows how very quickly
his style improved in freedom, and forms a landmark of
his first interest in antiquarian subjects.

These smaller efforts led to more ambitious flights,
and *Orra, a Lapland tale,* was published in 1822. As
the book has been out of print for many a lustre, and I
have never seen it, I can give no account of it. It is
possible that the first germ of the idea that prompted it
may have been the little Lapland love-song beginning—

"Thou rising sun, whose gladsome ray
Invites my fair to rural play,
Dispel the mist, and clear the skies,
And bring my Orra to my eyes."

This song, which appears in No. 366 of the *Spectator*, was ascribed to Addison's friend and Pope's rival, Ambrose Phillips. The name " Orra " in conjunction with Lapland would seem to point to William Barnes's knowledge of this poem, though his own was no doubt quite different in substance. That these early poems attracted a good deal of attention at the time, we gather from several complimentary letters addressed to him by admirers. One from a fellow poet, Mr.·Aubrey, presents him with a copy of his own poems; another tribute is from an appreciative fellow-townsman whose admiration is greater than his genius, for he addresses Mr. Barnes as " The Poet Laureate of Dorchester," and begins in this style, with plenty of capital letters :

> " Barnes, when thy muse inspires the song
>   My soul is all on fire,
> Thy numbers sweetly flow along
>   While I well pleased admire ; "

and so on for seven verses.

Orra was published by the help of the author's first efforts in wood engraving. A Mr. James Criswick was at the time printing a book named *Walks round Dorchester*, and the young Barnes engraved the following blocks for it :—

Lulworth Castle.	Bindon Abbey.
Milton Abbey.	Corfe Castle.
Cerne Abbey.	Arched rock at Lulworth.
Roman Amphitheatre.	Poundbury.

These first trials show a raw and unpractised hand, which however soon improved into a more forcible style, but they served their purpose in providing the artist with funds to publish *Orra* in 1822. It was illustrated with tailpieces engraved by himself. This talent for engraving seemed to some of his friends worthy of cultivation, and one of the most influential among their number sent specimens to the eminent London engravers, Scriven and Watson, both of whom wrote praising their promise, but advising further training in the technicalities of the art before adopting it as a profession.

The artistic training was not to be had just then, and he continued to work on by himself, obtaining several local commissions which were useful in giving him a more practised hand.

This time of his youth was the poet's *Vita Nuova* illumined by the faithful love which filled his whole life, for in 1822 he was betrothed to Julia Miles, and though they had very little prospect of worldly wealth, they had love and courage enough not to be dismayed at facing difficulties and working with and for each other. The future lay all in dreams, but the present was made delightful by happy walks and meetings, and by boating excursions on the Frome. One of these is very naïvely described in some impromptu verses on the back of a letter to Miss Miles, being evidently a recollection of a happy hour spent by them before he left Dorchester.

THE AQUATIC EXCURSION.

The glittering waters smoothly flow,
  The moon is shining bright,
My love is come that I may row
  Her up the stream to-night.

C

Lo ! in the rocking bark I stand,
　And Julia, by the river side,
To me holds out her lily hand
And quits, with trembling foot, the land,
　Upon the waves to ride.
Now put I out the bending oar
　The curling stream dividing,
And we, with light hearts, quit the shore
And o'er the waves are gliding.
Paris, I ween, the Trojan boy,
　When, in his bark so light,
He bore young Helen off to Troy
Did never feel a greater joy
　Than what I feel to-night.
Nor they who trade to mines of gold
E'er thought their barks so richly laden
As mine now seems while proud to hold
　My sweetly smiling maiden.
The stream is flowing wide and deep,
　We pause, and look around,
Where rocks are rising high and steep
Or hills with greenwood crowned.
Or where upon the verdant ground
　The wand'ring cattle feed,
Whose lowing is the only sound
　That passes o'er the silent mead.
Soft gliding we have sailed a mile,
　And Julia, sitting at the stern,
Looks on me with a winning smile
　And gently asks me to return.
I turn the boat, the stream is wide
And we are sailing with the tide
　And throwing down the oars to rest
I sit me down by Julia's side
　And press her to my breast.
She slyly turns the rudder round
　And in the bed of reeds we ride
And Julia she begins to chide
　" Away," says she, " away and guide

> The boat, or else 'twill run aground."
> I take the oar, on flies the boat
>   The boat strikes up the foam
> As o'er the glittering waves we float
>   And we again reach home.

These years of his life were also marked by a beautiful friendship, which I think must have had a great influence upon his mind and character. Edward Fuller—the Damon to his Pythias,—was at the time living in Dorchester, and the two had studied French together, walked and talked together on the banks of the crowfoot-studded Frome; and played music together in their bachelor rooms; for Fuller was a lover of the flute, and William Barnes at that time began playing the violin. Sometimes the duet became a quartette in the house of their mutual friend, Mr. Zillwood, who was a good violinist, while his sister Mary played well on the " Forte-piano," as it was called in those days.

When Barnes went to Mere, he and Mr. Fuller corresponded in French to keep up the language. He had also studied Italian, and began to translate Metastasio and Petrarch.

It is much to be regretted that his own letters are no longer extant, for if they were like Mr. Fuller's they would have thrown much light on his tone of mind at the time. His was the leading mind of the two, and Fuller looked up to him with an admiration which was very fresh and fervent. Fuller's letters are very charming, showing intellect, taste, and a delightful enthusiasm. An injustice or dishonesty excites him to a righteous wrath, a beautiful poem or picture calls forth ecstasies of appreciation.

Being almost exclusively thrown with such true
characters as Fuller, Carey, and the good rector, Mr.
Richman, who was one of the most simple-hearted
Christians that ever lived, it is no wonder that William
Barnes's first flight from the "Happy Valley" into the
world (not a very great world, it is true) did nothing to
quench his primitive faith in human goodness or to
lower his ideal of manhood. Not only was he "never
heard to say an unkind word of any human creature,"
as some of his old friends asserted, but he never
even thought ill of a living soul, and when the knowledge of evildoing in others was brought before him
unavoidably it caused him the deepest pain. To his
last day the thought of crime or injustice was to him
the saddest of all thoughts, and he invariably turned
away from such topics as soon as he could.

CHAPTER II.

THE POET TALKS.

WALKING HOME AT NIGHT.

Husband to Wife.

You then for me made up your mind
To leave the rights of home behind.
Your width of table rim and space
Of fireside floor, your sitting place,
And all your claim to share the best,
To guide for me my house, and all
My home, though small my home may be.

Come, hood your head; the wind is keen;
Come this side—here : I'll be your screen.

The clothes your mother put you on
Are quite outworn and wholly gone.
And now you wear, from crown to shoe,
What my true love has bought you new;

That now, in comely shape, is shown,
My own will's gift, to deck my own ;
And oh ! of all I have to share
For your true share a half is small.
Come, hood your head ; wrap up, now do ;
Walk close to me : I'll shelter you.

And now, when we go out to spend
A frosty night with some old friend,
And ringing clocks may tell, at last,
The evening hours have fled too fast,
No forked roads, to left and right,
Will sunder us for night or light ;
But all my woe's for you to feel,
And all my weal's for you to know.

Come, hood your head.   You can't see out ?
I'll lead you right, you need not doubt.

CHANTRY HOUSE.

1823—1834.

THE next great step in the life of William Barnes was made at the instance of Mr. W. Gilbert Carey, who shared his rooms in Dorchester, and was—next to Edward Fuller—his most intimate friend.

Carey had been educated in the school of a Mr. Robertson, at Mere in Wiltshire, and as the latter was now leaving that town, Carey very strongly recommended Barnes to take his old master's vacant post. As his chief object at this time was to make a home, this opening, although perhaps not what he would have chosen, seemed too opportune to be lost; there is no doubt that a schoolmaster had more chance of being able to support a wife than a lawyer's clerk. He proposed the plan to Julia Miles, and she, so far from discouraging the idea of his leaving Dorchester, urged it; and by way of doing her part in assisting the object, proposed taking pupils at Dorchester herself to grow accustomed to teaching, so that she could help him in after years. This idea she actually carried out, and was all the happier in the thought that she was doing something for him while he was away working for her sake.

The remove to Mere took place in 1823, and for the first few years his life was very much what it had been at Dorchester. The office was exchanged for the school, and all leisure time was employed in study, none of the known languages coming amiss to him. He writes in his note-book, " I took up in turn Latin, Greek, French, Italian, and German. I began Persian with Lee's grammar, and for a little time Russian, which, as being wanting in old lore, I soon cast off. I luckily had a French master as a friend in M. Charles Masson, an old French surgeon, who had heretofore been brought to England as a prisoner of war, and had married an Englishwoman of this neighbourhood, and was living at Mere. For some time I kept a diary of short daily notes in Italian or German for the sake of improvement in those languages.

" I did not at Mere wholly forget my love of art in drawing and engraving. In 1826 I cut some little blocks for Mr. Barter, a printer in Blackmore, and was mostly paid in bookbinding and cheese.

" In 1827 and 1828, I engraved some blocks for Mr. John Rutter, of Shaftesbury. Most of them—all I think but three—were for his *Delineations of Somerset*, published in 1829."

Many of these illustrations are very artistic, showing a firm hand and good *chiaro-oscuro*. Mr. Barnes had also a compact little copper-plate press, and tried his hand on metal, with as good success as on wood. So good, indeed, that he writes : " I had at one time an idle day-dream for a week or fortnight of trying my fortune as an engraver at Bath."

Much of his spare time was occupied in a sprightly correspondence with his future wife—letters in which there is a great deal of *naïveté* and independence on his side, and of archness and repartee on hers. In one he tells her he does not like the form of her D's, which are "round-backed creatures, reminding me of nothing but bent old age, and I cannot reconcile them to your graceful figure." To which she answers that "the thought of one's latter end is very wholesome for youth, and that as a moral warning to him she should continue to make the round-backed D's."

In one, dated March 6th, 1826, the lover takes his mistress to task for some little autocratic speech, saying : " Not content with governing my heart you want to regulate my thoughts also, I see, as you give me some advice about it in the latter part of your letter, and since you take that liberty I shall offer you some in return. As you are perfectly mistress of my heart, I advise you to be content with your power, and, not like an ambitious Prince, to endeavour to extend your empire beyond its proper limits. I suppose that after a time you would want to order when I am and am not to use my hand in writing to you, and my feet in coming to see you, which would be indeed 'binding me hand and foot.' "

The peculiarity of these old love-letters is that whenever he gives a reproof of any kind there is certain to be a salve to the wound, in the shape of some verses " To Julia " on the back of the letter. In the epistle just quoted is a poem, of which one verse runs—

When thou, my love, art far away,
  My hours are gloomiest and slowest ;
When near, an age would seem a day,
  Because the smiles that thou bestowest
Divest my heart of every woe.
  Then should I not wert thou mine own
Prize thee more, since thou alone
  I find canst soothe me so.

Four lonely years were passed by William Barnes at Mere. He lived in lodgings, the school being held in a large public room. At last he saw his way clear to the greater enterprise of taking a house, and the lot fell on a large old-fashioned building named Chantry House, which had once belonged to the Grove family— Charles II.'s friends. It stood near the church, and had before the Reformation been used as a chantry or priest's residence.

His first action as soon as the house was taken was to write to Mr. Miles, telling him all his hopes and prospects. The result is summarised in his diary in the words: " In 1827 I took Chantry House at Mere, and on a happy day—happy as the first of a most happy wedded life—I brought into it my most loveworthy and ever-beloved-wife, Julia Miles, and then took boarders."

And now begins an idyllic life, traces of which are found in his Italian diaries. These diaries, which he continued to the end of his life, merely consist of a few words every day, but by putting them together the whole life stands revealed ; the peaceful happiness of a love-enlightened home, the gradual expansion of a great and varied mind, the extraordinary versatility of taste, and never failing occupation, which made his life so full and complete. Chantry House was a roomy old Tudor building, with large oak wainscoted rooms, whose wide stone mullioned windows were entwined with greenery. It had a large garden and lawn, at the bottom of which ran a flowing stream, here widening into a pond overshadowed with trees. Here were trout and dace, and sometimes a flight of wild ducks or other water-birds would swim by. Near this pond was a favourite nook where William Barnes often came with his Petrarch in his pocket to pass a few happy leisure moments. The lawn was always mowed by his busy scythe, and he rose early in the spring and summer mornings to cultivate his garden. A frequent entry in the Italian diary is the word "*Zappando*" (digging), or "Gathered my apricots and took some to our friends." He remembered a wonderful Mayday when it was so very warm he had to throw off his coat while mowing, and sat down to rest under a hawthorn tree in blossom. Within a few hours a sudden change came, wild clouds fled before the wind, and the ground was soon covered with snow. Speaking of sudden changes of wind recalls a sagacious dog he had in a kennel in the garden of Chantry. In the night a great east wind arose and brought frost and snow with it. The dog, feeling the cold and damp in his face, got up, and by pushing with his fore-paws turned his kennel completely round with its back to the east. William Barnes found the dog enjoying the "lewth" and dozing comfortably next morning, the footmarks on the ground and sides of the kennel being witness to his sagacious labours.

In those days the young couple were poor, but very

happy; the school was increasing, and the husband spent his spare time in engraving, and as he tells us in his notes, he spent the proceeds of this work of his leisure in buying trinkets or plate for " Julia." At one time a silver butter knife would appear on the table, and when Julia took it up wondering, she would find engraved on the handle her own name and his entwined together. Once a pair of silver sugar tongs suddenly appeared in the sugar basin, and were received with delight by the young wife, and once a whole dozen of tea spoons ciphered, greeted her glad eyes.

The daily walks with her are chronicled, the favourite one being to a certain " Hinch's Mill," for since leaving the home of his boyhood the poet always had a predilection for a river bank. Sometimes the walk was changed for a nutting expedition with friends.

But the most astonishing thing which these monosyllabic diaries show us is the immense amount of literary work and study Mr. Barnes got through, which, when one reflects that it was only the result of spare hours, when the labour of the school was over, seems little less than miraculous. Culling a word here and there we find that in 1830 he read Buffon, Josephus, Burns, Ossian, *History of Spain*, German and Russian books, Theology, Gray's *Connection* (?), and Rollin's *Ancient History*. In 1831, *History of France*, Sallust, in Latin, Logic, Hutton's *Mathematics*, Welsh grammar and literature, Shakespeare, Hebrew, Blackstone's *Commentaries, Germany*. In 1832 and 1833, Greek authors, Ovid, Herschel's *Astronomy*, Herodotus, Hindustanee language and writings, &c., &c. These are only the books he mentions by chance, and probably do not include the whole of his readings.

Petrarch was his beloved poetical companion, and in a great measure that poet first formed his style in verse. In 1830 we find him writing sonnets both in English and Italian. The first were, "A Father to his Child;" written on May 26th, "Evening;"[1] May 28th, "The Overthrow;" May 31st, "The Storm" and "Esther interceding for the Jews;" June 1st, "The Dead Child," "Dreams."[2] The ones entitled, "I saw a sunbeam," "Let me awake," &c., came later in the year; speaking of these, Mr. Barnes writes: "Some of these sonnets have been printed in my little book of English poems (publisher, J. R. Smith, 1846), though some of my trials in verse in those days have worthily perished." As these sonnets almost all belong to the early period, and were rarely repeated after he began writing in dialect, it will be well to give a specimen of them.

THE TRIAL.

O that the stormy sea of life would lie
With calmer bosom through the darksome night
Of ignorance and fear, or that the light
Of truth would burst upon me from on high.
O that the haven of my peace were nigh,
Or that some guiding beacon were in sight.
Or that my Lord would listen to my cry,
And come and steer my erring vessel right.

Oh, feeble is my bark, my sinking soul ;
And great its load : while only error steers

---

[1] *Poems, partly of Rural Life*, p. 39.   [2] *Ibid* p. 88.

Bewilder'd o'er the wide and stormy main ;
And while for break of dawn I wish in vain,
A wild Euroclydon of hopes and fears
Blows hard and drives me onward on the shoal.

Besides these sonnets, several papers were published
in the *Dorset County Chronicle* under the *nom-de-plume*
of "Dilettante." They seem to be a free outpouring
of his thoughts on many subjects. Under the head of
"Linguiana" "Dilettante" traces many words from their
Greek and Latin origin. Under the heading "Cant,"
he pours out his soul in righteous wrath against hypo-
crisy, in every rank and class, sparing neither king
nor subject. In another paper he criticises the too
lenient treatment of criminals as contrasted with the
hardships of the honest poor. In another he celebrates
Petrarch as the prince of melancholy poets, and instances his many imitators of the Medicean period in
a style which proved that he himself was well versed in
humanist Italian literature. In an article on "Human
Progression" he arrives, through tracing the tendency
of all things to progress either in good or evil, at a
conclusion which, though now widely endorsed, was
then far in advance of the age. "It is not because
children are taught to read and write at the charity
schools that those establishments are so beneficial to
the state, but because they 'train up a child in the
way he should go,' and consequently obviate his progress in a wrong course. From the consideration of
the progressive habits of man we find the demoralising
tendency of very low wages, and the plan of paying the
poor a fixed sum per man out of the parish funds ; for
when a man knows that he cannot better his condition

by exertion, his exertion ceases. And if his daily
wants should leave an odd shilling in his pocket he
spends it in the alehouse, and becomes 'progressive'
in sloth."

As early as 1829 a little book was published by
Whittaker, entitled *An Etymological Glossary of English
Words of Foreign Derivation, so arranged that the Learner
is enabled to acquire the Meaning of many at once.* This
pamphlet was the first of a long line of valuable
publications on philology. In 1831 William Barnes
first appears in connection with the *Gentleman's
Magazine;* the papers of that year are : in June, "On
English Derivatives;" August, "On the Structure of
Dictionaries;" October, "Pronunciation of Latin;"
December, "Hieroglyphics." These all prove the
gradual turning of his mind to the study of language
as a science.

Nothing came amiss to him, from making garden
arbours and carved chairs for his wife, and dolls' cradles
and carriages for his children, to the turning out of
Latin epigrams, one of which 'was an epitaph on a
friend's child who died before it was named.

Here is an epigram in four languages on a man who
steals some books :—

> Se l'uom che deruba un tomo
> Trium literarum est homo,
> Celui qui dérobe trois tomes
> A man of letters must become.

The Romans called a thief a man of three letters,
from *fur*, a thief.

In 1830, April 26th, William Barnes chronicles a new

invention,—nothing less than a pair of swimming shoes. They consisted, I believe, in a flat sole, like that of a snow-shoe strapped on to the foot. This flat sole was furnished with hinges, so that in drawing up the foot the valves closed together in such a way as to offer no resistance to the water, but in pushing against the stream they opened wide, and formed a strong resistance. On Mayday the inventor went to find a suitable piece of water to try the swimming shoes, but unluckily the straps broke ; a second trial was no more successful, so on May 25th he had another pair made on a different principle, but a trial on June 2nd proved these also to be impracticable. Some more important inventions had better success, one was a quadrant of his own making, another an instrument to describe ellipses.

Again, we find him artistically painting the doors of Chantry House,—then making a receptacle for his engraving tools. He played the flute, violin and piano, —he invested in a turning lathe, and turned his own chessmen. His lathe stood in the unused coach-house, and turning was one of his favourite amusements. The border of the chess-board was carved by him in a raised scroll. The friend with whom he played chess could not bear to be beaten, although his wrath was soon over. It is recorded of this friend that when once he played with his wife—who being his pupil had the temerity to beat him—he took up board and men and threw them all together into the fire and departed. The wife rescued them, but the black marks must have been a continual reproach to the irascible man.

From the back of the house it was only a few steps to the church, and William Barnes spent a good deal of time practising on the organ. His skill in music, and a good baritone voice made him a valuable member of the church choir, and for a short time he became a voluntary organist there.

In November 1832, the diary records the writing of a sermon by him, and on November 18th we find the entry, "*Alla chiesa (il mio sermone predicato)*," probably his friend the Rector preached it. The Sunday diary generally contains the announcement "*suonavo l'organo.*"

At one time a dramatic company came to Mere, and Mr. Barnes went to the theatre every evening for a week, a course of diversion which had the immediate effect of exciting his genius, for on March 21st he began writing a farce which was finished in three days, and an epilogue was added on the 25th of the same month. The obliging actors at the little theatre must have taken it up *con amore*, for on the 31st the *Honest Thief* was acted on the stage at Mere, the author having added another scene to it. The dramatic inspiration did not stop here, for in April we read, " I wrote a comedy which I read to Mr. Larkham." This critic must have been encouraging, for on April 27th the comedy was acted at Wincanton, probably by the same company who performed the farce at Mere. The author went to see the first representation, but the diary sadly remarks, "*La premiera fu mal representata ;*" the first in this instance being the new comedy the *Blasting of Revenge; or, Justice for the Just,* which was followed by the farce already familiar to

D

the company. The characters announced in the play
bill are :—

Lord Ethelstead, Mr. Palmer.
Truman, his tenant, Mr. Murray (of the Salisbury Theatre, who
    has kindly volunteered his services for one night only).
Mrs. Truman, Miss Melville.
Fanny Truman (with a song), Mrs. Mulford.
Marwell (Lord Ethelstead's steward), Mr. S. Davis.
Henry Tuffman (sailor), Mr. Mulford.
Holden (sheriff's officer), Mr. McLean.
Tom Gauge (merry exciseman), Mr. Stanton

In May we find the author revising his comedies,
which were sent to London, but, I suppose, never acted
there, for no further mention is made of them, and the
dramatic impulse died a natural death.

The life of the young couple at Chantry House
was a pleasant social life—they were surrounded with
congenial friends, and we read of evenings at chess,
nutting parties, and excursions, Dorcas meetings for the
ladies, with admission to musical husbands at eight
o'clock, and pleasant little supper parties, such as,
" Went to Stourton to Mr. C., where we supped, and
talked of science and the fine arts."

October 30th, 1832, "Suonando gli strumenti di musica
col Sig. Cosens ed altri amici." Again, November 8th,
" Played musical instruments at the house of Mr.
Mitchell." This appears to have been a quartette club,
meeting periodically at the different houses of the
members. There was a good deal of music when
Edward Fuller came to stay with them and brought
his flute. A party was made for him on May-day,

and sweet sounds were discoursed in the oak-beamed room of Chantry. This stirred up William Barnes's universal inventive genius, and he wrote a valse and a song, "There's a Charm in the Bloom of Youth," which he set to music himself, modestly announcing it as " *Faccndo un aria per la mia canzone.*"

On February 6th he wrote a comic song called the " Hopeful Youth," and as the sonnet on " The Mother's Grave " was composed the same day it would appear that he worked off a melancholy impression by a lighter one, in the same way that Canova found relief when sculpturing tombs by modelling dancing Graces.

The aroma of peace and happiness in these halcyon days breathes out in the little word " *Felice,*" which, like a sigh of content, ends many a day's short but pithy chronicle. Only once or twice is a breath of sadness heard, such as, January 25th, 1832, " *Giorno triste e perduto,*" perhaps the student was disturbed from his books or the idea of a sonnet nipped in the bud by some commonplace interruption. In January 1834 is the touching sentence, " *Giulia malata—giorno triste.*" And soon after follows his own illness from the same low fever, and a long time of struggling through daily duties with an enfeebled frame. No writing, and but little reading, is done in this sad time.

The holidays ·were generally spent in visits to the parents or friends of Mrs. Barnes. In one of these excursions to Abergavenny, in June 1831, Mr. Barnes writes, " I was quickened with a yearning to know more of the Welsh people and their speech." He ascended the mountain Blorenge, went to Abergavenny fair, and talked Italian with a wanderer from the sunny South;

he went fishing, and "studying Welsh on the shores of
the Usk;" took a twenty-mile walk to Llangelly and
Nant-y-glo, and came home after all this with the germ
of a new lore, which was destined to influence the
whole of his career in literature. In the Welsh language he recognised the pure British unmixed with
Latin and other streams, and from it he got his
appreciation of the beauty of purity in language, which
his whole aim as a philologist was to attain to. He
would have English retain its pure Saxon just as Welsh
had kept its British, and if his dreams were Utopian,
he was, as far as lay in his power, true to his theories.
The Saxonising of his style in English only began in
later life, when his researches had taken him deep into
the origin of Teutonic speech.

His first Welsh studies resulted in several papers,
which appeared in the *Gentleman's Magazine*, such as in
1832, "The Identity of National Manners and Language," "Songs of the Ancient Britons," "Origin of
Language," and "The English Language."

Besides these philological papers were several archæological ones on interesting buildings in Dorset, illustrated with his own woodcuts, such as, May 1833,
"Napper's Mite, Dorchester;" June, "Silton Church;"
July, "Sturminster Newton Church," and "Nailsea
Church;" September, "Chelvy Cross," &c. On the
occasion of making the sketch for Sturminster Church
Mr. Barnes stayed with the rector, Mr. Fox, and this
day of his return to his childhood's home is marked
"*Felice*," though he half sadly remarks that the
"inhabitants did not recognise him."

One of the most valued of his Mere acquaintances

was General Shrapnel, of Puncknowle House, a great mathematician, who was occupied at the time in the invention of his weapon of war the "Shrapnel shell." Mr. and Mrs. Barnes sometimes visited him, and the former was, I believe, useful in aiding some mathematical calculations connected with the shell. An *Essay on the Advantages of the Study of Mathematics*, published by William Barnes in 1834, was dedicated to General Shrapnel. These literary labours were alternated with engraving several wood blocks for Mr. Phelps's *History of Somerset*, which proved to be unprofitable work, for he says "poor Mr. Phelps never finished his too great undertaking, and I never received for my woodcuts even a copy of the *History*."

It was in the years 1833 and 1834 that William Barnes wrote his first poems in the Dorset dialect, which were some eclogues published in the *Dorset County Chronicle*, with the following classical titles:— *Rusticus dolens* (now entitled "The Common a took in"); *Rusticus gaudens* ("The Lotments"); *Rusticus emigrans* (probably "The House Ridding"); *Rusticus domi* ("Father come Home," March 1834); *Rusticus rixans* ("The Best Man in the Vield); *Rusticus res agrestes animadvertens* ("Two Farms in Woone"); *Rusticus procus* ("A Bit of Sly Courting").

These attracted much local notice, and were the occasion of some correspondence in the paper. The same train of thought and sympathy with the honest labourer inspired these, which we see in the articles on "Leniency to Criminals," and "Human Progression," mentioned above; and the idea of putting the expression of these sentiments into the speech and person of the labourer himself, was an artistic way of emphasising it.   From this time the poet more frequently wrote in Dorset than in English, finding that it more fitly clothed the simple life which he chose to portray.

CHAPTER III.

LEARNING

HEAVENLY source of guiltless joy,
  Holy friend through good and ill,
When all idle pleasures cloy,
  Thou canst hold my spirit still.

Give the idle their delights,
  Wealth unblest, and splendour vain ;
Empty days and sleepless nights,
  Seeming bliss in real pain.

Take me to some lofty room
  Lighted from the western sky,
Where no glare dispels the gloom
  Till the golden eve is nigh.

Where the works of searching thought
  Chosen books may still impart
What the wise of old have taught,
  What has tried the meek of heart.

Books in long-dead tongues, that stirred
  Living hearts in other climes;
Telling to my eyes, unheard,
  Glorious deeds of olden times.

Books that purify the thought,
  Spirits of the learned dead,
Teachers of the little taught,
  Comforters when friends are fled.

Learning! source of guiltless joy,
  Holy friend through good and ill,
When all idle pleasures cloy,
  Thou canst hold my spirit still.

Poems of Rural Life, 1846.

41

THE TEACHER.

1835—1849.

In the beginning of the year 1835, William Barnes began to think of change, feeling that a wider sphere would be beneficial to his school. One of his note-books says, "Mere was out of the way for pupils, and I always yearned for Dorset and Dorchester; and as I had strengthened my teaching power, and was told by friends at Dorchester that there was then an opening for a boarding school, I put my hopes of after life in work at that place, to which I returned in 1835, and was happy and thankful with an income on which I brought up my children."

As soon as the summer holidays began in June, several days were occupied in packing furniture, settling accounts, and bidding friends farewell. The two sonnets, "A Garden," and "To a Garden—on Leaving it,"[1] were both written in this month; the latter is a tender expression of his regret on leaving

[1] Sonnets xxi. and xxii. in *Poems, partly of Rural Life,* 1846.

Chantry House, where such happy days had been spent.

> Sweet garden ! peaceful spot ! no more in thee
>   Shall I e'er while away the sunny hour.
> Farewell each blooming shrub and lofty tree ;
>   Farewell the mossy path and nodding flow'r ;
> I shall not hear again from yonder bow'r
>   The song of birds or humming of the bee,
> Nor listen to the waterfall, nor see
>   The clouds float on behind the lofty tow'r.
>
> No more at breezy eve or dewy morn
>   My gliding scythe shall shear thy mossy green ;
> My busy hands shall never more adorn,
>   My eyes no more may see this peaceful scene.
> But still, sweet spot, wherever I may be,
>   My love-led soul will wander back to thee.

The Italian diary of June 26th, sighs "*Andammo da Mere a Dorchester, Dio ci benedica,*" and in his "*Memoranda for his Life*" he speaks of this change as follows :—

"June 26th, 1835. We left Chantry House and Mere, and came to Dorchester, to settle in a house which we had taken in Durngate Street.

"Boys came in very hopefully, and we had soon a fair and fast-filling school, though we did not feel the happiness of the change in the strait-pent house instead of the old Chantry House with its fine open garden.

"The little I had learnt of Hindustani or Persian now became handy, as one of my first pupils was Mr. C. V. Cox now General Cox, the son of the Rev. C. Cox of Cheddington, who came to read with me for Addiscombe.

"At Dorchester I rarely took up the graver, though after a while I began to string some more Dorset rhymes.

"Some may wonder how far I could work faithfully with my charge of a school, while I gave my mind so far as I did to writing or other kinds of knowledge than those which were needful for the day in the school-room. It was my way at Mere as well as at Dorchester to give the boys every morning a sentence or two of dictation and then to discourse on the substance of it, in words and matter, and this quickened me to study sundry subjects that I might keep ahead of the boys.[1]

"It was my way again through the school months to pass much of my time and evening in a study within sight of the playground or within call of boys or ushers,

[1] The Rev. J. B. Lock, an old pupil of Mr. Barnes, and now Senior Fellow, Assistant Tutor, and Lecturer in Mathematics and Physics in Gonville and Caius College, Cambridge, thus describes Mr. Barnes's method : " I was sent to his school in South Street when about eight years old, and I can still picture to myself the old school-room in which once a week Mr. Barnes used, punctually at nine o'clock, to give to the whole school a lecture on practical science. His lecture on electricity—he gave us some sharp shocks with a frictional machine—on the physical geography of the Alps, on the steam-engine—he showed us a model which his son, Egbert Barnes, had made—on bridge building—he had a model arch in wooden bricks—I can still remember in detail. We had each, big and little, to write an abstract of the lecture in the most approved modern fashion. It seems worth recalling that such lectures were given in Dorchester thirty years ago, just such lectures as are now given in most of the great public schools, in which such subjects were still un-taught much less than thirty years ago. These lectures of my old master were as wonderfully adapted to his audience, as they were clear and accurate in substance."

and so I worked even against the irksomeness of lone-some confinement, and I found the thoughts and work of the Dorset idylls refreshen rather than weary the mind."

It was aptly remarked by the Rev. E. M. Young, at the "Barnes Memorial Meeting" in Dorchester in December 1886, in reply to a proposition that a scholar-ship or some educational memorial of him would be the fittest tribute, "that though he was a man to whom numerous old pupils owed a deep debt of gratitude, yet he, Mr. Young, could not help thinking that fifty years hence Mr. Barnes would not be remembered as a school-master but just as a poet."

This is, I believe, perfectly true, but as the part of his life which was given to teaching was a very im-portant part, both in its influence on others, and on the development of his own mind, as well as on his career as a philologist and man of science, I propose to devote a chapter to the poet schoolmaster.

It was part of his character to be entirely thorough, and so, though he may have liked writing poems better than teaching boys, he gave his whole mind to make the teaching the best that could be done. It was also part of his poet nature to see the inner meanings of things, and so his conception of education took in more than mere putting of facts and rules into the boys' brains, it meant training them to be reasoning and reasonable men. Of course with these views he was not content to follow merely the curriculum of ordinary schools, nor to confine his teaching to ordinary school-books. He had methods of his own and compiled his own books, many of which were published at his personal expense. I have mentioned his *Etymological Glossary*, published in 1829. *A Catechism of Government in General and that of England in Particular*, was printed by Bastable of Shaftesbury in 1833. This was a useful book to ground the minds of future politicians, though not a branch of knowledge usually taught in the school-room. In 1841 a small book named *Investigations of the Laws of Case in Language*, was printed by Longman and Co., and Whittaker and Co. This was an amplification of an article " On the Laws of Case," which came out a short time previously in the *Gentleman's Magazine*. In it he deduces certain fixed laws which are the same in all languages, he brings his proofs from a comparison of fourteen tongues, and which when understood greatly facilitate the study of foreign languages as well as classic lore. This little book was the germ of the great philological grammar and almost entirely forms the treatise on cases of nouns in that remarkable but little known work. One of Mr. Barnes's former pupils then passing through one of the universities writes on December 1842 :—

My Dear Mr. Barnes,

I received your kind letter with the Mnemonic verses last month, for which I have to tender you my best thanks, for indeed I have found them of great use.

Having shown your very elegant treatise, " Laws of Case," to the Rev. H. Cope (my master), whose brother is Professor of Mathematics at Addiscombe, he so much approved of it as to introduce it to the notice of one of the highest classical men of the time, a Dr. Tate, Head Master of Richmond Grammar School (author of several classical works), and Canon Residentiary of St. Paul's, who requested that I would let him have a copy of it —fortunately I had two and consequently spared him one—he returned a letter to Mr. Cape stating his opinion, of which the following is a copy :—

"Mr. Barnes is a very ingenious and acute-thinking man, and with those grammarians who build grammar on a basis of logical or metaphysical origin, ought to enjoy a very high rank of esteem. I, who consider sensible objects with material qualities and local relations, as at the bottom of all language apparently so, and the names of such things as transferred by the necessity of the case to indicate the objects and notions of the mind, of course see $\nu\sigma\tau\epsilon\rho o\nu$ $\pi\rho\acute{o}\tau\epsilon\rho o\nu$ (I don't know whether you can understand my Greek writing?) in Mr. B's line of investigations; and if it had been our lot to live in the same neighbourhood much friendly discussion would have arisen when we met."

Another useful book with which Barnes endowed his scholars in the same year, 1841, was an *Arithmetical and Commercial Dictionary*, containing easy explanations of commercial and mathematical terms, and important articles of commerce, of all arithmetical rules and operations, and a set of tables. No pupil in Mr. Barnes's school could perform arithmetical problems without knowing the why and wherefore. In 1842 Whittaker brought out the *Elements of English Grammar*, which is certainly unique amongst schoolbooks. His objects in writing it were "to keep up the purity of the Saxon English language, to give pupils a comprehension of the principles of the English derivation, and to offer teachers a grammar so scientifically based, as to prepare the pupil's mind for further philological studies." The grammar has never, · I believe, been adopted by other schools, though Mr. Barnes found it very successful in his own. The great difference between his arrangement of cases and classification of verbs would render its introduction almost as subversive as the conversion of the English money and measures into the decimal system, yet if once accomplished the practical benefit would be great. For instance, what would the student of Murray say to having his three cases multiplied into nine? Here they are: nominative, vocative, genitive, possessive, dative, accusative, originative, local, and instrumental; add to these a further list of mixed or double cases in seven conjunctions. Lindley Murray's three simplify the boy's task of learning, but do not train his discrimination, nor are they reasonably philological.

In 1844 he printed two useful little books, *Elements of Perspective*, and *Exercises in Practical Science*.

Next it appeared to him that the geography as taught in schools was too bald and bare, containing none of that human interest which the study of the world and man should contain. Consequently in 1847 he published his *Outlines of Geography and Ethnography* for youth. This was printed for him by Mr. W. Barclay, of Dorchester, and certainly the student who learns from it will gain some wider ideas of geography than names of places and their situations on the map, for it is at once a physical and descriptive geography, besides giving a great deal of ethnography.

And now a word as to William Barnes's method of teaching. His theory was that minds should be trained and not crammed; that the school curriculum ought to contain the germs of all the knowledge which the man would require in after life. He held Mr. Herbert Spencer's views as to the importance of science in all branches of political life, and also its value in developing the reason and observation, which alone make knowledge practical — this was long before Herbert Spencer had written his *Essays on Education*, but he was not the first great thinker of whose views Barnes was a prototype. His object was to render science not only comprehensible, but interesting, so as to induce the boys to wish for more knowledge. This was done by a daily lecture, generally taking the first hour of the day. The subject was varied every day of the week, and in turns botany, natural history, physics, chemistry, electricity, and geology, were all discussed. The lecture (which combined dictation, orthography, and composition, in such a way as to make them all interesting) began with a short dictation; if on botany or natural history, the distinctive marks of an order or class formed the subject. Then some flowers or specimens were shown, and the boys had to find the distinctive marks of the class, or to reject the specimen as not apposite. This trained their discrimination; the master then gave a lecture on the subject, and the boys were required to take notes, and write them out in a clear form as a composition for one of the daily tasks. The walks were made both inter-

esting and profitable by following out the morning's
lesson. Sometimes the boys vied with each other who
should find the greatest number of "Cruciferous" or
"Composite" flowers; other days they went armed with
hammers and bags for a geological expedition, finding
specimens of *terebratulæ, echinus,* or *belemnite* in the
chalk cutting of the then new railway. These were
very delightful walks, and it was a pleasant thing to
see the master and his wife, and now and then a little
daughter, walking calmly through the heaths and lanes
with a skirmishing party of boys around them. First
one would rush up with a flower he did not know, to
ask its name and order; then another would come to
display with great pride a new butterfly. Sometimes
they saw very interesting things: one afternoon a boy
threw a stone at a bird on the wing, which being
stunned by the blow came fluttering down in circlets to
the ground, when another bird, probably its mate, flew
hastily to its assistance, and helped it to return to a tree.

A favourite walk was to Yellowham Wood, where the
boys climbed the steep banks of yellow sandstone to
explore the sandmartin's holes; and in the spring there
was a great deal of tree climbing in search of birds'
eggs. *A propos* of this was a standing joke about the
boy who spoke the truth.

"Come down, Blair," said the master to a boy on the
branch of an elm, "we are going on now."

"I'm coming directly, sir," cried Blair as well as he
could speak, with his mouth full of linnet's eggs. He
had hardly said the words when the branch cracked,
and the boy came suddenly down with a good deal of
clutching at saving branches in his descent.

E

As soon as William Barnes found that his pupil was not hurt, he remarked dryly, "You kept your word, Blair; I like a boy who speaks the truth."

"I did not mean to do so this time, sir," replied the boy rubbing himself ruefully, but in spite of his intentions the name of "the truthful one" stuck to him throughout the school.

The half-holidays were spent in cricket-playing in the summer, and "hare and hounds," or practice with the leaping-pole over the brooks and runlets of the water-meadows near the Frome, in the winter. Sometimes there were merry picnics to the hills of Maiden Castle, the old British earthwork, or to the green woods of Skippet, near Bradford. Or private theatricals took place in the school-room, where a lisping Henry IV. exclaimed excitedly:—

> "Now ith the winter of our dithcontent
> Made gloriouth by thith thummer thun of York."

And cried with a wild flourish of sword—

> "A horth, a horth, my kingdom for a horth."

And where a hoydenish Queen Anne, very much impeded by her unaccustomed skirts, came to grief at "What shall I do, what shall I say?" and, after repeating this distressed query, peering everywhere for inspiration, called in an agonised voice to the prompter, "Why don't you tell me? what a duffer you are;" all of which characteristic by-play delighted William Barnes, who sat laughing among the audience at finding high comedy in a Shakespearian tragedy.

But this is a digression, we will return to the lectures. There were of course in such a school as this all kinds of collections—birds' eggs, butterflies, fossils, dried flowers, &c. The chemistry, physics, and electricity lectures were always illustrated by experiments. Some of the "old boys" have since turned out eminent men of science, and bear testimony to the good fruit borne by these lectures. One of his former pupils, now a clever naturalist, writes: "I became a pupil of his forty-three years ago, and from the first day of our acquaintance to the end of his life we were friends, with never in pupilage or after it, any break either in the matter or manner of our friendship." [1]

William Barnes's system of moral training was as unique as it was successful. No obligatory tasks, no caning (except solely, and seldom, for lying), no restrictions and restraints, except only the natural consequences of wrong-doing. If a boy had done badly it lay entirely with himself to retrieve his position. The only visible register was an invention of the master's own, called the "topograph." It consisted of a large flat box in which lay a board pierced with holes and painted in lines of colour—white, red, blue, &c., and ending with black. The boys' names were placed at the top of the board opposite each file of holes, and according to his want of diligence the peg was moved down, only to be put up again on the completion of a voluntary task. Of course if the boy were too careless to redeem it he could leave it, but a low standing was a kind of disgrace which they all felt

---

[1] *Dorset County Chronicle*, November 25th, 1886.

so keenly, that generally the boys lost no time in re-instating themselves. To have one's peg in the "blues" caused the loss of a holiday; that a peg reached the "blacks" was a thing almost unheard of.

This method was proved by practical use to be more efficacious than all the canings and impositions in the world. The boy was kept up to his best—by, first, his conscience, secondly, his own interest, and thirdly, by fear of falling in the opinion of others, three motives which are all powerful. The conscience being the true ruler of the soul, moral influence of the mind, and self-interest governing the worldly career.

A more successful school, as far as regarded the moral and mental welfare of the boys and the cordial affection between them and their masters, could not exist. Boys left and went into the world abroad or at home, but as soon as they won any honour, their first care was to write to their master and thank him for it.

One who had passed first of all England for the Indian Civil Service—thanks to William Barnes's preparation in mathematics and Hindustani—rose to be a judge, and the same post which brought the news to his parents brought also a letter of loving gratitude to his master.

Another Hindustani pupil, now General . . . . getting promotion fast in the wars of Goolab Singh, sent home to his father a box of antelopes' heads, and other trophies of the chase, with injunctions to "send some of them to his dear friend and tutor." As a proof of William Barnes's power to win the love of his pupils we cannot more fitly close this chapter than by the insertion of a · letter which the news of the poet's death brought from an old pupil in South Africa.

"I have to thank some kind and thoughtful individual for sending me the *Dorset County Chronicle* of October the 14th, containing a notice of the death of 'our Dorset poet.' I say our poet, for, to quote the concluding lines of one of Barnes's latest and cleverest poems with slight alteration,

> "'For he in childhood's days, of playful hours,
> Belonged to us, and henceforth he is ours.'

My earliest recollections of Dorsetshire and childhood are associated with my first schoolmaster. How well I remember being carried on rainy mornings on the back of one of my father's old servants down the narrow ill-paved South Street, to the school near the Alms' Houses; there, I, together with many others now scattered far and wide, were taught. How we reverenced him! and yet how playful and kind he was in his manner with children. I think his sympathetic nature was touched by them, even more than flowers and blossoms, which he has painted so well, and which live again in many of his very charming poems, witness "The Zummer Hedge" and "Come out o' Door, 'tis Spring, 'tis May." Leaving the old school-room, in South Street, for Dr. Penny's "down to Crewkarne," and to Bath and onwards, into the world of an active and anxious life, we did not meet again. At the close of a hot steamy day on the east coast of South Africa I received from a friend *The Poems of Rural Life in the Dorset Dialect*, and my whole nature was so touched and refreshed by the word-pictures of schoolboy scenes, so cool and sparkling in contrast with my present surrounding, that I could not refrain that night from writing to the poet and thanking him, I daresay in a very gushing style, for the unexpected and very great treat I had enjoyed. A few months afterwards I received a very characteristic and kindly reply, in which, in memory of the old school, he called me " his mind's child," stating he was happy in affording me pleasure by his descriptions of meadows, and streams, and Dorset downs. After a few years I got another letter from him, in reply to one I had written, and any Dorset man will understand how they are prized and kept.

*   *   *   *   *

I had intended to have sent a wreath of South African "everlasting flowers" to be placed upon his grave, but missed the opportunity, and instead offer my heartfelt tributary words to the memory of the greatest man Dorset has produced

F. ENSOR,
Surgeon, South Africa.

CHAPTER IV.

SONNET TO DEAD FRIENDS.

DEPARTED spirits, living far away ;
Oh, could ye hear my whispers where you dwell,
Or could my prayer, like magic spell,
Bring back your beaming forms to where I stray,
How would I meet you, when the garish day
Had left calm moonlight in the wood and dell,
And talk with you of other times, and tell
The joys and sorrows of this mortal clay.

But ye are far away, no more to tread
The busy ways of men, or to be seen
In lonely path, or laughter-sounding room.

A gulf between the living and the dead
Is fix'd for ever, and our Lord has been
Our Resurrection only through the tomb.

LITERARY AND SOCIAL LIFE.

1839—1841.

WE must now return a few years, and trace the literary life of William Barnes during these first years of his residence in Dorchester, and read the thoughts which "freshen his mind" in the retired little study where he could look on the boys at play, but only hear their voices in a distant echo which did not interfere with his flow of thought. The house which he and his wife found so "strait-pent" after dear old Chantry with its gardens, was no longer large enough to hold, the increasing numbers of the school, and, in 1837, they removed to a roomy old house in South Street which had a two-storey annex at the back forming spacious school and play-rooms. The narrow house in Durngate Street seems to have cramped not only William Barnes's personal freedom but his genius, for no literary work of any kind is recorded during the two years he lived there.

In 1837 he put his name on the books of St. John's College, Cambridge, as a ten years' man, and he again began to write for the *Gentleman's Magazine*, the first

article being one on " Roman Numerals," in December
of that year ; this was followed at intervals during the
next year by papers on "Æsop" (June 1838), "On
some Etymologies" (July 1838), and "On the so-
called Kimmeridge Coal-money." This last paper was
à propos of an archæological problem which William
Barnes thought he had solved. Excavations were
being made in the Isle of Purbeck, and the beds of
oolite and slate had made some most interesting yields
of sea-saurians, such as an ichthyosaurus, and the
gigantic fin or swimming paddle of a plesiosaurus,
besides multitudinous small fish and shells. In one
part of the Kimmeridge clay stratum, however, antiquities of another kind were found by hundreds—
certain whorls of black shale, with square holes in the
centre. These circles were of varied circumference, but
generally about half an inch in thickness, the edge being
bevelled off to an acute sharpness. Dorset geologists
and archæologists (among whom the most earnest were
William Barnes and his two friends, Mr. Charles Hall
and Mr. Charles Warne, both enthusiastic collectors)
promulgated many theories, which brought other archæologists from London on the scene to add more theories.
Some thought they were money, and that the current
coin was carried about strung on strings and hung on
the man's shoulders as the savage carries his cowries ;
others suggested weapons of war—some less scientific
declared that the whole thing was an accident of
nature, and that it must be the tendency of that
especial shale to split in a circular form. William
Barnes came down on all these vague ideas with a
practical one that they were lathe turnings, and con-

sequently not pre-historic at all. He proved that the pieces thrown away from a modern turner's lathe were precisely of the same shape, and if people doubted the antiquity of a turning machine, had they not the potter's wheel to testify that the principle of the wheel for the formation of circular objects was not unknown to the earliest ages?

In those days no Dr. Schliemann had discovered the hundreds of similar whorls at Troy, nor had his theory of spindle weights been thought of as an explanation, though it is not really much more probable than the Kimmeridge money theories.

During the next three years the following articles from the pen of Mr. Barnes appeared in the pages of the *Gentleman's Magazine*.

February, 1839 : " On the Battle of Penn."

May : " On the Roman Amphitheatre at Dorchester," (with a woodcut by the author).

June : " Hindoo Shasters."

August : " Phœnicians."

September : " Hindoo Pooran and Sciences."

January, 1840 : " On the Hindoo Fakirs."

May : " On the Dorset Dialect compared with Anglo-Saxon."

November, 1840 : " The Old Judge's House at Dorchester," (woodcut).

February, 1841 : " Education in Words and Things."

" Fielding's House at Stower," (woodcut by author).

May, 1841 : " Goths and Teutonics."

December, 1843 : " The Laws of Case, and Harmonic Proportion in Building."

This is a respectable amount of work for a schoolmaster's spare hours, when we take in all the school-books mentioned in the last chapter and the poems in the Dorset dialect which were quickly growing into a volume in his desk. The varied character and depth of the articles indicate a very great amount of reading. He was no doubt led to the Hindoo subjects by his readings in Oriental languages with his old friend Major Besant, through whose kindness he had studied Hindustani some years before. The major, who had spent many years in India where he had acted as interpreter to the British Army, was a very fine Oriental scholar, and frequently came to spend a few hours in W. Barnes's study deciphering the laws of Manu and other Sanskrit writings. From Hindustani they went on to Persian and Arabic readings, the imaginative Persian tales having a charm for the poet, though so much less serious than the Sanskrit literature.

The article on " Harmonic Proportions " was a result of his studies in harmony and colour. The comparison of the chord and scale in music, with the chord of three primaries and scale of half tones, in colours, led W. Barnes to apply the same principles to form.[1] So much truth did he find in his discovery that he always had his pictures framed and books bound in Harmonic Proportion, and the result was certainly pleasing. The following letter to the writer of this memoir, though written at least thirty years later, will explain his theory and its practice in his own words :—

" As to Harmonic Proportion, three quantities are in

[1] He wrote a letter to the *Art Journal* on the same subject in January, 1855.

Harmonic Proportion when the 1st bears the same proportion to the 3rd, as the difference between the 1st and 2nd bears to the difference between the 2nd and 3rd. 6, 3, 2, are a harmonic threeness, for the 1st, 6, is three times 2 (the third) and the difference between 6 and 3, is 3, which is three times the difference between 3 and 2 which is thus, 6 : 2 :: (6 − 3) : (3 − 2). "To find the harmonic 3rd to two given numbers, multiply the 1st by the 2nd, and divide the product by twice the 1st minus the 2nd. To find the harmonic 3rd to 6 and 3 as fore-given, 6 × 3 = 18. 2 × 6 = 12 − 3 = 9. Divide 18 by 9 = 2. If you have any two of the three you may find the other by other formulæ. Of course the harmonic 3rd is often fractional. Now I mostly have my books bound thus, with six spaces off-marked by bands on the back, and the lettering piece on the third space from the top; thus I have six spaces, three below the lettering piece and two above it, a harmonic triad. I feel that if the lettering piece is shoved up above that place the book looks hunch-backed. Then again in the framing of a picture, I find a harmonic 3rd to the height and breadth of it, and take a 4th part of it for the width of the frame, and then four widths of the four sides of the frame make the harmonic 3rd. The harmonic 3rd to 20, 15, is 12, a quarter of which is 3, which I should take as the width of the frame. In wainscoting you might take half of the harmonic 3rd for the framing of the panels, and it might not be bad for a very fine and small picture. In the framing of prints I mostly take for them what would be the width of the frame for an oil painting, as the width both of the narrow frame and the margin. I feel that the very

common way of framing of prints with a broad wilderness of white margin to make them look precious is
shockingly bad.   In the building of a church we may
have the height of the tower, nave, and chancel, and the
ground lengths of the nave, chancel, and tower harmonic
measures.   You understand that nothing of harmonic
proportion is mine, but these and such like uses of it.
With fond love all round,

Your affectionate father,

WILLIAM BARNES.

P.S.—I hope to find you an answer about Pausanias.

The article on Harmonic Proportions in the *Gentleman's Magazine* attracted the notice of a clergyman who
had lately had his church restored with a high chancel,
and, wishing to justify himself he entered on a very
vigorous correspondence, which ended in his expressing
himself a convert to the theory of Harmonic Proportion
in everything "except a low chancel!"   ·

This was not the only paper that attracted notice;
for instance, on May 30th, 1840, a Mr. Petheram having
discovered that the writer of *Dorset Dialect compared
with Anglo-Saxon* was also the author of the poems
appearing from time to time in the *Dorset County
Chronicle*, writes that when the poems are published, he
proposes that the glossary which would be necessary
should be made a complete glossary, not only of Dorset
speech but that of Somerset and all the western
counties, which he says is almost a semi-Saxon dialect.
Mr. Petheram further suggests tracing the words to

their Saxon derivatives, and offers his assistance in the formation of such a glossary, which by his knowledge of Anglo-Saxon lore and Somersetshire-folk speech he was eminently qualified to do. The correspondence which began thus with Mr. Petheram, resulted later in the publication of the *Anglo-Saxon Delectus*, which will be spoken of in its place. In March, 1839, Mr. John Gough Nicholls, Editor of the *Gentleman's Magazine*, proposed William Barnes as Member of the Camden Society in the following letter :—

March 7th, 1839.

DEAR SIR,

I fear you may have thought it a neglect that your communication on the Indian Jugglers was not noticed in the last *Gentleman's Magazine*. There was not room for it, and I did not mention it in the Minor Correspondence, intending to write to you, and say that the accounts you propose of the Hindoo Pooran and Fakirs would I have no doubt, be an appropriate and interesting sequel to it. I am happy to say that we have got your plan of the Dorchester Amphitheatre very nicely litho-graphed. It will not be in the next Magazine, but in that for May.

I am induced to send you the inclosed Prospectus, thinking you may be glad to be afforded the opportunity of entering the Camden Society whilst there are vacancies and during its first year. Your writings evince how much you have read of old literature, and therefore I am inclined to think you may be glad to avail yourself of this Society; the subscription to which is suited to almost every pocket, a circumstance which has greatly contributed to its success,

I remain, Dear Sir,

Yours very sincerely,

JOHN GOUGH NICHOLLS.

The correspondence with Mr. J. Gough Nicholls was very frequent in these days and proved how much William Barnes's mind and writings were appreciated by that able editor. The following letter was the beginning of a long course of reviews chiefly of philological and scientific works in the *Gentleman's Magazine*.

March 3rd, 1841.

DEAR SIR,

I have several books on language, dialects, and etymology now waiting for review in the *Gentleman's Magazine*. It has occurred to me that they might form acceptable acquisitions in your collection, and if you would like to accept them on the terms of writing a few critical remarks upon them for our pages, they are very much at your service.

There is a publication of your own of this nature, of which I noticed a prospectus among the waste paper of one of your parcels, and I think I saw the same very recently noticed (favourably) in the *Athenæum* or *Literary Gazette*. I do not recollect that a copy has come into my hands for our magazine; but if you like to send one by the next opportunity, I will endeavour to find some other friend to pay attention to it. We have now two letters of yours waiting an opportunity for admission. One of them, which was in type for the last number, will have an early chance for insertion in one of the first sheets we print.

I remain, Dear Sir,

Yours very sincerely,

JOHN GOUGH NICHOLLS.

The work spoken of was *An Investigation of the Laws of Case*, which was very favourably reviewed in the *Gentleman's Magazine* for April 1841, proving that Mr. J. G. Nicholls lost no time in fulfilling his promise.

In the midst of all this literary activity William Barnes did not neglect social life. His love of music was as strong as ever, and the *suonando gli strumenti musicali*, which had been so pleasant at Mere, was revived at Dorchester. A little quartette society was formed, which used to meet in the large schoolroom when the scholars were asleep, and fill it with the strains of Beethoven and Haydn. The first violin was Mr. Frederick Smith, the father of the well-known composers, Boyton and Sydney Smith—a man of such musical taste and genius that he might have become famous had circumstances made him known to a wider world. No amateur 'cellist being found, a worthy man, the clerk of St. Peter's Church, and leader of the choir orchestra, was called in to take the part; another church player, named Bailey, took the viola; and W. Barnes either played the second violin or flute, as the occasion required. Sometimes a lady friend, or a little daughter who, at a very early age was a good pianist,

F

took the piano part. Friends were often invited as audience to these delightful readings of the old masters. To this day the younger members of the family remember waking in their little cribs at night and hearing the beautiful harmonies penetrate the stillness of the night from afar off, and then falling asleep to dream of Paradise. To this day the sound of music in the night awakens in some of them a rush of happy childish memories. They also remember the more humble fireside music, when the children sat on their stools at their parents' feet in the flickering fire-light on a Sunday evening, and William Barnes and his wife sang hymns in which their shrill weaker trebles joined. The tiny children used to say, "Father's voice was the big drum, and mother's like the flute." On week-day evenings the husband and wife would sing duets, such as "Drink to me," and "O Pescator dell' onda," &c. Sometimes the tiny children got the ascendant instead of the music, and then there were romps under and over father's knees, and a great scrambling of little dogs on all fours away from a great roaring bear who hunted them out, and when caught there were shrieks of half-frightened delight.

Among his educational labours William Barnes taught his sons to play marbles, and they had a great respect for his prowess at "ring-taw," until they learnt to beat him. He turned in his lathe three whip-tops in box-wood, a very large one for himself, a moderate-sized one for the elder boy, and a small one for the younger. The three used to adjourn to the children's playroom, in the garret, each armed with a leathern whip, and spend half an hour before breakfast in trying who could keep his top spinning the longest. It was only in after years that the sons began to think this game was instituted as much for their physical development as for amusement. Those children never had in the remotest corner of their memories the shadow of an unkind word from their father, who was as ready to play "bears" with them as to study the deepest roots of language. Only once was a direct punishment given by him, which was found afterwards to be undeserved. It was when the four younger children were all condemned to be locked up in a room for a whole day, on an accusation of breaking a young fruit tree. They denied it, and the denial in the face of what seemed to be proof, was taken by the grieved father for a concerted lie. The four little captives, with easy consciences, made the best of their "arrest," and played together quite happily till evening, when the father discovered that the real culprit was the accuser —one of the scholars, whose peg was forthwith put down to the blacks on the Topograph—and he came to release the quartette of prisoners with a face which would have touched their hearts, had they only understood the deprecatory tenderness which was in it. That is the one and only personal chastisement that William Barnes's children can remember from him. When they grew older he rarely even gave them a prohibition, his theory being that every mind must learn to rule itself. If his advice were asked whether they ought or ought not to do a certain action, he would calmly reason on what were likely to be the consequences of each course of action, and then say, "Now do as you yourself think best." It was very rare for them not to choose the way that he intended they should, but the absence of arbitrary restraint was at the same time a great boon to the children in giving them a sense of freedom, and also a great moral trainer in making them depend on conscience and reason as their guides.

In the year 1840 William Barnes had the trial of losing his early friend Edward Fuller. He too, had married, but his young wife lived a very short time, dying of consumption in 1838. After that Fuller travelled a great deal, adding to a mind already refined the study of foreign art and scenery, and writing very long and descriptive letters of foreign scenes and art galleries to his friend. They made several plans for an excursion together into France, but William Barnes was not such a free agent as Fuller, and the journey was never taken. Mr. Fuller went alone to travel on the Continent, partly in search of health, but the cough of which he speaks in several letters deteriorated into consumption, and in 1840 he died, leaving a void in William Barnes's heart which was never filled up. The entry in his notebooks says : July 17th, "This day I have lost my early, worthy, and much-loved friend, Mr. Edward Fuller, who died at Staple Grove, near Taunton." His will contained the bequest of a small legacy to W. Barnes as a "token of long-standing friendship." To the memory of this friend who died so young, the following poem is dedicated :—

The Music of the Dead.

When music in a heart that's true,
Do kindle up wold loves anew,
An' dim wet eyes, in fëairest lights,
Do see but inward fancy's zights ;
When creepèn years wi' with'ren blights
'V a took of them that wer so dear
How touchèn 'tis if we do hear
    The tuèns of the dead, John.

CHAPTER V.

VULL A MAN.

No, I'm a man, I'm vull a man,
You beät my manhood, if you can
You'll be a man if you can teäke
All steätes that household life can meäke ;
 The love-toss'd child, a-croodlèn loud,
The buoy a-screamèn wild in play,
 The tall grown youth a-steppen proud,
The father staïd, the house's stay.
No ; I can boast if others can
   I'm vull a man.

A young cheäk'd mother's tears mid fall,
When woone a-lost, not half-man tall
Vrom little hand, a-call'd vrom pläy,
Do leäve noo tool, but drop a täy,
 And die avore he's father-free
To sheäpe his life by his own plan ;
 An vull an angel he shall be
But here on e'th not vull a man
No ; I can boast if others can
   I'm vull a man.

I woonce, a child, wer father-fed,
And I've a-vound my childern bread;
My eärm, a sister's trusty crook
Is now a faithvul wife's own hook;
    An I've a-gone where vo'k did send
An' gone upon my own free mind
    An' of'en at my own wits' end
A-led o' God while I wer blind.
No; I could boast if others can
            I'm vull a man.

An' still, ov all my tweil ha' won,
My loven maid an' merry son,
Though each in turn's a jäy and ceäre
'Ve a-had, an still shall have, their sheäre;
    An' then, if God should bless their lives,
Why I mid zend from son to son
    My life, right on drough men an' wives,
As long, good men, as time do run,
No, I could boast if others can
            I'm vull a man.

THE DORSET POEMS.—FIRST SERIES.

1844.

THE fugitive poems constantly appearing in a certain corner of the *Dorset County Chronicle* had become "familiar as household words" to many readers, and were beginning to attract wider attention; many guesses as to their authorship being set on foot. One writer in the *Gentleman's Magazine*, remarking on a previous paper on Provincial Dialects, called "Mr. Urban's" attention to these poems (quite unnecessarily by the way, for "Mr. Urban" and the poet were already friends and correspondents) where the "sweet pastoral spirit graces both the grave and the gay; and the rustic Muse is pure as the atmosphere of the downs on which she is indigenous." "The author of the lays" adds the writer, "is said to be an Archdeacon of the Established Church." It was for some time believed by many that the Rev. Lord Sydney Godolphin Osborne was the poet, till the *Gentleman's Magazine* set doubts at rest by giving William Barnes's name.

They attracted sympathetic admiration from two gifted women, Lady Dufferin and the Hon. Mrs. Norton,

who were then staying at Frampton House, and
wished much to make the personal acquaintance of
the poet.

Mr. Richard Brinsley Sheridan has himself described
the beginning of an acquaintance which was much
valued by William Barnes.

" I was well acquainted," he writes, "with the Dorset
poet. Our friendship and intimacy dates from as far
back as about 1844. I made his acquaintance under
peculiar and interesting circumstances, which, if not
wearying you I will relate. In 1844 the following distinguished persons were my guests at Frampton :—the
then Lord Bishop of the Diocese, Bishop Dennison,
Philip Pusey, the editor of the *Royal Agricultural
Journal*, Dr. Buckland, afterwards Dean of Westminster,
Fonblanque, the Editor of the *Examiner*, Archdeacon
Huxtable, two of my sisters, Lady Dufferin and Mrs.
Norton, a brother, and other members of my family.
Several short pieces of poetry had at that time
appeared in the *Dorset County Chronicle*, and were
greatly admired by Lady Dufferin and Mrs. Norton.
They earnestly begged me to write to the author, and
to invite him to join the party. In this request Bishop
Dennison, with other of my visitors joined. I wrote as
desired to Mr. Barnes. He gracefully and courteously,
in the first instance, declined the invitation, on the
ground that he was unaccustomed to society. I again
wrote to say that my sisters and others in the house
admired his poetry and were anxious to make his
acquaintance, and that I and my wife would feel greatly
honoured by his acceptance of our invitation. He came
and remained in the house until the party separated. I

should be occupying too much of your time if I described all that passed during his instructive visit. It is sufficient to say that all the distinguished persons that formed the party were greatly struck by the simplicity, varied knowledge, and information he imparted on so many subjects of interest. Dr. Buckland found in our lamented friend a kindred spirit, and was much impressed with his knowledge and information on geology."

As a sign of the poet's appreciation of this early recognition of his genius may be noticed the following autographic inscription on the fly-leaf of a presentation copy of the collected poems in 1879 :—

"To Mr. and Mrs. Brinsley Sheridan, with a happy memory of their invitation to Frampton Court, in April, 1844, to meet Mrs. Norton :—

> "Sweeter to me
> Your early praise
> Than now could be
> A crown of bays.

"W. Barnes.

"*November* 6th, 1879."

The Hon. Mrs. Norton had been known to Barnes before this, only as a fellow poet whose works he much admired. Some of her lyrics had pleased him so much that he set them to music. The meeting with her in person made a great impression on him and called forth the following sonnet :—

To the Hon. Mrs. Norton.

When first I drew, with melting heart, alone
(O gifted vot'ry of the tuneful Nine)
Entrancing melody from songs of thine
Sweet echo'd words of one as yet unknown ;
    How much I wondered what might be the tone
Of her true voice, as yet unanswering mine,
And what the hue with which her eyes might shine,
And what the form in which her soul was shown
To sons of men. How busy fancy brought
Before me lineaments of love and grace.
But who can tell what joy was mine at last,
When I beheld the object of my thought
In bright reality before my face,
And found the fairest of my dreams surpassed ! "

This bit of poetical homage was acknowledged by the
following letter :—

24, Bolton Street, Piccadilly.
May, 1844.

Dear Sir,

I must have appeared very uncourteous if not
very ungrateful in having allowed so long a time to
elapse, without acknowledging your letter and your
beautiful sonnet. I caught cold at Her Majesty's
drawing-room, and was confined to bed for some days,
leaving much business undone, which had accumulated
during my absence from town, and which has since been
my sole occupation.

You must now let me thank you very cordially for
the verses, which will take their place in a book of
autographs I am collecting for my boys ; and I assure

you most sincerely that I shall prize them more highly than many there, though other authors may have had the advantage, by chance or favourable opportunity, of becoming better known in the world of literature than your name is as yet.

A friend of mine who greatly admires your poems, told me that Sir Thomas Acland spoke of them; that Sir T. A. had read them at intervals in the newspaper, and was not aware till my friend mentioned the fact that they were now published in a collected form. He spoke in terms of the greatest praise, and wondered his son had not sent him word of the publication. I do not know if Sir T. Acland be a good critic, but I feel sure he must love real poetry by his praise of yours. I much wish you would put some of them into more cockney English. Perhaps you would let me send a list of those which are most liked, and would easiest bear the transmuting power proposed to be applied to them. Then you would judge if we were right in our selection.

If ever you find a day for busy London, during the pauses of your many occupations, I hope you will write me word beforehand, that I may have the pleasure of seeing you here to dine, or in any other way that may suit the planning of your spare hours. Perhaps some Saturday during the season, when we could hear a good opera by way of finishing the day well. Repeating my thanks for your letter, without even going through the form of deprecating the too complimentary lines addressed to myself,—I beg you to believe me, etc., etc.

C. NORTON.

The invitation given in this was repeated in June, when William Barnes went up to London for a few days, probably to arrange about the sale by a London publisher of the volume of Dorset Poems · now just printed in Dorchester by Mr. G. Simmonds, proprietor of the *Dorset County Chronicle*. Mr. John Russell Smith undertook the sale for the London market and the trade generally. Some events of this his first visit to London, may be gathered from the following letter from Mrs. Norton.

Monday, 17th June, 1844.

DEAR SIR,

I shall be extremely happy to see you on Saturday, and will arrange what we City folks call an early dinner for the opera, that is a dinner at 6.30, and expect the pleasure of your company.

Professor Wheatstone told me that he would show me on that day the working of his galvanic telegraph between London and Slough. Perhaps that also would interest you, and I will ascertain the exact hour from him and let you know by letter before Friday, if you have leisure on the morning of Saturday to come with us.

I write in great haste—which I trust you will excuse —and beg you to believe me, dear Sir,

Yours truly,

CAROLINE NORTON.

On Mr. Barnes's return from London, he was much disappointed to find the sympathising wife to whom

he had so much to tell had been called away by the
sudden illness of a near relative.   He wrote to her:

July, 1844.

My Dear Julia,

Here am I your unhappy husband, hurried home
for your society and finding you gone.   I should like to
see Mr. and Mrs. T., but really I have spent too much
on my London trip to make a second long one, though I
hope this circumstance will not affect your stay at N.,
since it is only fair that I should bear for your grati-
fication what you have borne for mine.   I am unwilling
to say much of my visit in writing as I think it a breach
of the laws of hospitality, but you will be pleased to
know that among those invited to meet me were
Lady ———, whom I took into dinner, Lord ———
son of the Earl of ——— and one of our first English
philosophers (Prof. Wheatstone) of whom I learned
something that I should like to show Mr. T.   I do not
know whatever I shall do until you come home.

I am, etc.

William Barnes.

My Dear Julia,

Your pretty winning offer to come home at my
bidding has quite ravished my heart, so that I cannot
now limit your stay, but if the N. smoke should
as usual give you headaches in a day or two, I trust that
you will immediately try a change of air which you
know did you so much good formerly.

Mind that you walk out and eat strawberries and

cherries. I should like to have a chat with Mr.
T. but I am fearful, I must not think of it now.
God bless you.

Your affectionate husband.

W. BARNES.

P. S.—I am very lonely, but occupied in work or
study. Tell Mr. T. I was working the whole of
yesterday in constructing apparatus for following up
Professor Wheatstone's discoveries on vision.

I have been trying to-day an experiment shown me
by him, but am fearful I shall not do it till after much
experience. I have learnt from him a vast deal that
will be available in my lectures, as I have seen all his
philosophic apparatus and all the scientific museums
of King's College. Lord ——— told me that my
book was making quite a sensation in the west end
of the town. I had yesterday an invitation from Mr.
Knight, of Piddlehinton, to go over there this week.
How are you spending your time ? Have you been to
Clevedon or Bristol ? Ask Mr. T. if like me he coveted
one of the model steam-engines at the Polytechnic ?
The children are well, but unluckily one has broken
one of the plaster figures on the bookcase, and another
has run her head through the window—on a Sunday
—as usual. E. is getting on wonderfully fast in
talking.

To-day is Dorchester Fair, and I have been out in
search of a small addition to my natural history in the
contemplation of lambs and piglings.

May God bless you, and very soon restore you to him

whose life you have made so happy and prosperous, and who loves you with undiminished affection.

Your faithful husband,
W. BARNES.

So the Dorset poems were now fully launched, and Russell Smith seems to have found a good sale in London, for he writes once or twice for fifty copies more to be sent to him. Indeed, considering how limited was its public—for in the first instance people looked on Dorset as a foreign tongue—the book achieved a decided literary success, and made quite a mark in its sphere. The Honourable Mrs. Norton did an immense deal to bring it before cultivated readers by her enthusiastic advocacy.

The author, thinking some enlightenment necessary to explain the use of the dialect, furnished the book with a dissertation and glossary, which were both so learned that the critics were puzzled, and hardly knew whether to review it on artistic or scientific grounds, whether the poems were merely illustrations of philological lore, or the half Anglo-Saxon glossary and learned dissertation were to make the poems intelligible.

The dialect was a great stumbling-block to those first critics, some of whom coolly translated the poems into English, thus taking off all their bloom, and one assures his readers that " If they will take a little trouble to penetrate the mysteries, they will not find the labour lost."

Local papers contented themselves by culling the

G

most telling sentences from the prose, and involving
themselves in allusions to Saxon and Doric, as if they
were two dialects of the same speech. The more
literary journals were generally more appreciative,
though one of them questioned the utility of compos-
ing poems in such a dialect ("which nobody will
read")!

Some critics took up the book on very unexpected
grounds—that of its political influence; one article,
after quoting the "Summer Evening Dance," and its
genial effect on the heart of the reader, adds :—

" And this, we would trust, may be among the
consequences of the present publication, to keep alive
in some measure the interest in the affairs of the poor,
which has been largely awakened in this neighbourhood
of late. If the landlords and upper classes generally
may thus be led to a more intimate acquaintance with
their feelings and habits, and to a more sincere
sympathy with their wants and hopes, and for their
homely and household prejudices, which are far too
frequently violated and despised, we are convinced that
Mr. Barnes will feel that his poems have aided in a
work, whose success he would value far above any fame
or emolument that may accrue to himself. We are
satisfied that all the poor want is to be known, and to
be communicated with directly by refined and honourable minds, instead of being left to the tender mercies
of an ill-educated class, whose own bargains have been
often hardly driven, and whose prosperity, therefore,
depends upon oppression and illiberality. Against this
treatment their only weapon is deceit; and the con-
sciousness of deceiving produces a savage gloom in their

character, and a suspiciousness of the upper classes most unfavourable to both parties. Still we are confident that matters might easily be made up between them ; and that a little real and personal condescension, a little study of the actual state of things, and a disposition to provide for their recreations as well as for their labour, might soon effect a happy reconciliation. The truly pleasing garb in which Mr. Barnes has dressed their 'short and simple annals' is likely to aid in effecting this; and we heartily recommend him to the diligent perusal of our readers."

Another critic says: " It is a great boon to the class which Mr. Barnes describes, to have this justice done them. Anything which exalts a man in his own opinion as a member of an honest and honourable class ennobles him. Anything which causes him to appreciate more fully the blessings he enjoys as a class member of the Church and of the State is an addition to his sense of happiness, an incitement to grateful reflection, and a joint security for his being a good citizen and a good Churchman." These seem very grave and serious views of " nature sketches " of village life in the cottage, the field, and the woodland, but it is not too grave, for all these things are there.

The difference between William Barnes's earlier and later critics seems to be that the earlier ones recognise the moral tendency and science of the poems, the latter ones, such as Mr. Patmore, Mr. Palgrave, &c., realise their artistic perfection. To the former they are deep teachings from nature, to the latter poems of art. They are both in fact, for they are, as all real poetry should be, the pure expression of a true and gentle mind,

seeing nature through a poet's eyes, and raising human
nature by showing what is highest and best in it; and
at the same time works of art, inasmuch as the form of
the poems was the result of immense study of the
poetical forms of all nations and ages.

The poet gives his own explanation as to the
philological researches which led him to adopt the
dialect, for when he began, it was as much the spirit
of the philologist as the poet which moved him. His
studies had traced the dialect of Dorset through all its
pedigree from the followers of Cerdic and Cymric who
brought it into England through "Eald Saxon," as
King Alfred called Holstein and Denmark, back to its
still remoter forefathers, the Frisians.

"Thus derived," he says, "the Dorset dialect is a broad and
bold shape of the English language, as the Doric was of the
Greek. It is rich in humour, stong in raillery and hyperbole;
and altogether as fit a vehicle of rustic feeling and thought, as
the Doric is found in the *Idyllia* of Theocritus. Some people,
who may have been taught to consider it as having originated
from corruption of the written English, may not be prepared to
hear that it is not only a separate offspring from the Anglo-Saxon
tongue, but purer and more regular than the dialect which is
chosen as the national speech, purer, inasmuch as it uses many
words of Saxon origin, for which the English substitutes others
of Latin, Greek, or French derivation; and more regular, inasmuch as it inflects regularly many words which, in the national
language, are irregular. In English, purity is in many cases
given up for the sake of what is considered to be elegance."

In many ways Dorset is richer than English,
especially in its distinguishing adjectives, its expressive affixes and the absence of words which have two
meanings.

It was, therefore, with a hope of preserving, and a dream of restoring, this pure ancient language and character to England, that Barnes began to write in dialect. The success of the first few experiments was enough to convince him that the simpler Saxon English was not only more forcible, but also more poetical than Latinised speech, and he soon found that no other form so well suited the rural scenes he loved to paint. The medium being so congenial, his soul found full expression, and poem after poem flowed from his mind, suggested by every memory of childhood and every scene in his country walks. Thus in course of time the poet reigned alone, and the philologist found other means of expression, in grammars and dissertations; and this is no doubt why the critics of the first series recognise science, and those of the later ones see only poetry.

CHAPTER VI.

THE WOODLAND HOME.

My woodland home, where hillocks swell,
With flow'ry sides, above the dell,
And sedge's hanging ribbons gleam
By meadow withies in the stream,
And elms with ground-beglooming shades
Stand high upon the sloping glades,
When toilsome day at evening fades,
And trials agitate my breast,
     By fancy brought
     I come in thought
To thee, my home, my spirit's rest.

I left thy woody fields that lay
So fair below my boyhood's play,
To toil in busy life that fills
The world with strife of wayward wills ;
Where mortals in their little day
Of pride, disown their brother clay.

But when my soul can steal away
From such turmoil, with greater zest,
    By fancy brought
    I come in thought
To thee, my home, my spirit's rest.

For I behold thee fresh and fair
In summer light and summer air,
As when I rambled, pulling low
The hazel bough, that when let go
Flew back, with high-toss'd head upright,
To rock again in airy light;
Where brown-stemm'd elms and ashes white
Rose tall upon the flow'ry breast
    Of some green mound
    With timber crown'd,
My woodland home, my spirit's rest.

And there my fancy will not find
The loveless heart or selfish mind,
Nor scowling hatred, mutt'ring aught
To break my heart-entrancing thought;
But manly souls above deceit,
The bright'ning eyes they love to meet,
The fairest in their looks, and best
    In heart I found
    On thy lov'd ground,
My woodland home, my spirit's rest.

THE DORSET COUNTY MUSEUM.

1845 TO 1847.

IN 1845 the South Western Railway was projected
from London to Dorchester, causing great excitement
among the inhabitants, and producing many results
which would seem at first sight to be quite irrelevant.
Landowners were aghast at threatened cuttings
through their land, artists were rabid at the destruction to the picturesque, geologists were excited at the
anticipated "finds" of fossil treasures in the chalk,
and—here comes the unexpected result—the Dorset
County Museum was founded, and William Barnes
became one of its secretaries! As a proof of the new
railway being the cause of the founding of the museum,
it is enough to glance at the resolutions of the preliminary meeting held on October 15th, 1845, wherein
it was resolved :

1st. That, in consideration of the importance of this
district with respect to natural history and both British
and Roman antiquities, and, more especially at this
time, when the disturbance of the surface of the country
in the formation of railroads is likely to bring to light

specimens of interest in these several departments of science, it is advisable to take immediate steps for the establishment of an institution in this town containing a museum and library for the county of Dorset.

.   .   .   .   .   .

5th.   That the Right Honourable Lord Ashley, M.P., be requested to become president of the institution.

6th.   That the Rev. C. W. Bingham and Mr. William Barnes be appointed honorary secretaries, and Herbert Williams, Esq., treasurer.

All the archæologists of the county came forward to assist the project of which Barnes was one of the most energetic promoters, and funds enough soon accumulated to make a modest beginning.   A house was taken in Back South Street, and Mr. Barnes, with his three clerical colleagues, the Revs. Charles Bingham, Osmund Fisher, and Henry Moule, were soon constantly at work arranging and classifying.   Specimens began to pour in as well as funds; William Barnes's two old friends, Mr. Charles Hall of Osmington House, and Mr. Charles Warne, F.S.A., sent duplicates from their respective collections of British and Saxon antiquities.   The naturalist, the Rev. J. C. Dale, of Glanville's Wootton, contributed butterflies and stuffed natural history specimens.   The antiquarians in the Isle of Purbeck placed in the museum their treasures, the ichthyosaurus, the fin of the plesiosaurus and other minor fossils, found in the Kimmeridge clay and oolite; and William Barnes took all his pupils—who for the time had a mania for fossil-hunting—geologising in the new railway cuttings.

It was amusing to see the dignified way in which these young *savants* started, with bag and hammer, and the undignified return, covered with chalk soil and showing very juvenile excitement over their *terebratulæ, echini*, and *belemnites*. Many of their "findings" went in with more important specimens, and thus formed the germ of the museum, with which William Barnes's name and labours have been connected for forty years. Sometimes the secretary's science was not quite adequate to the calls on it, and higher authorities had to be appealed to. In October, 1846, Professor Anstead wrote to William Barnes, saying: "Nothing can give me greater satisfaction than to be able to assist any one labouring in the field of geology. If you will have the kindness to send any specimens directed to me at the Geological Society, Somerset House, I will look at them, and if I am not myself able to help you, I doubt not there will be somebody to tell us what the doubtful specimen may be."

Sometimes undoubted rarities were found, for there is a letter from Mr. J. R. Jones, of the Geological Society, saying that the fossils sent him from Dorchester by Mr. Barnes, "prove to be a very interesting group of chalk forms of the brachiopod species." Some casts of shells found in the flint also attracted the notice of geologists.

About the same time Mr. Dale writes in great glee, sending some rare butterflies for the museum. He says: "I have a new genus (to Britain), *cærulas*, just arrived from Scotland, with a few other things new to me, and I have lately seen a new moth (as British), taken near Peterborough, and I have ascertained the names of some more to be inserted as Dorset specimens.

Mr. Wollaston took here a specimen, new to Dorset, of "cassida sanguinolenta."

William Barnes, always an archæologist by natural taste, was now by office bound to become a preserver of Dorset antiquities. Accordingly when in 1846 the Great Western line was planned to cut right through the interesting Roman camp of Poundbury, extra-ordinary efforts were made to save it. Mr. Colfox, of Bridport, wrote to give notice of the plan, but from the following reply of W. Barnes it would seem the Dorchester Museum had already been active.

DORCHESTER, *May* 15th, 1846.

SIR,

I beg to give you my most hearty thanks for your kind communication, and for your good and earnest endeavour to save our "Poundbury." Two friends of mine, with myself, first agitated the Archæo-logical Association in behalf of the amphitheatre,[1] which I am so happy to find will be saved; and when we found Poundbury likely to be cut we prepared a petition to Parliament in behalf of it, though we were not early enough to get it into the House before the Company's Bill went through it, and therefore refrained from sending it off; but the threatened intersection of Poundbury has been laid before the Archæological As-sociation, and we have reason to hope that the earthwork will be tunnelled, and therefore remain unmutilated. The institution we are trying to establish here is a county museum, supported simply by subscriptions and

---

[1] One of these was Charles Warne, F.S.A., who personally appealed to Brunel, and got the line diverted to save it.

donations, and therefore is not, I fear, a body that has any means of bringing up influence against Mr. Brunel, though I feel confident that he will not be negligent of the representations which have been already made to him on behalf of our earthwork.

I shall make known to all my antiquarian friends your truly good and not-to-be-forgotten endeavours to help us, and am, dear sir,

Yours respectfully,

WILLIAM BARNES.

A meeting of the museum council was called, and it was decided to beg the directors to tunnel under Poundbury. This not meeting a decided response, Mr. Colfox came forward in September and made application to the Master-General of the Ordnance, who in reply promised that the most important part of Poundbury should be tunnelled under, and thus saved from utter destruction. This correspondence was the beginning of a long friendship between Mr. Colfox and W. Barnes, which was kept up by their congenial tastes and frequent meetings, for when the poet went to lecture or read at Bridport, he always became the guest of the former.

About this time the head mastership of the Dorchester Grammar School fell vacant by the resignation of Mr. Cutler, and Barnes became a candidate. The school, being one of Edward VI.'s foundation, was under the power of a committee, whose members bore the quaint title of *feoffees*, the Earl of Shaftesbury being head of this council. It would have seemed that the candidate had every chance of success; his friends, which were legion, got up a memorial, signed by 104 householders of Dorchester, and there were besides spontaneous and warm testimonials from J. Gough Nicholls, the members of Parliament for town and county, Colonel Damer, and other influential people. But neither merit nor recommendation was of much use in this case; William Barnes was scarcely allowed the justice of a vote, for on the very day of the election the feoffees came to a preliminary resolution that none should be elected but a man in holy orders. This of course cut off Barnes's certain majority, and the feoffees' candidate was perforce elected, as there were no rivals left on the field. The excuse was after all a futile one, for William Barnes was already in the tenth year of his membership of St. John's College, Cambridge, and was in fact ordained by the Bishop of Salisbury in January the following year. This treatment, which galled his sense of justice, was for the time a cause of sadness to him, more especially as some of his supporters became partisans to the other school. The only unpleasantness approaching to a quarrel that is recorded in his life, was with his country publisher, Mr. G. Simmonds, who, on Barnes's feeling hurt at his change of sentiments about the school, made the relations between publisher and author very unpleasant by unfair claims on the edition of the *Dorset Poems* lately printed by him.

There is little literary work to record for this year, the poet's mind not being at rest. Besides the articles on the " Bromsgrove Greek Grammar," the "Cornish Dialect," and on " Wild Flowers" in the *Gentleman's Magazine*, the only literary event was the publication of

Poems, partly of Rural Life, in national English, printed by Simmonds and published by Russell Smith. This collection—which never reached a second edition—contains all the sonnets which he thought worth preserving, and many lyrics, together with a narrative poem entitled, "Erwin and Linda," a tale of tales, which opens thus :—

> There bright-lipp'd smiles, and rings of glossy hair
> Were shining softly in the flick'ring glare ;
> The ruddy-burning fire was flinging o'er
> The lofty-sided hall, and stonen floor.
> For while Orion, glitt'ring with his bright
> Three-spangled girdle, climb'd his southern height,
> And laurel leaves were gleaming in the sheen
> Of downcast moonlight on the grassy green,
> And chilly winds, that now no longer found
> The summer's leafy boughs and dewy ground,
> With shrilly-whistling eddies idly play'd
> Through prickly holly in the house's shade ;
> There neighbours, in a widely spanning bow,
> Were sitting merry round the fire's red glow,
> Each ready, as his turn might come, to hold
> The other's minds with tales as yet untold.

The story of the young lord of the manor is then told by the different speakers. Though there is some pretty word-painting here and there, the narrative poem was not William Barnes's forte, and after this he never repeated the experiment. Of the sonnets we have given two or three already. "My Woodland Home," which illustrates this chapter, is a good specimen of the lyrics, many of which prove that the author could be a poet even out of the groove of the Dorset

speech.   To emphasise this assertion we will give a few
verses from another :—

Moss.

O rain-bred moss that now dost hide
The timber's bark and wet rock's side
Upshining to the sun, between
The darksome storms, in lively green,
And washed by pearly raindrops clean,
     Steal o'er my lonely path, and climb
     The wall, dear child, of silent time.
          O winter moss, creep on, creep on
          And warn me of the time that's gone.

Green child of winter, born to take
Whate'er the hands of man forsake,
That makest dull in rainy air,
His labour-brighten'd works ; so fair
While newly left in summer's glare ;
     And stealest o'er the stone that keeps
     His name in mem'ry where he sleeps.
          O winter moss, creep on, creep on,
          And warn us of the time that's gone.

Come, lowly plant, that lov'st like me
The shadow of the woodland tree,
And waterfalls where echo mocks
The milkmaid's song by dripping rocks,
And sunny turf for roving flocks,
     And ribby elms extending wide
     Their roots within the hillock's side.
          Come winter moss, creep on, creep on,
          And warn me of the time that's gone.

Come where thou climbedst fresh and free
The grass-beglooming apple tree,
That hardly shaken with my small

Boy's strength, with quiv'ring head, let fall
The apples we lik'd most of all ;
    Or elm I climb'd with clasping legs,
    To reach the crow's high-nested eggs.
        Come, winter moss, creep on, creep on,
        And warn me of the time that's gone.

Or where I found thy yellow bed
Below the hill-borne fir-tree's head,
And heard the whistling east wind blow
Above, while wood-screen'd down below
I rambled in the spring-day's glow
    And watch'd the low-ear'd hares upspring
    From cover, and the birds take wing.
        Come, winter moss, creep on, creep on,
        And warn me of the time that's gone.

Some of the poems in this book are remarkable as
experiments in rhythm. The most curious are the
alliterative verses, written on the principle of old
Teutonic poetry. In the Anglo-Saxon this form is
found without rhyme, the alliteration being enough,
especially as the consonant repeated was always on the
syllable emphasised. The two first alliterative words
are placed in the first line, the third and last in the
first emphasised word of the second line.[1] Thus

    " But when the *m*oonlight *m*arks anew
    Thy *m*urky shadow on the dew,
    So *s*lowly o'er the *s*leeping flowers,
    O*n*sliding through the nightly hours,

---

[1] The principle is explained in Dasent's Rask's *Icelandic
Grammar*.

While smokeless on the *h*ouses' *h*eight
The *h*igher chimney gleams in light
Above yon *r*eedy *r*oof where now
With *r*osy cheeks and lily brow,
No *w*atchful mother's *w*ard within
The *w*indow sleeps for me to win." [1]

---

[1] " The Elm in home ground.''

CHAPTER VII.

OUR CHURCH.

How brightly our church, this sunny time,
Shows out on the hill its light grey wall,
Above the dark yew and leafy lime,
And flinging its merry sounds of bells
Out over the many-fielded dells.

Though I have my roof beside the spring,
And yours is beside the hollow oak ;
And some by the street may send up smoke,
And others' lone doors by fields may swing,
Still there are the chimes that sweetly call
Us all to the house that stands for all.

For all, at our Lord's high call to go
To share of His graces glad but meek,
And hear the good words His love may speak

As unto His children high and low;
Our own to go up that He may bless
Our fast-wedded loves with holiness.

Our own where Our Lord in goodness takes
Our children to make them all His own;
And kindred, beneath cold earth or stone,
May sleep till their souls' bright morning breaks
Through every change of good and ill,
We there have our church beside the hill.

ORDINATION.

1847.

On January 1st, 1847, Colonel Damer, of Came House, offered Whitcombe to William Barnes as a title to orders. This almost infinitesimal parish is neither a living nor a curacy, but what is called a *donative*. It is a tiny rustic hamlet which had been given before the Reformation to the Abbey of Milton, whence the little church had its pastor. Henry VIII. took it away from the monks and gave as curate's salary a kind of prescriptive stipend of thirteen guineas a year, and it then ranked as a separate parish. In the course of centuries, the 13*l.* remaining nominally always the same, its material value was so much depreciated that the parish became a mere adjunct to the adjoining living of Came, being held and served by the rector of that parish. In accordance, however, with Colonel Damer's wishes the Rev. George Arden kindly ceded Whitcombe to the new candidate for holy orders, but as a deacon could not hold preferment he proposed that W. Barnes should be nominated as his curate. The Bishop of Salisbury, however, preferred to make

a special case, for he wrote to Mr. Arden on
February 9th :—

PALACE, SALISBURY,
February 9th, 1847

REVEREND AND DEAR SIR,

I do not know whether you have yet done anything about Whitcombe—I mean whether you have
received the gift of donation. If not, I think I should
on the whole prefer that Mr. Barnes should present
himself to me with this as his title for Holy Orders,
rather than be nominated as your assistant. In any
case there will be a departure from my general practice
respecting Ordination, but I think the inconvenience
will be least in this way.

I remain, &c.,

E. SARUM.

In pursuance of this desire of the Bishop, the candidate presented himself for examination at Salisbury in
1847, whence he wrote to his wife :—

SALISBURY, *Wednesday, February 24th.*
Past Three o'clock.

I am just come back for a respite till 5 o'clock
from the ordeal of the examination, which turns out to
be rather severe. We had first to write a sermon off
from a given text, and then to turn a long piece of
English (from Hooker's works) into Latin. Both these
exercises I hope I have done pretty well. In the evening I think we shall have Ecclesiastical History.

I have had a very satisfactory and encouraging
interview with the Bishop.

I like my lodgings very much, having two prettily furnished and cheerful rooms on the sunny side of the street.

Friday, Three o'clock.

"I wish every day at the cathedral that the children could hear the service, which is heavenly, and see the building. . . .

"We have had a 'stunning' paper amongst those of to-day—to write an essay embodying the arguments of Hooker's first book of *Ecclesiastical Polity.*"

The Ordination took place on February 28th, at Salisbury, and William Barnes entered on his new duties as pastor of Whitcombe, a cure which entailed a course of long walks, the parish lying about three miles from Dorchester.

A propos of Whitcombe, it was some years later when a curious event happened in the little church one Sunday while the clergyman was preaching. The windows of the church were low, and looked on the farm-yard; the clerk, whose eyes had been gradually dilating with horror, at last rose with a sudden cry of "Fire," and flung his two hands into the air. In the course of a few seconds the whole congregation had rushed out, leaving the priest speaking alone. He, too, followed his flock, and was soon in the midst of them, handing on buckets of water and encouraging the workers. Two of the hay ricks were injured, but the others were saved, though it was found that trains had been laid to them all, probably some dastardly revenge on the farmer. In after days William Barnes, recalling the incident, used to say quaintly, "That was the only time my flock forsook their shepherd."

This year, 1847, was marked by another event, the purchase of a large lifehold house in South Street, and the removal of the school there in the summer. A more interesting purchase was made in October, at Sturminster, where William Barnes bought two fields near the banks of his beloved Stour, at Bagber. They were not precisely the land held by his forefathers, but were near enough to be dear to him by association, and the possession of them was a source of pleasure to the poet, who has illustrated his feelings in his own manner in "The pleace our own agean." The fields were let to a worthy Vale farmer, who came with due regularity on Dorchester fair days to pay his rent, and whose quaint Dorset speech was a never-ending delight to the young Barnes who entertained him. On one point landlord and tenant did not agree, and that was on the custom of pollarding trees. Farmer —— had an idea that a certain row of graceful elms along the banks of the stream would look much more "tidy-like if they were pollarded, so if Mister Barnes did agree he'd see about having it done." The landlord looked quizzically at the good farmer and asked, "Would you let me cut off your arm, or even your thumb?"

"Bless me, no, sir; why whatever should I do without un?"

"And what do you suppose the elms would do without their limbs?"

He scratched his head, "Well, sir, when you put it like that, I don't ezactly know, but I 'spose they'd grow some more."

"Yes, they would, poor, little stunted limbs, and look like mops instead of trees. No, Mr. ——, God made elms, and man made pollards; I like God's work best, so please leave the elms as they are."

The good farmer looked perplexed, and rather rue-fully gave in, to his landlord's veneration for the beautiful, his own theories of good farming.

William Barnes always had the greatest love for the Vale of Blackmore. The writer of this memoir has a recollection, dating some time before this, of a long drive taken by the poet and his wife in a friend's gig, lent for the occasion, with the tiny child at their feet on a little hassock. They drove to Ham Hill, up whose slopes they walked, until on the summit they looked over to the lovely valley of Blackmore, sur-rounded by its green hills. The Stour wound its flowing course in vagrant curves through green meadows and woodlands. Towns, and villages, and lonely farmsteads were dotted about, some forming a cluster of warm red or thatched roofs, others only suggested by curling smoke amongst the trees. The poet pointed out each place to his wife. "There was the farm of my grand-father;" "that was the house my great-grandfather possessed;" "there was one of my favourite haunts when a boy," and so on, every place seemed to be full of story to him. The child listened, not under-standing half the talk; but when after a time a sud-den rising cloud on the opposite hill became fringed with rain, and swept like a magic broom across the valley, making it glisten like diamonds, she asked, "Is that God's broom sweeping the country?" and the poet kissed her. One of his English poems, "On the Hill," [1] recalls a little the experiences of that long ago excursion.

Although already in deacon's orders W. Barnes had not yet taken his degree at Cambridge. By some University decree he was allowed to˙pass over the B.A. and M.A. degrees, and to compete for the higher ones in divinity, but to obtain these it was necessary that three terms should be spent in residence. Accordingly in June of this year 1847, we find him in St. John's College, Cambridge, making use of his boys' summer holidays by deeper studies of his own. His letters to Mrs. Barnes tell much of the story of his life at *Alma Mater* during the term which was marked by the installation of Prince Albert as Chancellor.

June 4th, 1847.

MY DEAREST JULIA,

I have little to tell you to-day, for I have been working hard in my own room. I have nearly finished my Latin sermon, which, however, I am fearful I shall have no chance of preaching this term. I believe I am to preach my English one before the professor and a large congregation on Sunday.

June 6th.

Thank God I have done one of my exercises, my English sermon, to-day. It is rather an arduous one, as it is preached in the public University Church (St. Mary's, which your mother knows) before the Vice-Chancellor, the Regius Professor of Divinity, and other

---

[1] *Poems of Rural Life in Common English,* page 76.

great men of the University, who sit weighing every
word of it. I hope it passed off pretty well. I have
some hope of getting my Latin sermon done this term.
I have taken my dessert with my tutor at his rooms
this afternoon, a good token that he is satisfied with my
exercise.

I find it is very lucky that I have given some
attention to logic. It is impossible to get a divinity
degree without it. I am now working up a Cambridge
book on the logic of the schools for my divinity disputations.

June 12th.

I have got into work here. I go to do two services
at Horningsea on Sunday for one of our fellows who is
called away, and I read prayers for him at the hospital
here every day till he comes back. I shall not forget
Saturday, the anniversary of the day which brought so
much happiness into the world for me. I am not joking,
and pray you may have a long series of repetitions
of it.

June 28th.

You are not to laugh at my tea-party. I was not so
silly as to make the tea myself. The other man
brought a tea-making thing called a wife ; and of course
I put the teapot into her hands, and made her wait on
me with her husband. When I have a single man,
however, I do make the tea for him. Preparations for
the installation are now thickening fast. They are
putting up an immense tent in our grounds, I think
it will be as large as the shed of our railway station.
I am to preach my *Clerum* (Latin sermon) to-morrow
morning.

July 6th.

It is a mercy you have a husband with sound limbs, as we have had such a squeeze to-day in Trinity College as you can hardly conceive. Members of the University up to many hundreds, possibly nearly two thousand, assembled in the outer square to receive the Queen, who arrived soon after one o'clock, and on its being announced that we were to go into the hall to present our addresses to her, a great rush was made to get in. I went with an impetuous wave that carried everything before it; and in which doctors with their red robes were pushed into scarecrows, and masters had their hoods torn off, and your unworthy admirer got his silver chain broken. We wore bands, and pretty things they were made in the scuffle. I got up to the head of the hall near the Queen before she withdrew. Our noble old college has appeared in her glory to-day. We have had two halls (dinners), one for pensioners and sizars at four o'clock, and a fellows' hall at six, when I sat down to a most superb dinner with about 200 sons of our *Alma Mater*; most of these men come up from the provinces to the installation.

God bless you and the children,

Your affectionate husband,

WILLIAM BARNES.

Sunday Eve.

I have made the acquaintance of another of our men' who paints in oil admirably, and is a good musician; he has introduced me to a friend of his at Queen's College, who is learned in architecture. There are certainly many superior minds here.

In the June of next year, 1848, he kept another term but was unable to get a turn to do either of his "opponencies."

The first was performed on October 19th, 1848, the opponent being Mr. Cole of Trinity, who was going in for his doctor's degree. The "questions" disputed were :—

(1) " Testamentum vetus novo contrarium non est."

(2) " Male sentiunt qui veteres tantum inpromissiones temporarias sperasse confingunt."

The second against Mr. W. Minen, of Sidney Sussex College, took place on November 2nd, when he thus wrote to his wife :—

ST. JOHN'S COLLEGE.

MY DEAREST JULIA,   *November 1st,* 1848.

I came up in exactly the way I marked out, but from the slipperiness of the rail I was late in London, and arrived at the Eastern Counties' station at the last minute.

Mr. B. (my tutor) had found me a room and sent in a sack of coals and a bedmaker ready to receive me, and a porter met me at the lodge to show me the way to my abode. I am in that part of the college which the men call "the wilderness," one side of the first or oldest court.

I ascend to my room by a dismal dusty decayed staircase of dark oak, trodden by gownsmen of many generations. My room is large and lofty, and is partially lighted by a great window with stone mullions, but unluckily the fireplace is in the same

wall as the window and therefore in a dark corner, so
·that I can hardly read in the luxurious attitude in
which I indulge myself at home, with my feet on the
hobs, or with my nose roasting over the grate. I guess
the room might have been so built to give the students
a hint of the difference between light and heat.

I am making something of my time by reading.
You might have found me if you had come this
morning with a huge folio (the works of an ancient
church father) before me. I wish to do as well as
possible at my examination, and can have from the
library books that I should not and could not buy.

He speaks modestly of his reading, but there is
recorded in some notes which have been found, a list
of the books he took from the University library, which
is remarkable as showing the omnivorous food he fed
his intellect withal. Here are some headings :—

June 29th, 1848.—*Grammatica Lapponica ; Aperçue
de la langue des Iles Marquises; Elementa Grammatices
Tyzoena* ; Lattain's *Egyptian Grammar ; Elemens de la
Grammaire Mandchoud.*

January 25th, 1850.—David's *Modern Greek Gram-
mar ;* J. W. Pol, *Bohmusche Sprache ;* Ziegenbalg,
Grammatica Danubica ; Vassalle, *Grammatica Maltez ;
Evangelia Gothice and Anglo-Saxonice ;* Endlicker's
Chinesischen Grammatik ; Blazewicz's *Wallachian
Sprache ;* Armenian *Grammar ;* Albanesen *Sprache*
(Xylander); *El Arte del Bascuenze ; Chaldee Grammar.*
The almost entirely philological nature of these
readings proves that he was already preparing the
scheme of his great work, the *Philological Grammar.*

Having come successfully through all his acts and
disputations, William Barnes finally had his B.D.
degree conferred on him in October, 1850. He had
been ordained Priest, at Salisbury, on March 14th, 1848.

With all these extra and deep studies he still found
time for writing. The correspondence with Mr.
Petheram, spoken of in Chapter IV., had the effect
of turning Barnes's mind to the great benefit which a
study of Anglo-Saxon would confer, in preserving the
purity of the English language. He believed that the
English spoken in our days is not, as many think, cultivated into a better form, but that it has been corrupted
for the worse, having lost many of its case-endings
and inflections, and it has besides lost in richness by
rejecting good old Saxon words to take in less intelligible ones from the Latin and Greek. He thought,
too, that Anglo-Saxon literature if more studied would
be found to contain a great deal that is interesting to
the scholar and the historian. These were the sentiments which gave rise to the *Anglo-Saxon Delectus*,
published by Russell Smith in 1849, a second
edition being called for in 1866. His object in
writing was always to do good more than to gain
money, and so closely did he keep this end in view that
he accepted without demur the following offer from
Russell Smith :—

4, OLD COMPTON STREET,
January 15th, 1849.

DEAR SIR,

Your MS. came safely to hand ; I have casually
looked it over, and I think it will make a 2s. or 2s. 6d.
book. Of its goodness I am no judge ; but if you feel

disposed to part with it for 5*l.* and a few copies, say
twenty, when printed, I will undertake it; this is what
Mr. Vernon asked me for his Guide [1] and which has not
yet repaid me, still I live in hopes of a good time
coming for Anglo-Saxon yet.

I am, etc.,

JOHN RUSSELL SMITH.

The Delectus was published under the title of *Se
Gefylsta* (the Helper) and was well reviewed, the
Athenæum, October 20th, 1849, saying that, " A philo-
sophic spirit pervades every part, &c."

In 1849 a short work entitled *Humilis Domus; some
Thoughts on the Abodes, Life, and Social Condition of the
Poor, especially in Dorset*, was printed. It contained
some just views of the condition of the poor, and was
probably to some of the Dorset landowners suggestive
of improvements which have since been made. The
farms in that county have now such model cottages
that the old cry of the half-starved Dorset labourer has
passed into an obsolete proverb, or is used ironically
when the peasants look particularly flourishing.

[1] *A Guide to the Anglo-Saxon Tongue*, by E. J. Vernon, B.A.

CHAPTER VIII.

PLORATA VERIS LACHRYMIS.

O NOW, my true and dearest bride,
Since thou hast left my lonely side
My life has lost its hope and zest.
The sun rolls on from east to west,
But brings no more that evening rest
Thy loving-kindness made so sweet,
And time is slow that once was fleet,
    As day by day was waning.

The last sad day that show'd thee lain
Before me, smiling in thy pain,
The sun soar'd high along his way
To mark the longest summer day,
And show to me the latest play
Of thy sweet smile, and thence, as all
The day's lengths shrunk from small to small,
    My joy began its waning.

I

And now 'tis keenest pain to see
Whate'er I saw in bliss with thee,
The softest airs that ever blow,
The fairest days that ever flow
Unfelt by thee, but bring me woe :
And sorrowful I kneel in pray'r
Which thou no longer now canst share
    As day by day is waning.

How can I live my lonesome days ?
How can I tread my lonesome ways ?
How can I take my lonesome meal ?
Or how outlive the grief I feel ?
Or how again look on to weal ;
Or sit at rest, before the heat
Of winter fires, to miss thy feet
    When evening light is waning.

Thy voice is still I lov'd to hear,
Thy voice is lost I held so dear.
Since death unlocks thy hand from mine,
No love awaits me such as thine;
O, boon the hardest to resign !
But if we meet again at last
In heav'n, I little care how fast
    My life may now be waning.

·

SORROW.

In the summer holidays of 1851 William Barnes
took his wife and two eldest children to London to see
the Exhibition. They had rooms in the house of a
person who had once lived in Dorchester. When they
visited the Exhibition, the very first thing they went to
see was Powers' Greek slave, which made a great
impression on the poet, who purchased a copy of it in
plaster, with which to adorn the mantel-shelf of his
study. A good deal of time was spent at the British
Museum, where the Nineveh marbles, then lately
brought to England by Sir H. Layard, proved intensely
interesting. The visit to town was not without its
adventures, for one of the children got nearly run over
—her terror-stricken mother pulling her out bodily from
beneath the feet of some pawing horses, which their
driver had pulled up on their haunches to save her.

A very amusing episode was the meeting with a well-
known Vale of Blackmore man, who looked thoroughly
out of place in the streets of London. He was a huge
fellow, so broad that when he drove his tax-cart about
his native lanes he took up the whole width of the

I 2

seat. The adventures of this mountain of humanity in the busy crowds of London were so funny that William Barnes put them in verse with great humour. When people looked at him and asked, "Who is that?" it was John Bloom's delight to chuckle, and say over his shoulder, "A half-starved Dorset man. Hee! hee!" This is how John Bloom fared with the London cabman :—

In Lunnon, John zent out to call
A tidy trap that he mid ride
To zee the glassen house, and all
The lot o' things a-stow'd inside.
"Here, Boots, come here," cried he, "I'll dab
A sixpence in your han' to nab
Down street a tidy little cab."
"A feäre," the Boots then cried ;
"I'm there," the man replied,
"The glassen pleäce, your quickest peäce,"
Cried worthy Bloom the miller.

The step went down wi' rattlen slap,
The zwingen door went open wide :
Wide? no ; vor when the worthy chap
Stepp'd up to teäke his pleäce inside
Breast foremost, he wer twice too wide
Vor thik there door. An' then he tried
To edge in woone an' tother side.
"Twont do," the driver cried ;
"Can't goo," good Bloom replied ;
"That you should bring theäse vooty thing,"
Cried worthy Bloom the miller.

"Come," cried the drever, "pay your feäre,
You'll teäke up all my time, good man."
"Well," answered Bloom, " to meäke that squäre,
You teäke up me, then, if you can."

" I come at call, the man did nod."
" What then ? " cried Bloom, " I han't a-rod,
And can't in thik there hodmadod."
" Girt lump," the drever cried ;
" Small stump," good Bloom replied !
" A little mite to meäke so light,
O' jolly Bloom the miller.

" You'd best be off now perty quick,"
Cried Bloom, " an' vind a lighter lwoad,
Or else I'll vetch my boot, and kick
The vooty thing athirt the road."
" Who is the man ? " they cried, " meäke room."
" A half-starved Do'set man," cried Bloom ;
" You be ? " another cried.
" Hee ! hee ! " wóone mwore replied.
" Aye, shrunk so thin, to bwone an' skin,"
Cried worthy Bloom the miller.

About this time the establishment of the Literary
Institutes for working men began to attract great
attention among the thoughtful; and William Barnes,
who always had the good of the people at heart, became
one of the most earnest supporters of the new move-
ment, and was willing at any time to lecture, or to teach
the young men. The Dorchester Institute was founded
chiefly under the active interest of three clergymen,
C. Bingham, H. Moule and W. Barnes, and was soon in
a flourishing condition. Barnes's lectures here led to
his being invited to speak at other Institutes. The
first of these was at Weymouth in November, 1851 ;
the second at his native town Sturminster, where, in
January, 1852, he lectured on " the Anglo-Saxons, and
the founding of the English kingdom, comprising the
relation of the Saxons to other Teutonic tribes, with

their settlement, institutions, laws, language and literature." The subject treated of seems a deep one for the
taste of working men, but it was evidently made clear and
interesting to them; a local significance being given to
it, as the old castle of Sturminster was once a residence
of King Alfred.

It was always pleasant to Mr. Barnes to be called to
the Vale of Blackmore for any cause, for his heart clung
to it through all changes, and to say a man was " a
Blackmore man " was a sure claim to his sympathies.
At this time there lived in Sturminster a most promising
young artist, named Thorne, a *protégé* of the good
rector, Mr. Lane Fox, who having discovered his extraordinary talent sent him to study under a good
master in London. William Barnes was one of Thorne's
most constant employers. He invited him to Dorchester,
where Thorne made portraits of the poet and his wife
and eldest little daughter, and whenever he had a few
pounds to spare, Barnes would order a landscape from
this compatriot. Thorne might have become a second
" Constable," if his character had not been too much
that of " Morland." He gave way to intemperance, and
at length his art became to him a mere means of
obtaining money to drink with. The walls of Mr.
Barnes's house were in time rich with the charming
landscapes, which, as far as their truth to nature and
happy treatment of rustic subjects goes, were worthy
illustrations of the Dorset poems themselves. Thorne
could pencil sunshine and storm effects as no one else
could, and several of his cattle pieces are worthy of
Cuyp.

The best way to get a picture done was by setting the

artist down before a lovely " bit" and giving him a commission on the spot. The fascination of the subject
generally made the erratic artist finish the picture. In
this way Barnes obtained some delightful paintings,
one of an old willow near Herringston, and some trees in
Frome Park amongst the number. When Thorne lay
dying, almost at the outset of what might have been a
fine career, he exclaimed " O that I could hold a brush,
I could paint such scenes ! such pictures as I have
never done before ! "

But it was too late, the life was wrecked even then,
and the poet often sighed as he looked at his pictures,
" Poor Thorne—he might have been great if he had
given himself a chance."

Early in 1852 the Bishop of Salisbury accepted the
resignation of the cure of Whitcombe, which William
Barnes tendered in the following note :—

DORCHESTER, Jan. 15th, 1852.

MY LORD,

I beg to signify to your lordship that I should
wish by your lordship's permission to give up the curacy
of Whitcombe at Easter next. I hope I have not been
unfaithful ·to the trust which your lordship put into my
hands, and which àt Easter I shall have holden five years;
and I trust I shall still serve the Church in my school,
and in any other Christian work which I can undertake
for her good.

Your lordship is aware that Whitcombe is holden
with Came by Mr. Arden, to whom with your lordship's
permission I leave it.

I am, etc.

There were several reasons for this resignation, one being the great distance of Whitcombe from his other duties, which entailed a six-mile walk every Sunday, so that with his weekly work in the school he got no necessary rest. Another still stronger reason was probably the failing health of his wife. There is a perfect blank of literary work in the first half of this year, nothing beyond a few short reviews of books in the *Gentleman's Magazine*. His was evidently a mind which required freedom from anxiety to be productive. In June 1852, he began again to keep his Italian Diary, a practice which he had left off on coming to Dorchester several years before and had never resumed till this sad time, after which the custom was never again broken. The first entry on June 5th was "*Infelice, mia moglia malata.*" The walks with the boys had still to be taken, and the cricket-matches played, the master following alone, and with a heavy heart. There is mention of his writing a poem called "Soul and Body," but as no trace of such a poem remains, it was probably an expression of some feelings too personal for publication. The holidays came just in time to release him from duties which his grief made almost impossible to him. Unfortunately he had made an engagement to preach twice at Frampton on June 20th, but he never knew how he got through that day of awful anxiety before he could return to the bedside of the invalid. No words but his own can tell the next day's woe,—a dark Midsummer day.

Monday, 21st.—"Oh, day of overwhelming woe! That which I greatly dreaded has come upon me. God has withdrawn from me his choicest worldly gift. Who

can measure the greatness, the vastness of my loss? I
am undone. Lord, have mercy upon me. My dearest
Julia left me at 11.30 in the morning."

June 22, 23, 24, 26, 27.—"*Giorni d'orrore.*" For
many days after this the single word "Sorrow," or the
sigh, "Oh, my loss," are eloquent and touching enough.
After a time he was able to relieve his heart by poetical
expression in the "*Plorata Veris Lachrymis,*" which
illustrates this chapter. In his own first writing the
first line runs, "My Julia, my dearest bride." This
sorrow took the deepest root in his heart. Hardly a
day for years but contained a sigh, such as, on May
19th, 1853: "Sad for my dearest wife." May 28th,
1853: "Heavy-hearted for my astounding loss." June
5th, 1853: "This day twelvemonths I began this diary:
Oh, day of sorrow! which has lasted until now." As
years went on these paroxysms of grief became less
violent, but to the time of his death, the word "Giulia"
was written like a sigh at the end of each day's entry.
Thirty-five years of constant loving remembrance! Is
it any wonder that the poems are eloquent of the
beauty and fullness of married love and of reverence
for the beautiful bond of married life? It is recorded
of Dr. Johnson that he was in the habit of writing
his dead wife's name in his journal after recording some
good resolution—merely the word "Tetty." He made
her the sharer of his most elevated moments, but the
daily "Giulia" showed a constant and never-ending
spiritual communion. He could say, with Stuart Mill,
"her memory was to me a religion." Memories of her
are enshrined in many of the most beautiful poems,
"Wife a Praised," p. 293; "Wife a Lost," p. 295;

"Woak Hill," p. 347 of the collected edition ; "Married
Pëair's Love-walk ;" the "Fireside Chairs," and "Walking Home at Night," in the English poems, and the
beautiful poem, "The Wold Wall," which I give here.

THE WOLD WALL.

Here Jeäne, we vu'st did meet below
The leafy boughs a-swingen slow
Avore the sun, wi' evenen glow
Above our road, a beamen red ;
The grass in zwath wer in the meads,
The water gleamed among the reeds
In air a-stealen round the hall
Where ivy clung upon the wall.
Ah ! well-a-day ! O wall adieu !
The wall is wold, the grief is new.

An' there you walk'd wi' blushen pride,
Where softly-wheelen streams did glide
Drough sheädes o' poplars at my zide,
An' there wi' love that still do live,
Your feäce did wear the smile o' youth,
The while you spoke wi' ages truth
An' wi' a rosebud's mossy ball,
I decked your bosom vrom the wall.
Ah ! well a-day ! O wall adieu !
The wall is wold, my grief is new.

But now when winter's rain do fall,
An' wind do beät ageän the hall,
The while upon the wat'ry wall
To spots o' gray the moss do grow ;
The roof noo moore shall overspread
The pillar ov our weary head,
Nor shall the rwose's mossy ball
Behang for you the house's wall.
Ah.! well-a-day ! O wall adieu !
The wall is wold, my grief is new.

The young wife had been in her lifetime the inspirer of the pretty "I Know Who," page 281, "The Maid for my Bride," page 134, and "Woone Smile More," page 339, &c.

Friends did all they could to console him in this sad time, and he rarely refused to be drawn out of his lonely house. In the middle of July, when he had preached at East Stoke on the Sunday, and dined and slept at Heffleton House, his old friends, Mr. and Mrs. Smith, brought his children to meet him at Wool, and spent the sunny July day in the ivy-grown ruins of Bindon Abbey. He never neglected to take his little girls for the country walks to which they had been accustomed, but the country seemed to him to have lost its beauty. His best solace was after all in hard work, and he says, " I took in my sadness to constant work out of school as well as in it," and turned to the *Philological Grammar* and wrote some papers for J. R. Smith's *Retrospective Review*.

The *Retrospective Review* was a venture of Mr. Barnes's publisher, Mr. J. Russell Smith, who writes thus about it on July 1st, 1852 :—

" I am going to start a *Retrospective Review* of old English literature, perhaps you may like to write some articles. In first starting I cannot offer a great remuneration; what I have offered to two or three is 2*l.* 10*s.* per article, to be not less than a sheet of sixteen octavo pages, one-third of it to be original composition, the remainder extracts, or more original matter if the writer chooses, but then I pay no more. I leave the subject to the writer, but it must not be on any doctrinal point of religion, or a classical

subject, except an old translation of a classical author
by an Englishman. . . . No review of the writings of
any living author will suit, but no objection to any
modern edition or first printed work of any ancient
writer. . . . I purpose publishing Part I., price 2s. 6d.
quarterly, in October. The two last sheets will be
devoted to the printing (for the first time) of short
MSS. in Anglo-Saxon, Norman, or Early English, &c.,
from the public libraries, and also to correspondents on
literary subjects of a larger kind than 'Notes and
Queries.' This correspondence I expect will flow in
without payment. The articles in the Review to be
anonymous. Please to let me hear what you think of it.

" Yours very truly,

" J. RUSSELL SMITH."

The reply must have been favourable, for during the
years 1853-4 Barnes contributed the following articles
to the *Retrospective*, Vol. I. Art. 4 : " Population and
Emigration at the beginning of the Seventeenth Century ; " " Anecdota Literaria ; " " Extracts from the
Diary of John Richards, Esq." pp. 97-201.

This diary was an old MS. book of about the date
1680, the journal of a Dorsetshire Squire, which fell by
some chance into William Barnes's hands, and caused
him great pleasure and amusement. The cost and
management of the writer's estates and household,
even the " farthingales for my wife Alice," and his own
amusements, are all chronicled there, and make a good
picture of life in the seventeenth century.

Some of William Barnes's papers present great contrasts of thought, such as the " Pyrrhonism " of Joseph

Glanville, and one on Waterhouse and Fox, and the
" Utility of Learning in the Church."

For an article on "Leland" Mr. Russell Smith sent
him down a precious batch of old tomes; these were
the life of Leland, Leland's *Cygnea Cantio*, Leland's
Assertio Asturin. Then came a paper on "Astrology,"
written after poring over such books as *Vox Piscis*,
Heydon's *Defence of Astrology*, Enderlie's *Astrologer*,
Life of Emin, Meltoni's *Figure Caster*. At this
time there was a good deal of amateur astrologising
in the household. Some of the children tried hard
to unravel the mysteries of their "ruling houses."
The poet himself, who had a retired study up in the
attics, learned to rule horoscopes, but I do not remember that any great truths were foretold. *A propos*
of that attic study, the student of astrology once very
nearly lost his life in it. He had invested in a new
stove which burned coke and gave a great heat, and
was revelling in the delight of writing in a genial
atmosphere, when his ideas became imperceptibly dulled,
and, pen in hand, he sank into immobility in his arm-
chair. It was only when he failed to appear at the
supper-table that Mrs. Barnes came to seek him; and
though nearly paralysed with horror, she managed to
drag him outside the room before calling for assistance ;
fortunately the pure air soon revived him. The maker
of this stove may possibly have been the inventor of a
new warming apparatus for the large church of St.
Peter's, Dorchester, which had a most alarming effect.
The carbonic acid gas which rose from beneath the
floor of the aisles had first the effect of making the
little children drop down insensible, and one by one

they were carried out. Next the more delicate young people succumbed, among whom were two or three of William Barnes's household. At length even the strong ones began to suffer, and went out in groups, leaving the rector preaching to empty benches, very much bewildered to know what was happening, for the heavy fumes had not yet reached him in the pulpit. The streets were full of groups of suffering people, helping to support others more suffering than themselves. One young woman fell into a swoon which lasted three hours, and William Barnes and his family were in all stages of racking headache, which he induced them to try and walk off by a long stroll in the country, though he himself felt the effects of it for some days after.

Some correspondence between Russell Smith and the Dorchester poet shows that in 1852—just after his bereavement—the new edition of the poems was in danger of being lost to him.

July 30, 1852.

DEAR SIR,

There is some difficulty about getting the copies of the *Dorset Dialect*. Mr. Clark has left business, and all the printed books have been sent to an auction room. The party who holds the books cannot act on your order without Mr. Clark's concurrence; will you please to write to this gentleman? . . . I think you had better put the whole of the copies into my keeping.

Yours very truly,

J. RUSSELL SMITH.

A second appeal in September brought the result that the whole edition was placed in Russell Smith's hands, with the following letter from the worthy but unfortunate printer, which proves him to have been better able to take care of his friend's interests than his own.

LONDON, *September 4th*, 1852.

MY DEAR SIR,

I am truly concerned that circumstances should have combined to render you so much inconvenience and uncertainty respecting the printed stock of your *Dorset Poems*, and I am very desirous of explaining to you that many little incidents seem to have conspired to occasion vexation, which at length is now remedied by a delivery into the charge of Mr. J. R. Smith. You are possibly aware that many months since my business was dissolved, when I secured protection for your work on the premises of my successor in business—my former partner. Success, however, not attending the arrangement, I was compelled, as the guardian of your interests, suddenly to remove the stock to a place of safer refuge until I had an opportunity of conference with you. I have received your two notes on the subject, but both having been sent to my former address did not reach my hands until some days after the time you intended; when being suddenly called to Liverpool on a business affair of emergency, I was compelled to postpone immediate compliance with your request. Mr. R. Smith has now received 402 copies in gross, for which I wish a speedier sale than of late. I trust this statement will remove any possible supposition of inattention or unfriendly neglect. I had thought some opportunity of a personal interview might have occurred previous to a necessity for removal, but time really seems to glide through one's fingers with the slipperiness of an eel, and to mock our puny endeavours at detention or delay . . . .

The letter ends with very feeling sympathy in the poet's domestic loss, and is signed George Clark.

In 1853 a series of lectures was begun in connection with the museum at Dorchester. The Rev. Osmund Fisher gave an interesting geological series, and the Rev. C. Bingham followed with antiquarian and historical subjects. William Barnes took his turn November 30th, 1852, on "Light and Heat," and again on February 8th, 1853, in a lecture on "Gold and Social Wealth." This was the germ of a future book, *Labour and Gold*, just as the Sturminster lecture on "The Anglo-Saxons" was the germ of *The Saxons and Saxon English.*

All through this year the Italian diary shows how grief ran through every occupation and under every change. It followed him when he took the well-known country walks with the pupils which she had so often shared, those excursions to the yellow cliffs and purple heaths of the Yellowham wood, the strolls by the flowing Frome, with the crowfoot white on its breast.

Here is a day, one of many. "September 1st, 1852. In school. Walked with the boys round Red-pit lane. Writing verses, 'The young that died in beauty.' Sad with my forlorn life." His kind friends did all they could; they came to chat in the evening

and to sup with him. Mr. Smith played chess with
him. Mr. L—— took him for drives, the chaplain of
the prison made little suppers for him, and talked of
all things under the sun to amuse him. His lost wife's
sister came in September to stay with the motherless
children, and took two of them home with her. As far
as he could, he occupied his mind; but too often the
strain of thought for the great task he had set himself,
the *Universal Grammar*, melted into sad poesy, and we
find him, on October 4th, " Writing some verses on
dearest Julia, ' Oh, had she been as many are,' &c.
Heavy rain all day." It was probably by a further
effort of William Barnes's good friends to draw him
out of himself that the " madrigal evenings were instituted. The first record of these pleasant meetings
was on October 27th, 1852 : " In school. Rearranging
and cleaning my books. Walked in the afternoon with
Julia " (his young daughter) " to Stafford. Mr. Patch
and Mr. Arden with us in the evening. Sang some
madrigals."

Mr. Patch, formerly a chorister, afterwards sub-
organist of Wells Cathedral, and at the time I write of,
organist to the Church of St. Peter, was gifted with a
magnificent bass voice of three complete octaves in
compass, and it was the great enjoyment of the young
Barneses to hear him roll out Polyphemus's song in
" Acis," " Oh, ruddier than the cherry," or Tom Purcell's
glorious " Mad Tom." Mr. Arden, a young surgeon,
was an amateur of great taste and with a beautifully-
cultivated tenor voice. These, with William Barnes's
useful baritone and the girls' clear young trebles, re-
inforced by some young friends with good contralto

K

voices, made up the harmony. The first trial led to weekly meetings, which proved a great solace to the poet. It was delightful to see him in his arm-chair by the fire listening with his eyes shut (which was always his favourite way of enjoying music) to the tender harmonies of "Blow, gentle gales," or "When winds breathe soft," and sometimes joining the singers in the chorus to the "Chough and Crow," or "Ye spotted Snakes."

The Sundays were rarely passed without preaching, though the curacy of Whitcombe. was given up. Clergymen were always in need of help, either from illness or engagements elsewhere, and we find him starting off on long drives to Godmanston, to Forston, to Milton Abbas, and elsewhere, serving the churches of his friends. These engagements were a boon to him, for on the only disengaged Sunday for a long time we find the day epitomised: "At church, walking, reading; supped at Mr. S.'s; very sad. My sabbaths, which were so happy with J. at my side, are now my saddest days."

It was about this time that the craving for constant employment induced him to take up the resource of painting in water-colours. He would carry his block and paint-box slung by a strap round his shoulders, and while the pupils played cricket or climbed trees in search of eggs, he made a rapid sketch of some favourite "bit." These sketches were very free, but most of them were in too low and melancholy a tone of colour, and seemed to be Nature at her saddest, having, strange to say, none of the joyous sunlight which marks the word-painting in his poems. An artist named Graham

came to settle in Dorchester, and W. Barnes often joined
him in sketching excursions.

On Wednesday, February 23rd, another loss befell
William Barnes in the death of Mrs. Miles, his mother-
in-law, who for the twenty-one years of her widowhood
had lived under his roof. She had been a great
consolation to him in her care of the motherless
children, and the remark on the day of her funeral,
" I sink a step lower in sadness," only faintly expresses
his feelings. The charge of the house now fell heavily
on the shoulders of young girls barely out of the
schoolroom.

CHAPTER IX.

TWEIL.

In wall-zide sheädes, by leafy bowers,
   Underneath the swayen tree,
O' leäte, as round the bloomen flowers
   Lowly humm'd the giddy bee,
My childern's small left voot did smite
Their tiny speäde, the while the right
Did trample on a deäisy head
Bezide the flower's dousty bed.
An' though their work wer idle then
   They, a-smilen an' a-tweilen,
Still did work an' work ageän.

Now their little limbs be stronger,
   Deeper now their vaïce do sound ;
An' their little veet be longer,
   An' do tread on other ground ;
An' rust is on the little bleädes
Ov all the broken-hafted speädes ;

An' flow'rs that wer my hope an' pride
Ha' long agoo a-bloom'd an' died;
But still as I did labour then
    Vor love ov all them children small,
Zoo now I'll tweil an' tweil ageän.

When the smokeless tun's a-growen
    Cold as dew below the stars,
An' when the vier noo moore's a-glowen
    Red between the window bars,
We then do läy our weary heads
In peace upon their nightly beds,
An' gi'e woone sock [1] wi' heavèn breast,
An' then breathe soft the breath o' rest
Till day do call the sons o' men   [ness
    Vrom night-sleep's blackness, vull of sprack-
Out abroad to tweil ageän.

Where the vaïce o' the winds is mildest
    In the plain their stroke is keen;
Where their dreatnèn vaïce is wildest
    In the grove, the grove's our screen.
An' where the worold in their strife
Do dreaten most our tweilsome life,
Why there Almighty ceäre mid cast
A better screen ageän the blast.
Zoo I won't live in fear o' men,
    But, man-neglected, God-directed,
Still will tweil an' tweil ageän.

[1] Sock—sigh.

THE PHILOLOGICAL GRAMMAR.

By the middle of the year 1853 the MS. of the *Philological Grammar* was in the hands of Mr. J. Russell Smith, who, doubtful of the financial success of such an astounding book, dared not improve on his usual offer of £5 for the copyright. This was accepted without demur—what would Mr. Anthony Trollope have thought of such a price?—and proofs began to come in, though the book was not really published till 1854. The *Philological Grammar* is perhaps one of the most extraordinary works a man has ever conceived, forming as it does a Universal Grammar. William Barnes had been led to the design through the readings of many years. It dawned upon him when he began, in the days at Chantrey, to compare Anglo-Saxon with English, and in Abergavenny, when he was so struck with the purity of Welsh. It grew upon his mental view when he discovered that the same laws of case ruled the fourteen different languages he had studied at Mere, when he wrote his pamphlet. Then he began to investigate further rules of grammar and wider laws, when his leisure time at Cambridge threw open to him the treasures of the University library, and he studied that polyglot list of books, which I have before quoted. By this time he had gained such a lucid view of the grammatical rules which have the same power in all languages, and knew so well the points of speech which were most likely to change under different influences, that he could acquire enough of a new language in a week or two to enable him to write and read it with a dictionary. The more he studied philology the more he felt sure that the science of grammar would be simplified by a clearly expressed epitome of these rules which are found in all tongues; and in avowing this aim he begins his preface :—

" There are three sciences which are of great service for the strengthening of the mind and the sharpening of wit, and for the helping of the understanding in its search after truth—Geometry, Logic, and Grammar ; but if we would make Grammar truly worthy of its two fellow-sciences, we must seek to conform it to the universal or to some common laws of speech, so as to make it the science of the language of mankind, rather than the grammar of one tongue.

" A knowledge of the forms which have grown out of common laws, working with peculiar elements in one tongue, cannot be fairly taken for the science of Grammar, any more than a knowledge of the organs of one plant (when some even of them are misformed from accidental causes) is the science of Botany.

" The formation of language is always a conformation to three things in nature—(1) the beings, actions, and relations of things in the universe ; (2) the conceptions of them by the mind of man ; and (3) the actions of the organs of speech: and inasmuch as the beings, actions, and relations of things and the mind and the organs of speech are the same in kind to all men upon earth, and a need of conformity to them is itself a law, so far it is clear that some common laws must hold in the formation of languages; and the science of those laws, when they are unfolded, is Grammar."

The moment one opens the book one feels in a strange land; even our native English is given a new sound, for it is here that the Saxonising of Barnes's English first becomes especially marked. For instance, vowels are called "breath-sounds," and consonants "clippings," because they clip or cut off the open vowel sounds.[1] Of course a mind like his would begin at the very foundation of language, and thus he traces the different modes of communication of thought, such as the symbolic or logographic mode, which he simplifies as "sight speech:" to this belong the ancient Egyptian hieroglyphics and the Chinese language. Sight speech, modified into the raised alphabet for the blind, becomes "finger speech" in his apt definition. He speaks of the "half language" of signals, which is for hearing and sight; of "breath-sound language" (speaking), which is for hearing alone, and of "type language" (printing), which is for sight and brain.

"Type language has been of great help in the exaltation of man's moral nature, for the enlarging of his knowledge, and for the weal of his social life.

---

[1] In a later work, *Speechcraft*, Barnes has taken the word "breath-penning" for consonants, because by them the breath-sound (vowel) is "pent" up.

as corps (*corpus*), viscount (*visconti*), autumn (*autumno*), debtor (*debitor*). Of English spelling he says, " It seems clear that the type-form of a language should be true to its 'breath-sound' form; and that there should be one letter, and no more than one, for every breath-sound and setting of the organs of speech. As our alphabet is short of the breath-sounds and clippings by many letters, and as letters of words borrowed abide in our language, in words from other tongues or from the older form of our own, . . . and as letters of words borrowed from other languages stand sometimes for the breath-sounds and clippings which they betokened in the word-giving languages, and at other times to those which they mark in our own, therefore our type-language is not true to the breath-sound speech, and it is very anomalous and puzzling, hard to learn and keep in mind. This untruthfulness of our spelling is a great hindrance and evil to our children and others in their learning of our type-language," &c. Here follows a plea for phonography, and Mr. Pitman's alphabet is explained, though he agrees that judgment must be used before meddling with the spelling of words, not to destroy too much the clue to their pedigree which superfluous letters often give. The most phonotypic languages are the Ancient Greek and Latin, Modern Italian, Spanish and Portuguese, Persian, Hindustani, Khoordish, and Turkish. Hebrew and Arabic read with points are also fairly spelt according to sound, so is Welsh, excepting only in its double consonants.

The " Canons of Clippings " (p. 31), or laws of consonants, is a most markworthy chapter. In it are

traced through all languages, from the older to the
newer, the special tendency to change in each consonant. By this we learn two general rules, that
kinsletters have a tendency to drop into the softer
form in course of time, and that in the meeting of two
consonants not kinsletters, the stronger often crushes
out the weaker. Barnes gives thirty-six cases of these
changes throughout all languages. So we learn that
B before F has a tendency to get lost in the stronger
power of the F, as in the Latin *subfocare*, now "suffo-
cate;" the B also softens to V, as in the Saxon *haben,*
our "have;" *silber*, "silver." V before T also goes out, as
Latin, *civitas;* Italian, *città.* The same with M before
N—Latin, *condemnare ;* Italian, *condannare.* T softens
to D—Latin, *patronus;* Italian, *padrone :* Saxon, *traum ;*
English, "dream;" and so on through all the thirty-six
cases of change. These rules thoroughly learnt would
greatly simplify the knowledge of derivatives, and make
comparative philology a very interesting study.

In "Etymology" the formation of words forms an
interesting chapter. Words are classed as notional
(nouns, adjectives, and verbs) and relational (all the minor
parts of speech). Some notional words are root words,
as " man," " good," "drive;" others are derivatives, as
"manful," from "man;" driver," "drift," &c., from "drive."
A cursory glance at the chapter on " Derivatives " gives
the idea of some abstruse algebraical dissertation, and
is possibly rather alarming at first glance to the student.
For instance, to be told of the word forms $5+3$ or
$3+$ or $2+1$, seems very difficult to take in ; but when
once the preliminary table is understood—that 1 stands
for Noun, 2 Adjective, 3 Verb, 4 Adverb, and 5 pre-

position, it is clear enough that 5 + 3 is a word formed
of a preposition and verb, such as "overcome;" that
3 + is a verb with a termination such as 3 + ing,
" loving " or " being ;" 3 + ly, " lovely ;" and that 2 + 1 is
a union of adjective and noun, as " blackbird." Taking
these numerical signs for the parts of speech, the same
rule will hold for any language.

Thus the form 2 + will express as well the English
" blackness," " softness " (2 + ness) as they do the Latin
dulcedo, rubigo (2 + do ; 2 + igo), or the Japanese *sige*
" thick," *sighe-sa* " thickness " (2 + sa), which could
never be completely classified in English words. The
rules of gender and number are brought under the same
comprehensive classification. All languages have the
singular and plural form, but only the " Shemetic
languages, such as Hebrew, Arabic, and Maltese, together
with Greek, Tonga, and possibly Welsh," have the dual
form for two things of their name such as we express
by the separate words, " pair," " twin," &c.

The chapter on Case is a masterly treatise, which was
enlarged from a former work called *The Laws of Case*,
spoken of in Chap. III. It begins, " Case is a most
weighty and powerful division of grammar, wielding
with great might the syntax of languages ; but although
its laws are highly worthy of our search, they are as yet
ill understood." To prove this he quotes from dozens
of grammars of all languages the weak or clashing
definitions of case and the varying number of cases ;
from M'Culloch's English Grammar, which gives only two,
nominative and possessive, to the eight cases of the
Basque and Hindustani, the thirteen of the Grammatica
Lapponica, and the sixteen of the Lingua Syrjoena, a

Finnic tribe. Setting aside both the inefficient and superfluous laws of cases, William Barnes then expounds his own scheme of classification (page 107), which may be found useful and true in every language. The list is a long one of twelve cases, for which, though he gives the Latin name, he also finds a very expressive English equivalent that, as usual, simplifies the apparent difficulty. I have epitomized them thus :—

Latin.	English.	Example.
1. Nominative	or Main-speech case	as The man rides.
2. Vocative	or Calling case	as O man ! hear me.
3. Possessive	or What's case	as John's field.
4. Genitive	or Whereof case	as The fear of death.
5. Originative	or Wherefrom case	as He went from London.
6. Accusative	or Whereunto case	as John went to London.
7. Objective	or Wheretowards case	as He threw a stone at John.
8. Locative	or Where case	as He sat in the hall.
9. Dative	or What-to case	as I spoke to the man.
10. Associative or Instrumentative }	or Wherewith case	as He writes with a reed.
11. Abessive	or Wherewithout case	as I wrote without a pen.
12. Assecutive	or Whereafter case	as He walks along by the canal.

Besides these there are the several twofold or mixed cases; and if it seem to the student that these endless combinations are puzzling, we have the author's words in answer :—

"It may be said against a system of natural cases, that to discriminate so many classes of the logical relations of things upon what may be deemed slight differences or likenesses, and to unfold as many shiftings of two-fold cases, is to make grammar needlessly perplexing. To this it may be answered that all the logical relations of things are in nature, and if they are manifold there is no help for it. We may shut our eyes to them, but we cannot lessen them. They have been brought in sundry classes before the thought of men of all nations as they have shown by the structure of their languages, and our minds will miss the good of what should be a wit-sharpening exercise, the learning of grammar, if we would wilfully keep them out of thought. . . . .

" Botanists tell us that there are three or four hundred orders of plants and more than a thousand species of the *Leguminosæ.* It is not by an idle wish that one can know them all, but there is no help for it. Botanists might, it is true, have stopped with the discrimination of the five great classes of plants, but still they would not have therefore lessened the number of the orders and species or made them more like or unlike one another, nor have left the knowledge of plants of more easy attainment " (p 14).

The chapter on adjectives is most exhaustive. There are the stem adjectives from verb roots, such as from " fill " we get " full," from " heat," " hot ; " and the stem adjectives from noun roots, as " stone," " stony ; " " hope," " hopeless." Of these last are many stems. Thus in Form 1 + y, by taking, as before, the " 1 " as the sign of a noun, it would stand for all words made of a noun with the ending " y," such as " cloudy," " noisy." This form is of universal application, by the explanation that " y " means " many " or " much," the Latin form being 1 + osus, *gramminosus,* or 1 + tus, *funestus.* In Anglo-Saxon tongues it might be 1 + ig, *Dreor-ig* (germ), *traur-ig,* and so on through many speech-forms. The other stems, 1 + ish " womanish ; " 1 + ful, " harmful ; " 1 + less, " shapeless," &c., &c., are all treated in the same way, as also the Forms 2 + ish, and other

endings,—2 being the formula for adjectives, this
branch includes such words as blackish, longish. Then
come the many verb roots (Form 3 +) such as 3 + some,
frolicsome, 3 + ly, lovely, &c. There are on the whole
32 different forms of the derivations of adjectives,
illustrated from the living and dead languages.

Verbs for which the formula number is 3 are treated
in the same kind of classification. Form 1 or 1 + "to
butter" or "sparkle," being words derived from nouns.
Form 2 + 1, adjective and noun, as "to blackball"
and Form 2 + 3, adjective and verb, as "whitewash."
Then there are Form 2 + to chuck, chuckle, spring,
sprinkle, &c.

Form 5 + 3 preposition and verb, such as inscribe,
circumscribe, overflow, undersell.

So it may be easily conceived that when once the
formulæ are understood, and they are very simple, just
the five numbers for the five parts of speech, the whole
system of classification becomes easy, and can be applied
to any language. It would take too long to follow the
classification of moods and tenses of which a comparative table is given. The part dedicated to syntax is
most clearly logical and comprehensive ; and though the
Latin terms are used, they are so explained in Saxon
English, as to make them easy to the dullest student.
For instance Pleonasm, an overfilling of speech;
Metonymy, a name changing; Euphemism, a fair-
speaking.

Of all this wonderful book, perhaps the part on
Prosody is the most remarkable, analysing as it does
the poetical and rhythmic forms of all nations, from the
Latin, "quantity," the Welsh "accent," the Saxon

L

" alliteration," the Hebrew " thought-rhyme," the Norse
" half-rhyme," the varied Persian metres, to the Italian
sonnetto, *rispetto*, and *stornello*, and modern English
rhyme.   It shows that his own poems are the result of
the deepest study, for nearly all these different national
forms may be traced in them.

The *Philological Grammar*, though treated with respect by all the critics, as " a learned and philosophical
treatise ; " " a most valuable monument of a well-read
man's mental capacity," found but little favour with the
general reader.

The time for Comparative Philology was not yet
come, and the look of the book needlessly alarmed the
casual reader, who probably shut it up with the verdict,
" Oh, this is dry, and beyond me ; one must be a linguist
or a mathematician already to understand it."   A little
more patience would have shown him that the book
might go far to make a man a linguist, who was not
one previously, for it teaches the science of language
from its foundation.   I cannot help thinking that since
the more general uses of steam and electricity annihilate
space so much that it is necessary for every man to
know something of foreign tongues ; the time will come
when this grammar, which shows at one glance the
general framework of all languages, may in a measure
take the place of the many special grammars which
students have to plod through to acquire even an un-
practical knowledge of languages.   We have rumours
of the necessity of a universal language ; but seeing
the impossibility of teaching it to every one, lettered
and unlettered, the next best thing is to study the
science of grammar on a wider basis, so that it may

assist us to understand the different languages which do and must exist. When the time arrives that this want is felt, the student will find Barnes' *Philological Grammar* ready to his hand, and will realise that when once the general laws which rule all speech are learned, the labour of studying a new language will consist mainly in learning the root-words, from which he will be able to build up the rest. The author himself had by these means so reduced the study of grammar to general rules, that he could, with the help of a dictionary for the root-words, learn to read or write a foreign language in a few weeks. The last proof of the grammar was sent to the printer on February 24th, 1854, and Barnes received the first copy of the book on March 27th the same year.

CHAPTER X.

OUR EARLY LANDSCAPE.

Ah! with what little shoes we trod,
  At first this path on upland ground,
Or else with elders took our road
  That leads to other homes around,
And pointing little finger tips
  Towards the yonder hills of blue,
Have cried with little boasting lips,
  " I've been out there," or " I have too."

And yonder, down beneath us, crawls
  The Stour towards the eastern hills,
To drive by many foaming falls
  The mossy wheels of many mills,
To clustered houses on its brow,
  Each village with a name full dear
To folk in other lands, who now
  Have left for aye their birth-homes here.

Stour's olden minster town, our own
  Dear birthstead, glides he slowly through,
Beneath its hoary bridge of stone,
  On both sides old, on one called new.
And Shillingston, that on her height
  Shows up her tower to op'ning day,
And high-shot Maypole, yearly dight
  With flow'ry wreaths of merry May.

And Durweston, the meadowy head
  Of Blackmore, where, as wanders on,
The stream, I see athwart its bed
  The high-heaved bulk of Hambledon.
Our sight or thought can reach by bridge
  And road, and parish towers,
From Thornhill spire on yonder ridge,
  To Blackmore's longsome rim of hills.

(Unpublished.)

"HWOMELY RHYMES."

1853—1858.

THE newly awakened love of sketching had the effect of stirring up William Barnes's innate artistic tastes in all directions. He became not only an amateur artist, but an enthusiastic collector of pictures. Hitherto he had been content to enrich his walls with the work of his compatriot Thorne, but now this no longer sufficed. A sale of books and pictures at Wincanton first attracted him; and in the next year while with his daughters visiting friends at Shepton Mallet, an auction of some collector's treasures took place, which he attended, and came home the happy possessor of landscapes and sea-pieces. From this time there was no escape for him, the mania of a collector had taken a firm hold, and his well-known figure was seen giving meaning nods at many an auction. The antiquarian shops knew him well, for if a dark old painting were hung at the door William Barnes might be seen stopping to examine it, and many a time he returned with a dusty picture under his arm, in which nothing but blackened varnish could be seen. With this he would retire to his den, and subject the dark canvas to a mysterious process of restoration known only to himself; it was a process which required him to don his oldest coat, and which filled the house with a smell of oils and varnish. After some days he would come down stairs with a beaming face, and display the astonishing results of his labour; very often a fine old work of art had emerged from the many layers of dust and old varnish. A beautiful *St. Joseph with the Infant Jesus*, one day came from obscurity, which connoisseurs attributed to Ribera. It was only of late years that the writer discovered a certain Guido in Florence which was the facsimile of it, and of which the picture at Came must have been a replica, or a very old copy.

Some signed pictures—notably a Gainsborough, a Backhuysen, a Serries, &c.—were thus rescued from obscurity, and took their places on the walls of Barnes's home, increasing so fast that they overflowed from drawing and dining rooms into lobby and staircase.

Their uses in the education of his children were as great as his own delight in them; for they trained the tastes which have in more than one instance been of practical benefit. He had an equally strong love of old engravings, of which he made a fine collection. He always thought it necessary to excuse himself for these innocent tastes, saying, "I spend no money on wines, or tobacco, or horses, don't you know?" and his listeners would smile at the incongruity of the idea. He never learned to smoke, and when asked the reason replied, "I do not wish to create a want which I have not by nature."

In 1854 the pleasant Hindustani and Persian readings with Major Besant were resumed. The two
scholars met alternately at each other's houses once a
week, for reading and supper. On March 17th, they
began the *Gulistan* of "Saadi," after which they took up
the *Bagh-o-bahar*.

Mr. Barnes's intercourse with his two antiquarian
friends was also very frequent. Sometimes he went to
stay with Mr. Charles Hall at Osmington, where the
two archæologists would hold discussions on Roman,
Celt and Saxon, amid the well-filled cases of antiquities
that lined the walls. Nearly every vacation we find him
spending a few days with Mr. Warne, who at the time
was engaged in a great work on Dorset, and there was
a very brisk interchange of ideas on "stone-girt duns,"
Roman roads, British "caers" and hut circles, &c.

Sometimes in the pleasant summer vacations he took
his daughters for a trip, such as the one to the Isle of
Wight, which was taken with some friends in June 1853,
where, after seeing the launch of the *Princess Royal* gun-
boat on Thursday the 23rd, they spent several pleasant
days in excursions about the island which he thus
humorously summarises in a playful letter to one of
his absent little daughters :—

DORCHESTER, July 1853.

My Very Dear L.

I am very happy to find that you are enjoying
yourself so highly, though I am almost bewildered with
the thoughts of your pleasures, past, present, and anticipated. Your dances on the green, and frolics in
other places, blowings of cornopeans, squeaking of

flutes! tweedling of fiddles! laughings of girls! glee singings! hoppings, skippings, and jumpings! Oh, it makes me quite giddy to think of it all! . . .

Your sisters will tell you of our trip, and how we saw the *Princess Royal* swimming in the sea, and went on board the *Victory*, and how I *stood up* where Nelson *fell*—am I not a great man!—and how we saw great sheets of canvass hung, and men standing before them with the *yards*, as we were told, though we did not see them measuring and cutting them for sale; and how we went down in the *cock-pit* and did not see in it so much as a single little *bantam*, and how the sailors called the ship *she*, and said she had (*beaux*) bows, which might have been some bigger ships in the harbour; and how we were carried away from Portsmouth in a steamboat, and forced to *appear* (a pier) before the inhabitants of Ryde, in the Isle of Wight, and had to pay sixpence to be let out again. These are only a few of the wonders of our voyage, you shall hear more of them when you come home.

Your affectionate Father.

The next summer's excursion was a visit to the Vale of Blackmore, to show the poet's birthplace to his children. There is an old, ill-written diary by the child to whom the above letter was addressed, which contains an account of this memorable day.

" *Thursday, June 29th*, 1854. This is a 'white day' of my diary. The sun rose brilliantly, and the sky was quite free from clouds. We were all up by five o'clock, and had a very early breakfast. The carriage was at the door by six, and we started in the full anticipation

of a very pleasant day. We were sorry to be obliged
to leave I.... at home, but father thought she would
not be able to walk quite so far, so she is going to
spend the day at the Castle. The drive was charming in
the clear morning air, the sun shone brightly, the birds
were singing and we were in the best possible spirits.
It seemed like going into the Promised Land, for it is
a pleasure that has been promised us many years, and
seeing dear father's birthplace has been anticipated by
us a very long time. The first place of any note we
passed was a rather large village called Lydlinch. A
quack once lived here who professed to, and I believe
did, cure the king's evil or scrofula by a charm. It was
only beneficial in the beginning of May at a particular
phase of the moon. The principal part of it consisted in
giving the afflicted person a small bag containing a toad
sewed up in it, which was to be worn round the neck.
Soon after passing Lydlinch we entered the Vale of
Blackmore, that most lovely picture of rural English
scenery. The vale of sunny slopes, shady lanes, woody
dells, picturesque trees and rivulets, not forgetting the
cottages which are scattered about—you cannot go a
quarter-of-a-mile without seeing a pretty cottage with
its honeysuckle porch, pretty garden and healthy-looking
children playing near. At the entrance of the Vale is
an inn called the 'King's Stag' because a gentleman
named Sir John de la Lynde once shot in that place a
stag which was a favourite of one of our early kings.
The king was so angry at the loss of his stag that he
taxed all Sir John's lands, and a tax is paid in that part
of the Vale of Blackmore to this day, which is called
the ' White Hart Silver.'

"At Bagber we let the carriage go on to Sturminster and began our walk of a mile across Bagber Common, of which I will say nothing, as there is a new stiff straight road through, and ugly brick houses. The first interesting place we saw was a large farm-house which is approached by a pretty avenue of trees and is the scene of the poem, 'Fanny's birthday.' It has the poetical name of Woodlands. Not far from here dear father pointed out to us a cottage at which he used to buy plums when he was a little boy; it was then inhabited by a misanthrope, who for some strange fancy would not allow any one, more especially a woman, to enter his door. He washed, scrubbed, and mended his things, even his stockings, himself. When boys went to buy his plums, which were very good, they were always served in the garden, but never crossed the threshold. This was the original of 'Gruff moody Grim.' About 200 yards from here father said, 'There is my birth-place.' I looked round, expecting to see a very venerable farmhouse; imagine my disappointment when I saw a new stiff square brick house with walls all round the garden. Here was all the interest of the place gone! I felt quite angry that the people should have had the disrespect to pull down the Rushay house in which father was born. Here the new road termi-nated, and we continued our walk through a lovely lane overshadowed with elm trees, till we came to a very old but most picturesque cottage. I was just admiring it when father said, 'That is the house where "Poll's Jack Dà" was.' The elm, however, in front, on which the cage hung has been cut down. I made an outline sketch of the cottage, intending to make a drawing of it at my

leisure. The walk was now intensely interesting, every
turn of the lane bringing to his recollection some incident
of his boyhood, or one of his poems.   Here was the
'Haunted House' a rambling stone building that
looked half deserted, there the 'Girt Wold House of
Mossy Stwone,' a large mansion full of gable-ends, and
stone mullion windows, and ivy growing over its walls.
Then at the end of a lane we saw the river Liddon ; it is
shallow in this place, and there is a pretty bridge over
it.   The water-lilies were just in bloom, and their broad
glossy leaves overspread the river.   I gathered one or
two of them.   We now returned and continued our
ramble to Pentridge Farm, where he spent most of his
boyish days with his cousins.   Here the farmer would
make us come in and taste his cider.   Thence we
proceeded through 'Home Ground' and many fields
remembered by father for 'Auld Lang Syne,' and after
a delightful ramble we reached his own field, where we
intended to eat our sandwiches and rest some time.   It
is a very pretty irregular field with a dear little brook
running through it, such a picturesque stream !   Willie
fished a little while here, but his line was not long
enough.   While   we   were   here   the   sky   became
cloudy, and feeling a few drops of rain we hurried on to
the lane leading to Sturminster.   Presently a heavy
thunderstorm came on, and we got under the hedge and
remained there till the rain penetrated the leaves, then
we changed our quarters to the shadow of a 'girt elm
tree' where we sang glees and danced, to while away
the time till the storm cleared up.   When the clouds
began to show their 'silver linings' we walked on to
the town.   First we saw Newton, then went up a winding

path to the bridge, from which there are lovely views of
the river. We next saw the Coombe, and part of the
ruins of the castle where King Alfred once lived, indeed
the whole Manor of Sturminster belonged to him. I can
describe the scenery in no other word than *noble*, it is truly
grand. We then went into the town of Sturminster, a
most irregularly built town, and very old-fashioned. We
dined at the inn, and were regaled with a large pike
caught in the Stour, &c., &c. After dinner we went to
see the church, which is a very handsome one with
transepts. We saw the very font at which father was
christened. After leaving the church we were over-
taken by a man who was running after us quite out of
breath. He wanted to know if this was really Mr. Barnes
of Dorchester, he was quite 'frighted' to see him again,
he said. His name was Gass, and he used to run errands
for father. He told us a very interesting piece of news,
that 'his grandmother was dead :' he himself must have
been more than sixty ! We took tea at Mr. Colbourn's.
I like the whole family very much, including the seven
boys. At seven o'clock we set off on our homeward
drive, very sorry to leave 'the home of our fathers' and
so ended this memorable day."

The autumn of this year is marked by a very painful
illness,—articular rheumatism,—which kept William
Barnes in bed in a critical state for a month, from the
end of November till Christmas. It left a very trying
result behind it, the muscles of the hand remained so
cramped that for some time he could not hold a pen in
the usual way, but wrote with his fist. He had great
fears that he would never regain the full use of the hand,
but though in course of time he obtained more power over

his fingers, his handwriting was never again so free and legible as it had been; its curious up and down pointed style becoming more strongly marked. He went to complete his convalescence in January, 1855, by spending a week or two in London with his friend Mr. Charles Warne, F.S.A. The antiquaries went together to the British Museum, the " Osmana " collection and National Gallery, and they visited Mr. C. Roach Smith, of the Society of Antiquaries, and attended the meeting of the Syro-Egyptian Society.

About this time a new theory occupied his mind, the study of colours. The theory was that nature never makes mistakes, and that the colours she brings into juxtaposition must be the true harmonies. He used in his walks to collect leaves and mosses, flowers and fruits, and try the effect of their contrasting colours in painting, until he got a collection of examples of the tints which Nature most often puts together.

This theory he applied practically to the binding of his books, the mounting of his water colours, the colours of clothing in his children's frocks, and in the hues of the furniture of his house. Once he had purchased two old high-backed chairs at a sale, and to cover them he chose a certain green-grey damask with a yellow-brown binding, the tints found on the upper and under side of a beautiful lichen. One of his discoveries was that strong contrasts rarely touched in nature, even the blue and red of the " morning glory " (*Convolvulus major*) being divided by a white line intervening.[1]

The summer holidays of this year included visits to

[1] An article by him on this theory appeared in the *Art Journal* in 1855, it was written on Feb. 12th.

Mr. Hall, the antiquary at Osmington, Rev. J. Dale, the naturalist at Glanville's Wooton, and a week at Stourton Caundle with an elderly lady of the old school, who had a delightfully antique country house. Her drawing-room was hung with large portraits by Lely and Reynolds, and the quaint garden was bounded by a cloister cut in yew, beneath whose arches Charles I. had walked in a bye-gone century. But the room which most pleased William Barnes was the quaintly styled "Book-room," on whose shelves reposed the most attractive old parchment bound tomes, and such old-fashioned books as *Ye Arte of Ingenyouslie Tormentynge*, and *Tears from Ye Bottle of Jonas Mickelthwayte*. In this room the poet generally spent his mornings, engrossed in ancient literature; the afternoons were passed in long drives and visits to country houses.

The diary of much of this year is written in Spanish instead of Italian, and records a great deal of reading of Welsh and Hindustani. For the following year it is in Welsh and consequently rather untranslateable.

This was probably caused by his summer holiday having been spent in Wales, where the poet walked in the vales of Neath and Taff, talking to peasants and thus gaining a more practical knowledge of the language.

A great deal of lecturing is recorded during these years. William Barnes was a warmly welcomed and well-known figure on the platforms of the Town Halls and Institutes all over the county. A lecture on the "Britons" was given at Dorchester, to the "Working Men's Mutual Improvement Society," the report of which in the local papers brought several letters from strangers. One from John Gifford Croker, Bovey

Tracey, Devon, gives an interesting account of some
rock cisterns discovered on Dartmoor.   For a month or
two William Barnes alternated his subjects of thought
by writing one day on the Saxons, and another on
the Britons; he gave lectures on both subjects at
Sturminster, Wimborne, Corfe Castle, Wincanton, and
Sherborne.   He went to the latter town on the warm
invitation of Macready the tragedian, who had settled
down into active and benevolent private life there. This
last visit brought him into personal acquaintance with
the Rev. Edward Nares Henning, who was one of the
most valued friends of his later years.   Mr. Henning
was, I think, the first to introduce public readings of
the Dorset poems, of which he had long been an
ardent admirer, cutting them out from the Dorset paper
as they appeared, and making a book for himself. Here
is his account of the first reading in 1856 :—

SHERBORNE, *Jan.*, 1856.
My DEAR SIR,

I am much obliged to you for your kind
acknowledgment of my poor endeavour to make known
at Sherborne the beauties of your Dorset rhymes, and
delighted that I did not do them so much injustice as I
expected.   The pieces I read (for they are too much on
an equality for selection) were " The Woodlands " " The
Girt Woak Tree," " Woodcombe Feast," " May," " Jenny's
Ribbons," " Whitsuntide," " Jenny out vrom Hwome,"
" What Dick an' I done," " Grammer's Shoes," " The
Vaices that be Gone," " The Bells of Alderburnham,"
" The Times." I never saw anything like the reception of
this selection, and I hope it will lead to the increased sale

M

of the book.   I believe the audience would have sat
patiently to hear the whole volume; as it was, I kept
them an hour and half beyond their usual time.   Miss
Macready sent for the poems next day, and has been
employing herself (on her own account) in modernising
some of them; which I told her was like polishing up
a Queen Anne's farthing.   And last night I was at a
party where I was so fairly pestered for a few more
specimens that I was obliged to go home for the book.
I see there is a very good notice of the reading in the
Dorset County Chronicle of Thursday last.   Burns never
beat the two last lines of "Jenny out vrom Hwome" or
the third stanza of "Vaices that be Gone." I very much
regret I had not asked you the other day to read one
or two to me, which when I am next in Dorchester I
shall with your permission do, though even that could
not raise my admiration for them.

I am, etc., etc.,

EDWARD NARES HENNING.

The Christmas holidays from New Year's Day, 1859,
were spent at Mere, visiting his old friends there.   The
associations, dear as they were, must have been very sad,
for on January 8th the diary says in pathetic Italian,
"Dined at Chantry House (loved place) with Mr. L.; a
very courteous and cultivated man.   Who can tell what
I felt at my heart, seated in the room of that sweet old
home, of which my dear Julia was once the mistress!"

On February 23rd, 1857, William Barnes, going as
usual to take his class at the Working Men's Institute,

found a surprise prepared for him. The youthful diary before quoted gives the following account of it :—

"Monday, February 23rd. 'A white cross day.' My sister and I accompanied father to a debating class of the Young Men's Improvement Society. He was chairman. After a very interesting discussion on 'dreams, clairvoyance,' &c., the young men unexpectedly presented to him a framed testimonial, and a very handsome pencil-case. They spoke of his kindness in giving them lectures and instruction, and in encouraging their society when it was first begun, and looked down on by many people. I felt so proud when they spoke so heartily of him. One of the working men, named Cole, spoke wonderfully well, every word showing a refined mind and good feeling. Then father rose to return thanks ; he began by sympathising with them, and said that he himself was not nursed in the lap of luxury, but was, like themselves, a working man, so he cheered them on the path they had chosen, of cultivating their minds and refining their tastes. It *was* a happy evening."

In 1857, a second series of Dorset poems, entitled *Hwomely Rhymes*, was ready for the press, and William Barnes proposed publishing them by subscription. His publisher, Russell Smith, however, thought that as he was now so well known this course was unnecessary, and added, "If you will ask no unreasonable sum I will buy the MS. right out and save you all further trouble and risk." The poet did not, fortunately, accede to these terms, and the second series was published in 1858, he receiving 15*l*. from Russell Smith, the publisher, for liberty to print 400 copies. This collection contains

M 2

some of the most beautiful poems, among which are
" Hallowed Pleäces," " Angels by the Door," " My Love's
Guardian Angel," " Vo'k a-comen into Church," and
" The Water Crowfoot," a tribute to the floral beauty of
the river Frome, which was second only to " Cloty "
Stour in his affection. Some of the humorous poems
in this collection are very graphic. " The Waggon a-
stooded " is a perfect scene from life. " The Shy Man,"
and " Gammony Gay," are very laughable. " The
Lady's Tower " was one of the poet's especial fancies,
written after his wife's death. In imagination he reared
a beautiful tower to her memory, making exact drawings
of it with the architectural measurements just as he
describes it in the poems. It had eight pillars and a
winding external staircase, leading to the room with
marble floor,

> " An' there—a-painted zide by zide
> In memory o' the squier's bride
> In zeven paintèns true to life
> Wer zeven zights o' wedded life."

Mr. Henning was provoked by the receipt of the
Hwomely Rhymes to write a long letter of acknowledgment in good Dorset rhyme ; and a very ardent admirer,
Mr. Charles Tennant, wrote on October 2nd, 1858, a
warm invitation to his house in London with a view to
introducing the poet personally to his London readers.
He says, " I have long thought that the Dorsetshire folk
have not shown a due appreciation of their own poet
by allowing him to have been so long in comparative
obscurity. But he has only to make his appearance in
the great metropolis to insure for Barnes, the Dorset

poet, a celebrity equal to that of Burns, the Scotch poet, whose hundredth anniversary is now about to be celebrated." Then follows an invitation to stay with Mr. Tennant during the season, and give some private readings in higher circles, with " if we do this well, you will wake one morning and find yourself famous." In a second letter, after William Barnes's acceptance of this kindness, Mr. Tennant writes, " I have heard to-day from a friend on a visit in Scotland, where he met Mrs. Norton, both great admirers of your poetry, that we may count upon the Duchess of Sutherland placing her rooms at our disposal for your readings of your inimitable Dorset poetry. Easter is considered an unfavourable time, as all who can then leave town. But immediately after Easter a tide of fashion sets into London for the full flush of the season." In the March of the following year, 1859, Mrs. Norton wrote, saying :—

DEAR SIR,

The Duchess of Sutherland has written me a kind note respecting your future lecture, saying she will be too happy to do as we proposed, and let one be given at Stafford House. I have written to your friend Mr. Tennant about it, that he may make what plans he thinks best, and with all wishes for your success,

Believe me, yours very sincerely,

CAROLINE NORTON.

The same day Mrs. Norton wrote to Russell Smith ordering copies of the poems to be sent in her name to the Duchess of Sutherland and the Right Honourable Sidney Herbert.

A letter from Mr. Tennant on April 4th, 1859, fixes the first week in May for this first reading, and names several of his favourite poems, which he hopes will be in the list selected. Unfortunately, just at the last moment the reading was postponed, on account of the illness of some member of the family of the Duchess of Sutherland. The correspondence begun on this subject with Mr. Tennant never ceased, but ripened into a close literary friendship, and they became collaborators in several articles on political and social economy, in which their opinions harmonised well, although they differed amicably on some political questions.

The *Hwomely Rhymes* brought William Barnes into another interesting acquaintance, with the Chevalier de Chatelain, who was at the time editing a work entitled *Beautés de la Poésie Anglaise*, in two volumes, and wrote to beg permission to translate for it some of the Dorset poems. He tells the poet that he thinks he has succeeded in giving a fair rendering of " Trees be Company," and some other poems, but adds, " J'ai voulu, mais en vain, tenter de traduire ' The Wold Wall,' j'en suis convaincu que votre charmant dialecte était souvent intraduisable. Adieu, A Dieu je vous confie, et j'espère bien qu'il vous laissera enrichir la littérature anglaise de nouvelles *Hwomely Rhymes*, &c., &c.

" LE CHEVALIER DE CHATELAIN."

The Chevalier succeeded well in " The Vaices that be Gone," and " The Beam in Grenly Church."

He published some of his translations in the *Gazette de Guernsey*, from which they were copied into other French papers. The letter-friendship between William

Barnes and his translator was cemented when the
Chevalier and Madame de Chatelain made a pilgrimage
to Dorchester in 1860 to visit the poet.

It was doubtless with a view to the London reading
spoken of above, that the poet tried his hand as a public
reader, by giving a selection of his poems to the members
of the Working Men's Institution at the Town Hall in
Dorchester. It was an evening to be remembered. The
hall was thronged almost to suffocation with rich and
poor, and seldom has an audience been more excited by
various emotions. At one moment the whole mass of
people would be breathless with interest at such descriptive poems as "Jeane's Weddèn'-day in Mornen',"
"Grammer's shoes;" the next, the women would be
sobbing audibly over "Meary Ann's Chile," or "My
Love's Guardian Angel;" then *hey presto!* sorrow would
flee away, and the multitude of faces relax into smiles,
with now and then a burst of hearty laughter, at "What
Dick and I done," or "A bit o' Sly Courten'." It seemed
to one of the poet's children that the crowd of human
beings was a magic harp on which he played, bringing
forth at his will the emotions he chose.

If this seem exaggerated, let it be remembered that
it was the first time a Dorset audience had heard its
feeling, language, and daily 'life portrayed in its own
common speech, and the effect was all the greater
from the newness of the emotion.

After the success of this reading, all the other institutes would have no other subject from their favourite
lecturer than "the Dorset Dialect," in which readings
were given at Sherborne, Wincanton, Poole, Wareham,
Corfe Castle, Blandford, Mere, &c., during that season,

and all met with the same hearty reception. So much notice did they attract that an enthusiast, writing to the *Dorset County Chronicle* under the signature of "*Palmam qui meruit ferat,*" pleaded earnestly for a cheap edition of the poems, so that Barnes may take his true place as a "poet of the people," one who "is fighting the battle side by side with rich and poor under the banner of Him who is Maker of them all." A man wrote from Westbury to the lecturer that he had walked nine miles to hear him and would willingly do as much again.

The same year in which *Hwomely Rhymes* appeared is marked also by the publication of *Britain, and the Ancient Britons.* Mr. Russell Smith seemed very doubtful about the success of this venture, and wrote on March 24th, 1858, "I have dipped into it here and there, and rather like it, as it is not quite so dry as some other books I have published on the ancient Britons, none of which filled my exchequer—so that I am doubtful of venturing further; but if you can make up your mind to accept a few copies when printed, I will take the risk, as it will not make a large book." A memorandum to this letter in the author's hand runs, "Yes, for the copies (with a copy also of *Talicssin*), on condition that you will bring it out at once."

I suppose there never was an author so easy for a publisher to make terms with as W. Barnes, who by this time had a firm conviction that his books were not for the million, but only for the few, and that therefore he could not command a price for them. I do not think he even kept the copyright of most of them, except fortunately the poems. There is however this to be said, no other publisher would probably have been so

persistent as Russell Smith in bringing out one abstruse
book after another, which were so far over the heads of
the paying public.　But he being an antiquary himself,
preferred publishing works of that kind, and had to the
last a firm belief that his client's genius must succeed in
the long run.　This book as usual proved a literary, if
not a pecuniary success.　An entirely new light was
thrown on the Ancient Britons which showed them to
be anything but the wild savages hitherto supposed.
The *Athenæum* cavilled at this view, and evidently
agreed with the schoolboy's idea that the skins worn by
the Britons were mere rough skins not made into any
form of garment (skins were never worn by the Britons
more than in these days of fur garments, by the by),
and seems to doubt his assertion that " The government
of the Britons was a limited monarchy of a form affording the people the greatest freedom," yet it has the
justice to add, " But although the author takes as we
think too Welsh a view of his subject, and is moreover a
hobbyhorse man (as may be seen by perusing his chapter
on the Triads where he treats of the threenesses of
things), yet is this little book of much value.　Mr.
Barnes has applied himself to the study of British and
Welsh literature, which he truly says has been too often
neglected by antiquaries.　He has evidently thought
deeply on the social and political features of British life,
and he communicates his conclusions in language which
is clear, concise, and forcible."

The legends of Arthur could never have sprung from
a savage and uncivilised people, and that they were,
although much idealised, founded in a measure on real
life is almost certain, in the same way as Homer gives a

true idea in a poetical form of life of the Ancient Greeks. How could the garments of Enid—the tapestry of Guinivere's maidens—the embroidery of Elaine on Lancelot's shield cover, or the furniture of the Castle, be described if garments, and elegant works, and artistic handicrafts, were unknown, as they would be in a savage race whose idea of clothing was the mere wearing of undressed skins ? William Barnes was not far wrong in the conclusions he drew from his *Taliessin, Morvryn, and other Bards*. The chapter on Triads is peculiarly interesting, and worthy of study.

Being perhaps discouraged at the limited number of his readers, he about this time took the idea of writing a novel. A letter from Mr Tennant, who was much in the poet's confidence says :—

" I am very glad, as everybody would be, to know that you entertain the idea of writing a work of fiction, and are only waiting for the plot. I hope you will soon hit upon something which will please your critical fancy. How often I wish I had you here with us in this little old-fashioned house near the ' Pantiles ' [at Tunbridge Wells], where Samuel Johnson in his plum-coloured coat, ditto shorts, and scarlet and gold waistcoat, used to walk with the beautiful Miss Chudleigh and close to the most beautiful common I ever saw."

This work of fiction never got written, or as far as I know even begun. It would probably have been a story of rustic life, but as the plot did not suggest itself, most likely the idea faded from his mind before the sad realities of the next few years.

CHAPTER XI.

THE TRIAL PAST.

How sorrowful was life, the while
My God, in love, withheld His smile ;
And though He kept me in His sight,
Yet gave my pining soul no light
To show my darksome goings right :
And yet would find me holding fast
To promises of seasons past,
　　　Enduring to the end.

So by His Spirit's sweet control
In patience I possess'd my soul,
And walked my guileless path, and drew
Sweet solace from His plants that grew
So blest by sun, and air, and dew ;
And all that lived around me, fed
By His love given daily bread,
　　　Enduring to the end.

But now his smile at last has blest
My heart again with joyful rest,
How melting is the backward thought
That 'twas His love again that wrought,
What I had deem'd His anger brought.
So blest is he that can abide
His day of sorrowing when tried,
Enduring to the end.

TROUBLOUS TIMES.

1858.

THE next literary venture was the publication of *Views of Labour and Gold*, a *résumé* of several lectures, which had been delivered during the past two years. Like all William Barnes's works, these "Views" were original, but original in such a good and high sense that one would wish them to be more than "Views." His social science is as different from Malthus and Bentham and the materiality of the earlier writers on the subject, as it is from Henry George and Chamberlain, who look only on one side of the question, and while claiming "rights" for all, propose wrongs to some as a means of obtaining them. Like Ruskin, Barnes bases his social science on Christian principles; the rights he allows to every man are the right to justice, and to practise and receive loving-kindness. He raises his voice earnestly against all shams, frauds and commercial injustice, by which traders obtain money by giving less than it is worth. He pleads thus for care of the rights of the working man: "But our deductions of unproductive hands are not great enough; for very few work till

they reach their eightieth year, and the production of
the nation's income lies heavier on some classes than on
others; and thence arise the stern calls for a lengthening
of the daily labour of the toilworn body, which so often
leaves a man no evenings wherein his mind may wander
free, while his body may rest on the bench by the
cottage door, or by the hearth amid the gambols of his
smiling children; and which leaves him no time to
strengthen the hallowed bonds of kindred; no time to
solace himself with the gifts of his God, the *domus et
placens uxor;* no time to enlighten and purify his soul by
a peaceful reading of the Word of Life; we were going
to say, no time for the ordinances of grace, for too often
the overworked body, if it has the rest of a Sabbath, is
on the Sabbath thrown listless on the bed of indolence
if not sickness. If it is not healthy to work for ever at
a business in which, for example, the thumb and fingers
shall gain skill while all the rest of the body shall
wither from inaction, so neither is it good for the man
of soul and body to be holden too long in work in which
the body only is in action, while the soul and mind are
left in a dulness almost below rationality. Man goeth
forth to his work until the evening, the Word of God
tells us; but the life of the overworked man in some
parts of England almost belies it, as the stern calls of
toil leave him no evening, but keep him from the peace
of his solace and rest almost till the dead of night.
Cheerless to him are both the going forth and the coming
home. A day's toil should be sweetened by the foretaste of
the evening of freedom that looms from behind it; and
the week's labour should be like a walk through the
nave of a cathedral, bright from the light at the end of

it, and not like a cave leading only from deep to deeper darkness.

" It is to the house that we must look for the growth of the most lovely social Christian graces ; the affections of kindred, a reverence for the kindly feelings, and a love of home, which in its full outgrowth becomes that bulwark of the safety of a community and constitution, *amor patriæ*, the love of one's fatherland.   For what is England that she should be dear to me, but that she is the land that owns my county ?   Why should I love my county, but that it contains the village of my birth ? Why should that village be hallowed in my mind, but that it holds the home of my childhood ?

" The holy affection of kindred for kindred grows out of the happier hours of freedom and rest in house-life ; it rises out of the harmless play of the summer evening ; the cheerful talk that beguiles the stormy winter's night, the daily teaching of a father's and mother's care, the godly exercises and talk of the Sabbath ; the love that so carefully folds up the little play-tired children on their evening beds, and gathers them with a smile to their morning meal.

" These graces therefore grow out of incidents and services for which some time, with freedom from toil, is needful.   Good fathers and mothers (and there are good ones among the poor, and there would be more with a happier house-life) are the best teachers of children, and a good home is the best school for the formation of the mind.

" Let the poor therefore have some time, if it can anyhow be afforded to them, to seek light for their own minds, and grace for their own hearts, by reading or kindly talk, or at least to refresh their bodies and minds by an evening's rest and peace, and to train their children in the wholesome love of English house-life and the social virtues."

His distinctions between capital and wealth, real and commercial value, labour and compound labour, &c., are clear and logical, as are all his definitions. The chapters on "Dignity and Disdain of Work," "Labours with a good Reaction," "True Wealth," contain many deep truths. The latter ends with one of Barnes's favourite "threenesses," which shows his views of "sociality."

"There are three divine gifts which are the elements of true happiness or wealth: the spiritual one of righteousness, the bodily one of health, and the social one of good government; but the more common kinds of worldly wealth are of uncertain effect, though the peace of a community is none the safer for a greater inequality of wealth, such that one class may be over-rich to wanton luxury, while another is poor to naked hunger."

The following letter from his hitherto unseen correspondent, Mr. Tennant, is one of the best *critiques* possible of the book.

LONDON, 17th *June*, 1859.

MY DEAR SIR,

I am very much pleased with your views on "Labour and Gold" which I obtained from your publisher the other day.

You touch lightly on the difficulties of the Currency Question, and I am not sure that I understand what your opinion really is on that question. But some of your views are quite original; and especially so your mode of expressing them, and altogether, what you write comes very fresh and forcible to my mind. But if the book contained nothing more than the pages 170 and 171 [1] it would be a valuable gift to the present generation and to posterity.

What I so much like is the tone of Christian Philosophy which pervades your Political Economy, and I see the same delightful tone through all your Pastorals, which first charmed me when I accidentally met with your volume of Dorsetshire poems many years ago, in Dorsetshire. In short I must, with your leave, make your personal acquaintance, for I fancy there is a great deal to be picked out of you, and that the serene rays of your genius have been too long buried in the unfathomed depths of Dorsetshire.

Would you like me to write and send a short review of *Labour and Gold* where I think it will be received and extensively circulated and may help the sale? for the public seem to have a stupid disinclination to books on this subject, which makes it difficult to know how to set about letting in any light on their frightful ignorance.

If you approve, I will try my hand at a short notice, which, at any rate, will serve as an *avertissement appétissant*, if nothing more, and, if you like, I will send it to you, to be dressed up a little before I forward it for insertion.

Etc., etc.,

C. TENNANT.

[1] The two pages quoted above.

N

In a letter of July 16th, 1859, Mr. Tennant writes
that his critique will appear in September in the
Financial Reformer, an organ of the Association for
extending the knowledge of the Government scheme of
taxation. The Association was under the presidency of
Mr. Robertson Gladstone, elder brother of the late
Premier, then Chancellor of the Exchequer. He adds,
" I confess it does appear to me quite hopeless to expect
by any moralizing to lift a people out of their moral
degradation and misery, without enabling them at the
same time to lift themselves out of their physical
destitution. . . . You will excuse me for having cut you
up about your chapter on " Machinery." I could have
minced you for that. But I have dealt tenderly with
you for your own sake.

Etc., etc.,

C. TENNANT.

The chapter on " Machinery " here referred to goes to
prove it not an unmixed good.

In the same month Mr. Tennant writes again about
the reading of the poems at Stafford House, which had
been postponed the previous season. The time was not
now propitious. " The dissolution of Parliament and
the distraction of parties have quite deranged the
London season and, I am afraid, have driven pastoral
poetry out of the people's heads. But whether the
readings come off or not at Stafford House, I
hope you will keep to your promised visit to us—
and we should be glad to know when this would
best suit your convenience." The letter finishes by
naming the 15th of that month (June), but the visit did

not take place; probably William Barnes was not feeling
in cue for London gaieties, and was unwilling to incur
the expense. For a long time he had great anxieties;
his literary works, deep and clever as they were, never-
theless were not of the kind to pay.   His sons had to
be provided for, one entering at St. John's College,
Cambridge, and the other wishing to follow the career
of an engineer, all of which entailed sacrifices with a
diminishing income. Then came sickness and other
troubles, the result of underhand dealing on the part of
one whom William Barnes had trusted for years—but
we need not enter into this, for he, with his characteristic
shrinking from the thought of injustice of any kind,
always put away the memory of this especial injury as
soon as ever its effects had ceased to wound him. Whatever were the cause, the school diminished, pupils were
withdrawn one by one for no expressed reason, and
great anxiety preyed on the master.   One day in
especial is remembered when he came in with a sad
face, holding some of these dreadful letters in his hand
together with others eulogising the poet.

   " What a mockery is life," he exclaimed ; "they praise
me and take away my bread ! They might be putting
up a statue to me some day when I am dead, while all
I want now is leave to live.   I asked for bread, and
they gave me a stone," he added bitterly.

   He little knew then how prophetic this bitter remark
was.   The following letter to Mr. Warne touches upon
his feelings at this time:—

DORCHESTER, 20*th September*, 1860.

DEAR MR. WARNE,

Do not think I have forgotten you, or lost my affection for you. I have had for nearly two long years a very unprosperous time, with great expenses, and I had made up my mind not to write to you till I had some definitely better news to tell you. As St. Paul puts it, " If I make you sorry, who is he then that maketh me glad, but the same which is made sorry by me ? " I have not written a word for the press these ten months, for I have not had an assistant.

*   *   *   *   *   *   *   *

The experience of your heart with the thought of the lost angel of the house is my own. My great consolation is that I can hope I was a good husband, so that she is not gone with aught against me to the Great Judge. If I had not this balm, oh ! . . . . My daughter J—— is at Berlin, and the Princess Frederic William has most graciously given her, at Her Highness's cost, a first-rate master in singing, so that if it be needful she can do very well, and I am told that Lord Palmerston has promised another of the Ministers—my friend in the case—that he will place my name on the Civil List. He has certainly sent me, through the Lords of the Treasury, £30, as of Her Majesty's Royal Bounty. It is, however, still an anxious time. . . . . Last year the " Hundreds Barrow " at Culliford Tree was opened by Captain Damer—4 skeletons east and west, one beside the other, at about 2 feet asunder; on a lady's neck a necklace of a substance unknown to us ; Captain Damer has promised to show it to the learned in London. He dug a little into the tops of two other barrows and found skeletons. A fine urn, now in the D. C. Museum, was found under a barrow at Winterbourne by Mr. Mansfield, and as there are some interesting British relics from Dorset barrows in the Museum, you ought to come down a day or two and take your own notes. I am so tied up that I could not satisfy my own mind, though I might yours, with particulars I might give you; for as you are going before the world in print, you ought to trust as little as you can in others' descriptions and opinions.

Etc.,

W. BARNES.

A few days after this Barnes had a more personal antiquarian discovery to tell his friend :—

DORCHESTER, 27*th September*, 1860.

DEAR MR. WARNE,

I find by a sewer just dug through my garden that I am on the site of a Roman house. The men have cut through a Roman rubbish pit, and we have picked out of their earth Samian and black pottery, with very many pieces of the painted frescoed plaster of a room (some of them are at your service when I see you), a bone hair-pin, and stone stud.

Yours truly,

W. BARNES.

There were gleams of sunshine even in these dark times, when the mantle of anxiety fell heavy on the young shoulders of the motherless girls, as well as on those of their father. One especially happy gleam was on a certain Sunday, when, after taking the service at Came for the absent rector, William Barnes dined at Came House with Captain Damer, who had once been a private pupil of his, and always kept a warm affection for him. While the two sat quietly over their dessert, Captain Damer remarked that "it was not probable his cousin would retain the Rectory for many years," and promised that when the living became vacant his guest should have it. This promise was the greatest solace to the whole family—it was as though they were in a disabled ship, tossing on the sea in troubled waters, and saw a far-off shadow of land, which kept up hope, even though many leagues of breakers might yet lie between it and them. William Barnes did not let himself build on a far-off promise, but continued his life as though it had not been made. He became a candidate for the chaplaincy of the Asylum, and also in June for the head mastership of the Bath Grammar School. His failures to obtain them caused some disappointment at the time, though after events proved that God knew best.

Quite a long spell of sunshine came in the summer of 1858, when he went to live at Came Rectory as *locum tenens* during the rector's absence. The happiness of the girls at this delightful change may be gathered from the same old diary quoted before. After describing the settling in on June 21st it adds : " W., I., and myself, finished the evening by walking arm in arm round the garden, giving vent to a little of our superfluous joy in sundry songs, duets, trios, &c., much, I fear, disturbing the repose of the birds in the shrubbery, who were not accustomed to hear the night echoes awakened in such a noisy manner."

Their first efforts at choir practice were rather unpromising :—

"June 22nd. We went to Whitcombe to practice— quite a hopeless case, I fear; none of the six children can sing, and three of them cannot read."

"June 28th. How charming this country life is! The perfect peace and happiness of it is doubly pleasant to us who have anything but a tranquil life at home." In the end of July this bright gleam faded, the family went back to the routine and anxieties in the old home on July 25th, where "there is a great smell of paint and many other discomforts. There is also a great deal of disagreeable work to be done. Father wanders about looking miserable, and sits all day in the empty schoolroom with no pupils, and the house, though very light and roomy, seems to hang over us like a cloud of trouble."

One of the chief events of the summer of 1859 was a visit from Prince Lucien Buonaparte, who had been very much attracted by the poems, and came to make William Barnes's acquaintance. He took him for a drive to Weymouth, and they talked philology all the day, for Prince Lucien was a great linguist, and had given many years to a comparative study of local dialects. He had collected specimens of all the dialects of Italy and France, and now wanted to add the English ones. The subject chosen for his comparisons was a curious selection—"The Song of Solomon," which he had caused to be translated into scores of different dialects.

Mr. Barnes undertook the arrangements for the Somerset and Devonshire translations, the first of which he put into the hands of Mr. Thomas S. Baynes, the latter

into those of Mr. George Pulman. Of the poet's own
translation into Dorset the Prince writes: " I thank you
for the trouble you have taken in the Devonshire,
Wiltshire, and Somerset translations. I expect them
with anxiety. I have been exceedingly pleased with your
clever observations on the Dorset dialect. They will add
a great value to your translation. . . . I hope soon to be
able to send you St. Matthew in the Milanese and
Bergamese dialects, as well as the Cornish ' Song of
Solomon,' and twelve copies of your own." The Prince
kept up for many years an interesting literary correspondence with him, sending him copies of all his
works, and keeping him *au courant* with all his
labours in the field of comparative philology. The
Italian diary for 1859, Sept: 12th, says: " Returned
from Lulworth, and found 30 books which Prince
L. L. Buonaparte has given me." In October of the
same year Prince Lucien returned to Dorchester to
consult with his collaborator there, who dined with him
at the hotel.

In the end of 1860, Mr. Tennant, through Thomas
Hughes, introduced William Barnes to David Masson,
the editor of *Macmillan's Magazine*, who wrote at once a
warm welcome to him, as one of his staff, saying, " It
would please me much if we could have the advantage
of an occasional paper from your pen, and bearing your
name. . . . I doubt not there are subjects on which your
knowledge and your opinion in the form of such brief
papers as our limits allow would be very welcome
to our readers."

The first article by the new contributor was a paper
on " Beauty and Art," published in May, 1861. In

acknowledging this with the usual cheque Mr. Macmillan himself writes :—

I have only been able to look it over partially as yet, but have read enough to convince me that I shall have a great admiration of it, as our editor told me I should—the style and thought seem so fresh and genuine. I trust this is by no means your last contribution to our magazine. Mr. Venables has several times promised us an article on your poetry, which I hope he will fulfil before long.

I am, Dear Sir,
Yours very respectfully,
ALEX. MACMILLAN.

Here is the enthusiastic Mr. Tennant's verdict, in a letter to the author :—

DEAR MR. BARNES,

I am sure you are a most remarkable man. I must see you somehow or other. If you won't come to me, I must go to you. I want to see you. I picture you to myself with the head of Socrates. You don't care much about Plutus, and if you worshipped any heathen deity it must be Pan.

You don't care much about commerce, but you delight in the "Beautiful," and you know what is beautiful.

If I were rich I would offer you £1000 a year to undertake the education of my son, a little boy of nine years old. I think you could make him just such a man as I should wish him to be; though you don't dot your i's or cross your t's. It has taken me two days to make out "Cincinnatus" in your last letter, and, but for those five acres of yours in the Vale of Blackmore I never

should have made it out. I could make nothing out of
it but "Canaanites," and that did not make sense.
But I like your handwriting because it is your own, and
unlike anybody's else. It puts me in mind of a fly
escaped from drowning in a bottle of ink, and crawling
over your paper. But I like it all the better for that,
because it is so unlike my own.

There is a good deal of original thought in the paper
on " Beauty and Art."   To begin with, the definition of
Beauty is terse and comprehensive.   *" The beautiful in
Nature is the unmarred result of God's first creative or
forming will, and the beautiful in Art is the result of an
unmistaken working of man in accordance with the beautiful
in Nature."*   By saying. God's *first* will one must not
understand the author to mean that God has two conflicting wills, but that where man has marred His created
work, His will often remedies this by afterwork.   Thus
it is God's first will that the ash tree should grow from
one single stalk with a certain type of grace and proportion in its branches.   When man had polled the ash, and
marred its natural grace, God, still working through
nature, gives it other branches and leaves, but it is not His
primary will that it should be a stunted, round-headed
tree, consequently the polled ash is less beautiful than the
natural tree.   *" If the beautiful be the good of God's first
forming will, then beauty must be good."*   And so it is. In
the first chapter of Genesis we read that God saw everything that He had made, and behold it was very good; here
the Hebrew word for good (*tov*) means, also, beautiful; as in
the Septuagint it is given by the word καλά, beautiful.
The beautiful is also the good, by reasoning of a fitness

or harmony which it possesses. But fitness, again, may be of sundry kinds." Here the writer traces the different kinds of fitness—fitness of quantity, of strength, of form, of number, of harmony. A great deal of his theory of harmonic proportion and nature's matchings of colours is woven in. The theory of fitness or unfitness is applied to landscape and decorative art. The sixth part, "Art true and false," is an application of the theory of beauty to moral art, such as poetry and the drama and human character. "The aim of high art is the seeking and interpreting the beautiful of God's works, and a working with His truth," says the writer; this, when his definition of the beautiful is admitted, is much deeper than Mr. Ruskin's aphorism. "That art is the greatest which conveys to the mind of the spectator, by any means whatever, the greatest number of the greatest ideas, and I call an idea great in proportion as it is received by a higher faculty of the mind, and as it more fully occupies, and in occupying exercises and exalts the faculty by which it is received." [1]

Gleams of light and shadows of darkness followed each other quickly in the poet's home in these last years, before all the troubles melted away. There came a certain April day, when the only daughter who was at home was arranging some primroses she had just brought from a long country ramble, when two gentlemen entered, saying they had come to offer their hearty congratulations to Mr. Barnes.

" On what ? " asked the girl, wondering.

" On having received a Civil List pension of £70 a year," and they showed her a *Daily Telegraph* with the

[1] *Modern Painters*, vol. i. chap. ii. p. 12.

list of newly-granted pensions, and there truly was her father's name as one of the chosen recipients.

"Let us go and tell father directly," said the girl, hastily taking up her hat; "he is gone to the station to see a friend off."

So she and her two friends set off in eager haste to bring the good news, which was to him a veritable godsend. The official notice from Lord Palmerston followed the next day, April 17th, 1861, and then began to pour in letters of hearty congratulation from all the county.

The memorial asking for it had been signed by forty magistrates, and by all the Members of Parliament who had a personal interest in him, such as R. Brinsley Sheridan, H. Ker Seymer, Mr. Floyer; and Mr. Sturt (since Lord Alington), had written private and spontaneous letters on his behalf to the Premier; and all were now hearty in their joy at their success. In acknowledging the grant to Lord Palmerston's Secretary, and rendering thanks to Her Majesty and to him, William Barnes concludes: "I hope that my future writings may not disgrace the literature of Her Majesty's kingdom, and that those works in the dialect of my own county may promote peace and good will among her rural subjects in the west, so that his Lordship (Palmerston) may never have the pain of finding he has recommended for the Civil List an unworthy name."

But the joy and relief in the family were soon damped, for almost the next post brought the news of the death of one who had lately entered the home circle.

So mingled were the two conflicting elements that many of the letters from friends are a touching mixture of congratulations and condolence. The "silver lining" is but the heavenly reverse of a "dark cloud."

It was in the end of this eventful year, November, 1861,[1] that the most extraordinary of all Barnes's philological works was published. This was *Tiw; or A View of the Roots and Stems of the English as a Teutonic Tongue.*

On August 1st he wrote to Russell Smith :—

DEAR SIR,

The books are come to hand, but your printer is very slow with my hopeful brat, *Tiw.* Will he go faster after a while ?

Yours truly,

W. BARNES.

To which the publisher answered laconically, "Been standing still for you; he has not enough MS. for a third sheet.—J. R. S."

The "hopeful brat," *Tiw,* was one of the author's pets among his literary children, and for nearly all his life after its publication he followed up his labours among roots and stems. His theory was that in primitive times language was limited to a few fundamental sounds or words, and that in the course of ages and different uses these roots expanded into many distinctive forms, each class of which he calls a stem. The roots treated of are those of the Teutonic speech, and the book is entitled *Tiw,* because the god from whom the Teutonic race took their name was so called.

---

[1] It was dated 1862, as books published in the winter season are generally dated for the new year.

By tracing back English words through the dialectic and older Saxon forms, comparing them with German, Icelandic, &c., the author arrives at these primitive Teutonic roots, of which he gives a list of about fifty in this form, $b*ng$, $fl*ng$, $sw*ng$, &c. The first consonants forming the unchangeable root, which is retained in all words derived from it ; the asterisk is in place of a vowel sound, which is not radical but changeable ; and the ending ng figuring the consonant closing the word, which changes for each of the stem forms. This ending may become intensified into nk, so that from the root $cr*ng$ we get " crank," or it may soften into nge, and form " cringe " or diminish into g, so that $d*ng$ gives " dig," and $pr*ng$ " prig," or augment into dge or tch, forming " bridge," " ridge," " pitch," " ditch," &c. Sometimes it goes out altogether, leaving only the root with a vowel, such as " die," " fry," " cry," &c.

Besides the stems formed from the primitive ng by speech wear, and which are distinguished as root stems, there are other stem forms made by replacing the ending ng by the different consonants or clippings, such as the st " stem," in which from $p*ng$ we get " past," the sh, $bl*ng$, " blush," the M stem, $pr*ng$ " prim," the B, D, N, L, and R stems.

The development of this ingenious theory occupied many years of William Barnes's life ; his lists of stem words grew longer and fuller with every new word which in dialect or common speech struck him as helping his proof. The study became quite engrossing when he could build up a whole root into its many branching stems, with good proof that the stems were the real off-spring of the root.

William Barnes seems to have had the idea that the roots of all tongues, if thoroughly investigated, would prove to be identical, for he finds Latin and Greek words may equally be traced to these same fundamental sounds, and discovers traces of some primitive roots even in the Indo-Teutonic languages.[1]

The appearance of the book is so mysterious—until one takes the trouble to really study it, when it becomes simple and clear, opening out to the mind a vast deal of thought and investigation—that few critics took the trouble to analyse it. One merely gives it a few lines in a long notice of the third series of the poems, saying, " The book he has called *Tiw* appears to open up a secret but certain page in the history of human civilization—that page which lays bare the first mainsprings that guide the utterances of thought, and shape the philosophy of language. Mr. Barnes has done in this department enough to place his name by the side of those of Horne Tooke and Max Müller, and that is more than any other British philologist has achieved."

Among the many whom the outward look of *Tiw* prevented from trying to understand it was Mr. Tennant, who facetiously writes, " I have got *Tiw*, and though it bears witness to much labour and learning, I cannot think it will ever be found in the list of entertaining literature. . . . Some of your distinctions between roots and stems seem to me to require a nice discernment. But though I know nothing about it, I can see that you know a great deal. I am expecting in April a learned German, Dr. Kramer, from Berlin, on a visit to

[1] A lecture on this subject by Mr. Barnes was read at the Philological Society on December 4th, 1863.

me for a month or six weeks I shall make him study *Tiw*.

LONDON, 21*st April*, 1862.

DEAR MR. BARNES,

Dr. Kramer is with us, and I expect will remain with us into June. I hope you will come and stay with us before he goes. He has got your *Tiw*, but I don't think he will be able to throw any new light on it. Your P.S. interests me. . . .

CHAPTER XII.

VO'K A COMEN INTO CHURCH.

The church do zeem a touchen zight,
When vo'k a-comèn in at door
Do softly tread the long-aïl'd vloor
Below the pillared arches' height,
Wi' bells a-pealèn,
Vo'k a kneelèn,
Hearts a-healèn, wi' the love
An' peäce a-zent em vrom above.

An' there, wi' mild an' thoughtvul feäce
Wi' downcast eyes, an' vaïces dum',
The wold an' young do slowly come
An' teäke in stillness each his pleäce,
A-zinkèn slowly,
Kneelèn lowly,
Seekèn holy thoughts alwone
In pray'r avore their Meäker's throne.

o

An' there be sons in youthful pride,
　An' fathers weak wi' years an' pain,
　An' daughters in their mother's train
The tall wi' smaller at their zide;
　Heads in murnèn
　Never turnèn,
Cheaks a-burnèn wi' the het
O' youth, an' eyes noo tears do wet.

There friends do zettle, zide by zide
　The knower speechless to the known;
　Their vaïce is there vor God alwone,
To flesh an' blood their tongues be tied.
　Grief a-wringèn
　Jäy a-zingèn
Pray'r a-bringèn welcome rest,
So softly to the troubled breast.

THE RECTOR.

1862.

THE year 1862 dawned brightly. The Christmas holidays were occupied by visits to friends in different parts of the county, and in giving gratuitous lectures to the Literary Institutes. The " Dorset Dialect with Readings " was chosen for Sherborne on the 7th of January, Mere on the 8th, Shaftesbury on the 9th, and Bridport on the 13th. At Weymouth and Blandford the lectures were on " Trial by Jury," a subject which Mr. Barnes afterwards worked up into an article for *Macmillan's Magazine*, in which it was published in March, 1862. On the 15th, William Barnes and his daughter were spending the evening with a clerical friend, when they heard a report that the rector of Came had accepted another benefice. This caused a great deal of hopeful excitement among the young people, who for many days ardently expected the postman's knock, hoping for a letter showing that Captain Damer had remembered his promise. Some friends suggested writing to remind him but this William Barnes utterly refused to do, for nothing would ever make him stoop to ask a favour for himself. " If it is Captain Damer's wish that I shall have the living he will give it me, if not, the forcing him to maintain a word perhaps forgotten, perhaps repented of, could bring no happiness to him or to me," was his argument. A friend who had a warm interest in the poet, did indeed, unknown to him, write on his behalf to the patron on Jan. 31st. It was however needless, for even as she wrote, the following letter was in the future rector's hands.

MORETON HOUSE, *Jan. 30th*, 1862.

MY DEAR MR. BARNES,

I am not unmindful of my promises I can assure you, and I have delayed till this day, when I was officially assured of my cousin's resignation of Came living within the next six months, to offer for your acceptance the same, which I do with the most heartfelt pleasure in the world, hoping you will long live to enjoy it. I may hope to see you next week in Dorchester. Remember me kindly to all your family, and with Mrs. Damer's kindest wishes,

Believe me,
Very truly yours,
SEYMOUR DAWSON DAMER.

Great was the delight of all and every member of the family. The poet saw before him peace and ease of mind, genial work among the poor he loved, and leisure for his studies. The girls, remembering that happy summer they had once spent in the nest-like little rectory, rejoiced in the idea that henceforth it would be their home. They were elated with the relief of feeling that the mantle of responsibility, which had rested so heavily on their shoulders, in a household which was difficult to guide, was slipping off, under the sunny rays of a more congenial future. Friends who had grieved with them now rejoiced in their joy, and letters of congratulation poured in by every post. Only one witty friend sent a lament instead of rejoicing, in the form of a parody on a popular song.

IN PARADISO (a new version).

A schoolboy sat by Napper's Mite,
  Tho' long the sun had set,
He seemed with grief o'erburdened quite,
  His cheek with tears was wet.
"And where is he," I asked the boy,
" To whom all languages were joy,
  Who every tongue did know ?"
He pointed eastward, out by Came,
And sobbed—he scarce the words could frame,
  "In Paradiso—in Paradiso.

" He left me here alone," he said,
  "An uninstructed boy ;
The teacher from his pupil fled
  To dwell in peaceful joy.
No more my tutor he will be,
No more—alas !—he'll punish me ;
  I own that I was slow.
Damer has borne him from the school,
O'er Came's glad parish folks to rule,
  All at his ease, oh !—all at his ease, oh."

The happy days were still half a year distant, but those last six months before the now small school was dissolved for ever flew by on the wings of hope, and the summer holidays made an end of the irksome days of teaching.

A curious instance of the irony of fate marked the close of William Barnes's teaching. The very week his last few scholars left him the lists came out in the *Times*, recording his pupil Tolbort's name at the head of the Indian Civil Service Examination, and forthwith the master was deluged with letters offering pupils. "I told them it took two to do it," he said afterwards, thus dividing his honours with the scholar. At the time his feeling was figuratively expressed, "When I was drowning no one offered help; now I have come to land, hands are held out to me."

On the 30th of July the outgoing rector called to bid good-bye, and handed over the key of the rectory. In August the family moved into residence, but the new rector was not really instituted till November 4th, when he went to dine and sleep at the palace at Salisbury, and the ceremony took place in the chapel of the palace after morning prayers.

On December 1st, the curious ordeal of induction was performed at Came Church, and he was presented with a sod of earth, and had to ring the church bell, besides other ancient ceremonials. The midday of life had been with the Dorset poet a season of clouds and storms, coming after a sunny morning, but now the calm, restful evening began, and not the shadow of a cloud dimmed the sunset. Anxiety, dread of the future, the restraint of uncongenial duties, the wear and tear of mind in a never-ending routine of teaching, were all gone, and in their place were peace and repose ; the country life he loved was his portion, and the rustic poor he sympathised with were his care. He found leisure too, so that when poetical thoughts were born, they were not crushed out of existence by sordid realities. The rectory of Came is a cosy little nest—a thatched cottage with wide eaves and wider verandah, on whose rustic pillars, roses, clematis, and honeysuckle entwine. It has a flowery lawn in front, and a sheltering veil of trees at the side. The poet's study was a room on the upper floor, which overlooked the sunny fruit garden, and here he could watch the blossoms expanding and falling from his apple and apricot trees, and see the breezes waving his feathery-headed asparagus. And how he enjoyed his garden and tended his shrubs! Sometimes he took a fancy to mow his own lawn, in memory of early days at Mere, but the use of a little mowing machine, the invention of later times, useful though it were, never gave him the same feeling as did the scythe of his earlier days, making its graceful curves.

The parish of Came is wide, with a nucleus of cottages and school round the church, in the very garden of the Squire's house; other groups of cottages with barns lie in different isolated portions on the outskirts of the wide park, and the farmer's house, with another little hamlet, two miles away, at the top of a down; while the dairy nestles in a woody hollow near the rectory.

Whitcombe, whose people received their former curate with joy as their rector, lies above a mile from Came along the high road. There is a long hill leading to it, between the cliffs of a deep cutting, where the fiercest winds and the hottest sun share the times of the year between them. Up this long hill the parson and his daughters would toil through rain or snow or sunshine every week, greeted when they appeared on the summit with the triple harmony of the village church bells. In summer a roof of blue overhung the deep cleft of ruddy soil, whose banks were covered with wild flowers— pinks, crow's-bill, golden pennyroyal, and tender silver-weed—and the poet read sermons in them all.

"See what a harmony of colour," he exclaimed one day; "look at these harebells by the tuft of green grass; pale blue and green—oh, that is lovely in the sunshine!" He often plucked a leaf, and would remark how the green of the outside was toned down by the grey beneath, saying, "We should make fewer mistakes in the arrangement of colour if we took hints such as these from Nature's book."

In winter he often stopped on his way home from church to watch the Winterbourne flowing under the bridge, across the road to the distant woods, where the red sun reflected level rays, and produced some enchanting effects of colour.

"Now if we could take a brush and paint the moment as it is—there's a picture!" Then after a long pause he would put his spectacles—which he only used at such moments as this—back into their case, take his stick down from under his arm, and walk on with a sweet pleased expression, as though he had had an insight into the mystic world.

It was not long before he arranged his parish duties on a definite system; he divided his parish into four districts, of which he took two, and his daughters two,

every week; in this manner a constant watch over all
his flock was kept up.

It was pleasant to see him starting out to visit his
district, a leather bag slung round his shoulder over his
flowing cassock. In the bag were prayer-books, or at
need a pocket font, or communion service. Sometimes
the well-filled pockets of the cassock coat bobbed against
the comely stockinged legs—for they were apt to be full
of sweets for the children—or now and then a doll might
be seen with its head peering out of the clerical pocket.
Thus accoutred he trod sturdily beneath the hawthorn
trees, and across the shadows of great elms in the
park, and knocked with his stick at the cottage doors
when he reached them. The housewives were always
glad to see him, and poured out all their confidences,
sure of comfort and sympathy. If he did not come on
the usual day they met him with a half reproach next
time, "Ah, sir, we thought you had forgotten us." The
children would creep nearer and nearer, peeping into
those big pockets from which "goodies" were wont to
come. I do not believe a child, however shy, was ever
afraid of "our parson."

One of the women once remarked to the writer,
"There, miss, we do all o' us love the passon, that we
do: he be so *plain*. Why, bless you, I don't no more
mind telling o' un all my little pains and troubles than
if he was my grandmother." Here she blushed. "I don't
mean any disrespec', miss, but o'ny to show how he do
understand us, and we do seem to understand him."

Weather was never allowed to interfere with these
parochial walks. He would leave his breakfast untasted
to visit a sick person, or baptize a weakly infant at the

other end of his parish in snow or rain. It was one of his sayings, " Oh, nonsense, how can the weather hurt us? We should be fit for nothing if we minded such trifles." Again, " Go out and rough it, then come home and enjoy a rest—you will have earned it."

He was quite as welcome a visitor in the Squire's house as in the cottage. The lady of the manor, the Hon. Mrs. Williams, of Herringston House, shall speak for herself on this point, in a letter addressed to his son. Herringston lies between the parishes of Came and Monkton, and thus forms a connecting link between the two rectors (father and son), and was the favourite resting place of the poet when on his way to Monkton, for he knew he was always welcome there. Herringston is a very perfect specimen of Tudor architecture ; the great arched drawing-room has some interesting carved oak panelling with quaint scenes from Scripture, and the central hall has been the scene of many a Christmas feast, such as the one described in the poem of *Herringston* (page 302 *Collected Poems*).

HERRINGSTON, *February,* 1887.

MY DEAR MR. BARNES,

I had no idea when you asked me to put on paper any reminiscences of your father, how hard I should find it to do so; but the fact is, he was so completely connected with our home life, that to write of him as we remember him is, in fact, to write about ourselves. He loved our old house, and the first time I ever heard his name was when we came to live here, and my husband told me there was a poem about it by the Dorset poet, and got the book for me to read it ; I was always fond of local dialect and word origin, so the volume interested me on other grounds, but it was not until Mr. Barnes became our rector (1862) that we made his personal acquaintance. From that time till his death we were in constant communication. He was a delightful companion, and among our large family party of all ages there was not one but felt this. The wonderful range of his information accounted for the interest of his conversation, but I think its great charm lay in his own perfect simplicity, and enjoyment of the talk of others ; his hearers always felt they were talked *with*, not talked *to*. His quaint modes of expression gave point to all he said, and his infectious laugh when he told a story of any of his people, especially if it told against himself, with the dry, " Ah, she (or he) was too sharp for me there," comes back to me as I write this. He used to talk to the cottagers on all points, religious and political, and his intimate acquaintance with their dialect and modes of thought gave him an opening where other men of his intellectual superiority would have been at fault, and have only excited suspicion or reserve.

He always saw the best side of individuals, but he was not so lenient or so hopeful about the times we live in. The increase of ready-made articles and of contrivances to save trouble did not commend themselves to him. He said it destroyed invention and self-reliance in childhood, weakened the sense of responsibility in later life, and reduced things to a standard of mere money cheapness, which he thought involved cheapness of character too. I remember his saying, " When I was a little chap if I wanted a top or a whistle I must make it ; but now

ever so smart a one can be got for a halfpenny, and it is
easier to ask 'mother' for the money than to make a
whistle." It distressed him that the cottage women no
longer baked, and the farmers no longer brewed. "You
can't take a pride in a thing which you don't make,"
he said.

I am glad to see that Mr. Palgrave's article in the
National Review touches upon the mention of children
so frequent in Mr. Barnes's poems. They were not only
an amusement, but a study to him. He used to say that
mothers should keep a book of their children's sayings,
and that attention to them would prevent some educational mistakes. The first time I remember his referring
to the subject was when I told him a question from one
of our children. "Mother, does God keep the angels in
bottles ? "

" No dear. Why ? "

" Because we keep our spirits in them."

" Ah," he said, " a child's reasoning is mostly right ;
its premises are often wrong from ignorance, but its
observation is right as far as it goes." And his love of
" speechcraft " as he called it, made their language interesting to him. I recollect his beginning an interesting
talk over early English, upon a child's saying to me,
' Better'nt we go out now ? " Instead of " Had we not
better ? " A long while after he was confined to his room,
he was told of children who called honey " bee-jam," and
at once remarked " That's valuable to a philologist."

All children loved him ; they knew their welcome
did not depend on company manners and clean pinafores,
and ours would rush across the lawn in all stages of
garden grubbings when he appeared at the gate. One

day I said, " I really must dress those creatures in sack-
cloth," and he replied with his hearty laugh, " And trust
them to find the ashes for themselves."

To young girls—" maidens ". as he called them—he
was the perfection of old-world courtesy, and to his
especial favourites would give names from the Persian
poets, " The gliding Cypress," " Rose of Paradise," and
such like.

But it was not only in sunshine that we learnt to
value him ; those who are gone from us could have told
more than I can, of his help and sympathy, which never
failed to high or low.   I think the burst of appreciation
of his literary work, which resounded when the news of
his death became known, came upon his parishioners
with an odd sense of surprise.   It was not that we did
not know and love his poems—they were household
words, but somehow " celebrity " was the last thing we
ever thought of concerning him, he was so genial and so
utterly unaspiring.

I remember Miss Barnes once laughing over a visit
from some strangers who wished to see the Dorset poet,
and one of them said, " Oh, I shall feel quite afraid of
any one so clever," and one of the children took it up and
said quite indignantly, " But no one ever was afraid of
Mr. Barnes."

I wish I could remember more accurately sayings
and words.   I retain only the general sense, and also
very much information about almost every subject upon
which we ever talked, and sad is the remembrance that
such talks are over now.

Yours,

S. W.

Came Church is as poetical a little church as one
would wish to see, with its ivied tower and nave half
hidden by tall elms, between whose trunks the sunny
slopes of the park appear. The churchyard is a veritable
garden, where the dead repose among the flowers. Here
the "parson" preached many a sermon, not in Dorset,
as one of his critics has said, but in that terse Saxon-
English which to strangers sounded so quaint, but was
quite plain to the simplest villagers. Some of these
sermons have been remembered, and the memory of one
in especial has since brought comfort in a dark hour to
many of us. It was at Easter time, and the text
was of the Maries saying on their way to the tomb,
"Who shall roll us away the stone?" and when they
reached it "the stone was rolled away." He applied it
so simply to the many trials we have and dread, and to
God's way of smoothing out the most difficult paths
before us, as the stone which the women would have
been helpless to move, was by Providence taken out of
their way. More than once the writer has heard the
cottagers, when speaking of their coming troubles, of
leaving Came, or of threatened illness, and wondering
however " they should get over it," suddenly remembering this sermon, and adding, " There, miss, I often think
I am like the Maries when I dread things so. I dare say
it will all come right, and I, too, shall find the stone
rolled away when the time comes."

At first he used to write his sermons, but this soon
gave way to jotting down mere headings in phonetic
spelling, but even if he forgot the sermon book entirely,
his people were no losers. One Sunday at Whitcombe
he went into the pulpit as usual, but with empty hands.

He soon discovered the absence of his book, and while the hymn was being sung he again descended to the vestry to seek it. Not finding it however, he returned to the pulpit Bible in hand, before the hymn was over, and preached a very good extempore sermon. The lost one was afterwards found between the cloth and the lining of his cassock, having slipped through a hole in the pocket.

William Barnes used to call his daughters his curates, for they shared all his work of schools and districts, and took much pleasure in training the village choir. The young men and maidens soon learnt to read music and to sing in parts. One brawny young blacksmith especially had a good bass voice. The rector was amused at a bit of his *naïveté* at practice one day when he stopped in a chant to exclaim, " Oh, please miss, do stop a bit, while I do fetch up that big note from the bottom." Having found and " fetched up " a resounding " *Fa*," he continued the chant with great satisfaction. Another of the village worthies who delighted the rector was his old clerk at Whitcombe, whom he used to call the " Archbishop of York," because he so prided himself on his office as to boast to the young men who misbehaved, " Now you 'ave a-got to mind I. I be the second man in the church—I be."

The rector's ministry at Came was suggestive of many of his poems, such as *Vo'k a Comen into Church* at the head of this chapter, *Righting up the Church*, in the English edition, *The Two Churches*, *The Village Playground* (unpublished), and the following pretty little bit, also unpublished, which describes part of his parish—the ruined chancel window of an ancient church, standing

alone in a wide grassy field, near Herringston, the only
remains of the once existing village of Farringdon. It
was one of the poet's favourite musing places, to sit in
the shadow of that old ruin and think of the parishioners
whose very homes had disappeared, leaving only uneven
spots in the waving grass to show where they had been.

THE DEPOPULATED VILLAGE.

As oft I see by sight, or oft
In mind, the ridges on the ground,
The mark of many a little croft
And house where now no wall is found,
I call the folk to life again
And build their houses up anew ;
I ween I shape them wrong, but who
Can now outmark their shapes to men ?

I call them back to path or door
In warm-cheek'd life below the sun,
And see them tread their foot-worn floor
That now is all by grass o'errun.
To me the most of them may seem
Of fairer looks than were their own,
Yet some of all their lives were shown
As fair's the fairest of my dream.

I seem to see the church's wall
And some grey tomb below a yew,
And hear the churchyard wicket fall
Behind the people passing through.
I seem to hear, above my head,
The bell that in the tow'r was hung ;
But whither went its iron tongue
That here bemoaned the long lost dead?

This church of the vanished dead took, in the rector's
mind, no small place in his ministry. He used to say,
" In the other churches I teach—here I come to learn."

It was on first coming to Came that William Barnes
habitually clad himself in the characteristic dress, which
was as quaint as it was clerical. Cassock and wide-
brimmed hat, knee breeches and large buckles on his
shapely shoes. He had passed through many phases of
costume before finally adopting this one, which he deemed
enjoined by the ecclesiastical canons. Just as he adapted
his theories of proportion to his books and picture frames,
his theories of colour to his furniture and children's garments, so did he adapt theories of fitness and utility to
dress. At one time a friend had brought a " poncho "
(the cloak of the South Amercan Guacio) from his
travels, and the shape of this struck William Barnes as
so beautifully simple, that he forthwith got a large square
of cloth, and making a central hole in it for the head,
wore this peculiar but efficient covering through the cold
and rain of more than one winter. At another time the
convenience of the Scotch plaid made that his favourite
out-of-door garment.

" You see," he said, " the beauty of this is that you can
just cover the side most exposed to the wind, and need
not be over covered elsewhere." A favourite article of
dress, which held its own even in the days of clerical
robes, was a red cap. His first one was a Basque cap,
which his friend, Mr. Colfox, had brought him from the
Pyrenees, the next a Turkish fez a friend had procured
in the East. In after years these were replaced by the
handiwork of his eldest daughter. In none of these
garments had he any idea of dressing for the sake of
appearance : comfort or utility was always his object,
united very often with a total disregard of appearance.
This disregard would at times have gone far to sacrifice

P

the dignity of his appearance if it could have been sacri-
ficed—as for instance when he walked down Dorchester
High Street and out to Came with a poker, shovel, and
tongs slung on his back, above the customary bag. On
his family remonstrating with him, he simply said, " As
I was coming myself, it was not worth while to give the
tradespeople the trouble of sending them over. Slung
like this the weight was nothing to me."

This same shrinking from giving any one trouble was
carried out through his life. Many a time when he wanted
coals in his study, he refrained from ringing the bell,
but would bring the scuttle down with a gentle " Oh,
Mary, *would* you be so kind as to give me some coals."
On which " Mary" would become intensely deprecatory.

The poet's days were passed in a gentle routine,
broken only by visits to and from friends. After
breakfast he took a stroll round his garden, noting this
and that blossom in its growth, then he gathered up
the letters which had strewn his breakfast table, and
proceeded to answer them. General correspondence
was always more or less irksome to him, and so to get
the thought of it off his mind he answered his letters as
soon as he received them. These written, he would
come down and place them in the green letter-box under
the verandah, which the postman cleared every evening,
and with a sigh of relief would start off to visit his poor.
The afternoon was spent in his study, and in the evening
his venerable head rested in his armchair in the drawing-
room, enjoying the music his daughters made for him. He
had one or two favourite pieces, which he always asked
for last, as soothing influences for the night. " Waft her,
Angels," and a few bits of Schumann were among them.

Like most authors, Barnes had a great many letters from strangers. His philological work, " Tiw " and the Grammar, as well as the reports of his speeches at archæological meetings, brought him a deluge of correspondence. Every one wanted to know the origin of the name of his family, or dwelling place, and not one of them was left without an answer. Some British, Saxon, or Roman origin was discovered for each name, and on further correspondence with the questioner was found to fit. A place beginning with *Mor* or *Mee* generally proved to be situated near a piece of water or the sea. *Cor* proved the site to have been once a round enclosure for civil or religious rites, as the old name of Stonehenge was Cor-gawr—the giants' ring. Cat from " Coit," would mean a place near a wood, as Cattistock. A great many letters contained appeals for autographs ; others besought for a cheap edition of the poems., One of the most touching was from a very learned man—a curate with a large family, who had been a member of the Philological and Royal Asiatic Societies, but who had been obliged by pecuniary distress to withdraw from both —who wrote to beg for a gratuitous copy of the Philological Grammar for use in his lectures on Language. Needless to say, the request was promptly granted. Then there came applications from compilers of selections, for permission to insert poems in their books. Coventry Patmore put him into *The Children's Garland*, Miss Martin into her *Poet's Hour*, the Rev. Charles Rogers gave him a place in the *Lyra Britannica*. Some of the humorous poems were published in *Poems of Wit and Humour*, and the Chevalier de Chatelain, who had already placed some translations from the poems in

Rayons et Reflets, dedicated to him in a very pretty poem, his new translation of the *Tempest* (Shakespeare's).

One of the most interesting letters to the poet was the following, written in an uneducated round hand :—

December 29th, 1869.

REVEREND SIR,

I wish you most heartily a happy New Year, and hope you will excuse a poor Woman writing to you. I had to dust some Books the other day that came from a sale, and amongst them was your poems in the Dorset dialect. Sir, I shook hands with you in my heart, And I laughed and cried by turns. The old Home of my Youth and all my dear ones now mouldering in the earth came back to mind. How happy we used to be at Christmas time.

And sometimes I sit down in the gloom of an underground London Kitchen and shut my eyes, and try to fancy I am on Beaminster Down, where I have spent many a happy hour years ago. But I try to think we must be content wherever the Lord has cast our lot, and not to hanker for the past. May God bless you and all yours, Is the true wish of an old Domestic Servant, who loves the very name of Dorsetshire."

As a pendent to this we may quote a most spontaneous outpouring of the spirit of a working shoemaker, who wrote to ask if there were a cheap edition, as anything expensive was beyond his reach, though he had contrived to possess himself of one volume.

"My ancestors," he said, "were Dorset people, and I love the book; it brings back the familiar words of the loved ones that are gone, and I love you—for the god-like goodness, kindness and affection of your kind and loving heart peeps out at every verse. I have tried for years to see you and hear you read, and I hope I shall yet; but if not, I hope I shall see you when earthly distinctions are passed; but may you long live to write, and may you long live to read, and may the earth be always blessed with such lights, and may they always be loved and honoured, and when earthly praise shall cease, may the music of a thousand voices bid you welcome and say "Well done." Trusting you will forgive me for taking the liberty of expressing my feelings.

I remain, &c.

Who shall say, after these spontaneous outbursts that the Dorset poems would be a sealed book to the poor? They would, on the contrary, offer the clearest proof of the refining effect it would have on the minds of the masses, were the poems given them in a form not beyond the reach of the poor man's pence. For these are only two out of many letters from would-be readers, whose poverty pleads for a cheaper edition.

CHAPTER XIII.

THE DO'SET MILITIA.

HURRAH, my lads, vor Do'set men
A-muster'd here in red agean ;
An' welcome to your files to tread
The steady march wi' toe to heel;
Welcome to marches slow or quick.
Welcome to gath'rens thin or thick ;
God speed the Colonel on the hill,
An' Mrs. Bingham, off o' drill.

When you've handled well your lock
An' flung about your rifle stock
Vrom han' to shoulder up an' down ;
When you've lwoaded an' a-vired
Till you do come back into town,
Wi' all your loppen limbs a-tired ;
An' you be dry an' burnen hot,
Why, here's your tea an' coffee pot
At Mister Greenèn's penny till
Wi' Mrs. Bingham off o' drill.

Last year John Hinley's mother cried,
" Why, my bwoy John is quite my pride,
Vor he've a-been so good to-year,
An' han't a-mell'd wi' any squabbles,
An' han't a-drown'd his wits in beer,
An' han't a-been in any hobbles.
I never thought he'd turn out bad
He always were so good a lad ;
But now I'm sure he's better still,
Drough Mrs. Bingham, off o' drill."

Jeäne Hart, that's Joe Dùntley's chaïce
Do praise en up wi' her sweet vaïce
Vor he's so straït 's a hollyhock
(Vew hollyhocks be up so tall)
An' he do come so true's the clock
To Mrs. Bingham's coffee stall ;
An' Jeäne do write an brag o' Joe,
An' teäke the young recruits in tow,
An' try, vor all their good, to bring 'em
A' come from drill to Mrs. Bingham.

God speed the Colonel, toppèn high,
An' officers wi' sworded thigh,
An' all the sargeants that do bawl
All day enough to split their throats
An' all the corporals, and all
The band a-playèn up ther notes,
An' all the men vrom vur and near
We'll gi'e 'em all a hearty cheer,
An' then another cheerèn still
Vor Mrs. Bingham, off o' drill.

LITERARY FRIENDSHIPS.

1862 TO 1865.

THE year 1862 brought William Barnes into connection with his brother poet, Coventry Patmore. The acquaintance began by Patmore sending a copy of *Macmillan* on June 5th, 1862, in which was an appreciative article on Barnes, the Dorset Poet, by his hand. His next letter runs :—

BRITISH MUSEUM,
June 10th, 1862.

MY DEAR SIR,

As the notices in the *North British Review* and in *Macmillan's Magazine* pleased you, I cannot resist the temptation to tell you that I wrote them myself. They but poorly express all the admiration and gratitude I feel. I am rejoiced at the hope of seeing you in London. Thank you much for your kind invitation to Dorchester ; but I fear that there is little prospect of my being able to venture from the bedside of my sick wife. I am glad to hear from Professor Masson that there is a prospect of a new edition of your poems. Etc., etc.

Mr. Patmore was soon called to pass through the fiery trial which even then loomed before him. His wife

"The Angel of the House," died early in July. A cordial invitation was given him to come for change of thought and scene to Dorchester, but he was not then in spirits for even that. On July 18th, 1862, the following year, he wrote fixing the ensuing month for his visit. "Ever since I first opened your poems, a pilgrimage to Dorchester has been a definite ambition and purpose with me. I shall not be content with 'little' walks. I am a great walker, and shall ask permission to relieve you of the duty of entertaining me for some hours at a time in order that I may visit the haunts of 'Blackmore Maidens' and other pleasant places made sacred by the truest rural poetry I know of."

Mr. Patmore brought his eldest little daughter with him, and their visit was greatly enjoyed by the family at Came. By this time the *Angel in the House* was published, and Barnes in his turn had become reviewer, in an article in *Fraser*, on the invitation of the editor, Mr. Froude. As the *Angel in the House* was just then the favourite reading at Came, the household volume being covered with marks of admiration, the article was written with all heartiness, and appeared in the July number of *Fraser*, 1862.

When Patmore's *Faithful for Ever* was published, Barnes asked to be allowed again the office of reviewer. To the end of the Dorset Poet's life the reciprocal pen of Mr. Patmore was always prompt in his praise, until the obituary articles in *St. James's Gazette* and the *Fortnightly Review* in October and November 1886, closed his tributes.

About this time also Barnes made the acquaintance by correspondence of Lord Tennyson, who wrote on February 28th to acknowledge a gift of the poems which he had for many years- known and admired. Some few years after visits were interchanged. Barnes made a stay of some days with the Poet Laureate at Freshwater, and I believe it was under the stimulus of this influence that the "Northern Farmer" was written, to try if the northern dialect would lend itself as well to poesy, as the western speech.

Another interesting correspondent was a friend of Mr. Tennant's, whom he styles "The old Anchorite of Guernsey—Georges Metivier."

"There is," remarks Mr. Tennant, a "peculiar charm in this eccentric old philosopher. He never moves away from his retired little hermitage, where he lives with one old Welshwoman as servant. I suspect that his worldly means are very small, and chiefly confined to very old books, of which he has a curious collection scattered about his little dark den, but he seems to have no wants. His memory struck me as something marvellous. . . . I should very much like to get M. Metivier over here in the spring, and set you together like the two Kilkenny cats, and myself to look on. Would this tempt you, if we can get Prince Lucien to make a third ? Let me know, Mr. Rector, what you think of this, and believe me, &c.

"CHARLES TENNANT."

M. Metivier was, in a way, a fellow worker with William Barnes, being a great student of French and insular dialects. He, too, worked for Prince Lucien, for whom he translated the "Song of Solomon" and the Gospel of

St. Matthew into · Jersey *patois*. His letters to the
Dorset Poet are chiefly philological.

In the spring of 1864, William Allingham, who had
introduced himself at Came by the welcome gift to his
brother poet of his charming poems, came to stay a few
days at the Rectory, a visit which much interested the
family. Mr. Allingham was then publishing *Laurence
Bloomfield in Ireland*, and the reckless way in which he
corrected his proofs, often rewriting the whole verse,
highly amused the Dorset Poet, who, out of tender
regard to his printers, made very few corrections. The
visit was returned in the autumn, when Barnes lectured
at Lymington in November, and became the guest of
Mr. Allingham. The same tour took him to Lyndhurst,
where Mr. Hamilton Aide, author of *Rita*, &c., was his
entertainer for a few days. They had pleasant excursions in the shades of the New Forest, one of the most
enjoyable being a lunch with "Dolores," in her flower-
embowered one-storied cottage. She sang some of her
pretty songs, and gave the poet a "good time" in the
way that he enjoyed best. Soon after this visit "Dolores" chose one of the Dorset poems to set to music as
a song. Madam Sartoris (Adelaide Kemble) also set
some of the poems to music.

It was early in 1863 that another literary acquaintance with Mr. F. Furnivall was begun by the
latter writing to ask for a paper on the Dialect, for
the Philological Society. This was written, and was
read by Mr. Furnivall at one of the meetings. It was
published for the Society by Asher at Berlin, in 1863,
under the comprehensive title of "*A Grammar and
Glossary of the Dorset Dialect*, with the history, out-

spreading, and bearings of south-western English." , The minute of the resolution of the Society about the publication of this paper was as follows :—" We recommend the paper of Mr. Barnes for printing in the transactions, provided that the author be good enough :

" 1st. To put it into printable shape, inserting stops, marking where paragraphs begin and end, &c. We also recommend—as well for the sake of greater clearness as for saving space—that all the less important matter, such as anecdotes &c., be printed in smaller type than the rest and be marked accordingly.

" 2nd. To substitute the usual terms for the unusual ones—as voice (sounds), voicings (vowels), clippings for consonants, mate-wording for synonyms, &c., there being no reason to introduce such quaint and unhappy words —what notion does clippings convey to one's mind ?— especially as other usual terms—diphthongs, pronouns, &c., are retained, and "vowels" is used more than once.

. " 3rd. To put the glossary in alphabetical order—*this is imperative*—and to omit the imaginary headings which imply etymological connections, the proof of which is not given, and should not be attempted, as many of them are extremely doubtful."

The Philological Society was clearly not inclined to become " pioneers in the effort to restore the Saxon language ;" they clung to their Latinized language, and were content to elucidate Saxon English as one treats of a dead language, but not to bring it back to its purity in daily use. William Barnes gave way on all these points substituted the usual grammatical words of Latin derivation and put his glossary into more correct arrangement before it went to the German printer of the society.

Other papers were written for the Philological Society
in the course of the year. On the 4th of December
two were read together ; one " Our elder Brethren, the
Frisians, their Language and Literature as illustrative
of those of England." The other "Trades of a Primary
Root f*ng or f* in the Indo-Teutonic Languages."

During the following year he supplied the Philological
Society with papers on " Language of the Stone Age,"
and on " Lost English words," which were read by Mr.
Furnivall, who wrote on June 4th :—

" I read your papers last night at our meeting, but I
am sorry to say that our members did not show much
sympathy with them. When the two words are both in use,
as ' desert ' and ' wilderness,' they thought that a distinction of meaning has grown up, and if not, they
would sooner have two words than one for the same
thing, as it prevents repetition. A few of the shorter
old words they liked, but all the old ones that have
become strange to them, they did not want revived:
The classical feeling was stronger than I had expected.

" The Stone Age they rebelled at. Your ' Tiw ' is not
accepted."

It is strange that Barnes found the least sympathy in
a society, the object of whose existence would have led
him to expect the most.

An article was published in *Macmillan* of March,
1863, on the *Rariora of Old Poetry*. In asking him to
write it, Masson, the editor, says, " The subject is a very
curious one, and in your hands, with the due trouble in
giving such interpretations as would be intelligible to
popular readers, the paper, I believe, would be very
interesting."

In this paper Barnes begins by proving the dramatic and odic poetry of the Greeks to have come from still older and less civilised sources. The chorus is traced through nearly all savage nations, with the same union of the three Graces—Dance, Tune, and Song. Thence we are carried on through the Norse, Druid, and Scald songs to the Welsh Bards; then to the Christian hymn, the Latin ode, the Saxon letter-rhymes, to the old English poets,—an intense compression of learned matter.

On February 14th, 1862, the editor of the *National Review*, who was then preparing a critique on the poems for its columns, wrote to ask William Barnes to become a contributor. He was at this time writing also for the *Reader*, at the solicitation of David Masson, who was editing that review, as well as *Fraser's*. In July, 1863, the article on Coventry Patmore's poetry appeared in *Fraser*, and in September, a paper on the "Credibility of old Song History and Tradition," a subject which he handled thoroughly from Homer to the Welsh Bards.

Whilst all these scientific writings were being thrown off here and there, the poet's mind was occupied by a new subject for his pen, a book on *Marriage*, which, however, his faithful publisher, Russell Smith, refused to bring out, it not seeming hopeful.

The Bridegroom's book was at last given to Mrs. Warren, editor of the *Ladies Treasury*, under the title of "A View of Christian Marriage," and was printed in the monthly parts of that magazine, during the year 1866. Besides taking up the subject on its Christian ground, it is treated exhaustively, both in its moral and historical aspect.

It was about this time that Stuart Mill's first work on *Utilitarianism* came out in *Fraser*. From the first, Mill's views had roused the spirit of confutation in William Barnes, so that he was quite ready to respond to the following letter from Mr. Tennant.

"I send you a remarkable book lately published by John Stuart Mill, entitled *Utilitarianism*. He is the son of Mr. Mill, the Political Economist, and author of *British India*, with whom I was acquainted, and who imbibed his false philosophy from his old friend and next door neighbour in Queen Street, Westminster— Jeremy Bentham. I have lost sight of John Stuart Mill since he was a boy, but he follows his father as a political economist, and is called *par excellence* the 'Great Thinker' and 'Master of Logic.'

"It is the more wonderful that he should have written such a book as this, and that such a doctrine should in these days have so many disciples."

The answer to this letter has perished, but it seems to have pleased his colleague, who, after thanking him, adds, "You have tried him more directly by the rules of logic than I could pretend to do, but I think we agree in our resolve of refuting him. I confess I was surprised at some of his reasoning, and I think his conclusions false and extremely objectionable. If so, they ought to be answered, coming as from a person who is looked upon as an authority."

There was a talk of a joint article, but the matter ended in both the friends writing refutations. Mr. Tennant's was published separately in 1864, and he did his utmost to get Barnes's article into one of the Quarterlies, but in both the ground was preoccupied, and the

MS. remained in the author's drawer as one of the
" handwrits not printed." The chief points in which he
disagreed with Stuart Mill were that Mill makes the
physical man almost an object of worship, quite forgetting the spiritual man ; also on his confusion between
" Utility," " Pleasure," and " Happiness," all of which
Barnes clearly defined and distinguished from each
other. Broadly stated, his distinction was that utility
was a purely material good concerning the body only ;
pleasure was good of body and mind; while happiness
reached still higher, including what was best for mind,
body, and soul.

During these few years (1863-4-5) the readings of the
poems extended greatly, and were no longer confined to
his own county. Mr. Barnes received and responded
willingly to earnest invitations from Salisbury, Buck-
land-Newton, Bristol, Christchurch, Trowbridge, Romsey,
Ryde, Portsea, Yeovil, Lymington, Lyndhurst, and Marl-
borough College, where he was invited, while on a visit
to the Head Master, to read to the boys. At Wellington
College, too, he was a guest of Dr. Benson, the Head
Master, now Archbishop of Canterbury. All these
readings, which were in every case gratuitous, were
enjoyable to him, as he had congenial friends at nearly
every town. One scarcely knows which he most enjoyed—a laugh over Dorset with his lively admirer, the
Rev. E. Nares Henning, at Sherborne ; an antiquarian
talk with Mr. Colfox, at Bridport ; a clerical chat with
the Rector of Buckland ; or a literary talk with Mr.
Allingham at Lymington ; they were all in turn delightful to him. But he did not give all his readings to
literary institutes. At Ryde it was the Young Men's

Q

Christian Association which benefited by them; at
Poole the fund for the new Temperance Rooms. He
was appealed to by philanthropic Mr. G. Ff. Eliot, who
had opened at Weymouth a reading-room for the
navvies employed on the railway, to come and help him
give these rough men a little rational entertainment,
which he did as willingly as he went to Wimborne to teach
a budding working man's society what "co-operation"
meant. Next the rectors of country parishes began to
appeal to him for readings to their villagers in the
parish schoolroom, and he read for the flock of his
old friend, Rev. J. Dale, the naturalist, at Glanville-
Wootton, and for Mr. Ravenhill, at Buckland, besides
many others, and these country audiences were more
sympathetic to him than the town ones. One of his
favourite audiences was that which assembled in the
militia barrack room, at times when the militia were
called out. Mrs. Bingham, the Colonel's wife, was very
earnest and energetic in giving the men good amusements during this time, which might have been injurious
to honest peasants, if spent in idleness. She opened a
coffee and reading room for them, and she often called
on the Dorset Poet to give "her boys" an evening's
entertainment. How they laughed and enjoyed the
Dorset rhymes! and what pictures the poems put before
them of their rustic homes in the vale! One night the
applause reached its height when the reader propounded
a riddle. "Tell me, my men, why is the Dorset militia
like blue vinne'yd (veined) cheese?" The rustics in
uniform showed puzzled faces and could not tell. "Because they'll stand vire (fire) and never run," said the
lecturer, himself bursting into a laugh as hearty as the

roar which greeted his joke against the unmelting moods of Dorset cheese.

Another evening the meeting was wild with enthusiasm on the reading of a poem written expressly for them, which if only as a tribute to the success of Mrs. Bingham's philanthropic efforts deserves quotation. Therefore I have chosen it as the poetical illustration of this chapter.

In 1865 began William Barnes's connection with the Archæological Institute, which in the summer of that year held its Congress in Dorchester. It may well be imagined that a man who knew all the British and Saxon history of his county, and could put his finger on every ruin or cairn worth studying, was sure to come to the fore on such an occasion. He was unanimously chosen guide of the Society, and it was a pleasant thing to see him pointing out the bits of old Roman wall and British earthworks to a listening crowd, all pressing near to gather his words. He did not have it all his own way, however, for there was, of course, the sceptical member, who would believe nothing, and the one idea'd member, who wanted to find in everything traces of Phœnician occupation in Britain, and the argumentative member, who knocked down by a flow of very hard words every assertion made by others. Many were the arguments the local antiquary allowed himself to be betrayed into by this fluent adversary, whose words were more overpowering than his logic.

There were delightful excursions to distant spots in a long procession of carriages, and when the archæological explanations were over, there were luncheons in some old abbey or Tudor manor-house, and here humour took

the place of dry learning in the speeches. The three
most prominent for humour were a remarkable trio, the
Bishop of Oxford (Wilberforce), Mr. J. H. Parker, and
the Dorset Poet. A certain thunderstorm in Sherborne
Park, when the whole Society was imprisoned for an
hour under an archway in Walter Raleigh's ruined
castle, will long be remembered ; for the trio above
mentioned kept them in fits of laughter the whole time
by one funny story after another.

The morning at Maiden Castle was a fatiguing one to
many, as the carriages had to be kept at the foot of the
earthworks, while the Poet led the members over the
" vallum " and mound, and up the steep walls of turf at
a rate more in accordance with his own eagerness than
the strength of their lungs. One very enthusiastic lady
was determined not to lose a word of wisdom from the
mouth of the guide for the day, and she literally hung
on to the skirts of his cassock as he clambered up the
sides of the hills. Arrived at the top a vigorous discussion took place, Barnes holding Maiden Castle as a
British work, and the argumentative and another member declaring that it was Roman. Barnes fled as usual to
philology for help. " It's very name is Celtic," he said.
" Mai dun, the stronghold by the plain, or with a plain
top." Here he glanced round on the wide expanse of
green turf which formed the summit of the earthwork.
The Rev. H. Moule confirmed this by quoting an Irish
friend's derivation of it from the Irish Magh dun, which
meant the same thing.

An interesting discovery was made of some subter-
ranean huts—which are described in the following
letter to Mr. Warne, who, to the poet's regret, was

not able to attend the Congress, but sent his paper to be read.

CAME RECTORY, August 17th, 1865.

DEAR MR. WARNE,

You will see in your MS. that I have written a few of your words in my own hand, lest I should hitch in my public reading of it, as I did when alone, and mar its effect.

Maiden Castle wants fifty pounds worth of digging. Mr. Cunnington has dug a little more in what we think hut-holes, two steined with rough stones, and affording in the soil, bits of rude and Roman pottery and tiles. Some man told him at the Congress that he thought the whole work Roman. So you must give up all your Celtic earthworks to the *gens togata*.

What say you of the rough stone pitching? Is that Roman? If so, the tesselated pavement of Dorchester may be British or Phœnician! But what if they find bits of Roman pottery? Must the work then be Roman? Is every pass in New Zealand an English work if English axes are found in it?

The man who took away the bases of the gate jambs was standing among us, and showed us where he dug them out. He is a homely Dorset swain, whose word is as good as his affidavit.

I have yet to "pull the torch" with you about Wareham. Long before Alfred and the Danes, Wareham was so called, and Wareham means the "mound, or fence inclosure." It is said of Brytric, " his lic lid aet Wareham (*Saxon Chronicle*, A.D. 784).. Therefore Wareham walls were up in his time. I don't read Asser as you do. He speaks of the castellum *called* Wareham ;

not *at* or *in* Wareham, " walled with mounds was the castle."

Castellum, a stem from *castra*, meant an ˙earthwork till stone castella were built in far later times.

It was my design to give a preface to the reading of your paper, and to have blown you at least one blast of praise, but I was cut out.

Yours very truly,

W. BARNES.

In September the Hon. Sec. of the Archæological Institute wrote to beg permission to print in the journal of the Society, the paper read by William Barnes at the Congress, and which was thought especially important as throwing light on many obscure place names. Another influential member, Mr. Thomas Purnell, wrote :—

19th August, 1865.

MY DEAR SIR,

I extremely regret I had to leave Dorchester without the pleasure and privilege of a chat with you, but hope at some future time I shall be so fortunate as to meet you again. I can assure you that I, like all who have spoken with me on the subject of the late " merry meeting " at Dorchester, carry away very pleasant recollections, not the least of which are your readings and courteous kindness during the week. I sent you the Welsh paper which I thought you might be pleased to see. The next day the editor printed your lecture. I

am sure he would be glad to print a note with
additional observations if you were to favour him
with it.

Believe me, &c.,

THOMAS PURNELL.

To the REV. W. BARNES, B.D.

Extracts from Diary　*Jan.* 21*st*, 1866.—The Hon.
Mrs. Norton came here to lunch.

Feb. 8*th.*—Sent my paper on "Tuscan Stornelli," to
Masson, for *Macmillan's Magazine.*

Feb. 11*th.*—A furious storm. The top of an elm by
the church tower was broken off and cast down on the
tower, and it broke off some of the battlement stones;
they fell on the roof, which was much broken.

(In spite of the bad weather, the rector, with his
daughter, struggled across the park, a work of difficulty,
they having often to hold on to each other, not to get
carried away in the blast which made the trees crack.
They waited in the empty church, but no congregation
came, and on their return home they found that a tall
fir tree in the shrubbery had been blown down, and lay
across the rectory lawn; fortunately it fell free of the
house itself. The church was newly roofed at the joint
expense of parson and squire, and on April 1st was
embellished with an organ, given by Mr. William Miles
Barnes, jun., who had developed a talent for amateur
organ building.)

May 28*th.*—Dined at the Rectory at Preston, and met
Mr. Martin Tupper.

June 19*th.*—Mr. Martin Tupper here.

June 22*nd.*—In Dorchester, examining the boys at the Grammar School.

June 25*th.*—Examining Grammar School boys in French.

The next event chronicled in the diary is a domestic one of a very gratifying kind. It runs :—

Sept. 5*th.*—I met Mr. Vyvyan (the outgoing Rector of Monkton) in Herringston Lane, coming to our house with a letter from the Hon. Mrs. Strangways (Lord Ilchester, the patron of the living, being at that time a minor), telling him that she gave to William the living of Monkton.

Her letter to young Mr. Barnes received the next day was a very graceful tribute to the father as well as the son. This appointment gave great pleasure to the Poet, who would now have his son near him for the remainder of his life, and this constant communication and mutual parochial assistance formed a great bond between them. On the day when the elder William Barnes took the district which led him nearest to Monkton, it was generally his custom, as I have before said, to lunch at Herringston House, where a place was always ready for him, and then to go on to Monkton to dinner. This was kept up through a long series of years, while the little grandchildren, one by one, were added to the group of welcoming faces that ran out to the gate to "watch for grandpapa," and while the music of babbling babies' voices which pleased him first, grew into the music of a trained choir and family orchestra, which was the delight of his old age.

The Rector of Monkton, when not engaged in assisting clerical friends, usually took a Sunday evening walk

to Came, joining the party at the tea-table in the rest
after duty, and adding his voice to the Sunday songs
which his father liked to hear from his daughters. The
two William Barneses dearly loved an argument, and
very often the younger would take up the adverse side
of a question for the sake of drawing out his father's
eager logic. No one ever had a greater dislike of
quarrelling than William Barnes the elder, but nobody
ever enjoyed more the sparring with a learned friend in
disputation. He was always rather hard on a woman's
reasoning, however, and said, " A woman could always
jump at a conclusion, but logically she never knew the
ground she stood on, or if she did, she could not stand
still on it."

CHAPTER XIV.

FANCY.

In stillness we ha' words to hear
   An' shapes to zee in darkest night
An' tongues a'-lost can hail us near,
   An' souls a-gone can smile in zight,
When Fancy now do wander back
   To years a-spent, an' bring to mind
   Zome happy tide a-left behind
In weästèn' life's slow beaten track.

When feädèn leaves do drip wi' rain
   Our thoughts can ramble in the dry,
When winter win' do zweep the plain
   We still can have a zunny sky.
Vor though our limbs be winter wrung,
   We still can zee wi' Fancy's eyes,
   The brightest looks ov e'th and skies,
That we did know when we wer young.

In päin our thoughts can pass to ease,
  In work our souls can be at play,
An' leave behind the chilly lease
  Vor warm-air'd meads o' new mow'd hay,
When we do flee in Fancy's flight
  Vrom daily ills avore our feäce,
  An' linger in zome happy pleäce
Ov me'th an' smiles, an' warmth, an' light.

ENGLISH POEMS.

1866.

"PRINKING ; A View of Bodily Ornament and Dress,"
by the Rev. W. Barnes. Such was the curious title of a
series of articles with which the feminine readers of the
Ladies' Treasury were instructed in 1866-7. It requires
a study of *tiw* to interpret even the title; there we
find that the root, pr*ng, has a meaning of to "put
forth." In its material sense this root yields such words
as " prong," " prick," " prim," &c., while in its moral
sense, as putting forth of one's self for admiration, or
adorning one's self, we come to the words "pretty,"
"pride," " priggish," " prance," " praise," &c., &c.
"Prinking," then, is nothing more nor less than the art
of adornment,[1] which is treated in a very polyglot
style. We have the " prinking " of the savage and
the civilised man, the " prinking " of the antique and
the modern human being, in all times and climates.
There is an article on " Tattoo ;" and headgear, bodygear,
and footgear are traced through all their forms, and even

[1] It is a curious fact that the word " to prink " is really in use
in America, meaning to adorn one's self.

the familiar names of "sash," "scarf," "shoe," &c., all carried philologically back to their original roots. "Prinking" was followed in the *Ladies' Treasury* by an equally exhaustive treatise on "The House and Home."

In the autumn of 1866, a correspondence with Mr. Richard D. Webb furnished William Barnes with some direct information about a part of Ireland, which for some time he had regarded with philological interest. This was an ancient English colony in the Baronies of Forth and Bargy in county Wexford. Legend says Forth was a Flemish colony in the ninth century. It is known as a fact to have been colonised by the followers of Strongbow and FitzStephen, in 1169, and as the dialect has more an old English than a Flemish form, it is probably to these latter settlers that it has to be traced. This dialect, which is quite unlike the Irish, has a great many Teutonic words, which, though now lost in our national English, are found in old English and some dialects. The first knowledge of the Forth and Bargy dialect came to Mr. Barnes in a curious way. A Quaker friend of his, Mr. Tanner, of Bristol, was reading the Dorset poems in a Somerset village one evening, when an Irish gentleman told him he had understood them quite well, as he had been accustomed to hear the country people, in a part of Wexford, speak a similar dialect. The united efforts of Mr. Barnes and Mr. Tanner were now given to find out the reason of a Saxon dialect in a Celtic land, and as it chanced they happened upon the very man who knew most about it, Mr. Webb, who possessed a great many papers written by his uncle, Mr. Poole, containing the result of his researches. These papers were handed over to the

Dorset poet, who found them so interesting that he gave them to the world, with a glossary and introduction by himself, as editor. The following verses will be enough to show the true Saxon ring of the language :—

"THE BRIDE'S PORTION.

A portion ich gae her was (its now ich have er-tolth)	The portion I gave her was (it's now I have told)
Dhree brailes o' beanes an' a keow at was yole.	Three barrels of beans, and a cow that was old,
A heeve o' been, an' dwanty shilleen.	A hive of bees, and twenty shillings."

The book was offered first to Prince Lucien Buonaparte, who showed great interest in it, but could not print it at the time. He wrote :—

15th May, 1866.

MY DEAR MR. BARNES,

I should have been very happy to have printed your interesting little work on the English dialect of the Barony of Forth, but unfortunately my linguistical budget is all absorbed for some years to come, by several publications on and in the Basque language. This language has always been the principal aim of my researches, and as such, it commands the preference. I hope you shall find some manner for not depriving the scientific world of this interesting publication. I shall be glad to subscribe for twenty-five copies. In a few weeks I shall send you some of the continuations which

I have edited, relating to the English, Italian, or French
dialects.
      And believe me, my dear Mr. Barnes,
           Yours truly,
               L. L. BUONAPARTE.

The book was at length published by Russell Smith,
and though it attracted some notice at the Philological
Society, it was not a good commercial investment, for
Russell Smith ruefully writes in December, 1867, " I
persuaded a Dublin bookseller to take thirteen copies,
and he informed me six months after that he had not
sold one !" It found one or two sympathetic readers,
however, in Ireland. The Principal of St. Patrick's
College, Maynooth, wrote to thank the editor for bringing an interesting philological fact before the world,
and Mr. A. Hume begged permission to incorporate
the glossary of the Forth and Bargy in his Dictionary of
Hibernian words. He was a well-known writer on
Celtic language, and a few years later a paper of
his won the Cunnington prize at the Royal Irish
Academy in June, 1869.

William Barnes contributed in 1867 some papers
and poems to a local journal edited by a clerical
friend, and entitled *The Hawk ; A Monthly Hover
from the Vale of Avon.* The Hawk was not a
long-lived bird, and fluttered to the ground after its
third hover.

The contributions to *Macmillan's Magazine* at the
time were a paper on " Bardic Poetry," in August, 1867
and one in November, 1866, on " Plagiarism," quaintly
called " Thought thieving and thought matching," a

curious proof that the same idea often springs up in two
or more minds at the same time, and that similarity of
idea and even expression is not always a proof of
plagiarism. *A propos* of this is a curious incident in
relation to the poem entitled the *Mother's Dream*. In
March, 1873, a poem appeared in the *Sunday at Home*,
by Mr. Alexander Grosart, entitled *Little Willie back
again*, in which the subject was so far identical with the
Mother's Dream, that it attracted the notice of the critics,
one paper printing the two poems side by side, with the
remark, " We do not think it likely that both of these
authors invented the dream, and we should like to know
whence it came into the mind of the latter one."

Mr. Grosart answers this letter in the same paper on
April 3rd, asserting, as a fact, that he had never seen or
heard of Mr. Barnes's poem, but that during his own
grief for his lost child, a lady told him a dream of her
own as a kind of consoling thought, and it gave him such
comfort that he felt inspired to express his emotions in
verse. He had written it in 1868, and had it privately
printed as a "leaflet" at that time, though it did not
appear in the *Sunday at Home* till 1873. He adds,
" this matter teaches two things. 1st. That alleged
plagiarisms are often merely coincidences. 2nd. That
in the dream world there are mysteries beyond our
fathoming, here assuming that this particular dream was
a reality in two cases. May not the dream in both
poems be used of the Master to stay the weeping of
Rachels refusing to be comforted ? " In 1876 William
Barnes received a letter from a lady, who said that she
had found the same idea, though less poetically expressed, in a poem by L.E.L., but that she was "strongly

R

impressed with the idea that the original legend is German." This is more surprising still, for Barnes had heard the dream as happening to a friend of his daughter in the north of England. But the strangest thing of all was that a third person had had the same inspiration. In August, 1879, a Mr. Hoskyns Abrahall wrote to beg to be allowed to call at Came on his way from Exeter to Salisbury, to make Mr. Barnes's acquaintance, and proposed an exchange of poems as a mark of friendship, adding, "Some years since I composed a poem (as yet unpublished) that is based on the story on which, as I have since found, you have founded your touching little poem of the *Mourning Mother*."

It would indeed seem as though such consoling dreams were a general consolation of Nature in excessive grief.

Besides the articles in *Macmillan*, several Dorset poems had appeared in its pages since 1864, when the editor had asked for them. After a few of the Dorset ones he wrote to the poet :—

LONDON, *November 3rd*, 1864.

MY DEAR SIR,

I enclose a cheque for your poem, which I admire greatly. But do give us one done into common English soon. I was in Cambridge the other day. A very accomplished and sensible lady there, whom I often talk with on literary matters, said to me what I have often said to myself, "What a pity Mr. Barnes *will* write that dialect! I really cannot, even after much pains, get at the meaning, and the effort too often exhausts the

interest." I read your last in such English as came to
me off-hand, and she was charmed. Do try the experiment with your next. I am sorry I can see little chance
of any good being done with the " Psalms " translation
you speak of. Have you done any of it ?

Yours, etc.,

A. MACMILLAN.

This appeal was followed by others. In one letter
Mr. Macmillan says: "Indeed you limit your audience
very greatly."

The combined persuasions of so many good judges so
far influenced the poet that he began translating a few
of his unpublished poems into English, and thus formed
the nucleus of the *Poems of Rural Life*, which was published by Macmillan in 1868. A reprint of this edition
was published in America, by Roberts Brothers, in December, 1868, illustrated by Homer and Billings, and
with an illuminated title-page.

One of William Barnes's reviewers in the obituary
notice in the *Saturday Review* for October 16th, 1886,
remarks of these, "That they read like translations
out of some original, and as though Mr. Barnes, which
was very probably the case, had thought them out in
Dorset, and had then translated them. His art and
magic, which are so remarkable in the dialect pieces left
him at once when he tried the common English."

The reviewer's literary acumen is not far out in the
first part of this assertion. Many of the poems in this
collection *are* literally translations, for the originals
exist in print in the dialect as cuttings from the *Dorset*

R 2

Chronicle. But as regards the assertion, that the poet's " art and magic " leave him as soon as he forsakes the folk speech, there might possibly be two opinions. I will quote a little poem, *Clouds,* in its two garbs, and I do not think the loss of art has been great in the translation.

CLOUDS.

Onriding slow, at lofty height	A-ridèn slow, at lofty height,
Were clouds in drift along the sky,	Wer' clouds a-blown along the sky
Of purple-blue, and pink and white,	O' purple-blue, an' pink, an' white,
In pack and pile, upreaching high,	In pack and pile, up-reachèn high,
For ever changing as they flew	A-shiftèn oft as they did goo
Their shapes from new again to new.	Their sheäpes vrom new ageän to new.
And some like rocks and towers of stone,	An' zome like rocks an' tow'rs of stwone,
Or hill or woods outreaching wide,	Or hills, or woods a-reachèn wide,
And some like roads, with dust upblown	And zome like roads, wi' doust a-blown
In glittering whiteness off their side,	A-glitterèn white up off their zide,
Outshining white, again to fade	A-comèn bright, ageän to feäde
In figures made to be unmade.	In sheäpes a-meäde to be un-meäde.
So things may meet, but never stand	Zoo things do come, but never stand
In life! They may be smiles or tears,	In life ! It mid be smiles or tears,
A joy in hope, and one in hand,	A joy in hope, an' one in hand,
Some grounds of grief, and some of fears ;	Zome grounds o' grief and zome of fears ;
They may be good or may be ill,	They mid be good or mid be ill,
But never long abiding still.	But never long a-standèn still.

Neither is the following serenade lacking in any of the qualities of true poetry. This, however, was not a translation; it was written first in English, and so is perhaps more free in style.

A NIGHT SONG.

Oh! do you wake or do you sleep
    With windows to the moonlit sky?
Oh! have you lost or do you keep
    A thought of all the days gone by?
Or are you dead to all you knew
Of life, the while I live to you?

May air, o'er wallside roses brought,
    Of charming gardens give you dreams,
May rustling leaves beguile your thought
    With dreams of walks by falling streams,
And on your lids be light, that yields
Bright dream clouds over daisied fields.

Our meeting hour of yesterday
    To me now deep in waning night,
Seems all a glory pass'd away,
    Beyond a year-time's longsome flight;
Though night seems far too short to weigh
Your deeds and words of yesterday.

While rise or sink the glittering stars
    Above dim woods, or hillock brows,
There, out within the moon-paled bars,
    In darksome bunches sleep your cows;
So sweetly sleep, asleep be they
Until you meet the opening day.[1]

---

[1] Page 22 of *Selection of Unpublished Rhymes*, printed privately at Monkton, by Rev. W. Miles Barnes, at the rectory press.

It is true that some of the poet's friends agreed in a measure with the critic before quoted. Mr. Coventry Patmore never liked the change of language. The Rev. E. N. Henning writes : " I have read it over, and am going through it again, with a view of picking out the pieces which I like the best; but I am so sorely puzzled to decide, that I have just given up the attempt, as I know it will end by my marking every one, as I have done with the old volumes. To me they lack but one charm, the very one purposely omitted by you, the dear old Dorset dialect. Putting them into conventional English seems to me like polishing a Queen Anne's farthing, and that refined language somewhat mars their simplicity. However, for my own purposes I doff their finery where I can, and find myself more at home." The poet himself had some fears about the success of the change of style, for in his preface he says he has written in common English, " not, however, without a misgiving that what I have done for a wider range of readers may win the good opinion of fewer."

The poems, whether in Dorset or in English, were the result of true inspiration. The writer did indeed so realise the scenes he described, that his imagination frequently took the form of a vision, so vivid was it. He said one day to the writer of this memoir, " The poem *Stay* is a metre I heard in a dream, and the refrain ' Stay, stay ! ' is the very same sound as in the dream. And again, *The Old Farmhouse* [see Chapter XVIII.] is a kind of vision of an ancient house at ——. I seemed to see the little girl running, and the straws moving and shining under her feet."

His favourite dreaming place was a certain corner of

the lawn at Came, where in May a red hawthorn tree
and flowering laburnum mingled their shades on the
grass, and feathery tamarisks, syringa, and lilac blos-
somed in the sheltering shrubbery behind.[1]   There was
a tall hop-pole too, sending its graceful wreaths up
luxuriantly against a background of sky; and nestling
near was a white rose, which had been transplanted from
the old home in town, in loving memory of her whose
hands had tended it there, and whose pale face its
blossoms had dressed for her last sleep.   In this floral
nook the poet would place his basket-work seat, and with
his eyes closed and face upturned into the sunlight, he
would sit for an hour at a time, sometimes brooding
poetry through the medium of visions, sometimes thinking out a deep question of ethics or philosophy, or
perhaps puzzling out a new metre.   His studies in metre
were thorough and wide.   No one reading his poems in
their seeming simplicity would imagine that the art
which created them was drawn from fountains of poetic
lore in all ages and hands.   Professor Palgrave remarks
on this art of metre and rhythm in his masterly lecture
on " William Barnes and his Poems," delivered at Oxford University, November 11th, 1886 (printed in the
National Review for February, 1887), and quotes the
rhythm and assonances of *Woak Hill* as a type of his
peculiarly rhythmical style.   The metre of *Woak Hill*
was one of the poet's favourite forms, the distinguishing
parts of it are not only the assonances which Professor
Palgrave remarks, but the hidden rhymes in the refrain.
The original of this metre is a Persian poetical form
called the " pearl," because the rhymes form a continual

[1] See Letter No. XII. Appendix, p. 346.

string, like beads on a thread. I give a few verses, italicising the " pearls."

WOAK HILL.

When sycamore trees wer a-spreadèn
  Green-ruddy in hedges,
  Bezide the red doust o' the ridges,
    A-*dried* at Woak Hill.

I packed up my goods all a-sheenèn
  Wi' long years of handlèn,
  On dousty red wheels ov a waggon
    To *ride* at Woak Hill.

The brown thatchèn roof o' the dwellèn
  I then wer a-leavèn,
  Had shelter'd the sleek head o' Meary,
    My *bride* at Woak Hill.

But now vor zome years her light vootfall
  'S a-lost vrom the vloorèn,
  Too soon vor my jay an' my children,
    She *died* at Woak Hill.

But still I do think that in soul
  She do hover about us,
  To ho' vor her motherless children,
    Her *pride* at Woak Hill.

Zoo lest she should tell me hereafter
  I stole off 'ithout her,
  An' left her uncall'd at house-ridden,
    To *bide* at Woak Hill:

I call'd her so fondly, wi' lippèns
  All soundless to others,
  An' took her wi' air-reachèn hand
    To my *zide* at Woak Hill.

On the road I did look round, a-talkèn
  To light at my shoulder,
An' then led her in at the doorway,
  Miles *wide* vrom Woak Hill.

That's why vo'k thought, vor a season
  My mind wer a-wandrèn
Wi' sorrow, when I wer so sorely
  A-*tried* at Woak Hill.

But no ; that my Meary mid never
  Behold herzelf slighted,
I wanted to think that I guided
  My *guide* vrom Woak Hill.

The Knoll (page 150, *English Poems*) is in the same
metre. Another Persian metre much used by him was
the *ghazal.* This is similar to the "pearl," having a
rhyme followed by an assonance at the end of each
verse, which in the *ghazal* is a couplet instead of a four-
lined metre. Here is a specimen :—

GREEN.

Our zummer way to church did wind about
  The cliff, where ivy on the *ledge* wer green.

Our zummer way to town did skirt the wood,
  Where sheenèn leaves in tree an' *hedge* wer green.

Our zummer way to milkèn in the mead
  Wer on by brook, where fluttrèn *zedge* wer green.

Our hwomeward ways did all run into one
  Where moss upon the roofstwone's *edge* wer green.

Lowshot Light and *Happy Times* in the English
edition are also *ghazal* poems.

There is another uncommon metre which is a little altered from a Welsh Bardic measure, called the *Hir a thoddaid,* the long or melting measure. The peculiarity is in the rhyme to the penultimate line being in the middle of the last line instead of at the end. All the previous lines rhyme in the ordinary way. *Fellowship* (*Poems of Rural Life in Common English,* page 169) is a specimen.

In *Meldon Hill* the poet has taken still further license with this Bardic metre, by introducing the middle rhyme three times in the verse, instead of merely at the end.

MELDON HILL.

I took the road of dusty *stone*
　To walk *alone* by Meldon Hill,
Along the knap with woody *crown*
　That slopes far *down* by Meldon Hill,
While sunlight overshot the copse
Of underwood, with brown-twigg'd tops,
By sky-belighted stream and *pool,*
　With eddies *cool* by Meldon Hill.

And down below were many *sights*
　Of yellow *lights* by Meldon Hill,
The trees above the brindled *cows,*
　With budding *boughs* by Meldon Hill,
And bridgèd roads and waterfalls,
And house by house with sunny walls,
And one, whence somebody may *come*
　To guide my *home,* from Meldon Hill.

White and Blue (page 14, English edition) is a kind of rendering into English of the Hebrew thought-rhyming. The first two lines of the verses show this :—

WHITE AND BLUE.

My love is of comely height and straight,
And comely in all her ways and gait;
She shows in her face the rose's hue,
And her lids on her eyes are white on blue.

When Elemley club-men walked in May,
And folk came in clusters every way,
As soon as the sun dried up the dew,
And clouds in the sky were white on blue,

She came by the down with tripping walk,
By daisies and shining banks of chalk,
And brooks with the crowfoot flow'rs to strew,
The sky-tinted water, white on blue.

She nodded her head as played the band,
She tapped with her foot as she did stand,
She danc'd in a reel, and wore all new
A skirt with a jacket, white and blue.

I single her out from thin and stout,
From slender and stout I chose her out;
And what in the evening could I do
But give her my breast-knot?—white and blue.

Of the Anglo-Saxon alliterative poems we have
already spoken in Chapter VI. Sometimes he tried
some Italian metres, such as the *rispetto* and the
terza rima. In fact, he drew the science of his art
from all the sources his philology could open to him.
But after all, the science was but the fashion of the
outer garb of his verse. Its most precious quality was
the love that produced it—the love of Nature and the
love of humanity. In speaking of some verses by
" Agrikler," an imitator who seemed to think that poems

in dialect (his was Somerset) must be either low or
satirical, William Barnes one day said : "There is no
art without love. Every artist who has produced anything worthy has had a love of his subject. The old
artists, as Raphael and his school, had a true love of
religion, and therefore painted true works of art in a
religious spirit. A scorn of the subject produces satire,
therefore satire, however clever, is no more true art
than a caricature is an artistic painting." It was this
love of his subject that gave him so much sympathy
with his people as a priest. He did not study them
merely as subjects for poems, though poetry was suggested by every cottage scene and rustic-life drama, but
he entered into their lives and feelings, saw their sorrows as they saw them, laughed in their joys as they
laughed, for his heart remained to his old age simple
as the heart of a child, though his head was stored
with the lore of a sage.

    The English poems were not, commercially, so suc-
cessful as the Dorset ones. Mr. Macmillan, in regretting
this, writes that " he grieves at such an evidence that
appreciation of fine, delicate, and truthful pastoral
poetry is not more widely spread. Our heated time,"
he adds, "needs such refreshment."

CHAPTER XV.

PROUD OF HIS HOME.

Up under the wood where tree tips sway
All green, though by skyshine tinted gray ;
Above the soft mead where waters glide
Here narrow and swift, there slow and wide ;
Up there is my house, with rose trimmed walls,
By land that upslopes, and land that falls
On over the mill, and up on the ridge
Up on the ledge above the bridge.

The wind as it comes along the copse,
Is loud with the rustling trees' high tops,
The wind from beyond the brook is cool,
And sounds of the ever-whirling pool,
Up there at my house, with well-trimmed thatch,
And lowly-wall'd lawn and archèd hatch
Beside the tall trees where blackbirds sing,
Over the rock and water spring.

And when from the north the wind blows cold,
The trees are my screen a hundred fold,
And wind that may blow from southern skies
Through quivering lime trees softly sighs,
And out in the west a tow'r stands gray,
And hills on the eastward fade away
From under the wood, above the mill,
Over the stream, below the hill.

As people along the road go by,
They suddenly turn their heads awry,
They slacken their canter to a trot
With, " Oh ! what a pretty little spot."
They take for their trot a walking pace
With " Heigh ! what a charming little place."
They lift up their hands with wond'ring look,
With, " Lo ! what a lovely little nook."

They see my laburnums' chains of gold,
And pallid blue lilac flow'rs unfold ;
They look at my fuchsias' hanging bells,
And calceolarias' yellow shells,
And cups of my lilies, white as snow,
And pinks as they hang their blossoms low ;
And then at my roses, fine and fair
As ever have sweeten'd summer air.

The foot-weary man that there may tread
The road, with no place to lay his head,
Will say, as he heaves his sighing breast,
" How blest is the man in that sweet nest."

THE ANTIQUARY.

1869 TO 1877.

"*Dec. 3rd*, 1868.—I sent my copy of *Early England and the Saxon English*, to J. R. Smith," writes W. Barnes in his diary. It was accepted on similar terms to the book on *Britain and the Britons*, and, with the same lack of pecuniary benefit to the author, was published in 1869.

As a history of the Anglo-Saxons in England it is perhaps the most fundamental one known. Tracing both Angles and Saxons from their earlier sources, the author particularises their conquests in England, and traces the landmarks of their first settlements, which are now left in the form of dykes.[1] The names o counties are traced to their Saxon roots, and a chronological chapter gives an account of Saxon-English feuds. The religion, laws, and social life, dress and customs are described very graphically. The latter part of the book is given especially to the Frisians, the "father-stock" of the English people. This part of the book—chiefly a reprint from a paper read before the Philological Society—brought the author into an

[1] See Letter VI. Appendix I.

interesting correspondence with a Dutch gentleman
named Halbertsma, whose late father had been working
on the same lines.   He writes in June, 1873, thus :—

MY DEAR SIR,

Having heard from your friend, Mr. Charles Warne,
the great interest you take in the works of my lamented
father concerning the Frisian language, I fulfil herewith
a promise made to your friend, of sending you a copy of
his *opus postumum*, which no doubt will claim your attention still more than his anterior publications, as he
had himself proposed to show the great affinity that
exists between the genuine English dialects and the
Frisian, from which fact he would most probably have
deduced another fact—viz., that it was especially the
Frisians who, at the time of the so-called Anglo-Saxon
invasion peopled a part of England and Scotland.

I hope you will accept of the book I offer you, and
remain,
                    Truly yours,

                              T. J. HALBERTSMA.

No better proof of the correctness of W. Barnes's
inferences could be given than that a scholar in a
different land had arrived independently at the same
conclusion, especially as it is not easy to trace the many
Teutonic tribes in their changes and emigrations.

A second proof of the kinship of the English and
Frisians was given when the gift of Herr Halbertsma
was acknowledged by a present of the *Dorset Poems*.
In thanking him for them the recipient says, " I imme-

diately perused your poems with great pleasure, and
became convinced that the Dorset dialect is a true
daughter of the Saxon, by the fact that only now and
then I had to take recourse to your useful glossary, as
most of the words were almost familiar to me, by their
resembling so much Friesic, Dutch, and Saxon words."

The publication of *Early England and the Saxon
English* led also to an invitation from Mr. Arthur
Kinglake,—who was bringing out an important work
entitled *Somersetshire Worthies,*—to furnish him with
some sketches of King Alfred. This William Barnes
did *con amore*, Alfred being one of the characters he
had studied most deeply. In thanking the author for
his " interesting Ælfred sketches," Mr. Kinglake writes:
" Your own thoughts of Alfred as a poet must be very
interesting to you as a poet. I have his character now
pretty well in hand from you. I must get some intelligent
barrister to record it as a great lawgiver and jurist.
Where can I get the little book *Dialogues of Ælfric
about Agriculture?* This seems to be very interesting."

A very different course of studies induced William
Barnes to make a new translation of the Psalms from
a comparison of the Hebrew and the Septuagint. His
object was to render them as literal and intelligible as
possible, and at the same time to preserve the rhythm
and " thought-matching" of the Hebrew poetry. His
translation was very melodious, and one or two of his
friends were so pleased that they thought this version
ought to form part of the new translation of the Bible,
then being made. Mr. Craig, rector of *Dilamger-bendi
Insula*, sent one of the Psalms, with the author's notes,
to Bishop Wilberforce in February, 1870, proposing

S

that Mr. Barnes should be made a "corresponding member of the committee of revisal," and another friend wrote on the same subject to Dean Stanley, who promised to submit his version to the Old Testament revisers. The translation was judged by them to be very correct and scholarly, but as it did not enter into their views to entirely change the existing translation, it was not literally adopted, although a letter from one of the revisers, in thanking him for it, says that "in some instances we have already adopted a rendering which, though not in your own words, gives the sense you prefer. We are now at work upon Isaiah xvi., and shall be glad of any hints which you may have to give us." The Psalms did not seem to promise well as an investment to any publisher, and they remained in the poet's drawer as "hand-writ," which was his way of saying manuscript.

In 1869 and 1870 the rector of Came had much pleasant intercourse with a new member of his congregation—Dean Close—who at intervals visited his daughter, Mrs. Prevost, then living at Came House. If the rector wished to have a holiday to visit his friends, the Dean—who playfully styled himself "curate of Came"—was always ready to take the duty at "our little church," as he called it. After one of these services he writes :—

CAME, *September 6th,* 1869.

MY DEAR MR. BARNES,

I plodded through all your duties yesterday without much terrible fatigue, and—barring a few additional nightmares, rather prospective than retrospective—I am none the worse to-day. I said a few words in favour

of your offertory and school, and hope I did not do
wrong. If I did your curate humbly asks pardon. I
enclose a cheque as my first annual subscription to
your school. Can I assist you in seeking a mistress
for it ?

I shall always take a deep interest in your pretty
little parishes. Displeased with what I had prepared
when I looked at the little flock at Whitcombe, I let off
a purely extempore address on "We do not know which
shall prosper—this or that." We leave for Carlisle to-
morrow. With kind regards to your circle,

Most truly yours,

F. CLOSE.

It used to be a favourite stroll of the Dean's, to walk
down to the Rectory and have a chat. Sometimes the
two ecclesiastics would discuss the revision of the Bible,
and other such grave topics: sometimes they merely let
their humour run away with them, and peal after peal
of laughter rang from the verandah-shaded windows of
the Rectory. The following little note refers to one
such witty meeting.

CAME, August 12th.

(The Murder of the Innocent Grouse.

DEAR MR. BARNES,

I find I have let a day drop out of my calendar.
I purpose to go to Weymouth next Sunday, and to
Swanage on the 31st, so the 24th of August intervenes,
and on that day, therefore, I shall be happy to assist

s 2

you at our little church. We had rather a merry meeting for grave parsons yesterday, but when I meet with wits, why you know the old axiom, " Action and reaction are equal, and in opposite directions."

Believe me, etc.,

F. CLOSE.

About this time the diary contains many an entry " *Scrivendo gli animali* " (writing animals), which would seem rather enigmatical, were it not explained by a remark in a letter from his friend, Mr. Tennant, " What an extraordinary undertaking for you—a dictionary, and etymological too, of animals.[1] I think you must be hard at work if you hope ever to get to the zebra. But surely that work ought to qualify you to make the animals talk appropriately."

This last remark was *à propos* of some political fables which Mr. Tennant was writing ; one, called *The Woods and Forests and the Monkeys*, is quoted in this same letter, which also contains an urgent invitation for the poet to visit him in London, with a further request for a reading of poems there. He accepted, and the next letter runs as follows :—

15*th June*, 1870.

MY DEAR MR. BARNES,

We have fixed Friday the 25th for the reading, and have sent out a good many cards. I enclose one to convince you that you are caught, and Mrs. Tennant begs you to write the " Hon. Mrs. Norton " on the back, and send it to her, as she will be delighted to take the

---

[1] This was never published—Messrs. Macmillan said it wanted amplification.

opportunity of meeting you, and we of making her acquaintance. We have asked Dawson Damer, and I am sure he will come if he can. Also Disraeli and other M.P.'s on both sides.

The reading went off very successfully, the audience being supplied with printed words of the poems chosen, so as to be the better able to follow the sense of the Dorset dialect, and a delightful week was spent in London by the poet. At one dinner-party they met Lord Tennyson and the Bishop of Gloucester. Lady Leslie made a pleasant little dinner for him, and they went to a concert at Lady Ashburton's, where Titiens, Gardoni, and other celebrities sang. Some of his friends insisted on taking the poet to the studio of a fashionable artist-photographer to have his likeness taken, and a very successful portrait was the result.

The friendship between Barnes and Mr. Tennant was cemented by this visit, and their correspondence on social and political questions was constant. Taxation, paper currency,[1] the Irish question, and the franchise were all discussed between them, and if they did not always take precisely the same view of things, they gave due weight to each other's arguments.

TELEGRAM.

W. Colfox to Rev. W. Barnes.   ˙ Oct. 28th, 1870.

"Mr. Moncure Conway, an American writer, is anxious to be introduced to you, and will call about half-past three."

---

[1] See Letters Nos. I., II., and III. in Appendix. Mr. Tennant died, greatly regretted by his friend, in March, 1873.

In this truly American style did an interesting visitor from the New World announce his coming. As he has published an account of it in *Harper's Magazine* for January, 1874, he shall speak for himself and give his own impressions. After a long drive from Weymouth, and one or two mistakes in the cross-country roads, Mr. Conway and his driver "came to the region of deep and shady lanes again. As we passed one of these, the sharp report of a gun close to our horses' heads, fired by some sportsman from whom we were separated only by a hedge, startled us. It seemed dreadfully out of keeping with the peaceful solitude, and a most incongruous salute for our arrival the next moment at one of the loveliest country cottages that ever gave a poet a sacred solitude. Before it, the trees stood like friendly guardians of a scholar's seclusion; on its doors climbed lovely roses, and into the windows the pendulous flowers peeped, as if each bore in its heart some secret it was commissioned to bear, from the sunbeam that wrote, to the eye that could read, the mystic cypher of their hues. . . . .

"But even the nestling tree-tops and flowers are forgotten when one enters the little drawing-room, with its unostentatious treasures of art and antiquity, still more when he meets the genial face of the gentleman and scholar, whose thoughts are as beautiful, and his virtues as fragrant as his roses. Mr. Barnes has a face of the finest Saxon type, its natural strength filtered, so to say, and refined, through generations of pure and thoughtful life. His features are regular, his forehead high, broad, and serene, his mouth wears a kindly smile, and his snow-white hair and beard--the

latter falling almost to his breast—form a fit frame for
a countenance at once venerable and vivacious. He
wears an antique Dorset gentleman's dress, with black
silk stockings fastened at the knee with buckles, a
costume decidedly quaint, and at first seeming to be
the Episcopal costume. What most struck me about
him was the look of spiritual and intellectual health,
and the expression of these in his soft blue eyes, and
in his clear, flexible voice. I could not help feeling
some surprise that he should be a clergyman, as the
traits and tone of the literary man seemed to be so
predominant in him."

The poet and his guest appear to have talked much
philology and folk-lore, of which there is a great deal
in the poems. They spoke of the *Weepen Leady*, the
Beam in Grenly Church, the witchcraft and fairy stories
of the poet's youth, and the *Haunted House*, and then
they got on the favourite subject of roots of words,
which lasted them the rest of the morning. After
luncheon they walked into Dorchester, the American
carrying with him, as a souvenir, a little book of
unpublished poems[1] with the poet's photograph, one of
which, *Proud of His Home*, we quote at the head of
the chapter as a pendant to Mr. Conway's description
of the Rectory.

" Winterbourne Came is but a mile or two from
Dorchester," says Mr. Conway, " to which city Mr.
Barnes walked with me. He mentioned one or two
Americans who had visited the neighbourhood in order
to discover connections between Dorchester in America

[1] The book was printed by Mr. W. Miles Barnes at his parish
press at Monkton, in aid of his School Fund.

and its 'mother town' here. But few facts concerning the Dorchester adventurers, who, under the Rev. John White, so speedily followed the Plymouth pilgrims, can have escaped the keen eye of Dr. Palfrey. Mr. Barnes called my attention to the occasional recurrence of the name of Channing in the earlier annals of the town, remarking that the ancestors of the famous preacher went from Dorchester. One of the records concerning the Channings was of a very unhappy character. It was that in the great Roman amphitheatre, the most important of the town antiquities, a crowd of 10,000 people gathered in 1705 to witness the execution of Mary Channing, who was strangled and burned for poisoning her husband."

The connection between this Dorchester and her child-town in America had long been an interesting topic to William Barnes, who had more than once received visitors from thence, and discovered a good many names of families which were identical with the old stock, still existing here. He was much interested to find many Dorset words extant in the speech of the American colony.

He held some correspondence on the same subject with another American writer, Mr. Daniel Ricketson, a poet, who began a correspondence with him in 1869, by a gift of his poems, *The Autumn Sheaf*, and continued it till Mr. Barnes's illness in 1884. Their letters were mostly on poetical subjects, often mutual descriptions of Nature in the Old and New Worlds, and the aforesaid Dorset colony was also a frequent topic.[1] It was in the autumn of this year, 1870, a little before Mr. Conway's

[1] See Letter No. II., Appendix.

visit, that the Somerset Archæological and Natural History Society met at Wincanton, on August 23rd, and three following days, during which William Barnes was the guest of Sir William Medlycott, at Venn House. The following letter gives some of his impressions :—

CAME RECTORY, *August* 29*th*, 1870.

MY DEAR MR. WARNE,

I thank you for your kind note, and hope that I shall soon ask you for a seat at your hearth, but I must not take a week just at once, as I spent the last week with the Somerset Archæological Society, with whom I was kindly taken round by Sir William Medlycott. I did not forget your book. We visited Cadbury Camp and the Barrows (so wrongly called) at Milbourne Wick, by Milbourne Port, and I enjoyed very much the men and the sights On the war and warring powers I find that your opinions tally with my own. I shall ask Dorset men (in the newspaper) to form an Archæological Society for this county. I feel ashamed for it with the Somerset club. One man said to me, " I suppose you have a Dorset Society ? " " No." " Tell it not in Gath," said he.

I am, dear Mr. Warne,

Yours very truly,

W. BARNES.

At this meeting a paper was read by him on " Somerset," which was printed in a pamphlet form by the society. His derivation of the name Somerset

from *som*, a root, meaning "softness," either in climate
or from a situation near marshy or moist land, was
productive of a great deal of discussion and correspondence. Mr. Price, an enthusiast on the point, made
it a subject of much research, and found an innumer-
able number of place-names all bearing the same
meaning—being near rivers or marshes. A few of
them are Sommervesle, the vale of Summerseat, Moor-
som, Chatsom, Sompting, Somerton, and many others.

The same society met again in October, 1874, when
another pleasant visit was made to Venn, and a paper
read at Sherborne, on "Ealdhelm, first Bishop of Sherborne," and the meeting of the two churches—English
and British—in Wessex. This early diocese of Sherborne was formed by King Ina in 705 A.D., who finding
the See of Winchester too wide, cut off the western
end, from Selwood westward, and placed Ealdhelm, a
kinsman of his own, as its bishop.

Ealdhelm was a great writer in prose and in verse.
Bede says his style was clear, and his verse was even
clearer than his prose. He wrote Latin hexameters as
freely as Saxon. The proof of the manner in which
the Saxons and British for a long time kept their
churches separate—each having their own place of
worship in different parts of the same town—is very
interesting. In 1871 the British Archæological Association held their congress at Weymouth, when the
Dorset poet was again the guest of Sir William Medlycott, and read a paper on "The Origin of the Hundred
and Tithing of English Law," which was afterwards
printed in the transactions of that society.

He thus writes his account of the week to Mr.

Warne, who had unfortunately been prevented from attending :—

CAME RECTORY, *September 22nd*, 1871.

MY DEAR MR. WARNE,

Oh, yes! You kindly thanked me for my small service anent the cromlech.[1] I was glad that I could send you a sunprint [photograph] rather than a drawing, as it might have been said that I had wilfully misdrawn it out of ill-will to the restorers.

I think the men of this congress have been earnestly working ones, and that they have brought out some good bits of history and knowledge. The *Times* bruised his own knuckles against the truth, in hinting that the association sponged on country houses, for they did not take or seek one free lunch in the whole week. I am very sorry for poor Dr. Smart, and should have enjoyed the week still more if you and he had been among us. Mr. —— went off his own ground, architecture, and handled what such men as Mr. Bond and Planché with the Celtic antiquaries understood better than he himself.

I with others laughed at Mr. ——'s theory of the work of the Roman *mensores*, but I like the man, who I believe is thoroughly good, albeit he is a seventh day saint. He is a most wonderful reader of old writings in abbreviated Latin, or queerly written old English, etc.

While we are speaking of Barnes as an antiquary,

[1] A cromlech at Portisham, visited by the association, and which had been restored.

we may as well anticipate a little, and say that the "Dorset Field Club," which he wished to see in his county, was not long in being established, and many a pleasant day did he pass with it in the following years.

At one period of their meetings a cromlech was opened at Fuzbury, under the superintendence of Mr. Cunnington. Within it the excavators found some skeletons, lying east to west, but no pottery, arms, or coins.

Some members thought the bodies were those of the slain in some tribal feud ; but Barnes's opinion was that a barrow did not contain the bones of ordinary people, but of the *penteulu*, or father of a household or kindred (chief, in fact).

He sat on the barrow surrounded by people, and gave his account of cromlechs and barrows, of British burial, wars, and history, concluding : " The very early lifetime of those who were buried in this barrow is betokened by the burials in it. They could not have been Britons of Cæsar's time, who were of the iron age, and so lived long after that of stone cutlery. The barrow shows no tokens of cremation, nor of the use of bronze tools, nor even of the grinding of stonen edge tools, but leaves only the tokens of the earlier life of the stone chippers, and between that form of life, while the Britons were coming slowly through the later ones, to the tribes of Cassibelaunus, with their war chariots and other carriages, and triad laws, and a school of poetry and music, we can hardly reckon a time less than a thousand years." (Mr. Barnes was loudly cheered as he finished his remarks.)

At another meeting William Barnes read a paper on

" King Athelstan, the Founder of Milton Abbey," which
he had compiled from the *Saxon Chronicle, Ethelward's
Chronicle*, Caradoc Llancarven's *History of Wales*, and
MacCullum's *Ancient Scots*. He disproved the legend
that Athelstan founded the abbey as an atonement for
the murder of his brother Edwin, and also the assertion
that he was the person who had the Bible or Gospels
translated into Saxon, for the Saxon version is clearly
of an earlier time than his.

The Roman and British roads had long been his
favourite study, and with the help of the *Antonine
Itinerary*, the *British Chronicles* or " Bruts," and his
own philological studies in the names of places, he had
succeeded in making a complete map of the great roads.
He found that these were in ancient times the *Ermyn
Street* and the *Akerman Street*, both British roads ; the
Watling Street, a road through dense forests, which led
to the north-western haven, whence ships departed for
Ireland ; and the *Erhen-ield* of East Anglia, or the *Via
Iceniana*, the road of the Iceni, whose way lies by so
many barrows that it has been styled the Appian way
of Britain.[1] The chief fact proved by these studies of
roads is, that the Britons were great roadmakers before
the Romans came, and that the Romans frequently
made use of the roads already existing, rather than
make new ones for themselves.

The third meeting of the Dorset Natural History and
Archæological Field Club was held at Shaftesbury, and
although the Dorset poet could not take his place as
cicerone in person, he sent in a paper on the " History
of Shaftesbury," which was read before the meeting by

[1] See Letter VIII., Appendix I.

Professor Buckman, and furnished subject for discussion during the whole day.

There was not a place in the county of which he could not give a history, nor a name which was not suggestive and pregnant with meaning in his hands; not an archæological query was put to him that he had not an answer ready to give to it, and nowhere was the quaint familiar figure more missed than when it ceased to be the peripatetic philosopher of the Dorset Field Club.

CHAPTER XVI.

WALK AND TALK.

COME up the grove, where softly blow
The winds, o'er dust, and not with snow,
A-sighing through the leafless thorn,
But not o'er flow'rs or eary corn.
Though still the walk is in the lew
Beside the gapless hedge of yew,
And wind-proof ivy, hanging thick
On oaks beside the tawny rick,
And let us talk an hour away,
While softly sinks the dying day.

Now few at evening are the sounds
Of life, on roads or moon-paled grounds ;
So low be here our friendly words,
While still'd around are men and birds,
Nor startle we the night that dims
The world to men of weary limbs;

But let us tell, in voices low
Our little tales, lest wind may blow
Their flying sounds too far away,
To ears yet out, as ends the day.

For what we tell and what we own
Are ours, and dear to us alone,
Past joys, so sweet in after thought,
And hopes that yet may come to naught;
But wherefore should we not look on
To happy days till all are gone ?
For if the day, so fair in dreams,
Should come less fair than now it seems,
Yet while a foreseen day seems gay
We have at once that happy day.

AUTUMN DAYS.

1875—1877.

THE calm autumn days of the poet's life glided on at this period in a busy and pleasant routine of parish and literary work, only broken by visits to this and that country house, where he was generally the life of the party, and by attending Field Club meetings, where he walked like any youthful member. The winters were still much occupied in the gratuitous lectures at the literary institutions, which had extended all over Hampshire, Wilts, Dorset, and Somerset. For the purpose of giving a little useful knowledge or even a little wholesome pleasure to others, no trouble or fatigue on his own part was thought too much.

As for the activity of his mind, the following extracts from his diary show how many subjects occupied him :—

" Jan. 5th, 1875. Began to write *Speechcraft*."

" March (several days). Writing verses."

" March 31st. Writing *The Beautiful*."

" April 3rd. Began to write on the local names of plants." (This was probably suggested by a letter from the president of a scientific society, who wrote to ask

T

what especial flower was called "greggles" or "grey-gles," in Dorset, the name having been given to both the wild hyacinth and the red lychnis in different counties.)

"Tuesday, April 13th. Writing on the Bible" (for the Committee of Revision, of which he was a corresponding member).

"Thursday, April 29th. Writing Persian."

"June 7th. Wrote on 'Elementary Schools.'"

"June 14th and 15th. Wrote on 'Norman Words in English.'"

"June 16th. Writing notes on my life for the *Conversations Dictionary* being published at Leipzig."

"July 23rd. Began to write on 'Feudal Laws.'"

In this varied manner his busy hand and brain were always employed.

The *Speechcraft*, which had been laid aside in 1875, was taken up again on January 8th, 1878, in alternation with *Studies of the Roman Roads*.

In April of that year it was finished, and published immediately by Messrs. Kegan Paul, who sent the author some early copies on May 22nd. His young friend and disciple, Mr. Truman, had been very energetic in obtaining subscriptions of names of purchasers to ensure success to the work.

In *Speechcraft*, which the "fore-say" (preface) announces as "a small trial towards the upholding of our own strong old Anglo-Saxon speech, and the ready teaching of it to purely English minds by their own tongue," the anglicising of William Barnes's speech reaches its climax. He boldly puts away all derived or foreignised words, and substitutes Saxon ones, or words formed by himself from Saxon roots, in their place. Vowels are designated as "free-breathings"; consonants "breath-pennings"; nouns are "thing names"; the classification of nouns, "thing sundriness"; adjectives are defined as "suchness," and their comparisons as "pitches of suchness"; while verbs are "time words"; and syntax becomes "thought wording." A kind of glossary of Latinised words put into true English is very curious and suggestive; we will give a few of the most apt definitions :—

Absorb, forsoak	Conjunction, a link-word
Accelerate, to onquicken	Democracy, folkdom
Accent, word-strain	Depletion, unfullening
Acoustics, sound-lore	Deteriorate, worsen
Aëronaut, air-farer	Emporium, warestore
Alienate, to unfrienden	Enthesis, an insetting
Ancestor, fore-elder	Equilibrium, weight-evenness
Aphorisms, thought-cullings	Equivalent, worth-evenness
Bibulous, soaksome	Foliate, leafen
Botany, wort-lore	Initial, wordhead

The book certainly shows that it is possible to keep language pure; but the hope that our mongrel English will ever by any national effort be purged from the foreign words which now form nearly half the language of general use, is the dream of an enthusiast. The tendency of modern languages seems, like that of the pure mountain brook, to be swollen with tributary streams which become incorporated in it, till no power can divide the different waters.

Speechcraft was one of William Barnes's favourite mind-children. He writes of it to one of his daughters in Florence :—

T 2

"CAME RECTORY, *August* 30*th*, 1878.
" MY DEAREST J.,

"I am glad you like my little book. Our speech will go to wreck if the half-learned writers for the press follow their own way. Hitherto no weekly or monthly but the *Athenœum* has given a word on the *Speechcraft*. The *Athenœum* thinks I am an enthusiast, but that my book will do good, as it teaches many overlooked (I say little known) points of speechlore. I hope God will send you to me in the spring. I am happy to find that the children are well, and gaining good strength and hardihood on the hills."

As early as 1874 Mr. Russell Smith had announced that the first two editions of the Dorset poems were exhausted, and recommended the author to publish the whole in a collected form, kindly promising to cede his interest in the third series still remaining on hand, at the cost price of the books. That a new edition was desirable may be gathered from the immense number of letters addressed to the author from strangers desiring to know where the books could be obtained, and the multitudinous regrets that all efforts to obtain them resulted in the answer, "Out of print." One or two publishers made offers for the publication of the book, but no terms were agreed on with any till 1878, when Mr. Kegan Paul published his edition in a size uniform with the collected works of Tennyson.

This again brought scores of enthusiastic critiques and letters, but nothing more substantial. If Barnes's name should live as an English poet, his fame certainly added little or nothing to his worldly wealth during life. He expresses his own feeling about this in a letter to his daughters :—

"CAME RECTORY.

"DEAREST J. AND L.,

"I send you each a flower petal and leaf or two, with my kisses, and have given Dolly, for dear L., some letters for her book of autographs. I am glad for Dolly's sake that she will have the great pleasure of a stay with you in Florence, but I feel on my side that the house is becoming sadly empty of children. I am working on as usual in the parish and my study, though with no markworthy fruit of good. I win more fame than worldly gain ; but I do not write down to the low taste which craves bad sensation. We are beginning here our great fight for Church and State, which we think in peril from Gladstone's attack on the Church in Ireland."

In one of his notebooks is the entry : "My writings are not of such a kind as may sell quickly, and therefore it would not be a wonder that the many things which I have in manuscript should never find a publisher." Regarding the poems, he wrote : "As to my Dorset poems and others, I wrote them so to say as if I could not help it. The writing of them was not work, but like the playing of music—the refreshment of the mind from care or irksomeness. They were almost all printed from time to time in the *Dorset County Chronicle*, and I did not look, as I sent them to the press, to their going beyond the west of England." So he sang from simple inspiration, without a thought of either fame or gain.

Among the results of this republication of the poems may be mentioned some of the literary acquaintance of his later days. One of his greatest appreciators, Professor Palgrave, Lecturer on Poetry at the University of Oxford, made one or two visits to Came, and Mr. Edmund Gosse was brought over to make the personal acquaintance of the poet by Mr. Thomas Hardy, who was building a house for himself near the Rectory, and often visited at Came. Many a talk and laugh did the Dorset poet and novelist have over old Dorset characters and bygone phrases of country life. Among these William Barnes might recall the honest old Vale farmer, who, seeing his neighbour's daughters going to their music lessons, said to him : " Goin' to spank the grand pianner at milking time ! That'll come to summat—that will." And it did indeed come to something, for they became bankrupt. Then there was the boy at school who " scrope out the ' p ' in psalm," and when asked by his master for a reason, replied, " 'Cos he didn't spell nothen."

Another day he would be reminded of a man with whom he had once made a joke about a donkey, and when the same man met him some time after, he said, referring to the story, " I do never see a donkey, sir, but what I do think o' you."

Another visitor was J. S. Udal, Esq., a barrister, who used to find time for a visit to the Rectory as often as his duties on circuit brought him near Came. Mr. Udal was of some assistance to the Dorset poet in sending him new words for the Glossary, which was

always enlarging itself under his hand, and he returned
the service by collecting legends and superstitions for
Mr. Udal's contemplated work on the *Folk-lore of
Dorsetshire*, for which, nearly ten years later, Barnes, at
his request, wrote an introduction. Folk-lore was to
him one of the most interesting subjects of investigation, and a long letter from an American correspondent, dated Yarmouth, Port Mass., February 2nd,
1874, proves how far he had gone in studying it in
its historical and international aspect. The American—
Mr. Amos Otis—gives him a most interesting comparison of the "folk-games" of the country people in
Massachusetts with those of Dorset, proving them to be
so similar as to add evidence to the connection between
the American and English Dorchesters. There are the
"Quaker dance," "Thread the Needle," "Queen Anne,"
and others, of which the words are nearly identical in
both countries. It gave William Barnes great regret
that these old games are dying out, for he found them
of much value in the international study of Folk-lore.
Barnes did not by any means confine his researches in
languages to the Teuton and Saxon. In a letter to one
of his daughters, dated December, 1877, he said : " I
am sure you like to know what I am doing in matters
of lore. I have sought, and feel sure I have found, the
cause of a phenomenon in Celtic speech,[1] and find that
the Professor of Celtic at Oxford (Professor Rhys) has
been at work on the same problem, and reached the
same outcome. He has now seen my paper, and I have
seen his, and in his letter to me he sets me on a level

---

[1] This was a key to the word-moulding, peculiarity of Celtic.
Zeuss, a German, had also an insight into it.

with himself. He says: 'It is so much in favour of those views, I think, that two men working independently should have elaborated them.' It gives a useful key to Celtic speech, as Welsh, British, and others. He asks me to continue my Celtic studies."

In answer to a question from this daughter, he wrote a long letter on the Runic characters, and their peculiarly angular shape, so suitable for cutting with a knife on the four-sided rods.

To another, who was at the time much interested in Etruscan antiquities and languages, he shows himself nearly as deeply versed in Etruscan lore as he was in British and Saxon—evolving the name "Tosca" or "Hetrusca" from its earliest roots, and going into their history and origin.

He says: "You are ahead of me with your historian Xanthus. I do not know of him. Where have you read of his works? As Herodotus is called the Father, we might call him the Grandfather of History. Herodotus is very trustworthy on what he tells you of his own knowledge, and his formerly so-thought fibs are found, on our wider knowledge of the world, to be true. He said that in India wool grew on trees, and he was thought very naughty for speaking thus of what we call cotton." The letter then goes on to quote Strabo, Herodotus, and Dionysius, &c., as to the origin of the Etruscans. A further correspondence led to his being supplied with Sardinian books, for he thought it might help him to discover the key to that mysterious language (the Etruscan), which Niebuhr said "he would give forty years of life to find."

In January 1875, he wrote: "I have not yet had

much time to work on the Sardinian speech-form with
Etruscan. I suppose that the Sardinian shapes of
words, as they differ by Grimm's Law from the Latin
ones, might have been owing to the taking of Latin on
the speech-laws of another tongue, and that if that
tongue were Etruscan, then, since for one case the
Sardinian had 'Vaddi' for 'Vallis,' 'd' for 'l,' so
would I see if, by turning the 'd' of Etruscan into 'l,'
I could find Etruscan words to have been akin to Latin
ones. But, alas! it seems to me at the outset that 'd'
is not at all common in Etruscan. Why, your collection
is becoming one of the lions of Florence, when wise
men come from north as well as west to see it."

In March of the same year he had given up this clue
as a false one, and wrote : " Tell T., with my love, that
I hope he will not take any more trouble about the
Sardinian Grammar. I see the shape of the Sardinian
speech, as far as it is an offshoot of the Latin, and do
not find in it any clue to the Etruscan. I think that
Mr. Taylor is not quite on the true grounds, although
he has shown some clever thoughts.[1] The two versions
of an inscription, as it was lately read by two men,
were about as much alike as the first verse of "God
Save the Queen" is to that of the Old Hundredth
Psalm. I have thought that the Etruscan might be of
kindred to the Coptic, but I have not tried it by some
Coptic that I have. I do not believe that the words of
the inscription you send are mostly at full length. Do
write an essay on ' Etruscan Goldsmithing,' as T. has so
good a gathering of their work," &c.

[1] Isaac Taylor's theory was that the Etruscans were a branch
of the Ugric or Tartar (nomadic) race.

But neither did the Coptic prove to be the key, and the mystery of ages is still locked up. I believe the Etruscan is the only philological puzzle which has entirely baffled William Barnes's mind, and the wish he expressed, "I should like to push back the veil from over the face of that venerable matron, the Lingua Etrusca," remained unfulfilled to him, as it had been to Micali, Lanzi, Niebuhr, and others before him. I give the remainder of the same letter, though on a totally different subject, for the advice he gives his correspondent is such a good illustration of his own feeling and practice in writing :—"Try your hand on the 'Essay on Education of Women.' Don't be careful to make it either long or short, but when you have good matter in your mind, pour it forth. Put no padding to lengthen it. There is no life in padding, as you know by men or women who eke out their shapes by cotton or wool.

"Do not begin with the thought, either, that the minds of the man and woman are of the same cast, or that one is higher than the other ; neither is the higher, but they differ that each may be the best for its mission, and each has that which the other lacks, and both make together the one full mind of mankind.

"Thank Tom for the newspapers. The opening of the sarcophagus of the Medici was very interesting; but why was it needful to handle and undo what was left of the bodies? Is the simple weight of the brain a sure measure of a man's power of mind ? Is not 'suchness' as well as 'muchness,' of some weight ? Is a pound and a half of coarse brain a mark of higher mind than a pound of very fine heading ? Is a bull or a donkey more clever than Dolly's doggie Cara ?

"We have had much sickness in the house. Mary, our cook, has been hovering between life and death, but is now better. On Sunday week we had a funny chain of little mishaps—

  "1. We were teased with some of the bolder of rats.

  "2. Had poison for them in the cellar.

  "3. Mary was ill and went not into the cellar.

  "4. The rats began to gnaw some hams.

  "5. George went down to fetch them up.

  "6. The dog went down with him and began to eat the rat poison.

  "7. Dolly had to go off to church, leaving the dog as he was.

  "8. I was fearful that she would play wrong, from a wandering of mind to the dog.

  "But the dog is unharmed, while we have still rats for many cats."

This same dog was one of the poet's constant companions, and well did the two understand each other. "Cara" accompanied him in all his country walks, and lay curled up at his feet when he sat dreaming under the shadows in his corner by the hop vine. As soon as the master appeared with his hat and walking-stick, Cara would dance round in an ecstasy of delight; but if he said with a shake of the head, "You cannot come to-day, Cara," then, after begging a little in vain, the dog would lie down on the path, and with a crestfallen, wistful look, watch his master go slowly up the avenue till the gate clanged. It was great fun to see the poet and the dog playing at "hide and seek" for stones, and how he would exclaim laughingly, "Ah! you are cold,

Cara," or "Now you have it !" with all the glee of a
child. When that game was over, the one player would
go back to his philology, and the other to bask in the
sunshine, in some corner of the lawn.

He used to say, " Why do we sometimes call a worth-
less fellow a dog ? The fidelity, long-suffering, and love
of dogs is so great that we cannot give the name to a
false friend without doing him too much honour." Cara
was the original of the poem which begins :—

"THE DOG WI' ME.

Aye then as I did straggle out
To your house, oh ! how glad the dog
Wi' lowset nose did nimbly jog
Along my path, an' hunt about,
An' his main pleasure wer' to run
Along by boughs, or timbered brows ;
An' ended where my own begun
At your wold door and stwonen floor."

No one enjoyed more the society of the young than
William Barnes did. There were generally some girl
friends of his daughters staying at the Rectory, and for
them he kept his most delightful table-talk and prettiest
old-world homage. He used to bring little posies from
his garden to put on their plates at breakfast time ; and
proud was the girl who got one of his favourite large
yellow oxlips—that was a special mark of favour.

His presence was never the bar to the lightest girlish
merriment. Once a laughing maiden said, "I fear you
must think we talk a great deal of nonsense, Mr.
Barnes."

" Oh, we don't want a lark to roar like a lion. Prattle

—prattle—I like to hear you," he replied in his quaint way. He used to give these young friends pet names. One was "The lady with the flaxen locks," and on her wedding day he wrote her a pretty epigram in verse. A tall and graceful girl was named the "Gliding cypress;" another who was gay and light-hearted he called "Hearts-ease." One of his favourites appeared one day with a scarlet flower on her fair head, and to her he wrote the little poem, *Lizzie* (p. 405, collected edition). In the book of another he wrote:—

> "May all your early friends be ever true ones ;
>   And if you lose
>   Some friends you choose,
> May then your Saviour Friend still find you new ones."

A girl who once asked for his name in her birth-day book found this written under it:—

> "Oh ! may those eyes for which is written here
>   My name, be aye unwetted by a tear."

The girl artists who competed for the School of Art prizes in Dorchester, where he was sometimes elected as judge, asked him for mottoes for their works for competition. Some of these are perfect aphorisms :—"A stern will winneth still;" "Good work, though crossed, is seldom lost;" "*Conari non est coronari*" (To try is not to be crowned). "*Hoc opus incipientis, dicasne insipientis*" (This work of a beginner do not call it that of a silly body); "This year's worst may be another's first;" "For one slight falling, take not to crawling."

An artistic friend of Miss Barnes, whom he named

"The light of the house," has given her memories of
one of her visits to Came, during which she made a
charming outline sketch of the Rector :—

"My visit to Came in August 1876 is one of my
dearest memories—a poem a fortnight long, of which
each day was a beautiful stanza.

"First the morning prayers, when the priest-master
read matins from a high lectern almost as if in church ;
the bright breakfast, at which he ate porridge and milk ;
and then the exact half-hour's walk round the garden.
He wore a sort of tunic of brown fustian with a large
worsted girdle, knee breeches, black stockings, shoes and
buckles, and a felt hat that had peaked itself in front.
When I saw him in this home-dress, I was always reminded of an Italian figure of mediæval times. The walk
round the garden after breakfast was a delightful very
short half-hour. He always went first to a leaden bath
for bleaching old engravings, which stood in a corner
under the trees, where one or two rare prints were under-
going restoration of some kind ; and I think his last visit
at night and his first in the morning were to these loves of
his. Then round the grass plot and flower beds, talking
of bird, leaf, and flower ; and of everything we talked
he had something lovely to say, showing the poetry and
the use of things, with sometimes a little antiquarian
lore.

"He spoke always in pure English, with a beautiful
simplicity and correctness, and never used an inappro-
priate term ; indeed, it was one of his small daily
troubles that people generally do not speak in truer
terms, and specially that they use words of foreign
origin or foreign words themselves, and he used to

laugh in an amused, gentle way at many a popular misnomer. When the half-hour's walk was done, he went up to work in his 'den'—which really did look something like a cave—a cave of books, all old, all rather ghostly-looking, in their curious dusty bindings of calf and vellum. It was very touching to see him handle them; each one had been a sort of friend, helper, or teacher to him, and he held them with a reverent tenderness that was extremely pretty to see. A large piece of old tapestry hung on one side of the room, and this he prized very much ; his writing-table stood near the one window, which looked over the fields. Here he wrote, and here, as he himself put it, had 'his visions.' The 'den,' the garden, the whole place, in its loveliness, was so far removed from all thought of what we call the world, that one hardly wonders to hear now that, largely sold as the *Rural Poems* have been in America and in England, he never gained as yet six pounds of money a year by them.

"After the pleasant mid-day meal, he went back to his study, and generally worked till tea-time ; he was engaged in writing a grammar (I think it was the *Grammar of the Anglo-Saxon Language*) when I was there, as well as poems.

"After the tea came the crowning hour of the day. 'In the cool of the evening' we had chairs under the verandah, and sat nearly facing the west, seeing the sunset through the slender beeches. Here we sat and listened to him, or conversed together of a hundred things, from sunbeams to dewdrops, angels to men, he adding some ancient story to everything. All was so simply said, with now and then a curious little

ejaculatory query peculiar to him, just a sound, ques-
tioning our sympathy and understanding.

"At the evening meal the Welsh bards often presided,
and very delightful presidents they were ! The dear
Dorset bard sometimes gave us a triad, which he dealt
out to us with great enjoyment, explaining to us the
darker sayings. Here is one of them : ' There are three
kinds of men—The man of God, who gives good for
evil ; the man of the world, who gives good for good and
evil for evil ; and the man of the devil, who gives evil
for good.'

"Walks with him were always full of interest. We
were walking once round what to commonplace people
would have been a very prosy field, but in his hands the
field became all poetry. He told me the English poetical names of all the weeds and grasses, pointing out why
they were named so—as, for instance, the ' Shepherd's
purse,' which is like the shape of the purses worn at the
girdle in olden days.

"He had a handsome presence and was a brave
gentleman. He did many things in his gentlehood that
a man of the world would never think of doing. I
remember he would not allow the gate to be shut when
I left."

CHAPTER XVII.

CHILDERN'S CHILDERN.

OH! if my lin'gren life should run
Drough years a-reckoned ten by ten,
Below the never tirèn zun
Till beäbes ageän be wives and men ;
And stillest deafness should ha' bound
My ears, at last, from ev'ry sound ;
Though still my eyes in that sweet light,
Should have the zight o' sky an' ground ;
  Would then my steäte
  In time so leäte
Be jaÿ or pain, be pain or jaÿ ?

When Zunday then, a-weanèn dim
As theäse that now's a-clwosèn still,
Mid lose the zun's down-zinkèn rim
In light behind the vier-bound hill;
       U

And when the bells' last peal's a-rung,
An' I mid see the wold an' young
A-vlocken by, but shoulдèn hear,
However near, a voot or tongue,
    Mid zuch a zight
    In that soft light,
Be jaÿ or pain, be pain or jaÿ ?

If I should zee, among 'em all
In merry youth a-glidèn by,
My son's bwold son, a-grown man-tall,
Or daughter's daughter, woman-high,
An' she mid smile wi' your good feäce,
Or she mid walk your comely peäce
But seem, although a-chattèn loud,
So dumb's a cloud, in that bright pleäce,
    Would youth so feair
    A-passèn there,
Be jaÿ or pain, be pain or jaÿ ?

'Tis seldom strangth or comeliness
Do leäve us lang. The house do show
Men's sons wi' mwore, as they ha' less,
An daughters brisk, vor mothers slow,
At dawn do clear the night's dim sky,
Woone star do sink, an' woone go high,
An' lovèn gifts o' youth do vall
Vrom girt to small, but never die ;
    An' should I view
    What God mid do
Wi' jaÿ or pain, wi' pain or jaÿ ?

THE GRANDFATHER.

1880 to 1884.

In the eightieth year of William Barnes's life his
book named *Redecraft* was published by Messrs. Kegan
Paul and Co. in a style uniform with *Speechcraft*. *Redecraft* means neither more nor less than the art of
reasoning, or "logic"; *rede* being an old English word
for reasoning. The matter of the book is very valuable,
and it forms a clear handbook to the art of logic;
but unfortunately for its popularity, the aiming
at extreme anglicising of style had led the author to
almost coin a new vocabulary of logical terms, which to
the general reader require as much to be learnt as the
usual Latin terms. "Kind" from "*kin*," is, it is true, a
very good substitute for "genus," as "*hue*," or "*make*,"
may be for "species," and "*odds*" for "differentia"; but
when we come to "selfliness" and "hapliness" instead
of "*proprium*" and "*accidens*," it requires a certain
effort of the mind to realise how appropriate they are.
A "proposition" is defined as "thought putting"; a
"syllogism" as a "three-stepped redeship." The
"syllogism" is illustrated in every possible inversion of

U 2

its three " steps." Here is the first shape : "Where the
middle step's end, is head-end in the first step, and latter
end in the middle one," as—

> Every breathsome being is lifely,
> Every man is a breathsome being,
> Every man is lifely.

The great use of the word-ending "some" is accounted for by the author as being more expressive
than any other term. Some people have said to him,
"Why could you not say a 'barking' dog instead of
' barksome '?" But the words are not synonymous.
" Some " from the Saxon "sam," means a set or class of
things, and to say "All dogs are barksome,"—meaning
the species which can bark—is not the same as saying
" All dogs are barking,"—i.e., in the act of barking.
Thus the ending " some " becomes of great use in logic,
as helping to discriminate between the power of action
and the act.

A " dilemma " is aptly put as a " two-horned redeship," and " induction " as "law-tracking."

Once realised, the expressiveness of Saxon-English
and Logic, under Barnes's explanation, becomes quite
simple. Of "flaws" (fallacies) he says : "A flaw or an
unsoundness in redecraft is a thought-putting which is
unsound or cheatsome, or guilesome." Twelve classes
of flaws are distinguished.

There are some words, however, which have quite
baffled the translator's power to find Saxon-English
equivalents for ; these are " civilisation," " river," &c., in
distinction to " stream," " brook," " beck," &c., and
" public " in the loose manner it is applied now. After

the publication of *Redecraft*, nearly all William Barnes's literary energies were given to "Speechlore," as he called Philology.

These days, when a hale and hearty old age had as yet done nothing but turn his hair and beard to a venerable silver hue, were very happy days in the Rectory.

HOME'S A NEST.

O, home is a nest by the spring
Where children may grow to take wing.

From that nest many of the children had flown long years ago, and now the younger birds sometimes flew to the old nest of their parents, from far and near, and again the poet heard merry young voices ringing about the shrubberies.

The days of his Herringston district still ended in the walk to Monkton, where, instead of tiny mites, tall maidens came running out to welcome grandfather and lead him in, and sit nestling beside him to hear his last quaint speech or humorous anecdote. After dinner the violin and 'cello were brought out, and the last new trio played to him ; then the harmonies of the piano and American organ would be added for an overture or symphony. Amongst his favourite concerted pieces were Mendelssohn's *Lobgesang* symphony, and the nocturne from the *Midsummer Night's Dream* ; but after even these he would ask for Handel's *Largo*, and sit listening to it with closed eyes, till the majestic peace that rings in it, seemed to grow into his soul, and he would get up and begin his walk home across the

quiet parks with the happiest of faces. A well harmonised melody or calm *andante* always pleased him
best; he did not like what he called "musical fire-
works."

Came Rectory was a happy meeting-place for all the
holiday grandchildren, and "grandfather" found delight
in all their sayings and doings, from the little half Floren-
tine, who sat at his knee and sang "Tre giorni son' che
Nina," to the boy from college, who boasted of the
victories of "our cricket club."

One tiny girl, on her first visit to church, greeted the
preacher with "I saw you in church, grandpa. You
were up in a box with a white frock on, and you were
talking so loud." They soon found out that he was their
best playmate, and the little hands that pulled his
cassock with "Now then, granny-pa, let us have a nice
play," were never denied. And what amusement their
queer sayings and doings caused him, especially when
they coined words which he considered valuable, such
as "put outer" for "extinguisher," or "baby cart" for
"perambulator."

He was not so pleased at his elder grandson's talk of
his velocipede. "Why don't you call it a wheel saddle?"
he asked.

Here are a few of his letters anent his grandchildren :—

CAME, 29*th April*, 1882.

DEAR C.,

E. is with us safe and sound, and I fancy begins
to show at times a little of English weather bloom on
his face. It so happened that our Bluecoat boy and his
sisters have been here for a fortnight, and yesterday

they and the Monkton children, and E. and A. from
Florence, were here all together, and I had so many
children that I should not have known what to do if I
had no ground round the house for their play.

I am revising to-day a proof of a paper of mine for
the Dorset Field Club, on the xvi. *Iter* of Antoninus,
" From Winchester through Dorset to Cornwall," on
which I have discovered the places of some stations from
the Welsh tongue, such, for a sample, as Londinis,
British Llynclaen, which turned into Anglo-Saxon
comes out " Brad-pol "—Broadpool by Bridport.

DEAREST L.,

I am very glad to have T.'s masterly observations
on his consular coins. It is very helpful in the study of
a time of Roman history. I hope G. has not forgotten
her " Granny-pa," or his gambols with her sprightly self.
She heard me say to W. that if a man were born in a
stable he would not therefore be a horse. Hence this
dialogue which I overheard :

" W. Are you Italian or English ? "

" G. I am Ingleesh."

" W. But you were born in Italy."

" G. Hee ! hee ! Well, if I were born in a basket I
should not be a kitten."

I sometimes hardly know off-hand how many I am.
I do not, like Jacob, reckon myself " few in number,"
and want you and J. to write out the names and birth
years of your children for my life-book. (This sentiment
he has put into poetry in " How great I am become.")
I have before me sun-prints of them.

I am happy to see that there is not in my little
sample of posterities any token of reversion to Darwin's
monkey. May God make them "good old men and
women."

The grandfather's Christmas greetings were a spe-
ciality peculiar to himself. They were generally in the
form of a quaint posy in rhyme. A few of them are
worth preserving :—

CAME, December, 1877.

MY DEAREST J.,

I give to all of you my New Year's greeting.

To C.

(Who is al mondo Carlo a me Caro) and

> May the love of God aye bless
> Julia his—but mine no less,
> And give new years of daily joys
> To May and both the jolly boys.

CAME, December, 1877.

To T. AND L.

And theirs at home.

Since I from you, my children dear,
By land and sea am sundered wide,
And cannot meet you voice to ear
This ever hallowed Christmastide,
I write my blessing—" Be ye blest
With all the good that God deems best."

W. BARNES.

December, 1879.

I send you all my fondest Christmas greeting.

A happy life	May many loves
To man and wife	E'er hold you dear,
Long lives of joy	And God e'er keep
To girl and boy.	You free of fear.

Your loving father,

W. BARNES.

The Christmas at the Rectory was always a busy time. There were ancient charities of meat and coal (a bequest of a certain Hugh Millar, whose sculptured effigy has lain on his tomb in Came Church for the last 300 years) to be given out to every family, so on the morning of Christmas Eve a constant coming and going of parishioners took place. In the evening the kitchen was full of guests, for the sextons and choir singers, and their families, from both parishes came to supper. When supper was over, a knock was heard at the kitchen door, and the Rector would enter to welcome them all and sit down amongst them. Then the men sang their songs to him, and the girls joined in some quaint old carols, and the grey-haired pastor would clap his hands or rap his stick on the floor for applause. He laughed with them and made some merry joke or told a story, chatting to each by name. But when he rose up from his chair his face and voice became earnest, and he gave them words of advice and encouragement, calling to their minds that they each had some work to do for God in His church, and that it should be done with reverence; then with a parting bow he left them. On Christmas Day all the members of the family who were in England, to three generations, met at the dinner table.

It was in the year 1880 that the Rector of Came was invited to preach in Salisbury Cathedral, the invitation being suggested by a remark of the Bishop to one of his canons, "I should very much like to see that venerable old man in the cathedral pulpit."

Once a friend remarked to him, "I suppose you have very little to do in such a country place as Came; merely a little row of cottages near the church." The Rector laughed and said, "I think you have never seen my parish." He knew well of the many leagues he walked from farm to hamlet over the downs on which Came was scattered. One memorable day's work done by this sturdy octogenarian deserves to be recorded from his daughter's note-book. Indeed, the whole fortnight was memorable, beginning from January 18th, 1881.

"Tuesday. Woke up to see everything covered deep with snow, and a violent snow hurricane continued the whole day. At dinner father amused us by singing the refrain of an old song—

> My dear, you cannot hunt to-day,
> It rains, it blows, it freezes, snows,
> You cannot hunt to-day.

"And it did snow! Trains were stopped or blocked up all night. We began to watch anxiously for the arrival of the coal waggon, and after days of waiting we saw it labouring along, drawn by four horses across a field, as being an easier way than the snow filled road."

"Sunday, Jan. 23rd. The roads still impassable, yet father was quite undaunted, and prepared to start for the service at Whitcombe. However, his kind friends at Came House sent over a sleigh to carry him to church, but once arrived there he very characteristically refused to keep either man or horse waiting, and returned on foot."

"Sunday, February 6th. The snow has disappeared, though the country ways are very muddy and much broken up. After his breakfast of porridge and milk, father put on his leather gaiters, and started at half-past eight for Came, to take a wedding there at nine o'clock. On his way a messenger met him and begged him to go on to Whitcombe, two miles in the opposite direction, to administer Holy Communion to a dying woman.

"The messenger was sent to the Rectory to tell his daughter to meet him at Whitcombe in an hour with the Communion plate. He married the couple at Came, and reached Whitcombe soon after ten, in time to perform the offices for the sick before the service in the church at eleven o'clock. On his return he could only take a hurried dinner, having to be at Came again before two, for a funeral service before the Evensong. So besides his walk of five or six miles to and fro, he had performed two full services, a wedding, a celebration, and a funeral service on this day ! Welcome was the quiet rest in his easy chair by the fire in the evening, and sweet to him the Sunday songs ' O lovely peace,' and ' Waft her, angels,' that he loved to hear his daughter sing."

In this same year his activities with the Dorset Field Club continued unabated. On May 31st they met at Dorchester, and on July 6th at Sherborne. At this time the diary notes " Wrote on King Athelstan," " Wrote on Britain, and on earthworks." On August 3rd he accompanied the Club to Milton Abbey, whence there was

an arduous walk to Eggardun, a fine British camp, the
history of which he explained to the members. The bad
walkers were provided with waggons stuffed with hay
for this rough excursion, but Barnes's eighty years
made, in his mind, no claim for any such indulgence.
On September 29th he went with the Dorset Club to
Blandford, and saw a barrow opened at Down Wood,
near the famous earthwork known as Busbury. In this
year the Dorset County Museum, which had counted
William Barnes as one of its foster-fathers from the
beginning of its existence, made a new step towards
permanency. The Old Ship Inn in High Street was
purchased and pulled down, and a new Tudor building
erected in its place for the Dorset Museum and Library.
Here the museum began a new and prosperous career,
Mr. Henry Moule undertaking the honorary office of
Curator. A portrait of the Dorset Poet, painted and
presented by Mrs. Stiles, adorns the vestibule of the
museum, and it is proposed to place a statue of him not
far from it. So the memory of one who reverenced the
past history of his native county, and did so much to
preserve it, is to be ever kept fresh within the walls
which enshrine the relics of that past epoch.

About the autumn of 1881 he took a new departure in literature, though only experimentally, by
dramatising in Dorset the story of Ruth. There is an
antique rusticity about the narrative which lends itself
very well to rustic speech. His idea was to make a little
drama suitable to village actors and village audiences,
but as it was never published (being only printed for
private circulation), the aim of the author was not
accomplished. During the next year an article on

"Dorset Folk : " it appeared in the *Leisure Hour* of January, 1883. It had been a matter of doubt with the editor whether he should ask Mr. Hardy, or his neighbour ✓ at Came Rectory, to write the article, but he chose the poet as having had the longer and more experienced knowledge of his subject. The article gives not only pictures of Dorset life, and sketches of its folk, but an analysis of their character, and the fundamental causes of their social position. He regrets that the good old-fashioned working squire had vanished, and that the thrifty labourer is now sundered from the farmer by a bailiff, and from the landowner by both the farmer and the bailiff. He has inserted in this article the pretty poem of "The Old Farmhouse" which embalms the semblance of the good old squire farmer of the Vale, and is the one of which he said he saw in a vision the child running about among the glistening straws. (*See* p. 246.)

THE OLD FARMHOUSE.

That many tunn'd farmhouse that stands
  A little off the old high road,
When landlords lived upon their lands,
  Was long its landlord's dear abode ;
And often thence, with horn-call'd hounds
  High-steeded through the gate he sped,
The while the whirring grey-wing'd doves
  Flew out of dovecots overhead.

And after that, below the tun,
  There burnt for happy souls the fire
Of one whose name has blest his son,
  A farmer fit to be a squire.
And while his barley-sowing sped,
  . On dusty mould, in springtide light,
From those old dovecotes' many doors
  The grey-wing'd doves arose in flight.

And while through days of longsome span
    His corn was sunn'd from green to red,
His son grew up from boy to man,
    And now is master in his stead ;
For him the loaded waggons roll
    To staddled ricks that rustle dry,
And there for him the grey-wing'd doves
    Around the mossy dovecots fly.

There oft his sister, then a child—
    That's now a mother, fair, though staid—
His merry playmate flitted wild
    And tittering, through light and shade
On tiptoe, fanning in her speed
    The gold-like straws beside her shoe ;
While to the dovecots, nigh at hand,
    The grey-wing'd doves in haste upflew.

And still with fondness, and with praise
    The brother's and the sister's mind
Behold their home-spent childhood's days
    So fair, and left so far behind—
As I behold, in thought, the time
    When first the lord of wall and sward
There dwelt, and first the grey-wing'd doves
    Flew out from dovecotes in the yard.

One autumn evening he came down from his room to
rest in his easy chair, seeming tired and overburdened
in his mind. He said with sadness, "Another work is
finished to be put away or to be buried." This was the
*Etymological Dictionary of our Common Names of Ani-
mals,* the book at whose beginning Mr. Tennant had
jested, and it was only now finished. He had made some
great philological discoveries in the names of animals,
which he found to be closely descriptive of their life and
habits, according to the roots of the names, as in *Tiw.*

His sigh was prophetic, the book is put away; it never got published.

A pleasant visit was made to Sherborne on June 15th, where Mr. Barnes was present at the commemoration day of the Sherborne School, and heard the prize essay read on "The Relation of the County of Dorset to English History," in which we may be sure his name was not forgotten.

Later on in the same year he paid his last visit to his birthplace, for an account of which we cannot do better than quote from the note-book of his son, the Rector of Monkton.

"In 1883, thinking that my father was not looking well, and that a change would do him good, we suggested three or four different places, and asked him to accompany us as our guest. He firmly refused them all till we suggested Sturminster, when he accepted at once, and the visit to the scenes and haunts of his boyhood and early life gave him intense pleasure. He took great interest in pointing out the old familiar spots—Sturminster Bridge, which he had so often passed over; the view of the 'rushy' Stour winding on amidst the meadows of the valley, the banks fringed here and there with overhanging trees, and its surface covered in places with water lilies then in bloom. The scene of the turnstile, however, has long since been done away with, and its place supplied by bars. The pathway leading to it is arched over by trees growing closely together, though here and there giving a glimpse of a sunny meadow, and the streak of a meandering stream beyond. There was the old school-house with its stone mullioned windows, where he went to school as a boy;

but we heard no sound of children's voices as we passed,
for it has long since been converted into a carpenter's
shop, and .the endowment, we believe, handed over to
the parish school.

"The view from the elevated churchyard was very
beautiful, overlooking the well-wooded valley of the
Stour. One of its picturesque spots was a parallelogram
of stately trees, which, in the dim light, looked like the
pillars in the nave of some noble cathedral. It is so
described in one of his poems. When we reached the
old market-place, he laughed merrily at a recollection of
a certain morning of his boyish days, when he leaped
down from the steps of the market cross, and with out-
stretched arms, and a horrid ' boo !' rushed in the front
of a herd of cows which a drover was bringing to market.
How the enraged drover pursued him, and with what
threats of dire vengeance and the punishment he would
inflict upon him when he caught him—which he never
did. After our first drive he urged us to go to the hotel
and pay for the carriage at once, to ease the landlord's
mind, ' Because,' he said, ' for aught they know, we
might be sharpers.' The simplicity of this was delicious,
and so delightfully incongruous to his appearance, which
would have spoken for itself, even in a place where he
was less known and reverenced.

" Mr. Marshallsay most kindly placed his boat at our
disposal during our stay, and many excursions were
made in it. Father would sometimes take an oar, but
generally asked to steer, and we meandered leisurely up
the stream, now lost amid the rushes, now in some quiet
nook or under a shady tree, or we gently floated down
the current, enjoying the quiet and the songs of the

birds, and reaching out for water lilies or other aquatic treasures as we passed.

"On most of our expeditions we passed over ground very familiar to him, and his remarks as he passed each well-known spot, showed how he was being carried back into the dim past, and how he was picturing the scenes as they once were, recalling voices which had been long silent, and persons who had long gone to their rest, and of whom the present generation knows nothing. I cannot recall his exact words, though I remember quite well the general sense of his remarks. 'Here is Elbow field; just step over the fence, and you will see that it is in the form of a man's elbow. How often I have come down here to play with ——; and yonder I used to take my books and sit under the tree there. It is not much altered. Further on to the left, my uncle lived, there was his farm. Yes, but the old house is gone; that must be a new one.' Here a little sadness came over his face; then, 'Now we shall come to my favourite walk. Here it is!—this shady lane; but there are fewer trees than there used to be; there were once fine elms overshadowing the lane. Ah! and the banks!—how many wild flowers used to grow upon them.'

"We went on to the 'Haunted House,' which seemed very attractive to him. A dark and gloomy lane ran towards it. Father's face beamed with old memories. 'That was the lane your great-grandfather was riding down, when all at once he saw the ghost in the form of a fleece of wool, which rolled along mysteriously by itself, till it got under the legs of his horse; and the horse went lame from that hour and

X

for ever after,' he concluded, with a humorous twinkle in his eyes."

He was very anxious to obtain a photograph of that house, and even a few weeks before his death, asked his son if he had yet got the " sun-picture " of the "Haunted House ? "

CHAPTER XVIII.

.

BED-RIDDEN.

THE sun may in glory go by,
  Though by cloudiness hidden from sight;
And the moon may be bright in the sky,
  Though an air-mist may smother its light;
There is joy in the world among some,
  And among them may joy ever be.
And oh ! is there health-joy to come
  Come any more unto me ?

The stream may be running its way
  Under ice, that lies dead as the stone,
And below the dark water, may play
  The quick fishes, in swimmings unshown;
There is sprightliness shown among some,
  Aye I and sprightly may they ever be,
And oh I is there limb-strength to come—
  Come any more unto me ?

LAST ILLNESS AND DEATH.

1884 TO 1886.

THERE were to be no more Field Club excursions, and few more long parish walks; for though the mind of the poet remained bright and clear as ever, illness and pain chained the active limbs, which had seldom known fatigue.

The first warning of this was a severe chill, caught from exposure to a winter's storm on January 26th, 1884. Mr. Thomas Hardy says he remembers the day, for he had himself walked from Dorchester with his neighbour through a cold driving rain across the exposed road to Max Gate, and though he begged Mr. Barnes to take shelter at his house, he declined, and pressed on drenched and chilled, to the Rectory. Although he recovered sufficiently from the rheumatic illness which followed to take his service once more in March, he was never the same again, and that one service was only possible with the help of a carriage. His daughter's diary records this last memorable day, when his parishioners received the Holy Communion from his hands for the last time on March 9th :—

" It was a scene never to be forgotten ; a bright ray of coloured light shining through the painted window, falling on him as he stood, chalice in hand, at the altar rails, and illuminating his reverent face and white robe as with a heavenly sign. It was a moment of peace, and a suggestion of consolation."

As long as he possibly could do his duties, nothing would make him give them up. He often said, "We should use to the utmost all the powers we have of mind and body, and by using we gain more." But with all his energy of mind he could not compel himself to work beyond his strength, and was fain to accept the willing and constant aid of clerical friends, who week after week took his services for him, until his hopes of returning health failed, and he consented to take a curate. Even now, whenever he could, he would take a stroll round the garden, or go to sit in his covered seat at the back of the shrubbery, facing a sunny field that sloped to the east.

On some of those sad spring days his strength only served him to sit in the veranda, but whenever he could, he went to see his favourite oxlips. I think he must have had some youthful memory connected with this flower, which ranked next the clote or water lily in his affections. He used to bring roots home from his walks and plant them, till there grew up a row of golden bells gleaming among the dark-leaved ferns under the trees of the shrubbery. Towards the autumn he was better, and wrote to his absent daughters.

Aug. 27th, 1884.

My DEAREST J. AND L.,

I greet you both, because I find you are happily and happy together. My ailing is a queer one, as I

believe that no organ is in itself diseased, but it came
in the form of rheumatic pains in the limbs and stomach,
and leaped and pitched about in neuralgic twinges, so
that the straining of some muscles was very painful.   I
hope it is now going off, and I have worked in my study
this week, and have taken my meals much as usual.   I
like the sweet-minded, and, I believe, much thinking
lassie May, and hope she is happy here with the two
homes and cousin playmates.   I have enjoyed the accounts of your high doings on the hills; they must have
afforded the *contadini* a bright time of life-shine.   I am
very thankful that dear J. is so much better.   Thanks
be to God.

L.'s handsome dog is the worse for his folly.   He
would not stay here, but haunted the town, and took to
running races up the line of railway with started trains,
and one day got too near a wheel, which cut off half his
tail, because he would not "come home and bring his
tail behind him."   God bless you, with love all round,

Your affectionate father,

W. BARNES.

No illness could dull his sympathy with others, nor
his joyous humour.   Neither could it destroy his
patience; for, though the diary for these months
contains little but the melancholy words, " *Poco fatto* "
(little done), or " *Niente fatto, sto male* " (nothing done,
feel ill), yet not a word of complaint ever passed his
lips; and when his limbs no longer obeyed his active
mind, he gave up the doing of what he wished with his
own simple resignation.

"Feb. 15th, 1885. Father was driven over to Whitcombe and took the very last service he was able to take. In the same little church in which his ministry began, there he ended it."

He would never allow arrangements for his duties to be made beforehand, for he always hoped to be able to take them himself, till the end of the week came, and found him still suffering. Some kind clerical friend was always ready to take his duty; how good they were in their hopeful sympathy in his time of need can never be forgotten. To the Hon. and Rev. H. Spring Rice, and Rev. W. Lock, of Keble College, a special debt of gratitude is due. The invalid often said, " God has raised me up many friends while I lie useless here."

But he was not useless. His advice and wisdom were sought by many at his bedside ; it was the brightest and most peaceful place in the house. Here came all his literary friends for pleasant half hours of chat about books and nature. Here he would talk literature with Mr. Edmund Gosse, dig up word-roots from Saxon and British soil with Mr. Truman, and discuss Church politics with his clerical neighbours. He maintained a constant interest in the doings of the Dorset Field Club, and when a programme for the season arrived, he desired that the days of the meetings might be noted in his diary, for said he hopefully, " I might be able to go by that time," quite oblivious for the moment, that he could not rise from his bed. When the proposal was made, to amalgamate the Somerset and Dorset Clubs, he exclaimed emphatically, " No, no ! it has always been the Dorset Club—keep it so." His vote was recorded on this subject at the next meeting, and the motion was negatived.

How cheery and bright he was, too, always giving some prompt and fitting answer. When his grand-daughter one day sent him some little delicacy to tempt his failing appetite, and he was told she made it herself, he smiled and said, " Tell her sweets from the sweet are doubly sweet. I am glad she gives her mind to cookery as well as bookery."

In the summer of 1885 Miss Bayley came from London to bid him good-bye, and he greeted her with a cheering smile, stopping her regrets with " I can think as well as ever." And he chatted with her as of old on his favourite Welsh poets and their Triads, from whom he had gained so much wisdom. " He was a lovely friend," she writes, strengthening one's faith in all that is true, and he himself was so humble. In ages to come, the student and lover of English will, I believe, value the Rev. W. Barnes's work and words, as we now value Chaucer. He was so sweet a soul and sang so sweetly."

Professor Palgrave and his son visited him, and they, too, have recorded their impressions in their own family newspaper in these words:—

" Frank and I are not likely soon to forget our visit last night to Mr. W. Barnes. This aged poet seems to me to stand second only to Tennyson, in the last half century. He has a truth united always to beauty in his drawing of character and of country ways—a pure love of nature, such as one sees in the best Greek or Roman writers, exalted and rendered more tender by his devout Christian spirit. I know not, also, if any of our poets have surpassed him in the number of original pictures

or motives which his three precious volumes display ;
his perfect sincerity of thought and style, gives life and
individuality to a hundred scenes of quiet country life,
lying all within the same little sphere, yet each shown
with a grace of its own. A perfect unity in treatment is
another charm of William Barnes's work. Horace himself does not round off his little odes with more finished
and lovely art.

" But from the work let us turn to the workman.
Though, I fear, very feeble in body, his mind was lively
and vigorous, and he took pleasure in telling of his visit
to Tennyson at Farringford, and of his own interest in
old English speech. In writing, he said he had looked
mainly at Homer, aiming at following him in a careful
selection of epithets, choosing always the one word
which should most characterise the object in place of a
crowd of less significant words.

" He was most gracious and kind ; but some flashes of
speech, and the look in his eyes showed me that, with
the youth-in-age proper to the poet, he had not lost a
poet's animation and fire. He sat crouched in an
armchair, clothed in a red upper dress lined with fur,
a darker red cap on his white hair. His face is
singularly fine and delicate in its lines, like one carved
in marble, the eyes bright, a long white beard over his
chest, his hands white and fine. I have never seen old
age look more beautiful and dignified. Titian or Tin-
toret might have loved to paint him ; no Doge of Venice
in their pictures looks more royal or noble-natured."

" DORCHESTER, 3rd Oct. 1885."

The echoes of the world reached him through the newspapers of the day, which were read to him by his two nurses—Miss Barnes and Miss Benson, who during his illness took quite a daughter's place to him—and every question of the day awoke his interest. The threatening of Dis-establishment was just agitating the country, and no one entered into it with more clear-sighted interest than he. He dictated articles on "Church Endowment," and "Who supports the Church?" for the local newspaper; sent a refutation to Mr. Miall's attack upon the Church, and another paper on the "Bill and the Ministry."

He wrote several leaflets for distribution among the labourers of his parish, putting the Church question clearly before them in language they could understand, and so from that quiet little room, knowledge and help went forth to the outer world. Sometimes a pleasant little tribute to his work was read to him in the daily paper, as on October 6th, 1885, when Lord Iddesleigh's speech on Dorset and the Dorset labourers, was given at the Conservative meeting at Sherborne.

It was noteworthy how he would eschew all the evil in newspapers; no theft or murder could ever be read to him. If a subject of this kind were begun, he showed his displeasure by " Tut, tut! I don't want to hear that; read something else." One day he said, " You will not find that in any of my poems I have ever made a hero of an immoral man or a criminal. There may be such in the world, but I never choose them as subjects, nor could I have written my poetry if I had done so." Speaking of poetry reminds one how strange it was that he so rarely read the works of contemporaneous poets. "I do not want," he used to say, "to be trammelled with the thoughts and styles of other poets, and I take none as my model except the Persian and Italian authors, on which I have framed some, as regards only metre and rhyme." Hafiz, the Persian poet, was much enjoyed by him, and so were Petrarch and Metastasio among the Italians.

The art of poesy had not forsaken him even yet; the sounds of the garden gate clanging after departed friends, and even the tapping of a spray of ivy or rose-bush on his window pane were suggestive. His daughter records: "Oct. 13th. Father dictated to me the poem "The Geäte a-vallèn to." It was a cold evening, and he was sitting in his easy chair by the fire with his fur-lined cloak and red cap and his feet in a fur foot muff. The firelight fell warm on his face, and even dimly brought out the figures in the ancient tapestry behind his bed. He dictated and I wrote :—

In the zunsheen of our summers
  Wi' the hay time now a-come,
How busy wer' we out a-vield
  Wi' vew a-left at hwome,
When waggons rumbled out ov yard
  Red wheeled, wi' body blue,
And back behind 'em loudly slamm'd
  The geäte a-vallèn to.

Drough day sheen for how many years
  The geäte ha' now a-swung,
Behind the veet o' vull-grown men
  And vootsteps of the young,
Drough years o' days it swung to us
  Behind each little shoe,
As we tripped lightly on avore
  The geäte a-vallèn to.

In evenen time o' starry night
  How mother zot at hwome,
And kept her blazing vire bright
  Till father should ha' come,
And how she quickened up and smiled,
  And stirred her vire anew,
To hear the trampèn hosses' steps
  And geäte a-vallën to.

There's moonsheen now in nights o' Fall
  When leaves be brown vrom green,
When to the slammèn of the geäte
  Our Jenny's ears be keen,
When the wold dog do wag his tail,
  And Jeän could tell to who,
As he do come in drough the geäte
  The geäte a-vallèn to.

And oft do come a saddened hour
  When there must goo away,
One well-beloved to our heart's core
  Vor long, perhaps vor aye.
And oh ! it is a touchèn thing
  The lovèn heart must rue
To hear behind his last farewell
  The geäte a-vallèn to.

" The last verse seemed a sad foreboding to me. When finished he said, ' Observe that word " geäte," That is how King Alfred would have pronounced it, and how it was called in the *Saxon Chronicle*, which tells us of King Edward, who was slain at Corfe's geäte.' After a pause he continued, ' Ah ! if the Court had not been moved to London, then the speech of King Alfred of which our Dorset is the remnant—would have been —the Court language of to-day, and it would have been more like Anglo-Saxon than it is now.'

" Sometimes he had quite gay and youthful fancies.

The ivy tapping at his window pane made his heart
young again, and this was the poem that came to him
as he lay there, eighty-six years of age, and helpless:

AT THE WINDOW.

(A girl is supposed to be thinking to herself.)

I had thought what is it whipping in the wind?
A-whipping whipping on the window pane?
Is it the ivy hanging from above
And shaken by the winds that briskly pass?

(*She sings*) The ivy is an evergreen,
          And does not die in Fall,
          My lover's love is ever true,
          And will not die at all.

I had thought what is it whipping in the wind?
A whipping, whipping on the window square]?
Is it the holly at the window side,
And shaken by the freshly blowing air?

(*She sings*) The holly is an evergreen,
          And lives the winter through,
          My true love's love will never die,
          But standeth ever true.

I had thought what is it whipping in the wind,
A whipping, whipping on my window panes?
And 'twas my lover's hand that flipped a twig
Off broken from the tree of golden chains;

          In the duskiness of twilight
          A hand I did not see,   `
          It meant, if you are there then fling
          The casement out for me.

I thought, oh wind, if thou wert very cold,
A warm heart is in the midst of thee,
And thou wilt not bring in to me a storm,
But words as sweet as ever words can be.

I opened then the casement wide
Before his welcome smile,
And then we chatted in the dusk
A while—too short a while.

" Oct. 17th. Father surprised us all by coming down to dinner once more. He sat in his easy chair with a plaid over him, but was soon weary, and after a cheery word to every one, returned to his own room.

" ' My day is short,' he sighed as he went. It was, alas, his last day downstairs. Those rooms never again echoed back his bright voice and laugh.

" Nov. 9th. He looked over the last proof of his *Glossary of the Dorset Language.*" The Glossary which was his first linguistic work in the earliest volume of poems, had been growing more full and complete, through friends' suggestions, and his own researches ever since, through half a century, and now in its completed form was his very last published work. It was printed by Mr. Foster at Dorchester, and the preface contained the names of the many friends whom he wished to thank for assistance.

" Nov. 21st. Mr. Foster came and brought him the first (author's copy) of the Glossary, and it seemed to be a great happiness to him to have been spared to take it into his hands. He said, ' I have done some little to preserve the speech of our forefathers, but I fear a time will come when it will be scarcely remembered, and none will be found who can speak it with the purity I have heard it spoken in my youth.' " A few weeks after this he received a letter from the Secretary of the Dialect Society, of which he was a member, offering to take 500 copies of this Glossary. He was much pleased, and said, "Ah; just as I am going out of the world things begin to mend." He began dictating to his daughter, his "pen-hand" as he called her—a table of signs for sounds, to assist the pronunciation of the words of the Glossary, but he grew weary very soon, and the work was never finished.

"Nov. 18th, 1885. Mr. W. Miles Barnes and some musical friends came over from Monkton to give the poet an impromptu serenade. Lamps and chairs were arranged on the arched lobby at the top of the stairs, and several glees and madrigals sung outside his chamber door. He was delighted, and clapped his hands, crying 'Bravi, bravi!—again, again!' His old favourite, 'By Celia's arbour,' was one of those he would have repeated over and over again." Sometimes some street musicians, who played harp and violin very creditably, were brought into the passage to make music for him, and better than this, the grandchildren from Monkton sometimes brought over their instruments, and played his favourite concerted bits.

"Christmas Day, 1885. Father was for the first time unable to join the united party at the dinner table, but they went to his room for his Christmas blessing, which he gave specially to each one. It was a scene which might have recalled the blessing of Jacob to his grandchildren, the venerable old man whose silver beard fell in wavy sheen on his breast, thus giving his benediction from the throne of his bed. 'My blessing this year is "May God guide your ways and bless your days." Some years ago when I gathered my offspring round me, they were dependent upon my hands; now I have fallen on my children's hands, and owe very much to them all.' Then he spoke of what each had done, not forgetting the 'stranger that was within his gates,' and who had been as another daughter through all his illness. Nor. were the far-off children left out. Then followed an allusion to the Mother of the Gracchi and her jewels, ending with, 'My grandchildren are my jewels richly set, for they are not wanting in those gifts of mind and character which will help to make them good men and women. It used to be the fashion to enter in the Family Bible, after the notice of a birth or baptism, "May God make him or her a good old man or woman." This good wish was twofold —it wished a long life and a good life, so I say of them, " May God make them good old men and women"; and for them and you all, " God guide your ways and bless your days." ' "

On Jan. 7th, 1886, the Bishop of Salisbury came to visit him and administer the Holy Communion. He was accompanied by Mrs. Wordsworth, who joined in the beautiful service round the bed, where the invalid reposed peacefully. Beside him was a vase of snowdrops and holly berries—spring and winter together, the beauty of the old life and the purity of the new one just opening before him.

The Bishop himself has written of this visit :—

" It was my privilege to minister to him twice at least during the last twelve months; and on both occasions I was impressed by him as a man of no ordinary abilities, even though he was then weak in body and slowly dying of old age. But I think that what we have most to thank God for in him, and what most struck myself, was his serene and guileless character, and his sympathy with the best side of English country life. I spoke to him,

Y

naturally, about his poems, and having a very practical interest in the character of the Dorset villagers, I ventured to ask him how far they might be considered true to nature, how far one might appeal to the feelings disclosed in his idyllic pictures of rural scenes and characters. He replied in effect as follows (I much regret that I cannot reproduce his own terse and graceful, though homely words) :—' That many persons thought that he had painted our folk in too bright colours, but that everything which he had written was true of some one in the classes described in the poems; that he was painting, in fact, from life, though the level might be somewhat above the average.' I do not doubt the truth of this statement, and I have seen much in Dorset villages to confirm it. But if society owes a debt to those poets and artists who make a nation conscious of its better self, and set before it, as true ministers of God, the ideal of excellence which is within its grasp as part of His creation, surely this is true, in one not insignificant province of England, of our Dorset poet. He has helped the people hereabouts to feel what they can be and do."

A few days after this the poet felt his weariness so much that he said, "Ah! it is time that I go, and I am ready—yes, ready."

It was one of his pleasures to hear the Psalms of the day read to him in the Hebrew antiphonal manner, one taking the leading thought and another the rhyme thought, which is the mark of Hebrew poetry, thus—

1st voice. "Thou broughtest out fountains and waters out of the hard rock."

2nd voice. "Thou driedst up mighty waters."

1st voice. "The day is Thine and the night is Thine."
2nd voice. "Thou hast prepared the light and the sun."
" Now think," he said, " how it was in the Temple of Jerusalem. How glorious, thousands of voices taking up in succession the grand poetry of the Hebrew Psalms! Our Blessed Lord must have joined in this when He went daily to the Holy Temple."

Rev. W. Miles Barnes's diary : " Jan. 26th, 1886. To Came in the afternoon. Father not feeling well, and not disposed to talk much ; was a little vexed that his last poem had not been sent to the *Dorset County Chronicle.* I asked him if he remembered Mr. ——'s request that he would write a poem to encourage Dorset lads to enlist. He replied, ' That is a subject connected with politics, not with poetry. I have never written any of my poems but one, with a drift. I write pictures which I see in my mind.' The only one written with a drift is the fable of *The Pig and the Crow*—that was directed against the Chartists, the socialists of those days.'

" Thursday. Feb. 4th. A restless night. Kind Miss Benson had sat up with him. About three in the morning she persuaded him to take some beef-tea, and then expressed a hope that he would go to sleep; to which he replied, in the words of Henry IV.'s apostrophe from Shakespeare—

" ' Sleep, gentle sleep,
Nature's soft nurse, how have I frighted thee
That thou no more wilt weigh my eyelids down
And steep my senses in forgetfulness ? ' "

The next morning he was so bright, that in return for Miss Benson's readings of little anecdotes to him, he told her many humorous tales, and laughed with her over them.

"April 28th, 1886. The following letter came to-day from the North-Western Literary Society, Sioux City, Iowa :

"'SECRETARY'S OFFICE, *April* 12*th*, 1886.

"'DEAR SIR,

"'The members of this Society, desiring to convey to you in some manner an expression of their appreciation of your verses, and in recognition of your great learning, have, as a slight token of their esteem, unanimously elected you an honorary member of the Society.

"'Very respectfully yours,

"'BEN. W. AUSTIN, *Sec.*'

"'This is an honour from afar, is it not?' said his daughter. He replied with a sigh, 'It has come too late; put it away now.'"

On May 3rd he dictated a pretty letter of thanks for the honour done to him, and sent a photograph with his autograph. In the same month he was much cheered by a visit from his youngest daughter, Mrs. T. D. Gardner. He enjoyed her songs, and got quite excited over the Philo-Israel theory, which she spoke of having heard discussed in London. He dictated an entire article to disprove it on philological grounds; the Teutonic and the Aryan tongues being built on an entirely different form from the Shemitic. He ended by saying, "The Lost Tribes of Israel are simply those

who lived amongst and married and took the false
religion of the surrounding nations, and gradually
lost the only knowledge which kept them a distinct
nation—the knowledge and laws of the One true
God."

So the time passed on. Through the long summer
months he "possessed his soul in peace," and saw his
friends once more, among whom were Captain and
Mrs. Damer, who had first placed him in his happy
Rectory, and again the Bishop of Salisbury ministered
to him. Mr. Gosse also once more paid him a visit,
which he has thus recorded in a letter to Mr. Coventry
Patmore : " Hardy and I went on Monday last to Came
Rectory, where he lies bedridden. It is curious that he
is dying as picturesquely as he lived. We found him in
bed in his study, his face turned to the window, where
the light came streaming in through flowering plants,
his brown books on all sides of him save one, the wall
behind him being hung with old green tapestry. He
had a scarlet bedgown on, a kind of soft biretta of dark
red wool on his head, from which his long white hair
escaped on to the pillow ; his grey beard, grown very
long, upon his breast; his complexion, which you
recollect as richly bronzed, has become blanched by
keeping indoors, and is now waxily white where it is
not waxily pink ; the blue eyes, half shut, restless under
languid lids. . . . I wish I could paint for you the
strange effect of this old, old man, lying in cardinal
scarlet in his white bed, the only bright spot in the
gloom of all these books. You must think that I
make too much of these outer signs, but it seemed to
me that this unconscious *mise-en-scène* in the solitude

of this out-of-the-way Rectory was very curious and characteristic."

With the autumn his strength failed gradually, till there came a morning, October 7th, on which he seemed to be especially peaceful. When prayers were read, he sighed softly, " Lighten our eyes, O Lord, that we sleep not in death ; " and then he soothed himself to slumber by repeating some characteristic little couplets, those epigrammatic couplets which he was so fond of making. The last one he spoke was—

> " Dry our eyes in weeping,
> Shut our eyes in sleeping."

With this he fell into a sweet slumber, and no one knew the moment when he stepped over the boundary into the invisible world and dreamed his way into Paradise. It was on the 11th of October that the poet fulfilled his own prophecy, and there came—

> " a saddened hour,
> When there must goo away
> One well-beloved to our heart's core
> Vor long or perhaps vor aye.
> And oh ! it is a touchèn thing
> The lovèn heart to rue,
> To hear behind his last farewell
> The geate a-vallèn to."

The clang of the gate behind the simple procession when the poet passed out of his home for the last time fell with a deep meaning on some of the mourners' hearts. Professor Palgrave describes it :—

" I was again before the gate leading down to the little Rectory, deep amongst trees as yet untouched

by autumn. There I saw the plain elm coffin carried
out and placed on a little hand-bier, covered only by
many wreaths and crosses of white, spring-like flowers;
then drawn forth and followed by a little crowd of the
poet's children and grandchildren. In company with
many friends and neighbours—words which in his case
were identical—I followed to his own gray little church,
where with the sweet, solemn words which he had
himself read over old and young, and the nosegays of
cottage flowers which the children shyly dropped into
his grave, in the "sure and certain Christian hope,
he was laid to rest from his labours."

But not dead—the true poet can never die.

APPENDICES.

APPENDIX I.

SOME LETTERS.

I.

To C. Tennant, *Esq., apropos of his new work entitled the*
" Sovereign Remedy."

Came Rectory,
September 25th, 1865.
Dear Mr. Tennant,

Your work so puzzles me that I know not what to
say of it.

It contains, like your other works, so vast a store of historical and statistical facts, which I not only cannot gainsay,
but am glad to meet, that I am much inclined to sit still at
your feet as a learner ; and yet I think that, on broad
grounds (first principles), I might not come to all your
conclusions. In the first place, I do not (as if I mistake
you not, you do not) hold paper currency to be itself capital,
that is, a concrete form of labour ; nor do I see that any
increase of it is an increase of capital.

All forms of life-gear which are won by labour are
capital as the concrete form of the labour ; but a promis-
sory note can be the concrete of only the labour that made

the paper and wrote the words of it. If the words on it
are a promise to pay a thousand sovereigns, which are the
concrete of the labour that brought them to hand, it represents the sovereigns only for some cases of exchange.

For as gold is better than heavy forms of life-gear for
the exchanging of rights into quantities of capital, so again
is a note often better than gold for exchanging of such
rights, and that is the only good of it ; while, if it exchanges
or is meant to exchange a right into a concrete of labour
not in being, it is an evil as it is a cheat ; as it would be a
cheat and a wrong for a man to give me for my true week's
labour, a right to a week's labour of his man John or of his
horse Whitefoot, when he has neither man nor horse.

Therefore I deem it pernicious that there should be any
paper currency that shall not have behind it the concrete of
the labour it represents ; and so that there should be any
bank notes payable on demand, beyond the gold that is ready
under the drawer's hand to be given on demand.

Thence I will give you my answer to a question which I
think you ask, as to what is an over-issue, or, at least,
what is over-trading.

If a man risks more capital than his own, so that by
any losses ever known in the chances of trade he sinks the
capital of unwilling losers as creditors, he overtrades,—by
a trading which the state ought not to foster ; and an issue
of promises to pay in gold beyond the gold under hand, is
an over-issue.

If the Bank of England should keep in its vaults only
gold enough to meet ordinary calls for it, who would be
bound to find for every note-bringing hand the gold for
extraordinary calls ? The state ? If so, where is the state
to keep it under hand, or gather it in a day ?

I do not myself think that the commercial mind in
England is in want of stimulation ; wherever there is a way
of making money, it is seen and followed—aye, *per fas et*

nefas—from the Atlantic cable to the most hollow of the trade companies, and from the most useful form of commerce down to the horrid trade of killing babes at so much a head; and the state has already done evil in fighting traders' quarrels in China and Japan, and especially seeing the way in which we cringe to powerful states, as we do not now even dare to tell Prussia and Austria of their wrongs to their faces.

I hope your change of air has done you all good.

I am, dear Mr. Tennant,

Yours very truly,

W. BARNES.

II.

To C. TENNANT, Esq.

CAME RECTORY,
January 5th, 1871.

MY DEAR MR. TENNANT,

I thank you much for the bookling of Mr. Tomline on the silver coinage, and I am very glad that he has taken so good a ground on behalf of a good Englishman's right, and against the debasing of our money, for I have understood, rightly or wrongly, that the debasing of the coinage is a token of the coming fall of a state. Pray let me know what happens between the Colonel and the tax-gatherer.

But now, alas! we seem to be all still at the Tower of Babel, with a confusion of tongues. I was awhile ago with three other men, and no two of us gave anything like the same definition of *dogma*, and now you and I mean two unlike things by the words *value* and *intrinsic value*. I took my commercial value of gold in my letter as its value in the hand of the chapman as it may be good for other commodities; and you are talking of the life-value of matter to man's bodily being, or what some call its *real value*. Air in our land is of the greatest life-value, but of very little commercial value. You say that there is no more value in the gold than in the paper. I say there is more *commercial* value in the gold of the sovereign than in the paper of a £5 note, because it will fetch much more in the market. And you say that if gold were not the generally accepted measure of value, it would no more exchange for *anything* than a bit of gravel; but I answer gold has been taken as a measure of value owing to its commercial value, and that if men were now to take gravel for a measure of value, a pound of gravel would not buy more bread than it would now buy. Whereas, although the diamond is not taken as a common measure of value, it would exchange for bread up to nearly its worth in the market.

We differ because we speak in a confusion of words as if we were at Babel, and I called a chisel by some name that to you meant a hammer.

With all good wishes,

Yours very truly,

W. BARNES.

P.S.—I and my three friends gave up our argument about dogma only because we could not understand each other.—W.B.

III.

To the same.

CAME RECTORY,
January 1871.

MY DEAR MR. TENNANT,

I thank you again for your last letter and its enclosures. I do not at all see that Colonel Tomline's course of behaviour is readily laughed down. The mint-handlers say that there is *enough* of silver coin. What is the proof of enoughness? Forgive the word. Enoughness, I can see, may be found between two points: 1st, That there should not be a gold or silver coin out of all the gold and silver brought to the land; and 2nd, At the other end that every pound of gold and silver in the land should be minted into coins. Now where between those two points is the minter's enoughness? and what is the proof that it is there?

Until these questions meet a sound answer, who has a right to laugh at any man who may hold that there is not, as I believe there is not, enough of silver coin?

I now see, notwithstanding our Babel mingling of words, that you and I are, as to what I call commercial value, of one mind. You say, and I say, that the value was not in the gravel or in the gold (of which I spoke), but in the human labour that brought the gravel to where it was wanted to hand, as I have said in *Labour and Gold;* and so I held that labour was the *measure* of *commercial value.* Well then, *measure* means one thing to you, and to me another. Labour gives and *gauges* commercial value; and shall I put the word *gauge* for *measure,* and say that labour is the *gauge* of commercial value, and let you keep your *measure* to your own meaning? But we have another misunderstanding, in that you seem to hold that there is no other *value* than what I call commercial value, and which is met by money; and I think you very far narrow the meaning of the old Latin *valeo* and the French *valoir*. Pliny says that a drug "*valet adversus morbum*"; and I think one may say in French, "*Les actions valent plus que les paroles.*" I value very highly your friendship, though I have not rated it in gold, but I will give you the word *worth* instead of *value* if you like to have it.

I like your fable of "The River and Canal." It is good and not overstrained. The other is good, but not quite original; it is taken from a Swedish poem, which you will find at page 85 of the *Little Swedish Grammar*, which I send you, with the English at the foot of the page. I had learnt much of it by rote from another book in my younger years. You may kindly send back the book when you have done with it.

With kind love to my dear London guide, D., and all of you singly,

I am, yours ever truly,

W. BARNES.

IV.

To the same.

CAME RECTORY,
January 20th, 1871.

MY DEAR MR. TENNANT,

More last words. I ran down on Tuesday to Chard in Somerset, to read to a Literary Institution, and the secretary to it is manager of a bank. Chard is a town of some factories, and he (the Secretary) tells me that he finds it hard, and often beyond his means, to find silver for the paymasters on their wages days, and mostly he can accommodate only his good customers; and some of them have told him that they pay their hands in clusters, by gold, which they must change and share among themselves as best they may, and that they often do so at the inns—most of them are women—where they pay a discount by the pewter pot. The banker says that although the silver is paid to town hands, it does not *float back* to him, and that there is a vast drain of our silver to China.

Yours very truly,

W. BARNES.

V.

To the same.

(Referring to a book on the Irish question written by Mr. Tennant.)

CAME RECTORY,
April 10th, 1871.

MY DEAR MR. TENNANT,

I should be glad to have your last proof, though I do not believe that I can improve it. I once knew a tuner of pianofortes, and he told me that a Dorset gentleman who was a fine musician, and had a fine ear, and hand-skill for tuning a pianoforte, had just tuned his own. Then he sent for the man of the screw-wrench, and said, " Oh! just see if my piano wants tuning." He found it in good tune, and said to the gifted owner of it, " Oh, sir, your piano is quite in tune, I can't improve it." " I am glad of that," was the answer, " but, here, take this note to Miss A., and this to Lady B., and one to Mr. C., and you will have all their pianos put into your hands." " Ah! " said the tuner, " how thankful I was that I did not fall into a snare! " Well now, you have tuned your Irish harp eight times over, and then say to me, " Here, just see if

Z

my harp is in good tune, and if not, tune it." My answer must be, "I cannot improve it." I *did* think, the other day, that one of the strings, that rough one, the "*chorda fiscalis*," was screwed up a bit too high, but when I meddled with it I let it down far too low, and I have no good one that I can put instead of it, or that you would be likely to take, so that you might sing with Anacreon, Ἥμειψα νεῦρα πρώην, "I lately changed a string." No, I cannot improve your tuning, but I shall be very happy to have the harp after the eighth or twentieth tuning, so that I may sweep out a little of its good music, and I am sure you will keep the old knotty string, and make it sound well, one way or another.

Yours very truly,

W. BARNES.

VI.

To C. WARNE, Esq., F.S.A.

CAME RECTORY,
August 20th, 1869.

MY DEAR MR. WARNE,

As to the so-called Belgic dikes in Dorset. I do not believe that the Belgæ ever held land in Dorset. Ptolemy gives the Belgæ as under or below the "Dobuni," with the head town Κορίνιον, and the Akebatii with the town Ναλκούα, and on the west and south of these tribes he puts the Durotriges, and westwards of these the Dumnonii; and since Ptolemy's mapping has never been falsified by any better or more trustworthy writer of the time, on what ground can it be maintained with Stukely that the Belgæ held all Dorset, or indeed, that they held any of it? Dikes or banks may have been dug for (1) tuns or fences, as of

cattle fields or corn ground ; (2) Landmarks of ownership ;
(3) Boundaries of jurisdiction, as of hundreds, or shires,
or boroughs or states ; (4) Defences against foes in war.

I should not hold that a dike was for No. 2 until I had
found it would not do for No. 1, nor for 3 if it would be
such as would be made rather for 1 or 2, nor for 4 if it
would seem rather to be a work for 1, 2, or 3.

I believe many dikes were made for peaceful jurisdiction
rather than for war walls, as we marked our borough
boundaries, the good of which is that we know without
strife whether a law-breach outside or inside of it is to be
tried by the county or borough magistrate ; so a wrong
on the English side of Offa's dike was under English law,
and a wrong on the Welsh side was under Welsh law.
Who can believe that the Britons, or Belgæ, or Saxon-
English could have manned scores of miles of a low bank
and shallow ditch, over which men or boys might have gone
anywhere with a leap or stride ? Grimsditch is said to part
Dorset from Wilts, and before we settle the uses of the
dikes we ought to have an account of every kind of
boundary of every shire, and hundred, and old borough.
Why may not the dike by Wareham, from the Piddle to
the Frome be just what the streams themselves may be
on their sides—Wareham land-marks ? It is interesting
to see that the Stour was called the Alawn (Alauna) from
the great mark of it now—the Alaw or water-city (Clote).
With kind love to Charles, ·

I am,

Dear Mr. Warne,

Yours truly,

W. BARNES.

VII.

To the same.

DEAR MR. WARNE,

I am glad to have your kind letter, and, while I am sorry for your ailings of body, to see that the higher man is ever young.

I had three charming days at Ranston, and was very glad to see Dr. Smart, and the earthworks of his most interesting neighbourhood. He and I had already written many times to each other, as he asked me a question, on which I put others to him. You, in your map and letter to Sir T. R., were our guide all the day through ; I felt that you of all men should have been with us there as well as at Hod.

It seemed clear to me, as we stayed on the dike, at the short *spur* of which you speak in your book, that the dike at first ended there, as it bent in somewhat roundly in that spur, and ended there at what was, as you say, woody land, and simply because it was woody land, which was at the time either of itself or as the Britons thickened it—a good fence and defence—and I believe that afterwards when the woods became thinner—for the thick population of herdsmen must have drawn much fuel from the woods— they cast up the rest of the banks towards the road. So I think that the short banks of which you speak, stopped at first a clear wood-free gangway, as Dr. Smart tells me that the dikes end where there was wood, or cliff, or some natural fence. These are my thoughts *valeant quantum.* I should like to have gone over the whole length of the dike, and I wish to see Knowlton, though from your book

I am convinced that your opinion is right, that it was not a *caer* for war, but a *côr* for the civil and religious business and gatherings of, it may be, the whole pastoral population. By the way, it is markworthy that the Welsh even now call Stonehenge *y Côr gawr,* " The Giant's Ring," a token of its high antiquity, since at the early time at which they first called it so, they knew nothing of its history. Knowlton is the head of Hundred of Knowlton, and I suppose was in the British times the place of the Hundred's court, or *L'lys ys cantrev,* a court well known to old Welsh law.

You may know that Dorset has begun to bestir itself for a Dorset museum. I am on the building committee, and I believe that at our meeting on Thursday we may choose a plan. Mr. Robert Williams has given the George Inn, with all of its ground, and I hope that in a short time Dorset may have its museum and library in its own freehold building.

I have had one of your maps, but I should be most glad to have a list of the "*coms.*"

With kind regards to your son,

I am, dear Mr. Warne,

Yours very truly,

W. BARNES.

VIII.

To his Son-in-law. ·

CAME RECTORY,
July 1878.

MY DEAR T——

I am glad to see in your handwriting a token of returning strength. The Romans made some roads in Wales and elsewhere, but I believe that the great roads, such as the Via Iceniana, of which a branch came down through Dorset to Land's End were British roads, taken and improved by the Romans. British history gives the making of them to Dyfnwal Moelmud, King of the Britons, about 440 years B.C. They are not made in the Roman way, nor does any Roman writer speak of the making of any such roads, and they ran to great British strongholds.

An essay by me on " British Roads " will most likely be printed in our *Transactions*. We had a good meeting last week at Glanville's Wootton, near Sherborne, and the secretary and I had a little sparring on an earthwork hard by. He holds it to be Roman, whereas the Roman castra had walls or banks of straight lines, and angles, and four gates, and this one has bending banks and only one opening. Then he called a nether quern stone found there a

Roman one, though it is as flat as this
The Roman millstone was surely taller than that, more like

 I dare say you have seen some old

Roman quern stones, and most likely the quern of the Italian *contadino*, if he has one, is still of the old form. Can you give me a sketch of an Italian one of the olden times, or of our days ?

I was much pleased to have the Sibyl inscriptions. I believe that the Sibyls were taken up by the Church for some of the Sibylline prophecies which were understood to speak of the Messiah and Christianity.

I thank you much for your thought of me with the Papal *Pauls.*

Yours truly,

W. BARNES.

IX.

To EDMUND GOSSE.

CAME RECTORY,
DORCHESTER, DORSET,
August 18*th*, 1879.

DEAR SIR,

It has not been my wont to complain of a critic who might have found fault with my homely rhymes, or to thank one who might have thought them worthy of any praise, as I have deemed that the business of a critic, so long as he is true to matters of fact, is between him and his readers.

But since you in the *Academy* have spoken so handsomely of my *Dorset Idylls and Ditties*, and openly in your own name, I cannot help telling you that I feel very happy with your praise. No critic would have daunted me from the writing of the pieces, as it was simply a refreshment of mind from cares and irksomeness, as is music to a man who may play an instrument alone.

I am, dear Sir,

Yours truly,

WM. BARNES.

EDMUND GOSSE, ESQ.

X.

To DANIEL RICKETSON, Esq., *New Bedford, Mass. U.S.*

RECTORY, WINTERBOURNE CAME,
February 7*th*, 1869.

DEAR MR. RICKETSON,

The friendly hand which you hold out to me with your kind and good letter, I take with the best feelings of a threefold fellowship : that of a brotherhood in song, and in race, and in our holy faith, and a threefold cord is not quickly broken (Ecclesiastes iv. 12). I am happy to find that my homely poems earn approving readers, and among them a poet in the great New England of the West. Poetry has to me been a solace, for like other men, I have had with many blessings, times of struggling and sorrow. Without doubt America will have her mind-stars of glory, and a literature and an art, the offspring of her own state life, but I hope Americans will always look kindly to the old land and their father stock, and the rock whence they are hewn and the quarry whence they are digged (Isaiah li. 1).

The old town of Dorchester, in the outskirts of which I am writing, has a daughter town in America, Dorchester, Massachusetts, next, I believe, to Boston, and I think it likely that your Channings were sprung from Channings till lately represented in our Dorchester, by men of the name.

" Ex ungue leonem."

I think from the poems of your *Autumn Sheaf*, that it will yield a fine sample of golden grain.

I am, my dear Sir,

With kindest feeling,

Yours very truly,

WM. BARNES.

XI.

To the same.

CAME RECTORY, DORCHESTER,
April 12th, 1869.

DEAR SIR,

I thank you for your kind letter and offer of a copy of your book, which of course I should like to see. Your letter which left New Bedford on the 19th of March, reached Dorchester on the 1st of April. Winterbourne Herringston, which you found in the *Beauties of England*, is a hamlet in my parish. There is a small stream through our valley called the Winterbourne, or Winterbrook, as it runs only in the winter, and a string of villages on it are called from one of their names, Winterbournes. Our lower land is meadow, and the upper ground is of sheep downs or corn ground on a chalk soil. Dorchester is on the pretty little river the Frome, which reaches the sea beyond Wareham, an old town of great note in the Saxon-English times. If you ever go to Dorchester, Massachusetts, you may find, I think, in the town library, a copy of the old edition of Hutchins's *History of Dorset*, which was given to the town by a friend of mine, a former mayor of Dorchester.

Our climate is mild, our south-west and west winds are moist, as coming over the Atlantic, and our east wind is cold. Our spring begins at the latter end of March, which is mostly a time of dry bracing winds, and our winter begins in November, usually a windy and rainy month. May is a charming month, in which our dry downs are covered with sheets, as it were of silver and gold, in daisies and buttercups. June is our hay month. We are rich in wild flowers: the snowdrop comes up in January; daffodils are now going off, and primroses are now coming into full bloom, and will soon be followed by cowslips and anemones or windflowers. On the Frome in May will bloom in snow-white patches the water crowfoot, or water ranunculus, a charming sight, with the water tinted blue from the sky, as it is given in my little poem, "White and Blue." The river Stour bears the yellow water-lily, *Nuphar Lutea*, which we call the clote. Our hedges, as the summer goes on, are tinted with the blossom of the blackthorn, whitethorn, honeysuckle, wild rose, and briony, goosegrass, and other plants.

I am now amid the chirping of birds, such as the black-bird, thrush, and sparrow. The lark will soon be soaring in song over our heads, and the rooks have nearly built their nests in the clusters of elms.

We have within three miles of us " Maiden Castle," so called, one of the finest British earthworks in England : and Dorchester was a Roman Castra.

I will bear in mind your wishes about your pre-elders in England, and be on the watch for any clue to their old abode. The name of Ricketts, not Ricketson, is known in Dorset. The Halls also yet linger in the county, and I am told the name of Hall is known in Massachusetts, and I once sent to the American Halls an old coin, a Dorchester tradesman's token, with the name Hall.

I do not know how your kind gift of one of your books could come better than from your publisher to mine, Mr. R. Smith or Messrs. Macmillan, publishers, London.

I am, dear Sir,

Very kindly yours,

WILLIAM BARNES.

15*th April.*—The cuckoo was first heard here yesterday.
W. B.

XII.

To the same.

RECTORY, WINTERBORNE CAME,
June 11*th*, 1869.

DEAR MR. RICKETSON,

Your kind letter was given to me on our lawn on May 26, where I read it, with a laburnum tree in full bloom before me, a pink maytree showing some blossom on my left, and on my right rose-trees and syringas bursting into flower, and before me, beyond the lawn were ash, beech and elm. If you have a greater rainfall than we, you have, I should think, fewer damp days. I should enjoy your dry-aired and sunny November. Most likely the ivy does not climb your walls and trees as freely as it overspreads ours. Have you many kinds of fern, and have you planted the yew in your graveyards as our forefathers have set them in ours?

I thank you much for the copy of your book of good pure-minded poems, which I can read with pleasure, unmarred in the way in which is too often marred the pleasure afforded me by the works of some of our high-ranked poets, who, when they have all but finished a charming scene, cast in some ugly touch of malice or mockery. I can trust myself to your poems without any shock to my better feelings; and they are the more interesting, as they show how the Englishman works in a new world of land and life. I thank you for the honour of the lines addressed to me, as they afford me all pleasure but that of feeling worthy of them. You have in one of your poems the name Walden, the name of a householder, a dairyman of this parish. There is, about twelve miles from us, a small old town, "Cerne Abbas," where in the earlier Saxon times was a noted abbey, one of the abbots of which was the learned Ælfric, and in that town is an old house which is said by tradition to have been the abode of Washingtons, the forefathers of General Washington. Of Washingtons it was the abode, and I send you some particulars of it and of its inmates, kindly given to me by Mr. Ball, the clergyman of the place.

I remain, dear Sir,

Yours very truly,

W. Barnes.

XIII.

To the same.

CAME RECTORY,
June 3rd, 1870.

DEAR MR. RICKETSON,

I am glad to receive a few more kindly words from
my brother bard, and now almost old friend. I, too, am
enjoying, like you,—though I am fearful with less of thank-
fulness that I owe to the Giver of all good,—the charm of
the opening summer. Our difference of longitude does not
give me a summer to your winter, though our Australian
kindred cannot have the spring when we rejoice in its
presence. We have had a rather cold May, and late
growth, but now the meadows and hedgerows are gay with
leaf and bloom. Our apple-trees have been as a sheet of
blooth, as we call bloom collectively in Dorset, and we are
likely to have a fair fruit year. I know the grave spot of
Henry Kirke White, at Cambridge.

I am writing a Dictionary of our common names of
animals, with the languages from which their names are
taken, and the meaning of the words as marking the
animals. Pray did your people call the Bob-a-link by its
name from its cry? Whip-poor-Will, I know, is a cry-
mocking name. Do you know whether the name racoon
was an Indian one? I have a Grammar of the Cree and
Chippaway speeches, and hope to have in a few days a
book by Barratt, of Connecticut, on the old speeches of
New England. I should be very thankful for the meaning of any Indian name that our people have taken for
any American animal.

I am writing to you in my study, before a window
through which I can see on a ridge of ground a very fine

old British barrow burial tumulus, with a clump of trees growing on it. Just under, though beyond it, is the pretty river Frome, and the town of Dorchester, the mother of Dorchester, Massachusetts.

With all Christian love,

Yours very truly,

WILLIAM BARNES.

APPENDIX II.

THE PUBLISHED WORKS OF WILLIAM BARNES.

1822. Orra, a Lapland Tale. A short poem. 8vo, pp. 28,
with four woodcuts by the author. Published
by I. Clark, Dorchester.
Some Small Poems, and Poetical translations of
Bion's Epitaph on Adonis, and some of the
golden verses of Pythagoras.

1827 Several Short Essays, signed "Dilettante," printed
to   in the *Dorset County Chronicle;* also several
1835.   Sonnets and other Poems.

1829. The Etymological Glossary, or Easy Expositor for
the Use of Schools and non-Latinists, wherein
the greater part of the English words of foreign
derivation are so arranged that the learner is
enabled to acquire the meaning of many at
once. Published in Shaftesbury by J. Rutter:
London, by Whittaker, Teacher, and Arnot.
1829.

1831 Papers in the *Gentleman's Magazine.*
to   On English Derivatives. June 1831.
1841. On the Structure of Dictionaries. August 1831.
Pronunciation of Latin. October 1831.
Hieroglyphics. December 1831.

Napper's Mite, Dorchester, with woodcut. May 1833.
Silton Church, with woodcut. June 1833.
Sturminster Newton Church. June 1833.
The English Language. June 1833.
Nailsea Church, Somerset. July 1833.
Chelvey, Somerset. September 1833.
Puncknowle Church, with woodcut. July 1835,
On Roman Numerals. December 1837.
On Æsop. June 1838.
Some Etymologies. July 1838.
On the so-called Kimmeridge Coal Money. Feb. 1839.
Battle of Pen. February 1839.
The Roman Amphitheatre, Dorchester. May 1839.
The Hindoo Shasters. June 1839.
The Phœnicians. August 1839.
Hindoo Pooran and Sciences. September 1839.
Hindoo Fakeers. January 1840.
Dorset Dialect compared with Anglo-Saxon. January
    1840.
The Old "Judge's House," Dorchester, with wood-
    cut. November 1840.
Education in Words and Things. January 1841.
Fielding's House at Stour, with woodcut. Feb. 1841.
Goths and Teutons. May 1841.
Laws of Case. May 1841.
1832. Papers in *Hone's Year Book*.
Dorsetshire Customs. Pp. 1172.
Single-stick and Cudgels. Pp. 1525.
Lent Crocking. Pp. 1599.
1833. A Catechism of Government in General, and of
    England in Particular. Bastable, Shaftesbury.
The Mnemonic Manual.
1834. A Few Words on the Advantages of a more Common
    Adoption of the Mathematics as a Branch of
    Education. London: Whittaker and Co.

1835. A Mathematical Investigation of the principle of
Hanging Doors, Gates, Swing Bridges, and
other Heavy Bodies. Dorchester : Simmonds
and Sydenham.

1840. An Investigation of the Laws of Case in Language.
London : Whittaker and Co. Price 2s. 6d.

1841. An Arithmetical and Commercial Dictionary.
London : Whittaker and Co. Price 1s. 6d.

A Pronouncing Dictionary of Geographical Names.

1842: The Elements of Grammar. London : Longmans
and Co.; Whittaker and Co. 1s.

The Elements of Linear Perspective and the Pro-
jections of Shadows, with sixteen diagrams cut
in wood by the author.

1843 to 1849. Reviews of various books in magazines.

1844. Exercises in Practical Science, containing the Main
Principles of Dynamics, Statics, Hydrostatics,
and Hydrodynamics, with fourteen diagrams.
Dorchester : Clark. Small 8vo.

" Sabbath Days " : Six Sacred Songs. Words by
W. Barnes, Music by F. W. Smith. London :
Chappell, 50, New Bond Street.

Poems in the Dorset Dialect, with a Dissertation on
the Folk Speech, and a Glossary of Dorset
Words. Printed by Clark, Dorchester ; published by J. Russell Smith, London. Price
10s. Second Edition printed by Maurice
and Co., published by J. R. Smith ' in
1847. Third Edition printed by Simmonds,
Dorchester. Fourth Edition published by J.
Russell Smith in 1862. Fifth Edition by same
in 1866.

1846. Poems, partly of Rural Life (in national English),
London : J. R. Smith, 4, Old Compton Street.
Price 5s.

1847. Outlines of Geography and Ethnography for Youth.
. Dorchester : Barclay, Cornhill. Price 3s. 6d.

1849. Se Gefylsta : An Anglo-Saxon Delectus. London :
J. Russell Smith. Second Edition in 1866.

Humilis Domus : Some Thoughts on the Abodes,
Life, and Social Condition of the Poor, especially
in Dorsetshire. Pamphlet.

1853 Papers in the *Retrospective Review*. Vol. I. Art. 4.
and "Population and Emigration at the beginning
1854. of the Seventeenth Century" "Anecdota
Literaria," pp. 97 and 201. "Extracts from
the Diary of John Richards, Esq." Art. 11.
"Pyrrhonism of Joseph Glanvill."

Vol. II. (Feb.) Art 6. "Leland the Antiquary."
(May) Art. 5. "Controversial Writers on
Astrology." (Aug.) Art. 3. "Waterhouse and
Fox on the Utility of Learning in the Church."

1854. A Philological Grammar grounded upon English, and
formed from a comparison of more than Sixty
Languages. Being an Introduction to the
Science of Grammar in all Languages, especially
English, Latin, and Greek. 8vo, pp. 312.
London : John Russell Smith. Price 9s.

1858 Hwomely Rhymes. A second collection of Dorset
Poems. London : J. R. Smith. Second Edition.
1863.

Britain and the Ancient Britons. London : J. R.
Smith. Small 8vo. Price 3s.

1859. Views of Labour and Gold. London : J. R. Smith.

The Song of Solomon in the Dorset Dialect. Printed
at the private press of H.R.H. Prince Lucien
Buonaparte.

1862. "Tiw," or a View of the Roots and Stems of the English
as a Teutonic Tongue. London : J. R. Smith.

A A

1861 Papers in *Macmillan's Magazine*—
to   The Beautiful in Nature and Art. May 1861.
1867.   The Rise and Progress of Trial by Jury in Britain.
      ·March 1862.
      The Rariora of Old Poetry. May 1863.
      Plagiarism. November 1866.
      On Bardic Poetry. August 1867.
      Several Poems at different times.
1863. Articles in *Fraser's Magazine*—
      On the Credulity of Old Song, History, and
      Tradition. September 1863.
      Coventry Patmore's Poetry. July 1863.
1863. A Grammar and Glossary of the Dorset Dialect,
      with the History of the Outspreading and
      Bearings of the South-Western English. Pub-
      lished for the Philological Society by A. Asher
      and Co., Berlin.
1863. Third Collection of Poems in Dorset Dialect.
      London : J. R. Smith. Second Edition in
      1870.
      Reviews in the *Reader*—
      Dean Hoare on English Roots and Stems.
      September 1863.
1864.   Coote's Neglected Fact in English History. July
      1864.
      A Guide to Dorchester. Published by Barclay,
      Dorchester.
1865. Paper on Dorset. Read before the British Archæo-
      logical Society at Dorchester. Published in
      their *Transactions*.
1863 Serial Articles in *Ladies' Treasury*—
to   Christian Marriage. 1863.
1867.   Prinking. 1866.
      The House. 1867.

1867. A Glossary and some pieces of verse of the Old Dialect of the English Colony in the Counties of Forth and Bargy. By Jacob Poole. Edited with Introduction and Historical Notes by W. Barnes. London: J. R. Smith. 8vo, cloth. 4s. 6d.

1868. The Church in Ireland. Logical anomalies of the Disendowment. *Dorset County Chronicle.*
The Rating of Tithes. Ditto.
Poems of Rural Life in Common English. London: Macmillan. American Edition, illustrated, published by Roberts Brothers at Boston on December 1st, same year.

1869. Paper on the "Farm Labourer," and Employment of Women and Children in Agriculture. Written for the Government Commission. Printed in the Blue Book, Appendix, Part II., to Second Report.

1869. Early England and the Saxon English. London: J. Russell Smith. Small 8vo. Price 3s.
A Paper on Somerset. Read before the Somerset Archæological Society at Wincanton. Published by F. May, Taunton. Reprinted from the *Proceedings.*

1871. On the Origin of the Hundred and Tithings of English Law. Read before the British Archæological Association at Weymouth. Printed in their *Transactions.*

1878. An Outline of English Speechcraft. London: Kegan Paul and Co. Price 4s.

1879. Poems of Rural Life in the Dorset Dialect. 8vo, pp. 467. Being a collected form, including all the three series previously published. London: Kegan Paul and Co. Price 6s.

1879. An Outline of Redecraft, or Logic. With English
wording. London: Kegan Paul and Co.
Price 3*s*.

1884. Dorset Folk in the Leisure Hour.

1886. A Glossary of Dorset Speech. Partly printed, but
never published, as the author's death prevented the final revisions.

APPENDIX III.

"HAND WRITS" NOT PRINTED.

Version of the Psalms in English measures (metre), un-rhymed, formed upon those of the Hebrew, with some original and other notes. Begun in 1864, finished 1874.

A Second Set of Poems in Common English. Some were printed in *Macmillan's* and the *Leisure Hour*.

Hymns—

On Church Opening.	Marriage.
Harvest Thanksgiving.	Choir Meeting.
Baptism.	School.

Word-building in English.

A Word List of English Words which have heretofore holden or would do instead of others that have been intaken from other tongues. Many of these words are used in "Speechcraft and Redecraft."

A Latin Word Book of Words ranked under their roots or main stemwords. Three upsewings.

Latin Word-building in the Noun and Verb endings.

Angria the Pirate, and the Indian Wars of his time. A Paper meant for the *Retrospective Review*. The *Review* was given up before this was published.

Utilitarianism.   An answer to John Stuart Mill.
Studies in Poetry of less known schools.
Notes on Persian Word-stems.
Notes on the Song of Deborah and Barak.   Judges v.
Notes on the Greek Verbs.
Alphabetical and Etymological Dictionary of the Common
  Names of Animals.
King Arthur, and Welsh Poetry of and since his time.
  Two upsewings.
Notes on the *Goel ha dum* or Redeemer of Blood under the
  Jewish Law.
A Word List of Grammar Terms, outcleared by wording,
  and English words in their stead.
Essay on the Maintenance of the Church of England as an
  Established Church.   Ten upsewings.
Dorset Dialogues.   One upsewing.
Preaching.   One upsewing.
Liturgy.   One upsewing.

THE END.

RICHARD CLAY AND SONS, LONDON AND BUNGAY.

MACMILLAN'S
BIOGRAPHICAL SERIES.

Crown 8vo, uniformly bound. Price 6s. each.

Spinoza: A Study of. By Rev. DR. JAMES MARTINEAU. With a Portrait. Second Edition.

The Life and Work of Mary Carpenter. By J. ESTLIN CARPENTER, M.A. With Steel Portrait.

Catherine and Craufurd Tait, Wife and Son of ARCHIBALD CAMPBELL, Archbishop of Canterbury: A Memoir. Edited, at the request of the Archbishop, by the Rev. W. BENHAM, B.D. With Two Portraits engraved by JEENS. New and Cheaper Edition.

A Record of Ellen Watson. Arranged and Edited by ANNA BUCKLAND. With Portrait.

Henry Bazely, the Oxford Evangelist: A Memoir. By the Rev. E. L. HICKS, M.A., Rector of Fenny Compton; Hon. Canon of Worcester; sometime Fellow and Tutor of Corpus Christi College, Oxford. With a Steel Portrait engraved by STODART.

The Life of Elizabeth Gilbert and Her Work for the Blind. By FRANCES MARTIN, Author of "Angélique Arnauld." With Portrait.

Bernard (St.).—The Life and Times of St. Bernard, Abbot of Clairvaux. By J. C. MORISON, M.A. New Edition.

Charlotte Brontë: A Monograph. By T. WEMYSS REID.

St. Anselm. By the Very Rev. R. W. CHURCH, M.A., Dean of St. Paul's. New Edition.

Great Christians of France: St. Louis and Calvin. By M. GUIZOT, Member of the Institute of France.

Alfred the Great. By THOMAS HUGHES, Q.C.

Biographical Sketches, 1852-75. By HARRIET MARTINEAU. With Four Additional Sketches, and Autobiographical Sketch. Sixth Edition.

Francis of Assisi. By Mrs. OLIPHANT. New Edition.

Victor Emmanuel II., First King of Italy. By G. S. GODKIN. New Edition.

MACMILLAN & CO., LONDON.

MESSRS. MACMILLAN & CO.'S PUBLICATIONS.

The Life of Ralph Waldo Emerson. By J. L. CABOT, his Literary Executor. 2 vols. Crown 8vo. 18s.

Reminiscences. By THOMAS CARLYLE. Edited by CHARLES ELIOT NORTON. 2 vols Crown 8vo. 12s.

Early Letters of Thomas Carlyle. Edited by CHARLES ELIOT NORTON. 2 vols. Vol. I. 1814–1821. Vol. II. 1821–1826. With Two Portraits. Crown 8vo. 18s.

James Fraser, Second Bishop of Manchester: A Memoir (1818-1885). By THOMAS HUGHES, Q.C. With a New Portrait. 8vo. 16s.

Memoirs of Mark Pattison, late Rector of Lincoln College. Crown 8vo. 8s. 6d.

Carlyle, Personally and in his Writings. Two Lectures. By DAVID MASSON, M.A., LL.D. Extra fcap. 8vo. 2s. 6d.

Louis Agassiz: His Life and Correspondence. Edited by ELIZABETH CARY AGASSIZ. 2 vols. Crown 8vo. 18s.

Francis Bacon: An Account of his Life and Works. By EDWIN A. ABBOTT, D.D., Author of "Bacon and Essex." &c. Demy 8vo. 14s.

Memoir of Daniel Macmillan. By THOMAS HUGHES, Q.C., Author of "Tom Brown's School Days," &c. With Portrait. Crown 8vo. 4s. 6d. POPULAR EDITION. Paper Cover. Crown 8vo. 1s.

Annie Keary. A Memoir. By ELIZA KEARY. With a Portrait. Third Thousand. Crown 8vo. 4s. 6d.

Professor Clerk Maxwell, A Life of. With Selections from his Correspondence and Occasional Writings. By LEWIS CAMPBELL. M.A., LL.D., Professor of Greek in the University of St. Andrews, and WILLIAM GARNETT, M.A. New Edition, abridged and revised. Crown 8vo. 7s. 6d.

Modern Guides of English Thought in Matters of Faith: Essays on Some of the. By RICHARD HOLT HUTTON. Globe 8vo. 6s.

Spenser, Wordsworth, and other Studies. A Volume of Collected Essays. By AUBREY DE VERE. 2 vols. Globe 8vo. 12s.

Lectures and Essays. By W. K. CLIFFORD, F.R.S., late Professor of Applied Mathematics and Mechanics at University College, London, and sometime Fellow of Trinity College, Cambridge. Edited by LESLIE STEPHEN and FREDERICK POLLOCK. With an Introduction by F. POLLOCK. Second and Popular Edition. Crown 8vo. 8s. 6d.

Amiel's Journal Intime. Translated from the French, with an Introduction and Notes, by Mrs. HUMPHRY WARD. 2 vols. Globe 8vo. 12s.

Duntzer's Life of Goethe Translated by T. W. LYSTER. With Illustrations. 2 vols. Crown 8vo. 21s.

Duntzer's Life of Schiller. Translated by P. E. PINKERTON. With Illustrations. Crown 8vo. 10s. 6d.

Berlioz, Hector. Autobiography of. Comprising his Travels in Italy, Germany, Russia, and England. Translated entire from the second Paris Edition by RACHEL (Scott-Russell) HOLMES and ELEANOR HOLMES. 2 vols. Crown 8vo. 21s.

Napoleon I., History of. By P. LANFREY. A Translation made with the sanction of the Author. New and Popular Edition. 4 vols. Crown 8vo. 30s.

MACMILLAN & CO., LONDON.

BEDFORD STREET, COVENT GARDEN, LONDON.

September, 1887.

MACMILLAN & *CO.'S CATALOGUE* of *Works in BELLES LETTRES*, *including Poetry*, *Fiction*, *etc.*

ABOUT MONEY; AND OTHER THINGS. A Gift Book. By the Author of "John Halifax, Gentleman." Crown 8vo. 6s.

ADDISON, SELECTIONS FROM. By JOHN RICHARD GREEN, M.A., LL.D. (Golden Treasury Series.) 18mo. 4s. 6d.

ADVENTURES OF A BROWNIE, THE. By the Author of "John Halifax, Gentleman." With Illustrations by Mrs. ALLINGHAM. New Edition. Globe 8vo. 4s. 6d.

ÆSOP.—SOME OF ÆSOP'S FABLES. With Modern Instances shown in Designs by RANDOLPH CALDECOTT. From New Translations by ALFRED CALDECOTT, M.A. The Engraving by J. D. COOPER. Demy 4to. 7s. 6d.

ALEXANDER (C. F.).—THE SUNDAY BOOK OF POETRY FOR THE YOUNG. (Golden Treasury Series.) 18mo. 4s. 6d.

ALICE LEARMONT. A Fairy Tale. By the Author of "John Halifax, Gentleman." With Illustrations by JAMES GODWIN, New Edition, revised. Globe 8vo. 4s. 6d.

ALLINGHAM.—THE BALLAD BOOK. Edited by WILLIAM ALLINGHAM. (Golden Treasury Series.) 18mo. 4s. 6d.

AMIEL.—THE JOURNAL INTIME OF HENRI FREDERIC AMIEL. Translated, with an Introduction and Notes, by Mrs. HUMPHRY WARD. Two Vols. Globe 8vo. 12s.

AN ANCIENT CITY, AND OTHER POEMS.—By A NATIVE OF SURREY. Extra fcap. 8vo. 6s.

AN UNKNOWN COUNTRY. By the Author of "John Halifax, Gentleman." With Illustrations by F. NOEL PATON. Royal 8vo. 7s. 6d.

ANDERSON.—BALLADS AND SONNETS. By ALEXANDER ANDERSON (Surfaceman). Extra fcap. 8vo. 5s.

ARIOSTO.—PALADIN AND SARACEN. Stories from Ariosto. By H. C. HOLLWAY-CALTHROP. With Illustrations by Mrs. ARTHUR LEMON. Crown 8vo. 6s.

ARNOLD.—Works by MATTHEW ARNOLD.
THE POETICAL WORKS OF MATTHEW ARNOLD. Vol. I. EARLY POEMS, NARRATIVE POEMS, AND SONNETS. Vol. II. LYRIC AND ELEGIAC POEMS. Vol. III. DRAMATIC AND LATER POEMS. New and Complete Edition. Three Vols. Crown 8vo. 7s. 6d. each.
SELECTED POEMS OF MATTHEW ARNOLD. With Vignette engraved by C. H. JEENS. (Golden Treasury Series.) 18mo. 4s. 6d.
DISCOURSES IN AMERICA. Crown 8vo. 4s. 6d.

ART AT HOME SERIES.—Edited by W. J. LOFTIE, B.A.
SUGGESTIONS FOR HOUSE DECORATION IN PAINTING, WOODWORK, AND FURNITURE. By RHODA and AGNES GARRETT. With Illustrations. Sixth Thousand. Crown 8vo. 2s. 6d.
MUSIC IN THE HOUSE. By JOHN HULLAH. With Illustrations. Fourth Thousand. Crown 8vo. 2s. 6d.

a

15,000. 9. 87.

ART AT HOME SERIES—*continued.*

THE DINING-ROOM. By MRS. LOFTIE. Illustrated. Fourth Thousand. Crown 8vo. 2s. 6d.

THE BED-ROOM AND BOUDOIR. By LADY BARKER. Illustrated. Fourth Thousand. Crown 8vo. 2s. 6d.

DRESS. By Mrs. OLIPHANT. Illustrated. Crown 8vo. 2s. 6d.

AMATEUR THEATRICALS. By WALTER H. POLLOCK and LADY POLLOCK. Illustrated by KATE GREENAWAY. Crown 8vo. 2s. 6d.

NEEDLEWORK. By ELIZABETH GLAISTER, Author of "Art Embroidery." Illustrated. Crown 8vo. 2s. 6d.

THE MINOR ARTS—PORCELAIN PAINTING, WOOD CARVING, STENCILLING, MODELLING, MOSAIC WORK, &c. By CHARLES G. LELAND. Illustrated. Crown 8vo. 2s. 6d.

THE LIBRARY. By ANDREW LANG. With a Chapter on *English Illustrated Books*, by AUSTIN DOBSON. Illustrated. Crown 8vo. 3s. 6d.

ARTEVELDE—JAMES & PHILIP VON ARTEVELDE. By W. J ASHLEY, B.A., late Scholar of Balliol College, Oxford. Being the Lothian Prize Essay for 1882. Crown 8vo. 6s.

ATKINSON.—AN ART TOUR TO THE NORTHERN CAPITALS OF EUROPE. By J. BEAVINGTON ATKINSON. 8vo. 12s.

AUSTIN.—Works by ALFRED AUSTIN.

SAVONAROLA. A Tragedy. Crown 8vo. 7s. 6d.

SOLILOQUIES IN SONG. Crown 8vo. 6s.

AT THE GATE OF THE CONVENT, and other Poems. Crown 8vo. 6s.

PRINCE LUCIFER. A Poem. Crown 8vo. [*In the press.*

AWDRY.—THE STORY OF A FELLOW SOLDIER. By FRANCES AWDRY. (A Life of Bishop Patteson for the Young.) With a Preface by CHARLOTTE M. YONGE. Globe 8vo. 2s. 6d.

BACON'S ESSAYS. Edited by W. ALDIS WRIGHT. (Golden Treasury Series.) 18mo. 4s. 6d.

BAKER.—Works by Sir SAMUEL BAKER, M.A., F.R.S., F.R.G.S., &c., &c.

CAST UP BY THE SEA; or, THE ADVENTURES OF NED GREY. With Illustrations by HUARD. New Edition. Crown 8vo, cloth gilt. 6s.

TRUE TALES FOR MY GRANDSONS. With Illustrations by W. J. HENNESSY. Crown 8vo. 7s. 6d.

BALLAD BOOK. — CHOICEST ANECDOTES AND SAYINGS. Edited by WILLIAM ALLINGHAM. (Golden Treasury Series.) 18mo. 4s. 6d.

BARKER (LADY).—Works by Lady BARKER (Lady Broome) :

A YEAR'S HOUSEKEEPING IN SOUTH AFRICA. With Illustrations. Cheaper Edition. Crown 8vo. 3s. 6d.

STATION LIFE IN NEW ZEALAND. With Illustrations. Cheaper Edition. Crown 8vo. 3s. 6d.

LETTERS TO GUY. Crown 8vo. 5s.

THE WHITE RAT, and other Stories. Illustrated by W. J. HENNESSY. Globe 8vo. 2s. 6d.

BEESLY.—STORIES FROM THE HISTORY OF ROME. By Mrs. BEESLY. Fcap. 8vo. 2s. 6d.

BERTZ.—THE FRENCH PRISONERS. A Story for Boys. By EDWARD BERTZ. Crown 8vo. 4s. 6d.

BIKÉLAS.—LOUKIS LARAS; or, THE REMINISCENCES OF A CHIOTE MERCHANT DURING THE GREEK WAR OF INDEPENDENCE. From the Greek of D. BIKÉLAS. Translated, with Introduction on the Rise and Development of Modern Greek Literature, by J. GENNADIUS, Chargé d'Affaires at the Greek Legation in London. Crown 8vo. 7s. 6d.

BJÖRNSON.—SYNNÖVE SOLBAKKEN Translated from the Norwegian of BJÖRNSTJERNE BJÖRNSON, by JULIE SUTTER. Crown 8vo. 6s.

BLACK (W.).—THE STRANGE ADVENTURES OF A PHAETON, Illustrated. Crown 8vo. 6s.

A PRINCESS OF THULE. Crown 8vo. 6s.

THE MAID OF KILLEENA, and other Stories. Crown 8vo. 6s.

MADCAP VIOLET. Crown 8vo. 6s.

GREEN PASTURES AND PICCADILLY. Cheaper Edition. Crown 8vo. 6s.

MACLEOD OF DARE. With Illustrations. Cheaper Edition. Crown 8vo. 6s.

WHITE WINGS. A YACHTING ROMANCE. Cheaper Edition. Crown 8vo. 6s.

THE BEAUTIFUL WRETCH : THE FOUR MAC NICOLS: THE PUPIL OF AURELIUS. Cheaper Edition. Crown 8vo. 6s.

SHANDON BELLS. Crown 8vo. Cheaper Edition. 6s.

YOLANDE : THE STORY OF A DAUGHTER. Crown 8vo. 6s.

THE WISE WOMEN OF INVERNESS: a Tale, and other Miscellanies. Crown 8vo. 6s.

JUDITH SHAKESPEARE. New Edition. Crown 8vo. 6s.

WHITE HEATHER. Crown 8vo. 6s.

SABINA ZEMBRA. Three Vols. Crown 8vo. 31s. 6d.

BLACKIE.—Works by JOHN STUART BLACKIE, Emeritus Professor of Greek in the University of Edinburgh :—

THE WISE MEN OF GREECE. In a Series of Dramatic Dialogues. Crown 8vo. 9s.

LAY SERMONS. Crown 8vo. 6s.

GOETHE'S FAUST. Translated into English Verse, with Notes and Preliminary Remarks. By J. STUART BLACKIE, F.R.S.E. Crown 8vo. 9s.

WHAT DOES HISTORY TEACH? Two Edinburgh Lectures. Crown 8vo. 2s. 6d.

MESSIS VITÆ: Gleanings of Song from a Happy Life. Crown 8vo. 4s. 6d.

BRIGHT.—THE ENGLISH FLOWER GARDEN. By HENRY A. BRIGHT. Crown 8vo. 3s. 6d.

a 2

COLQUHOUN.—RHYMES AND CHIMES. By F. S. Colquhoun (née
F. S. Fuller Maitland). Extra fcap. 8vo. 2s. 6d.
CONWAY.—Works by Hugh Conway.
A FAMILY AFFAIR. Crown 8vo. 6s.
LIVING OR DEAD. Crown 8vo. 6s.
CORBETT.—Works by Julian S. Corbett.
THE FALL OF ASGARD. Two Vols. Globe 8vo. 12s.
FOR GOD OR GOLD. Crown 8vo.   [In the press.
CORNWALL, AN UNSENTIMENTAL JOURNEY
THROUGH. By the Author of "John Halifax, Gentleman." With
numerous Illustrations by C. Napier Hemy. Medium 4to. 12s. 6d.
COWPER.—POETICAL WORKS. Edited, with Biographical Introduction,
by Rev. W. Benham, B.D. (Globe Edition.) Globe 8vo. 3s. 6d.
THE TASK: AN EPISTLE TO JOSEPH HILL, Esq.,; TIROCINIUM;
or, a Review of the Schools; and the HISTORY OF JOHN GILPIN.
Edited, with Notes, by William Benham, B.D. (Globe Readings Edition.)
Globe 8vo. 1s.
LETTERS OF WILLIAM COWPER. Edited, with Introduction, by Rev.
William Benham, B.D., F.S.A., Rector of St. Edmund the King, Lombard
Street. 18mo. 4s. 6d. (Golden Treasury Series.)
SELECTIONS FROM COWPER'S POEMS. With an Introduction by Mrs.
Oliphant. 18mo. 4s. 6d. (Golden Treasury Series.)
CRANE.—THE SIRENS THREE. A Poem. Written and Illustrated
by Walter Crane. Royal 8vo. 10s. 6d.
CRANE.—GRIMM'S FAIRY TALES: A Selection from the Household
Stories. Translated from the German by Lucy Crane, and done into Pictures
by Walter Crane. Crown 8vo. 6s.
CRANE (LUCY).—LECTURES ON ART AND THE FORMATION
OF TASTE. By Lucy Crane. With Illustrations by Thomas and Walter
Crane. Crown 8vo. 6s.
CRANE (T. F.)—ITALIAN POPULAR TALES. By Thomas Frederick
Crane, A.M., Professor of the Romance Languages in Cornell University.
Demy 8vo. 14s.
CRAWFORD—Works by F. Marion Crawford.
MR. ISAACS. A Tale of Modern India. Crown 8vo. 4s. 6d.
DOCTOR CLAUDIUS. A True Story. Crown 8vo. 4s. 6d.
A ROMAN SINGER. Crown 8vo. 4s. 6d.
ZOROASTER. Crown 8vo. 6s.
A TALE OF A LONELY PARISH. Crown 8vo. 6s.
MARZIO'S CRUCIFIX. Two Vols. Globe 8vo. 12s.
CUNNINGHAM.—THE CŒRULEANS. A Vacation Idyll. By H. S.
Cunningham, Author of "The Chronicles of Dustypore." New and Cheaper
Edition. Crown 8vo. 6s.
DAGONET THE JESTER.—Crown 8vo. 4s. 6d.
DAHN.—FELICITAS. A Tale of the German Migrations, A.D. 476. By Felix
Dahn. Translated by M. A. C. E. Crown 8vo. 4s. 6d.
DANTE; AN ESSAY. By the Very Rev. R. W. Church, D.C.L., Dean of
St. Paul's. With a Translation of the "De Monarchiâ." By F. J. Church,
Crown 8vo. 6s.
THE "DE MONARCHIA." Separately. 8vo. 4s. 6d.
THE PURGATORY. Edited, with Translation and Notes, by A. J. Butler,
M.A. Crown 8vo. 12s. 6d.
THE PARADISO. Edited, with a Translation and Notes, by A. J. Butler, M.A.
Crown 8vo. 12s. 6d.

DAY.—Works by the Rev. LAL BEHARI DAY:
BENGAL PEASANT LIFE. New Edition. Crown 8vo. 6s.
FOLK-TALES OF BENGAL. Crown 8vo. 4s. 6d.

DAYS WITH SIR ROGER DE COVERLEY. From *The Spectator*. With Numerous Illustrations by HUGH THOMSON. Small 4to. Extra gilt. 6s.

DEMOCRACY—An American Novel. Crown 8vo. 4s. 6d.

DE MORGAN (MARY).—THE NECKLACE OF THE PRINCESS FIORIMONDE, and other Stories. With 25 Illustrations by WALTER CRANE. Extra fcap. 8vo. 6s.

* Also an Edition printed by Messrs. R. and R. Clark, on hand-made paper, the plates, initial letters, head and tail pieces being printed on Indian paper and mounted in the text. Fcap. 4to. THE EDITION IS LIMITED TO ONE HUNDRED COPIES.

DEUTSCHE LYRIK. By Dr. BUCHHEIM. (Golden Treasury Series.) 18mo. 4s. 6d.

DE VERE.—SPENSER, WORDSWORTH, AND OTHER STUDIES. A Volume of Collected Essays. By AUBREY DE VERE. Globe 8vo.
[*In the press.*

DE WINT.—THE LIFE OF PETER DE WINT. By J. COMYNS CARR. Illustrated with 20 Photogravures from the Artist's Work. Medium 4to.
[*In preparation.*

DICKENS (CHARLES).—THE POSTHUMOUS PAPERS OF THE PICKWICK CLUB. By CHARLES DICKENS; with Notes and numerous Illustrations. Edited by CHARLES DICKENS the Younger. In Two Volumes. Extra Crown 8vo. 21s.

DICKENS'S DICTIONARY OF PARIS, 1885. An Unconventional Handbook. With Maps, Plans, &c. 18mo. Paper cover, 1s. Cloth, 1s. 6d.

DICKENS'S DICTIONARY OF LONDON, 1887. (Seventh Year.) An Unconventional Handbook. With Maps, Plans, &c. 18mo. Paper cover, 1s. Cloth, 1s. 6d.

DICKENS'S DICTIONARY OF THE THAMES, 1887. An Unconventional Handbook. With Maps, Plans, &c. Paper cover, 1s. Cloth, 1s. 6d.

DICKENS'S CONTINENTAL A.B.C. RAILWAY GUIDE. Published on the first of each Month. 18mo. 1s.

DICKENS'S DICTIONARY OF THE UNIVERSITY OF OXFORD. 1885-1886. 18mo. paper cover. 1s.

DICKENS'S DICTIONARY OF THE UNIVERSITY OF CAMBRIDGE. 1885-1886. 18mo. paper cover. 1s.

DICKENS'S DICTIONARY OF THE UNIVERSITIES OF OXFORD AND CAMBRIDGE. In One Volume. 18mo. Cloth. 2s. 6d.

DILLWYN (E. A.).—Works by E. A. DILLWYN.
JILL. Crown 8vo. 6s.
JILL AND JACK. 2 vols. Globe 8vo. 12s.

DOYLE.—THE RETURN OF THE GUARDS, and other Poems. By Sir FRANCIS HASTINGS DOYLE, late Fellow of All Souls' College, Oxford. Crown 8vo. 7s. 6d.

DRYDEN.—POETICAL WORKS OF. Edited, with a Memoir, by W. D. CHRISTIE, M.A. (Globe Edition.) Globe 8vo. 3s. 6d.

DUFF (GRANT).—MISCELLANIES, POLITICAL and LITERARY. By the Right Hon. M. E. GRANT DUFF. 8vo. 10s. 6d.

EBERS.—Works by DR. GEORG EBERS.
THE BURGOMASTER'S WIFE; a Tale of the Siege of Leyden. Translated by CLARA BELL. Crown 8vo. 4s. 6d.
ONLY A WORD. Translated by CLARA BELL. Crown 8vo. 4s. 6d.

ELBON;—BETHESDA. By BARBARA ELBON. New Edition. Crown 8vo. 6s.

ELLIS.—SKETCHING FROM NATURE. A Handbook for Students and Amateurs. By TRISTRAM J. ELLIS. With a Frontispiece and 10 Illustrations by H. STACY MARKS, R.A., and 30 Sketches by the Author. New Edition, Enlarged and Revised. Crown 8vo. 3s. 6d.

EMERSON.— THE COLLECTED WORKS OF RALPH WALDO EMERSON. Uniform with the EVERSLEY EDITION of Charles Kingsley's Novels. Globe 8vo., price 5s. each volume.

1. MISCELLANIES. With an Introductory Essay by JOHN MORLEY.
2. ESSAYS.
3. POEMS.
4. ENGLISH TRAITS: AND REPRESENTATIVE MEN.
5. CONDUCT OF LIFE: AND SOCIETY and SOLITUDE.
6. LETTERS: SOCIAL AIMS, &c.

ENGLISH ILLUSTRATED MAGAZINE, THE. Profusely Illustrated. Published Monthly. Number I., October, 1883. Price Sixpence.
YEARLY VOLUME, 1884, consisting of 792 closely-printed pages, and containing 428 Woodcut Illustrations of various sizes. Bound in extra cloth, coloured edges. Royal 8vo. 7s. 6d.
YEARLY VOLUME, 1885. A Handsome Volume, consisting of 840 closely printed pages, containing nearly 500 Woodcut Illustrations of various sizes, bound in extra cloth, coloured edges. Royal 8vo. 8s.
YEARLY VOLUME, 1886. A Handsome Volume, consisting of 840 closely printed pages, containing about 400 Woodcut Illustrations of various sizes bound in extra cloth, coloured edges. Royal 8vo. 8s.
YEARLY VOLUME, 1887. A Handsome Volume, consisting of over 822 closely printed pages, and containing nearly 400 Woodcut Illustrations of various sizes, bound in extra cloth, coloured edges. Royal 8vo. 8s.
Cloth Covers for binding Volumes, 1s. 6d. each.

ENGLISH ILLUSTRATED MAGAZINE, THE. PROOF IMPRESSIONS OF ENGRAVINGS ORIGINALLY PUBLISHED IN THE ENGLISH ILLUSTRATED. In Portfolio. 21s.

ENGLISH MEN OF LETTERS. Edited by JOHN MORLEY. Crown 8vo. 2s. 6d. each.

JOHNSON. By LESLIE STEPHEN.
SCOTT. By R. H. HUTTON.
GIBBON. By J. COTTER MORISON.
SHELLEY. By J. A. SYMONDS.
HUME. By T. H. HUXLEY, F.R.S.
GOLDSMITH. By WILLIAM BLACK.
DEFOE. By W. MINTO.
BURNS. By Principal SHAIRP.
SPENSER. By the Very Rev. R. W. CHURCH, Dean of St. Paul's.
THACKERAY. By ANTHONY TROLLOPE.

BURKE. By JOHN MORLEY.
MILTON. By MARK PATTISON.
HAWTHORNE. By HENRY JAMES.
SOUTHEY. By Professor DOWDEN.
CHAUCER. By A. W. WARD.
COWPER. By GOLDWIN SMITH.
BUNYAN. By J. A. FROUDE.
LOCKE. By Prof. FOWLER.
BYRON. By Prof. NICHOL.
WORDSWORTH. By F. W. H. MYERS.
DRYDEN. By GEORGE SAINTSBURY.

ENGLISH MEN OF LETTERS—*(continued).*

LANDOR. By SIDNEY COLVIN.

DE QUINCEY. By Prof. MASSON.

CHARLES LAMB. By Rev. ALFRED AINGER.

BENTLEY. By Prof. R. C. JEBB.

CHARLES DICKENS. By A. W· WARD.

GRAY. By EDMUND GOSSE.

SWIFT. By LESLIE STEPHEN.

STERNE. By H. D. TRAILL.

MACAULAY. By J. COTTER MORISON.

FIELDING. By AUSTIN DOBSON.

SHERIDAN. By Mrs. OLIPHANT.

ADDISON. By W. J. COURTHOPE.

BACON. By the Very Rev. R. W. CHURCH, Dean of St. Paul's.

COLERIDGE. By H. D. TRAILL.

SIR PHILIP SIDNEY. By JOHN ADDINGTON SYMONDS.

KEATS. By SIDNEY COLVIN.

[Other Volumes to follow.]

Popular Edition. One Shilling Each.

ENGLISH MEN OF LETTERS. Edited by JOHN MORLEY.

Now publishing Monthly. Vols. I.—IX. *ready.* Paper covers, 1*s.* each ; cloth binding, 1*s.* 6*d.*

JOHNSON. By LESLIE STEPHEN.

SCOTT. By R. H. HUTTON.

GIBBON. By J. COTTER MORISON.

HUME. By T. H. HUXLEY, F.R.S.

GOLDSMITH. By WM. BLACK.

SHELLEY. By J. A. SYMONDS.

DEFOE. By W. MINTO.

BURNS. By Principal SHAIRP.

SPENSER. By the Very Rev. R. W. CHURCH, Dean of St. Paul's.

THACKERAY. By ANTHONY TROLLOPE. [*October.*

BURKE. By JOHN MORLEY. [*November.*

MILTON. By MARK PATTISON. [*December.*

[And the rest of the Series in due course.]

ENGLISH STATESMEN.

Under the above title Messrs. MACMILLAN & Co. beg to announce a series of short biographies, not designed to be a complete roll of famous Statesmen, but to present in historic order the lives and work of those leading actors in our affairs who by their direct influence have left an abiding mark on the policy, the institutions, and the position of Great Britain among States.

The following list of subjects is the result of careful selection. The great movements of national history are made to follow one another in a connected course, and the series is intended to form a continuous narrative of English freedom, order, and power. The following Volumes are in preparation :—

WILLIAM THE CONQUEROR. By EDWARD A. FREEMAN, D.C.L., LL.D. [*In the press.*

HENRY II. By Mrs. J. R. GREEN.

EDWARD I. By FREDERICK POLLOCK.

HENRY VII. By J. COTTER MORISON.

WOLSEY. By Prof. M. CREIGHTON.

ELIZABETH. By the Very Rev. the Dean of ST. PAUL'S.

OLIVER CROMWELL. By FREDERIC HARRISON.

WILLIAM III. By H. D. TRAILL.

WALPOLE. By LESLIE STEPHEN.

CHATHAM. By J. A. FROUDE.

PITT. By JOHN MORLEY.

PEEL. By J. R. THURSFIELD.

EVANS.—Works by SEBASTIAN EVANS.

BROTHER FABIAN'S MANUSCRIPT, AND OTHER POEMS. Fcap. 8vo. 6*s.*

IN THE STUDIO: A DECADE OF POEMS. Extra fcap. 8vo. 5*s.*

FAIRY BOOK. By the Author of "John Halifax, Gentleman." (Golden Treasury Series.) 18mo. 4s. 6d.

FAY.—MUSIC STUDY IN GERMANY. From the Home Correspondence of AMY FAY, with a Preface by Sir GEORGE GROVE, D.C.L. Director of the Royal College of Music. Crown 8vo. 4s. 6d.

FINCK.—ROMANTIC LOVE AND PERSONAL BEAUTY: THEIR DEVELOPMENT, CAUSAL RELATION, HISTORIC AND NATIONAL PECULIARITIES. By HENRY T. FINCK. 2 vols. Crown 8vo. 18s.

FLEMING.—Works by GEORGE FLEMING.

VESTIGIA. New Edition. Globe 8vo. 2s.

A NILE NOVEL. New Edition. Globe 8vo. 2s.

MIRAGE. A Novel. New Edition. Globe 8vo. 2s.

THE HEAD OF MEDUSA. New Edition. Globe 8vo. 2s.

FO'C'S'LE YARNS.—Including "BETSY LEE" AND OTHER POEMS. Crown 8vo. 7s. 6d.

FORBES.—SOUVENIRS OF SOME CONTINENTS. By ARCHIBALD FORBES, LL.D. Crown 8vo. 6s.

FOSTER-BARHAM.—THE NIBELUNGEN LIED. Lay of the Nibelung. Translated from the German. By ALFRED G. FOSTER-BARHAM. Crown 8vo. 10s. 6d.

FRASER-TYTLER.—SONGS IN MINOR KEYS. By C. C. FRASER-TYTLER (Mrs. EDWARD LIDDELL). Second Edition. 18mo. 6s.

FREEMAN.—Works by E. A. FREEMAN, D.C.L., LL.D., Regius Professor of Modern History in the University of Oxford.

HISTORICAL AND ARCHITECTURAL SKETCHES; CHIEFLY ITALIAN. With Illustrations by the Author. Crown 8vo. 10s. 6d.

SUBJECT AND NEIGHBOUR LANDS OF VENICE. Being a Companion Volume to "Historical and Architectural Sketches." With Illustrations. Crown 8vo. 10s. 6d.

ENGLISH TOWNS AND DISTRICTS. With Illustrations. 8vo. 14s.

GARNETT. — IDYLLS AND EPIGRAMS. Chiefly from the Greek Anthology. By RICHARD GARNETT. Fcap. 8vo. 2s. 6d.

GEDDES.—FLOSCULI GRAECI BOREALES SIVE ANTHOLOGIA GRAECA ABERDONENSIS. Contexuit GULIELMUS D. GEDDES. Crown 8vo. 6s.

GILMORE.—STORM WARRIORS; or, LIFE-BOAT WORK ON THE GOODWIN SANDS. By the Rev. JOHN GILMORE, M.A., Vicar of St. Luke's, Lower Norwood, Surrey, Author of "The Ramsgate Life-Boat," in "Macmillan's Magazine." Second Edition. Crown 8vo. 6s.

GLOBE LIBRARY.—Globe 8vo. Cloth. 3s. 6d. each.

SHAKESPEARE'S COMPLETE WORKS. Edited by W. G. CLARK, M.A., and W. ALDIS WRIGHT, M.A., of Trinity College, Cambridge, Editors of the "Cambridge Shakespeare." With Glossary.

SPENSER'S COMPLETE WORKS. Edited from the Original Editions and Manuscripts, by R. MORRIS, with a Memoir by J. W. HALES, M.A. With Glossary.

SIR WALTER SCOTT'S POETICAL WORKS. Edited with a Biographical and Critical Memoir by FRANCIS TURNER PALGRAVE, and copious Notes.

GLOBE LIBRARY—*continued.*

COMPLETE WORKS OF ROBERT BURNS.—THE POEMS, SONGS, AND LETTERS, edited from the best Printed and Manuscript Authorities. With Glossarial Index, Notes, and a Biographical Memoir by ALEXANDER SMITH.

ROBINSON CRUSOE. Edited after the Original Editions, with a Biographical Introduction by HENRY KINGSLEY.

GOLDSMITH'S MISCELLANEOUS WORKS. Edited, with Biographical Introduction by Professor MASSON.

POPE'S POETICAL WORKS. Edited, with Notes and Introductory Memoir, by ADOLPHUS WILLIAM WARD, M.A., Fellow of St. Peter's College, Cambridge, and Professor of History in Owens College, Manchester.

DRYDEN'S POETICAL WORKS. Edited, with a Memoir, Revised Text, and Notes, by W. D. CHRISTIE, M.A., of Trinity College, Cambridge.

COWPER'S POETICAL WORKS. Edited, with Notes and Biographical Introduction, by Rev. WILLIAM BENHAM, B.D.

MORTE D'ARTHUR.—SIR THOMAS MALORY'S BOOK OF KING ARTHUR AND OF HIS NOBLE KNIGHTS OF THE ROUND TABLE. The original Edition of CAXTON, revised for Modern Use. With an Introduction by Sir EDWARD STRACHEY, Bart.

THE WORKS OF VIRGIL. Rendered into English Prose, with Introductions, Notes, Running Analysis, and an Index. By JAMES LONSDALE, M.A., late Fellow and Tutor of Balliol College, Oxford, and Classical Professor in King's College, London ; and SAMUEL LEE, M.A., Latin Lecturer at University College, London.

THE WORKS OF HORACE. Rendered into English Prose, with Introductions, Running Analysis, Notes and ¡Index. By JAMES LONSDALE, M.A., and SAMUEL LEE, M.A.

MILTON'S POETICAL WORKS, Edited, with Introductions, by Professor MASSON.

GOETHE AND CARLYLE.—CORRESPONDENCE BETWEEN GOETHE AND CARLYLE. Edited by CHARLES ELIOT NORTON. Crown 8vo. 9s.

GOETHE'S REYNARD THE FOX.—Translated into English Verse by A. DOUGLAS AINSLIE. Crown 8vo. 7s. 6d.

GOETHE'S FAUST. Translated into English Verse, with Notes and Preliminary Remarks, by JOHN STUART BLACKIE, F.R.S.E., Emeritus Professor of Greek in the University of Edinburgh. Crown 8vo. 9s.

GOLDEN TREASURY SERIES.—Uniformly printed in 18mo:, with Vignette Titles by Sir J. E. MILLAIS, R.A., T. WOOLNER, W. HOLMAN HUNT, Sir NOEL PATON, ARTHUR HUGHES, &c. Engraved on Steel by JEENS, STODART, and others. Bound in extra cloth, 4s. 6d. each volume.

THE GOLDEN TREASURY OF THE BEST SONGS AND LYRICAL POEMS IN THE ENGLISH LANGUAGE. Selected and arranged, with Notes, by Prof. FRANCIS TURNER PALGRAVE.

THE CHILDREN'S GARLAND FROM THE BEST POETS. Selected and arranged by COVENTRY PATMORE.

THE BOOK OF PRAISE. From the best English Hymn Writers. Selected and arranged by EARL SELBORNE. *A New and Enlarged Edition.*

THE FAIRY BOOK ; the Best Popular Fairy Stories. Selected and rendered anew by the Author of " John Halifax, Gentleman."

THE BALLAD BOOK. A Selection of the Choicest British Ballads Edited by WILLIAM ALLINGHAM.

THE JEST BOOK. The Choicest Anecdotes and Sayings. Selected and arranged by MARK LEMON.

GOLDEN TREASURY SERIES—*continued.*

BACON'S ESSAYS AND COLOURS OF GOOD AND EVIL. With Notes and Glossarial Index. By W. ALDIS WRIGHT, M.A.

THE PILGRIM'S PROGRESS from this World to that which is to come. By JOHN BUNYAN. Large Paper Edition. Crown 8vo. 7s. 6d.

THE SUNDAY BOOK OF POETRY FOR THE YOUNG. Selected and arranged by C. F. ALEXANDER.

A BOOK OF GOLDEN DEEDS of All Times and All Countries gathered and narrated anew. By the Author of "The Heir of Redclyffe."

THE ADVENTURES OF ROBINSON CRUSOE. Edited from the Original Edition by J. W. CLARK, M.A., Fellow of Trinity College, Cambridge.

THE REPUBLIC OF PLATO. Translated into English, with Notes, by J. Ll. DAVIES, M.A. and D. J. VAUGHAN, M.A.

THE SONG BOOK. Words and Tunes from the best Poets and Musicians. Selected and arranged by JOHN HULLAH, late Professor of Vocal Music in King's College, London.

LA LYRE FRANÇAISE. Selected and arranged, with Notes, by GUSTAVE MASSON, French Master in Harrow School.

TOM BROWN'S SCHOOL DAYS. By AN OLD BOY.

A BOOK OF WORTHIES. Gathered from the Old Histories and written anew by the Author of "The Heir of Redclyffe." With Vignette.

GUESSES AT TRUTH. By TWO BROTHERS. New Edition.

THE CAVALIER AND HIS LADY. Selections from the Works of the First Duke and Duchess of Newcastle. With an Introductory Essay by EDWARD JENKINS, Author of "Ginx's Baby," &c.

SCOTTISH SONG. A Selection of the Choicest Lyrics of Scotland. Compiled and arranged, with brief Notes, by MARY CARLYLE AITKEN.

DEUTSCHE LYRIK. The Golden Treasury of the best German Lyrical Poems, selected and arranged with Notes and Literary Introduction. By Dr. BUCHHEIM.

ROBERT HERRICK.—SELECTIONS FROM THE LYRICAL POEMS OF. Arranged with Notes by Prof. FRANCIS TURNER PALGRAVE.

POEMS OF PLACES. Edited by H. W. LONGFELLOW. England and Wales. Two Vols.

MATTHEW ARNOLD'S SELECTED POEMS.

THE STORY OF THE CHRISTIANS AND MOORS IN SPAIN. By CHARLOTTE M. YONGE. With a Vignette by HOLMAN HUNT.

CHARLES LAMB'S TALES FROM SHAKESPEARE. Edited by ALFRED AINGER, M.A.

WORDSWORTH'S SELECT POEMS. Chosen and Edited, with Preface, by MATTHEW ARNOLD. Also a Large Paper Edition. Crown 8vo. 9s.

SHAKESPEARE'S SONGS AND SONNETS. Edited, with Notes, by Prof. FRANCIS TURNER PALGRAVE.

SELECTIONS FROM ADDISON. Edited by JOHN RICHARD GREEN.

SELECTIONS FROM SHELLEY. Edited by STOPFORD A. BROOKE. Also Large Paper Edition. Crown 8vo. 12s. 6d.

POETRY OF BYRON. Chosen and arranged by MATTHEW ARNOLD. Also a Large Paper Edition. Crown 8vo. 9s.

SIR THOMAS BROWNE'S RELIGIO MEDICI ; Letter to a Friend, &c., and Christian Morals. Edited by W. A. GREENHILL, M.D., Oxon.

MOHAMMAD, THE SPEECHES AND TABLE-TALK OF THE PROPHET. Chosen and Translated by STANLEY LANE-POOLE.

GOLDEN TREASURY SERIES—*continued.*

WALTER SAVAGE LANDOR, Selections from the Writings of. Arranged and Edited by Sidney Colvin.

COWPER—SELECTIONS FROM COWPER'S POEMS. With an Introduction by Mrs. Oliphant.

COWPER.—LETTERS of WILLIAM COWPER. Edited, with Introduction, by the Rev. W. Benham, B.D.

KEATS.—THE POETICAL WORKS OF JOHN KEATS. Reprinted from the Original Editions, with Notes by Prof. Francis Turner Palgrave.

LYRICAL POEMS. By Alfred, Lord Tennyson, Poet Laureate. Selected and Annotated by Prof. Francis Turner Palgrave. Large Paper Edition. 8vo. 9s.

IN MEMORIAM. By Alfred, Lord Tennyson, Poet Laureate. Large Paper Edition. 8vo. 9s.

THE TRIAL AND DEATH OF SOCRATES. Being the Euthyphron, Apology, Crito, and Phaedo of Plato. Translated into English by F. J. Church.

GOLDSMITH.—MISCELLANEOUS WORKS. Edited with Biographical Introduction, by Professor Masson. (Globe Edition.) Globe 8vo. 3s. 6d.

——VICAR OF WAKEFIELD. With a Memoir of Goldsmith by Professor Masson. (Globe Readings Edition.) Globe 8vo. 1s.

GONE TO TEXAS. LETTERS FROM OUR BOYS. Edited, with Preface, by Thomas Hughes, Q.C. Crown 8vo. 4s. 6d.

GRAY.—THE WORKS OF THOMAS GRAY. Edited by Edmund Gosse, Clark Lecturer on English Literature in the University of Cambridge. In Four Vols. Globe 8vo. 20s.

GRAHAM.—KING JAMES I. An Historical Tragedy. By David Graham, Author of "Robert the Bruce." Globe 8vo. 7s.

GRAHAM, J. W.—NEÆRA: a Tale of Ancient Rome. By John W. Graham. New and Cheaper Edition. Crown 8vo. 6s.

GREENWOOD.—THE MOON MAIDEN; and other Stories. By Jessy E. Greenwood. Crown 8vo. 3s. 6d.

GRIMM'S FAIRY TALES. A Selection from the Household Stories. Translated from the German by Lucy Crane, and done into Pictures by Walter Crane. Crown 8vo. 6s.

GUESSES AT TRUTH. By Two Brothers. (Golden Treasury Series.) 18mo. 4s. 6d.

HAMERTON.—Works by P. G. Hamerton.
ETCHING AND ETCHERS. Illustrated with Forty-eight new Etchings. Third Edition, revised. Columbier 8vo.
THE INTELLECTUAL LIFE. With Portrait of Leonardo da Vinci, etched by Leopold Flameng. Second Edition. Crown 8vo. 10s. 6d.
THOUGHTS ABOUT ART. New Edition, Revised, with Notes and Introduction. Crown 8vo. 8s. 6d.
HUMAN INTERCOURSE. Third Thousand. Crown 8vo. 8s. 6d.

HARDY.—Works by Arthur Sherburne Hardy.
BUT YET A WOMAN. A Novel. Crown 8vo. 4s. 6d.
THE WIND OF DESTINY. Two Vols. Globe 8vo. 12s.

HARDY, T.—THE WOODLANDERS. By THOMAS HARDY. Author of "Far from the Madding Crowd." New and Cheaper Edition. Crown 8vo. 6s.

HARMONIA.—By the Author of "Estelle Russell." 3 vols. Crown 8vo. 31s. 6d.

HARRISON (F.).—THE CHOICE OF BOOKS; and other Literary Pieces. Second Edition. By FREDERIC HARRISON. Globe 8vo. 6s.
*** Also an Edition on Hand-made paper, buckram binding. Limited to 250 copies. 8vo. 15s.

HARRISON (JOANNA).—A NORTHERN LILY. Five Years of an Uneventful Life. By JOANNA HARRISON. Three Vols. Crown 8vo. 31s. 6d.

HARTLEY (MRS. NOEL).—Works by Mrs. NOEL HARTLEY.
HOGAN, M.P. Crown 8vo. 6s.
THE HONOURABLE MISS FERRARD. Crown 8vo. 6s.
FLITTERS, TATTERS, AND THE COUNSELLOR: WEEDS, AND OTHER SKETCHES. Crown 8vo. 6s.
CHRISTY CAREW. Crown 8vo. 6s.
ISMAY'S CHILDREN. 3 Vols. Crown 8vo. 31s. 6d.

HAWTHORNE (JULIAN).—THE LAUGHING MILL; and other Stories. By JULIAN HAWTHORNE. Cheaper Edition. Crown 8vo. 6s.

HEINE.—SELECTIONS FROM THE POETICAL WORKS OF HEINRICH HEINE. Translated into English. Crown 8vo. 4s. 6d.
A TRIP TO THE BROCKEN. By HEINRICH HEINE. Translated by R. McLINTOCK. Crown 8vo. 3s. 6d.
IDEAS "BUCH LE GRAND" OF THE REISEBILDER OF HEINRICH HEINE, 1826. A Translation by I. B. Crown 8vo. 3s. 6d.

HERRICK (ROBERT).—SELECTIONS FROM THE LYRICAL POEMS OF. Arranged with Notes by F. T. PALGRAVE. (Golden Treasury Series.) 18mo. 4s. 6d.

HILL.—Works by OCTAVIA HILL.
HOMES OF THE LONDON POOR. Popular Edition. Crown 8vo, sewed. 1s.
OUR COMMON LAND. Consisting of Articles on OPEN SPACES; and on WISE CHARITY. Extra fcap. 8vo. 3s. 6d.

HOBDAY.—VILLA GARDENING. A Handbook for Amateur and Practical Gardeners. By E. HOBDAY, Author of "Cottage Gardening," &c. Extra Crown 8vo. 6s.

HOLLWAY-CALTHROP.—PALADIN AND SARACEN: Stories from Ariosto. By H. C. HOLLWAY-CALTHROP. With Illustrations by Mrs. ARTHUR LEMON, engraved by O. LACOUR. Crown 8vo. 6s.

HOMER.—THE ODYSSEY OF HOMER DONE INTO ENGLISH PROSE. By S. H. BUTCHER, M.A., Professor of Greek in the University of Edinburgh; sometime Fellow and Prælector of University College, Oxford, late Fellow of Trinity College, Cambridge; and A. LANG, M.A., late Fellow of Merton College, Oxford. With Steel Vignette. Seventh and Cheaper Edition. Revised and Corrected. With new Introduction and Additional Notes. Crown 8vo. 4s. 6d.
THE ODYSSEY OF HOMER. Books I.—XII. Translated into English Verse by the Right Hon. the Earl of Carnarvon. Crown 8vo. 7s. 6d.
THE ILIAD OF HOMER. Translated into English Prose. By ANDREW LANG, M.A., WALTER LEAF, M.A., and ERNEST MYERS, M.A. Crown 8vo. 12s. 6d.

HOOPER AND PHILLIPS.—A MANUAL OF MARKS ON POTTERY AND PORCELAIN. A Dictionary of Easy Reference. By W. H. HOOPER and W. C. PHILLIPS. With numerous Illustrations. Second Edition, revised. 16mo. 4s. 6d.

HOPE.—NOTES AND THOUGHTS ON GARDENS AND WOOD-LANDS. Written chiefly for Amateurs. By the late FRANCES JANE HOPE, Wardie Lodge, near Edinburgh. Edited by ANNE J. HOPE JOHNSTONE. Crown 8vo. 6s.

HOPKINS.—Works by ELLICE HOPKINS.
ROSE TURQUAND. A Novel. Cheaper Edition. Crown 8vo. 6s.
AUTUMN SWALLOWS: a Book of Lyrics. Extra fcap. 8vo. 6s.

HOPPUS.—A GREAT TREASON: A Story of the War of Independence. 2 vols. Crown 8vo. 9s.

HORACE. WORD FOR WORD FROM HORACE. The Odes literally versified. By W. T. THORNTON, C.B. Crown 8vo. 7s. 6d.
WORKS OF. Rendered into English Prose by JAMES LONSDALE, M.A. and SAMUEL LEE, M.A. (Globe Edition.) Globe 8vo. 3s. 6d.

HULLAH.—HANNAH TARNE. A Story for Girls. By M. E. HULLAH, Author of " Mr. Greysmith." With Illustrations. New Edition. Globe 8vo. 2s. 6d.

HUNT (HOLMAN).—THE PRE-RAPHAELITE BROTHERHOOD. By W. HOLMAN HUNT. Illustrated by Reproductions from some of Mr. HOLMAN HUNT's drawings and paintings. Crown 8vo. [In the press.

HUNT (W.).—TALKS ABOUT ART. By WILLIAM HUNT. With a Letter by Sir J. E. MILLAIS, Bart., R.A. New Edition. Crown 8vo. 3s. 6d.

HUTTON.—ESSAYS ON RECENT ENGLISH GUIDES IN MATTERS OF FAITH. By R. H. HUTTON, M.A. Globe 8vo. [In the press.

IRVING.—Works by WASHINGTON IRVING.
OLD CHRISTMAS. From the Sketch Book. With upwards of 100 Illustrations by RANDOLPH CALDECOTT, engraved by J. D. COOPER. New Edition. Crown 8vo, cloth elegant. 6s.
    Also with uncut edges, paper label. Crown 8vo. 6s.
    People's Sixpenny Edition. Illustrated. Medium 4to. 6d.
BRACEBRIDGE HALL. With 120 Illustrations by R. CALDECOTT. New Edition. Crown 8vo, cloth gilt. 6s.
    Also with uncut edges, paper label. Crown 8vo. 6s.
    People's Sixpenny Edition. Illustrated. Medium 4to. 6d.
OLD CHRISTMAS AND BRACEBRIDGE HALL. By WASHINGTON IRVING. With Numerous Illustrations by RANDOLPH CALDECOTT. An *Edition de Luxe* on fine Paper. Royal 8vo. 21s.

JACKSON.—RAMONA. A Story. By HELEN JACKSON (H. H.), Author of " Verses," " Bits of Travel." Two Vols. Globe 8vo. 12s.

JAMES.—Works by HENRY JAMES.
THE PORTRAIT OF A LADY. Cheaper Edition. Crown 8vo. 6s.
WASHINGTON SQUARE; THE PENSION BEAUREPAS; A BUNDLE OF LETTERS. Cheaper Edition. Crown 8vo. 6s.
THE EUROPEANS. A Novel. Cheaper Edition. Crown 8vo. 6s.
THE AMERICAN. Cheaper Edition. Crown 8vo. 6s.
DAISY MILLER: AN INTERNATIONAL EPISODE: FOUR MEETINGS. Crown 8vo. 6s.
RODERICK HUDSON. Crown 8vo. 6s.
THE MADONNA OF THE FUTURE; and other Tales. Crown 8vo. 6s.
FRENCH POETS AND NOVELISTS. New Edition. Crown 8vo. 4s. 6d.
PORTRAITS OF PLACES. Crown 8vo. 7s. 6d.
TALES OF THREE CITIES. Crown 8vo. 4s. 6d.
STORIES REVIVED. Two Series. Crown 8vo. 6s. each.
THE BOSTONIANS. Crown 8vo. 6s.
THE PRINCESS CASAMASSIMA. Crown 8vo. 6s.

JAMES.—NOVELS AND TALES. By HENRY JAMES.

18mo, 2s. each volume.

THE PORTRAIT OF A LADY. 3 vols.
RODERICK HUDSON. 2 vols.
THE AMERICAN. 2 vols.
WASHINGTON SQUARE. 1 vol.
THE EUROPEANS. 1 vol.
CONFIDENCE. 1 vol.
THE SIEGE OF LONDON: MADAME DE MAUVES. 1 vol.
AN INTERNATIONAL EPISODE:

THE PENSION BEAUREPAS:
THE POINT OF VIEW. 1 vol.
DAISY MILLER, A STUDY: FOUR MEETINGS: LONGSTAFF'S MARRIAGE: BENVOLIO. 1 vol.
THE MADONNA OF THE FUTURE: A BUNDLE OF LETTERS; THE DIARY OF A MAN OF FIFTY: EUGENE PICKERING.

JOUBERT.—PENSÉES OF JOUBERT. Selected and Translated with the Original French appended, by HENRY ATTWELL, Knight of the Order of the Oak Crown. Crown 8vo. 5s.

KEARY (A.).—Works by ANNIE KEARY.
CASTLE DALY: THE STORY OF AN IRISH HOME THIRTY YEARS AGO. New Edition. Crown 8vo. 6s.
JANET'S HOME. New Edition. Globe 8vo. 2s.
CLEMENCY FRANKLYN. New Edition. Crown 8vo. 6s.
OLDBURY. New and Cheaper Edition. Crown 8vo. 6s.
A YORK AND A LANCASTER ROSE. Crown 8vo. 6s.
A DOUBTING HEART. New Edition. Crown 8vo. 6s.
THE HEROES OF ASGARD. Globe 8vo. 2s. 6d.

KEARY (E.).—Works by ELIZA KEARY.
THE MAGIC VALLEY: or, PATIENT ANTOINE. With Illustrations by E. V. B. Globe 8vo. gilt. 4s. 6d.

KEATS.—THE POETICAL WORKS OF JOHN KEATS. Reprinted from the Original Editions, with Notes by Professor FRANCIS T. PALGRAVE. 18mo. 4s. 6d. (Golden Treasury Series).

KINGSLEY'S (CHARLES) NOVELS AND POEMS.— EVERSLEY EDITION.

WESTWARD HO! 2 Vols. Globe 8vo. 10s.
TWO YEARS AGO. 2 Vols. Globe 8vo. 10s.
HYPATIA. 2 Vols. Globe 8vo. 10s.
YEAST. 1 Vol. Globe 8vo. 5s.
ALTON LOCKE. 2 Vols. Globe 8vo. 10s.
HEREWARD THE WAKE. 2 Vols. Globe 8vo. 10s.
POEMS. Two Vols. Globe 8vo. 10s.

KINGSLEY.—Works by the Rev. CHARLES KINGSLEY, M.A., late Rector of Eversley, and Canon of Westminster. Collected Edition. 6s. each.
POEMS; including the Saint's Tragedy, Andromeda, Songs, Ballads, &c. Complete Collected Edition.
YEAST; a Problem.
ALTON LOCKE. New Edition. With a Prefatory Memoir by THOMAS HUGHES, Q.C., and Portrait of the Author.
HYPATIA; or, NEW FOES WITH AN OLD FACE.
GLAUCUS; or, THE WONDERS OF THE SEA-SHORE. With Coloured Illustrations.
WESTWARD HO! or, THE VOYAGES AND ADVENTURES OF SIR AMYAS LEIGH.
THE HEROES; or, GREEK FAIRY TALES FOR MY CHILDREN. With Illustrations.
TWO YEARS AGO.
THE WATER BABIES. A Fairy Tale for a Land Baby. With Illustrations by Sir NOEL PATON, R.S.A., and P. SKELTON.

KINGSLEY (CHARLES)—*continued.*
THE ROMAN AND THE TEUTON. A Series of Lectures delivered before the University of Cambridge. With Preface by Professor MAX MÜLLER.
HEREWARD THE WAKE—LAST OF THE ENGLISH.
THE HERMITS.
MADAM HOW AND LADY WHY; or, FIRST LESSONS IN EARTH LORE FOR CHILDREN.
AT LAST; A CHRISTMAS IN THE WEST INDIES. Illustrated.
PROSE IDYLLS. NEW AND OLD.
PLAYS AND PURITANS; and other HISTORICAL ESSAYS. With Portrait of Sir WALTER RALEIGH.
HISTORICAL LECTURES AND ESSAYS.
SANITARY AND SOCIAL LECTURES AND ESSAYS.
SCIENTIFIC LECTURES AND ESSAYS.
LITERARY AND GENERAL LECTURES.

HEALTH AND EDUCATION. New Edition. Crown 8vo. 6s.
SELECTIONS FROM SOME OF THE WRITINGS OF THE REV. CHARLES KINGSLEY. Crown 8vo. 6s.
OUT OF THE DEEP. Words for the Sorrowful, from the writings of CHARLES KINGSLEY. Extra fcap. 8vo. 3s. 6d.
DAILY THOUGHTS SELECTED FROM THE WRITINGS OF CHARLES KINGSLEY. By His WIFE. Crown 8vo. 6s.
THE WATER BABIES: A Fairy Tale for a Land Baby. With One Hundred Illustrations by LINLEY SAMBOURNE. Fcap. 4to. 12s. 6d.
GLAUCUS; or THE WONDERS OF THE SHORE. With coloured Illustrations. Extra cloth. Gilt edges. (Gift-book Edition.) Crown 8vo. 7s. 6d.
THE HEROES; or, GREEK FAIRY TALES FOR MY CHILDREN. With Illustrations. Extra Cloth. Gilt Edges. (Gift-book Edition.) Crown 8vo. 7s. 6d.

KINGSLEY (H.).—TALES OF OLD TRAVEL. Re-narrated by HENRY KINGSLEY. With Eight full-page Illustrations by HUARD. New Edition. Crown 8vo, cloth, extra gilt. 5s.

KING ARTHUR: NOT A LOVE STORY.—By the Author of "John Halifax, Gentleman," "Miss Tommy," etc. Crown 8vo. 6s.

LAMB.—Works by CHARLES LAMB. Edited by ALFRED AINGER, M.A.
TALES FROM SHAKESPEARE. Edited, with Preface, by ALFRED AINGER, M.A. Globe 8vo, 5s. Golden Treasury Edition. 18mo. 4s. 6d. Globe Readings Edition for Schools. Globe 8vo, 2s.
ESSAYS OF ELIA. Edited, with Introduction and Notes, by ALFRED AINGER, M.A. Globe 8vo 5s.
POEMS, PLAYS, AND MISCELLANEOUS ESSAYS, &c. Edited by ALFRED AINGER, M.A. Globe 8vo. 5s.
MRS. LEICESTER'S SCHOOL; The Adventures of Ulysses; and other Essays. Edited by ALFRED AINGER, M.A. Globe 8vo. 5s.
LETTERS OF CHARLES LAMB. Edited by ALFRED AINGER, M.A. 2 vols. Globe 8vo. 5s. each. [*Immediately.*]

LANDOR (WALTER SAVAGE).—SELECTIONS FROM THE WRITINGS OF WALTER SAVAGE LANDOR. Arranged and Edited by SIDNEY COLVIN. With Portrait. 18mo. 4s. 6d. (Golden Treasury Series.)

LAWLESS.—A MILLIONAIRE'S COUSIN. By the Hon. EMILY LAWLESS, Author of "A Chelsea Householder." Crown 8vo. 6s.

b

LECTURES ON ART.—Delivered in Support of the Society for Protection of Ancient Buildings. By REGD. STUART POOLE, Professor W. B. RICHMOND, E. J. POYNTER, R.A., J. T. MICKLETHWAITE, and WILLIAM MORRIS. Crown 8vo. 4*s.* 6*d.*

LEMON (MARK).—THE JEST BOOK. The Choicest Anecdotes and Sayings. Selected and Arranged by MARK LEMON. (Golden Treasury Series.) 18mo. 4*s.* 6*d.*

LITTLE LAME PRINCE, THE, AND HIS TRAVEL-LING CLOAK.—A Parable for Old and Young. By the Author of "John Halifax, Gentleman." With 24 Illustrations, by J. McRALSTON. Cr. 8vo. 4*s.* 6*d.*

LITTLE PILGRIM, A, IN THE UNSEEN. Crown 8vo. 2*s.* 6*d.*

LITTLE ESTELLA, and other FAIRY TALES FOR THE YOUNG. 18mo, cloth extra. 2*s.* 6*d.*

LITTLE SUNSHINE'S HOLIDAY.—By the Author of "John Halifax, Gentleman." With Illustrations. Globe 8vo. 2*s.* 6*d.*

LOWELL.—Works by JAMES RUSSELL LOWELL.
COMPLETE POETICAL WORKS. With Portrait, engraved by JEENS. 18mo, cloth extra. 4*s.* 6*d.*
DEMOCRACY : and other Addresses. Crown 8vo. 5*s.*

LUBBOCK.—THE PLEASURES OF LIFE. By SIR JOHN LUBBOCK, Bart., M.P., F.R.S., LL.D., D C.L. Second Edition. Fcap. 8vo. 3*s.* 6*d.*

MACLAREN.—THE FAIRY FAMILY. A Series of Ballads and Metrical Tales illustrating the Fairy Mythology of Europe. By ARCHIBALD MACLAREN. With Frontispiece, Illustrated Title, and Vignette. Crown 8vo, gilt. 5*s.*

MACMILLAN.—MEMOIR OF DANIEL MACMILLAN. By THOMAS HUGHES, Q.C. With a Portrait engraved on Steel by C. H. JEENS, from a Painting by LOWES DICKINSON. Fifth Thousand. Crown 8vo. 4*s.* 6*d.* Popular Edition, Paper Covers, 1*s.*

MACMILLAN'S BOOKS FOR THE YOUNG.—In Globe 8vo, cloth elegant. Illustrated, 2*s.* 6*d.* each :—

WANDERING WILLIE. By the Author of "Conrad the Squirrel." With a Frontispiece by Sir NOEL PATON.

THE WHITE RAT, AND OTHER STORIES. By LADY BARKER. With Illustrations by W. J. HENNESSY.

PANSIE'S FLOUR BIN. By the Author of "When I was a Little Girl." With Illustrations by ADRIAN STOKES.

MILLY AND OLLY; or, A Holiday among the Mountains. By Mrs. T. H. WARD. With Illustrations by Mrs. ALMA TADEMA.

THE HEROES OF ASGARD; Tales from Scandinavian Mythology. By A. and E. KEARY.

WHEN I WAS A LITTLE GIRL. By the Author of "St. Olave's," "Nine Years Old," &c.

NINE YEARS OLD. By the Author of "When I was a Little Girl."

THE STORY OF A FELLOW SOLDIER. By FRANCES AWDRY. (A Life of Bishop Patteson for the Young.) With Preface by CHARLOTTE M. YONGE.

AGNES HOPETOUN'S SCHOOLS AND HOLIDAYS. By Mrs. OLIPHANT.

RUTH AND HER FRIENDS. A Story for Girls.

THE RUNAWAY. By the Author of "Mrs. Jerningham's Journal."

OUR YEAR. A Child's Book in Prose and Verse. By the Author of "John Halifax, Gentleman."

LITTLE SUNSHINE'S HOLI-DAY. By the Author of "John Halifax, Gentleman."

A STOREHOUSE OF STORIES. Edited by CHARLOTTE M. YONGE, Author of "The Heir of Redclyffe." Two Vols.

HANNAH TARNE. By MARY E. HULLAH. With Illustrations by W. J. HENNESSY.

MACMILLAN'S BOOKS FOR THE YOUNG—*continued.*

By Mrs. Molesworth.

With Illustrations by WALTER CRANE. Globe 8vo. 2s. 6d. each.

"CARROTS"; JUST A LITTLE BOY.
A CHRISTMAS CHILD.
THE TAPESTRY ROOM.
GRANDMOTHER DEAR.

THE CUCKOO CLOCK.
TELL ME A STORY.
ROSY.
THE ADVENTURES OF HERR BABY.

MACMILLAN'S MAGAZINE.—Published Monthly. Price 1s. Vols.

I. to LVI. are now ready. Medium 8vo. 7s. 6d. each.

MACMILLAN'S POPULAR NOVELS.— In Crown 8vo, cloth.

Price 6s. each Volume :—

By William Black.

A PRINCESS OF THULE.
MADCAP VIOLET.
THE MAID OF KILLEENA; and other Tales.
THE STRANGE ADVENTURES OF A PHAETON. Illustrated.
GREEN PASTURES AND PICCADILLY.
MACLEOD OF DARE. Illustrated.
WHITE WINGS. A Yachting Romance.

THE BEAUTIFUL WRETCH:
THE FOUR MAC NICOLS:
THE PUPIL OF AURELIUS.
SHANDON BELLS.
YOLANDE.
JUDITH SHAKESPEARE.
THE WISE WOMEN OF INVERNESS; A Tale; and other Miscellanies.
WHITE HEATHER.

By Charles Kingsley.

TWO YEARS AGO.
"WESTWARD HO!"
ALTON LOCKE. With Portrait.

HYPATIA.
YEAST.
HEREWARD THE WAKE.

By the Author of "John Halifax, Gentleman."

THE HEAD OF THE FAMILY. Illustrated.
MY MOTHER AND I. Illustrated.
THE OGILVIES. Illustrated.
AGATHA'S HUSBAND. Illustrated.

OLIVE. Illustrated.
MISS TOMMY A Mediæval Romance. Illustrated.
KING ARTHUR: not a Love Story.

By Charlotte M. Yonge.

THE HEIR OF REDCLYFFE. With Illustrations.
HEARTSEASE. With Illustrations.
THE DAISY CHAIN. With Illustrations.
THE TRIAL: More Links in the Daisy Chain. With Illustrations.
HOPES AND FEARS. Illustrated.
DYNEVOR TERRACE. With Illustrations.
MY YOUNG ALCIDES. Illustrated.
THE PILLARS OF THE HOUSE. Two Vols. Illustrated.
CLEVER WOMAN OF THE FAMILY. Illustrated.
THE YOUNG STEPMOTHER. Illustrated.
THE DOVE IN THE EAGLE'S NEST. Illustrated.
THE CAGED LION Illustrated.

THE CHAPLET OF PEARLS. Illustrated.
LADY HESTER, and THE DANVERS PAPERS. Illustrated.
THE THREE BRIDES. Illustrated.
MAGNUM BONUM. Illustrated.
LOVE AND LIFE. Illustrated.
UNKNOWN TO HISTORY. Illustrated.
STRAY PEARLS. Illustrated.
THE ARMOURER'S PRENTICES. Illustrated.
NUTTIE'S FATHER. Illustrated.
THE TWO SIDES OF THE SHIELD. Illustrated.
SCENES AND CHARACTERS. Illustrated.
CHANTRY HOUSE.
A MODERN TELEMACHUS.

b 2

MACMILLAN'S POPULAR NOVELS—*continued.*

By Annie Keary.

CASTLE DALY.
OLDBURY.
CLEMENCY FRANKLYN.

A YORK AND A LANCASTER ROSE.
A DOUBTING HEART.

By Henry James.

THE EUROPEANS.
THE AMERICAN.
DAISY MILLER: AN INTERNATIONAL EPISODE: FOUR MEETINGS.
RODERICK HUDSON.
THE MADONNA OF THE FUTURE, and other Tales.

WASHINGTON SQUARE: THE PENSION BEAUREPAS: A BUNDLE OF LETTERS.
THE PORTRAIT OF A LADY.
STORIES REVIVED. Two Series, 6s. each.
THE BOSTONIANS.
THE PRINCESS CASAMASSIMA.

By Mrs. Oliphant.

HESTER.
THE WIZARD'S SON.
A BELEACUERED CITY.

SIR TOM.
A COUNTRY GENTLEMAN.

By F. Marion Crawford.

A TALE OF A LONELY PARISH. | ZOROASTER.

By Hugh Conway.

LIVING OR DEAD. | A FAMILY AFFAIR.

By J. Henry Shorthouse.

JOHN INGLESANT. | SIR PERCIVAL: a Story of the Past and of the Present.

TOM BROWN'S SCHOOL DAYS.
TOM BROWN AT OXFORD.
REALMAH. By the Author of "Friends in Council."
ROSE TURQUAND. By ELLICE HOPKINS.
OLD SIR DOUGLAS. By the Hon. Mrs. NORTON.
THE LAUGHING MILL; and other Tales. By JULIAN HAWTHORNE.
THE HARBOUR BAR.
BENGAL PEASANT LIFE. By LAL BEHARI DAY.
VIRGIN SOIL. By TOURGÉNIEF.
VIDA. The Study of a Girl. By AMY DUNSMUIR.
MISS BRETHERTON. By Mrs. HUMPHRY WARD.

JILL. By E. A. DILLWYN.
BETHESDA. By BARBARA ELBON.
A MILLIONAIRE'S COUSIN. By the Hon. EMILY LAWLESS.
MITCHELHURST PLACE. By MARGARET VELEY.
THE STORY OF CATHERINE. By ASHFORD OWEN.
NEÆRA : A TALE OF ANCIENT ROME. By J. W. GRAHAM.
MY FRIEND JIM. By W. E. NORRIS.
AUNT RACHEL. By D. CHRISTIE MURRAY.
THE CÆRULEANS. By H. S. CUNNINGHAM.
THE WOODLANDERS. By THOMAS HARDY.

MACMILLAN'S TWO SHILLING NOVELS :—

By the Author of "John Halifax, Gentleman."

THE OGILVIES.
THE HEAD OF THE FAMILY.
OLIVE.

AGATHA'S HUSBAND.

TWO MARRIAGES.

MACMILLAN'S TWO SHILLING NOVELS—*continued.*

By Mrs. Oliphant.

THE CURATE IN CHARGE.
A SON OF THE SOIL.
YOUNG MUSGRAVE.

HE THAT WILL NOT WHEN HE MAY.

PATTY.

By Mrs. Macquoid.

By George Fleming.

A NILE NOVEL.
THE HEAD OF MEDUSA.

MIRAGE.
VESTIGIA.

By the Author of "Hogan, M.P."

HOGAN, M.P.

THE HONOURABLE MISS FER-
RARD.

FLITTERS, TATTERS, AND
THE COUNSELLOR: WEEDS,
AND OTHER SKETCHES.
CHRISTY CAREW.

By Frances H. Burnett.

HAWORTH'S
"LOUISIANA" and "THAT LASS O' LOWRIE'S." Two Stories.
Illustrated.

JANET'S HOME.

By Annie Keary.

A SLIP IN THE FENS.

MACQUOID.—PATTY. By KATHARINE S. MACQUOID. Globe 8vo. 2s.

MADAME TABBY'S ESTABLISHMENT.—By KARI. With
Illustrations. Crown 8vo. 4s. 6d.

MADOC.—Works by FAYR MADOC.
THE STORY OF MELICENT. Crown 8vo. 4s. 6d.
MARGARET JERMINE. 3 vols. Crown 8vo. 31s. 6d.

MAGUIRE.—YOUNG PRINCE MARIGOLD, AND OTHER FAIRY
STORIES. By the late JOHN FRANCIS MAGUIRE, M.P. Illustrated by S. E.
WALLER. Globe 8vo, gilt. 4s. 6d.

MAHAFFY.—Works by J. P. MAHAFFY, M.A. Fellow of Trinity College,
Dublin:—
SOCIAL LIFE IN GREECE FROM HOMER TO MENANDER. Fifth
Edition, enlarged, with New Chapter on Greek Art. Crown 8vo. 9s.
GREEK LIFE AND THOUGHT FROM THE MACEDONIAN TO THE
ROMAN CONQUEST. Crown 8vo *[In the press.*
RAMBLES AND STUDIES IN GREECE. Illustrated. Third Edition,
revised and enlarged, with Map. Crown 8vo. 10s. 6d.
THE DECAY OF MODERN PREACHING. An Essay. Crown 8vo. 3s. 6d.
THE ART OF CONVERSATION. Crown 8vo. *[In the press.*

MALET.—MRS. LORIMER. A Novel. By LUCAS MALET. Cheaper
Edition. Crown 8vo. 4s. 6d.

MASSON (GUSTAVE)—LA LYRE FRANÇAISE. Selected and
arranged with Notes. (Golden Treasury Series.) 18mo. 4s. 6d.

MASSON (Mrs.).—THREE CENTURIES OF ENGLISH POETRY: being selections from Chaucer to Herrick, with Introductions and Notes by Mrs. MASSON and a general Introduction by Professor MASSON. Extra fcap. 8vo. 3s. 6d.

MASSON (Professor).—Works by DAVID MASSON, M.A., Professor of Rhetoric and English Literature in the University of Edinburgh.
WORDSWORTH, SHELLEY, KEATS, AND OTHER ESSAYS. Crown 8vo. 5s.
CHATTERTON: A Story of the Year 1770. Crown 8vo. 5s.
THE THREE DEVILS: LUTHER'S, MILTON'S AND GOETHE'S; and other Essays. Crown 8vo. 5s.

MAURICE.—LETTERS FROM DONEGAL IN 1886. By a LADY "FELON." Edited by COLONEL MAURICE, Professor of Military History, Royal Staff College, Crown 8vo. 1s.

MAZINI.—IN THE GOLDEN SHELL: A Story of Palermo. By LINDA MAZINI. With Illustrations. Globe 8vo, cloth gilt. 4s. 6d.

MEREDITH.—Works by GEORGE MEREDITH.
POEMS AND LYRICS OF THE JOY OF EARTH. Extra Fcap. 8vo. 6s.
BALLADS AND POEMS OF TRAGIC LIFE. Crown 8vo. 6s.

MILTON'S POETICAL WORKS. Edited with Text collated from the best Authorities, with Introductions and Notes, by DAVID MASSON. With three Portraits engraved by JEENS. Fcap. 8vo Edition. Three Vols. 15s. (Globe Edition.) By the same Editor. Globe 8vo. 3s. 6d.

MINCHIN.—NATURÆ VERITAS. By GEORGE M. MINCHIN, M.A., Professor of Applied Mathematics in the Royal Indian Engineering College, Coopers Hill. Fcp. 8vo. 2s. 6d.

MINIATURE ART, A HISTORY OF. By AN AMATEUR. With Illustrations. 4to. *[In the press.*

MISS TOMMY. A Mediæval Romance. By the Author of "John Halifax, Gentleman." Illustrated by F. NOEL PATON. Crown 8vo. 6s.

MITFORD (A. B.).—TALES OF OLD JAPAN. By A. B. MITFORD, Second Secretary to the British Legation in Japan. With Illustrations drawn and cut on Wood by Japanese Artists. New and Cheaper Edition. Crown 8vo. 6s.

MIZ MAZE, THE; OR, THE WINKWORTH PUZZLE. A Story in Letters by Nine Authors. Crown 8vo. 4s. 6d.
The following Writers contribute to the Volume :—Miss Frances Awdry, Miss M. Bramston, Miss Christabel R. Coleridge, Miss A. E. Anderson Morshead, Miss C. M. Yonge, Miss F. M. Peard, Miss Mary S. Lee, Miss Eleanor Price, and Miss Florence Wilford.

MOHAMMAD, SPEECHES AND TABLE-TALK OF THE PROPHET. Chosen and Translated by STANLEY LANE-POOLE. 18mo. 4s. 6d. (Golden Treasury Series.)

MOLESWORTH.—Works by Mrs. MOLESWORTH (ENNIS GRAHAM).
US: AN OLD-FASHIONED STORY. With Illustrations by WALTER CRANE. Crown 8vo. 4s. 6d.
TWO LITTLE WAIFS. Illustrated by WALTER CRANE. Crown 8vo. 4s. 6d.
ROSY. Illustrated by WALTER CRANE. Globe 8vo. 2s. 6d.
SUMMER STORIES FOR BOYS AND GIRLS. Crown 8vo. 4s. 6d.
THE ADVENTURES OF HERR BABY. Illustrated by WALTER CRANE. Globe 8vo. 2s. 6d.
GRANDMOTHER DEAR. Illustrated by WALTER CRANE. Globe 8vo. 2s. 6d.
THE TAPESTRY ROOM. Illustrated by WALTER CRANE. Globe 8vo. 2s. 6d.
A CHRISTMAS CHILD. Illustrated by WALTER CRANE. Globe 8vo. 2s. 6d.

MOLESWORTH.—Works by Mrs. MOLESWORTH (ENNIS GRAHAM)—*continued.*

CHRISTMAS-TREE LAND. Illustrated by WALTER CRANE. Crown 8vo. 4*s*. 6*d*.

TELL ME A STORY. Illustrated by WALTER CRANE. Globe 8vo. 2*s*. 6*d*.

"CARROTS": JUST A LITTLE BOY. Illustrated by WALTER CRANE. New Edition. Globe 8vo. 2*s*. 6*d*.

THE CUCKOO CLOCK. Illustrated by WALTER CRANE. New Edition. Globe 8vo. 2*s*. 6*d*.

FOUR WINDS FARM. With Illustrations by WALTER CRANE. Crown 8vo. 4*s*. 6*d*.

PEGGY. With Illustrations by WALTER CRANE. Crown 8vo. 4*s*. 6*d*.
[*In the press.*

MORISON.—THE PURPOSE OF THE AGES. By JEANIE MORISON. With a Preface by Professor A. H. SAYCE, of Oxford. Crown 8vo. 9*s*.

MORLEY.—WORKS BY JOHN MORLEY.

THE COLLECTED WORKS OF JOHN MORLEY. A New Edition. In 9 vols. Globe 8vo. 5*s*. each.
VOLTAIRE. One Vol.
ROUSSEAU. Two Vols.
DIDEROT AND THE ENCYCLOPÆDISTS. Two Vols.

ON COMPROMISE. New and Revised Edition.
MISCELLANIES. Three Vols.
ON THE STUDY OF LITERATURE. Crown 8vo. 1*s*. 6*d*.

MORTE D'ARTHUR.—SIR THOMAS MALORY'S BOOK OF KING ARTHUR AND OF HIS NOBLE KNIGHTS OF THE ROUND TABLE. (Globe Edition.) Globe 8vo. 3*s*. 6*d*.

MOULTON.—SWALLOW FLIGHTS. Poems by LOUISE CHANDLER MOULTON. Extra fcap. 8vo. 4*s*. 6*d*.

MOULTRIE.—POEMS by JOHN MOULTRIE. Complete Edition. Two Vols. Crown 8vo. 7*s*. each.
Vol. I. MY BROTHER'S GRAVE, DREAM OF LIFE, &c. With Memoir by the Rev. Prebendary COLERIDGE.
Vol. II. LAYS OF THE ENGLISH CHURCH, and other Poems. With notices of the Rectors of Rugby, by M. H. BLOXHAM, F.R.A.S.

MUDIE.—STRAY LEAVES. By C. E. MUDIE. New Edition. Extra fcap. 8vo. 3*s*. 6*d*. Contents:—" His and Mine "—" Night and Day "—"One of Many," &c.

MURRAY.—ROUND ABOUT FRANCE. By E. C. GRENVILLE MURRAY. Crown 8vo. 7*s*. 6*d*.

MURRAY.—AUNT RACHEL: A Rustic Sentimental Comedy. By D. CHRISTIE MURRAY, Author of "Joseph's Coat." New and Cheaper Edition. Crown 8vo. 6*s*.

MUSIC.—A DICTIONARY OF MUSIC AND MUSICIANS (A.D. 1450-1886). By Eminent Writers, English and Foreign. With Illustrations and Woodcuts. Edited by Sir GEORGE GROVE, D.C.L., Director of the Royal College of Music. 8vo. Parts I. to XIV., XIX. to XXII., 3*s*. 6*d*. each. Parts XV. and XVI., 7*s*. Part XVII. and XVIII., 7*s*.

Vols. I., II., and III. 8vo. 21*s*. each.

Vol. I.—A to IMPROMPTU.

Vol. II.—IMPROPERIA to PLAIN SONG.
Vol. III.—PLANCHE to SUMER IS ICUMEN IN.

Cloth cases for binding Vols. I., II., and III., 1*s*. each.

MYERS (ERNEST).—Works by ERNEST MYERS, M.A.

THE PURITANS. Extra fcap. 8vo. 2s. 6d.

POEMS. Extra fcap. 8vo. 4s. 6d.

THE EXTANT ODES OF PINDAR. Translated into English, with Introduction and Short Notes, by ERNEST MYERS. Second Edition. Crown 8vo. 5s.

THE JUDGMENT OF PROMETHEUS, AND OTHER POEMS. Extra Fcap. 8vo. 3s. 6d.

MYERS (F. W. H.).—Works by F. W. H. MYERS, M.A.

ST. PAUL. A Poem. New Edition Extra fcap. 8vo. 2s. 6d.

THE RENEWAL OF YOUTH, and other Poems. Crown 8vo. 7s. 6d.

ESSAYS. 2 Vols. I. Classical. II. Modern. Crown 8vo. 4s. 6d. each.

WORDSWORTH (English Men of Letters Series). Crown 8vo. 2s. 6d.

NADAL.—ESSAYS AT HOME AND ELSEWHERE. By E. S. NADAL. Crown 8vo. 6s.

NEW ANTIGONE, THE. A Romance. 3 vols. Crown 8vo. 31s. 6d.

NINE YEARS OLD.—By the Author of "St. Olave's," "When I was a Little Girl," &c. Illustrated by FRÖLICH. New Edition. Globe 8vo. 2s. 6d.

NOEL (LADY AUGUSTA).—HITHERSEA MERE. By LADY AUGUSTA NOEL, Author of "Wandering Willie," &c. 3 vols. Crown 8vo. 31s. 6d.

NOEL.—BEATRICE, AND OTHER POEMS. By the HON. RODEN NOEL. Fcap. 8vo. 6s.

NORRIS.—MY FRIEND JIM. By W. E. NORRIS. New and Cheaper Edition. Crown 8vo. 6s.

NORTON.—Works by the Hon. Mrs. NORTON.

THE LADY OF LA GARAYE. With Vignette and Frontispiece. Eighth Edition. Fcap. 8vo. 4s. 6d.

OLD SIR DOUGLAS. New Edition. Crown 8vo. 6s.

OLIPHANT.—Works by Mrs. OLIPHANT.

THE LITERARY HISTORY OF ENGLAND in the end of the Eighteenth and beginning of the Nineteenth Century. Cheaper Issue. With a New Preface. 3 Vols. Demy 8vo. 21s.

AGNES HOPETOUN'S SCHOOLS AND HOLIDAYS. New Edition, with Illustrations. Globe 8vo. 2s. 6d.

THE WIZARD'S SON. New Edition. Crown 8vo. 6s.

HESTER: a Story of Contemporary Life. New Edition. Crown 8vo. 6s.

SIR TOM. Crown 8vo. 6s.

A SON OF THE SOIL. New Edition. Globe 8vo. 2s.

THE CURATE IN CHARGE. New Edition. Globe 8vo. 2s.

YOUNG MUSGRAVE. Cheaper Edition. Globe 8vo. 2s.

HE THAT WILL NOT WHEN HE MAY. Cheaper Edition. Globe 8vo. 2s.

A COUNTRY GENTLEMAN AND HIS FAMILY. Crown 8vo. 6s.

THE SECOND SON. 3 vols. Crown 8vo. 31s. 6d.

THE MAKERS OF FLORENCE: Dante, Giotto, Savonarola, and their City. With Illustrations from Drawings by Professor Delamotte, and a Steel Portrait of Savonarola, engraved by C. H. JEENS. New and Cheaper Edition with Preface. Crown 8vo. Cloth extra. 10s. 6d.

THE MAKERS OF VENICE. A Companion Volume to "The Makers of Florence." With Illustrations. Demy 8vo.   [In the press.

THE BELEAGUERED CITY. Cheaper Edition. Crown 8vo. 6s.

DRESS. Illustrated. Crown 8vo. 2s. 6d.   [Art at Home Series.

OUR YEAR. A Child's Book, in Prose and Verse. By the Author of "John Halifax, Gentleman." Illustrated by CLARENCE DOBELL. Globe 8vo. 2s. 6d.

OWEN.—THE STORY OF CATHERINE. By the Author of "A Lost Love" (ASHFORD OWEN). Crown 8vo. 6s.

PALGRAVE.—Works by FRANCIS TURNER PALGRAVE, M.A., Professor of Poetry in the University of Oxford, late Fellow of Exeter College, Oxford.
THE FIVE DAYS' ENTERTAINMENTS AT WENTWORTH GRANGE. A Book for Children. With Illustrations by ARTHUR HUGHES, and Engraved Title-Page by JEENS. Small 4to, cloth extra. 6s.
LYRICAL POEMS. Extra fcap. 8vo. 6s.
ORIGINAL HYMNS. Third Edition, enlarged 18mo. 1s. 6d.
VISIONS OF ENGLAND ; being a series of Lyrical Poems on Leading Events and Persons in English History. With a Preface and Notes. Crown 8vo. 7s. 6d.
GOLDEN TREASURY OF THE BEST SONGS AND LYRICS. Edited by F. T. PALGRAVE. 18mo. 4s. 6d.
SHAKESPEARE'S SONNETS AND SONGS. Edited by F. T. PALGRAVE. With Vignette Title by JEENS. (Golden Treasury Series.) 18mo. 4s. 6d.
THE CHILDREN'S TREASURY OF LYRICAL POETRY. Selected and arranged with Notes by F. T. PALGRAVE. 18mo. 2s. 6d. And in Two Parts, 1s. each.
HERRICK: SELECTIONS FROM THE LYRICAL POEMS. With Notes. (Golden Treasury Series.) 18mo. 4s. 6d.
LYRICAL POEMS. By ALFRED, LORD TENNYSON, Poet Laureate. Selected and Annotated. (Golden Treasury Series.) 18mo. 4s. 6d.
THE POETICAL WORKS OF JOHN KEATS. Reprinted from the Original Editions. With Notes. (Golden Treasury Series.) 18mo. 4s. 6d.

PANSIE'S FLOUR BIN. By the Author of "When I was a Little Girl," "St. Olave's," &c. Illustrated by ADRIAN STOKES. Globe 8vo. 4s. 6d.

PARKER.—THE NATURE OF THE FINE ARTS. By H. PARKER, M.A., Fellow of Oriel College, Oxford. Crown 8vo. 10s. 6d.

PATER.—Works by WALTER PATER, Fellow of Brasenose College, Oxford:
THE RENAISSANCE. Studies in Art and Poetry. Second Edition, Revised, with Vignette engraved by C. H. JEENS. Crown 8vo. 10s. 6d.
MARIUS, THE EPICUREAN : His Sensations and Ideas. Second and Cheaper Edition. Two Vols. 8vo. 12s.
IMAGINARY PORTRAITS. Extra Crown 8vo. 6s.

PATMORE.—THE CHILDREN'S GARLAND, from the Best Poets· Selected and arranged by COVENTRY PATMORE. New Edition. With Illustrations by J. LAWSON. (Golden Treasury Edition.) 18mo. 4s. 6d. Globe Readings Edition for Schools, Globe 8vo, 2s.

PEEL.—ECHOES FROM HOREB, AND OTHER POEMS. By EDMUND PEEL, Author of "An Ancient City," &c. Crown 8vo. 3s. 6d.

PEOPLE'S EDITIONS. Profusely Illustrated, medium 4to, 6d. each; or complete in One Vol., cloth, 3s.
TOM BROWN'S SCHOOL DAYS. By an Old Boy.
WATERTON'S WANDERINGS IN SOUTH AMERICA.
WASHINGTON IRVING'S OLD CHRISTMAS.
WASHINGTON IRVING'S BRACEBRIDGE HALL.

PHILLIPS (S. K.).—ON THE SEABOARD; and other Poems. By SUSAN K. PHILLIPS. Second Edition. Crown 8vo. 5s.

PINDAR.—THE EXTANT ODES OF PINDAR. Translated into English, with Introduction and short Notes, by ERNEST MYERS, M.A., late Fellow of Wadham College, Oxford. Second Edition. Crown 8vo. 5s.

PLATO.—THE REPUBLIC OF. Translated into English with Notes by J. LL. DAVIES, M.A., and D. J. VAUGHAN, M.A. (Golden Treasury Series). 18mo. 4s. 6d.
THE TRIAL AND DEATH OF SOCRATES: Being the Euthyphron, Apology, Crito, and Phædo of Plato. Translated into English by F. J. CHURCH. 18mo. 4s. 6d. (Golden Treasury Series.)

POEMS OF PLACES—(ENGLAND AND WALES). Edited by H. W. LONGFELLOW. (Golden Treasury Series.) 18mo. 4s. 6d.

POETS (ENGLISH).—SELECTIONS, with Critical Introduction by various writers, and a general Introduction by MATTHEW ARNOLD. Edited by T. H. WARD, M.A. Four Vols. New Edition. Crown 8vo. 7s. 6d. each.
Vol. I. CHAUCER TO DONNE.
Vol. II. BEN JONSON TO DRYDEN.
Vol. III. ADDISON TO BLAKE.
Vol. IV. WORDSWORTH TO ROSSETTI.

POOLE.—PICTURES OF COTTAGE LIFE IN THE WEST OF ENGLAND. By MARGARET E. POOLE. New and Cheaper Edition. With Frontispiece by R. FARREN. Crown 8vo. 3s. 6d.

POPE.—POETICAL WORKS OF. Edited with Notes and Introductory Memoir by ADOLPHUS WILLIAM WARD, M.A. (Globe Edition.) Globe 8vo. 3s. 6d.

POTTER.—LANCASHIRE MEMORIES. By LOUISA POTTER. Crown 8vo. 6s.

REALMAH.—By the Author of "Friends in Council." Crown 8vo. 6s.

REED.—MEMOIR OF SIR CHARLES REED. By His Son, CHARLES E. B. REED, M.A. With a Portrait. Crown 8vo. 4s. 6d.

ROBINSON CRUSOE. Edited, with Biographical Introduction, by HENRY KINGSLEY. (Globe Edition.) Globe 8vo. 3s. 6d.—Golden Treasury Edition. Edited by J. W. CLARK, M.A. 18mo. 4s. 6d.

ROPES.—POEMS. By ARTHUR REED ROPES. Fcap. 8vo. 3s. 6d.

ROSS.—A MISGUIDIT LASSIE. By PERCY ROSS. Crown 8vo. 4s. 6d.

ROSSETTI.—Works by CHRISTINA ROSSETTI.
POEMS. Complete Edition, containing "Goblin Market," "The Prince's Progress," &c. With Four Illustrations by D. G. ROSSETTI. Extra fcap. 8vo. 6s.
A PAGEANT, AND OTHER POEMS. Extra fcap. 8vo. 6s.
SPEAKING LIKENESSES. Illustrated by ARTHUR HUGHES. Crown 8vo, gilt edges. 4s. 6d.

ROSSETTI (D.G.).—DANTE GABRIEL ROSSETTI: a Record and a Study. By WILLIAM SHARP. With an Illustration after Dante Gabriel Rossetti. Crown 8vo. 10s. 6d.

RUNAWAY, THE. By the Author of "Mrs. Jerningham's Journal." With Illustrations. Globe 8vo. 2s. 6d.

RUTH AND HER FRIENDS. A Story for Girls. With a Frontispiece. New Edition. Globe 8vo. 2s. 6d.

ST. JOHNSTON.—Works by ALFRED ST. JOHNSTON:
CAMPING AMONG CANNIBALS. Crown 8vo. 4s. 6d.
CHARLIE ASGARDE. A Tale of Adventure. A Story for Boys. Crown 8vo. 5s.

SCOTT (SIR WALTER).—POETICAL WORKS OF. Edited with a Biographical and Critical Memoir by FRANCIS TURNER PALGRAVE. (Globe Edition.) Globe 8vo. 3s. 6d.
THE LAY OF THE LAST MINSTREL; and THE LADY OF THE LAKE. Edited, with Introduction and Notes, by FRANCIS TURNER PALGRAVE. Globe 8vo. 1s. (Globe Readings for Schools.)
MARMION ; and THE LORD OF THE ISLES. By the same Editor. Globe 8vo. 1s. (Globe Readings for Schools.)

SCOTTISH SONG.—A SELECTION OF THE CHOICEST LYRICS OF SCOTLAND. By MARY CARLYLE AITKEN. (Golden Treasury Series.) 18mo. 4s. 6d.

SEELEY.—THE EXPANSION OF ENGLAND. Two Courses of Lectures. By J. R. SEELEY, M.A., Regius Professor of Modern History in the University of Cambridge, Fellow of Gonville and Caius College, &c. Crown 8vo. 4s. 6d.

SELBORNE (EARL).—THE BOOK OF PRAISE. From the best English Hymn writers. By the Right Hon. the EARL OF SELBORNE. (Golden Treasury Series.) 18mo. 4s. 6d.

SERMONS OUT OF CHURCH. By the Author of "John Halifax, Gentleman." Crown 8vo. 6s.

SHAKESPEARE.—The Works of WILLIAM SHAKESPEARE. Cambridge Edition. Edited by W. GEORGE CLARK, M.A., and W. ALDIS WRIGHT, M.A. Nine Vols. 8vo, cloth. [A New Edition in the press.

SHAKESPEARE'S COMPLETE WORKS. Edited, by W. G. CLARK, M.A., and W. ALDIS WRIGHT, M.A. (Globe Edition.) Globe 8vo. 3s. 6d.

SHAKESPEARE'S SONGS AND SONNETS. Edited, with Notes, by FRANCIS TURNER PALGRAVE. (Golden Treasury Series.) 18mo. 4s. 6d.

SHAKESPEARE.—CHARLES LAMB'S TALES FROM SHAKE-SPEARE. Edited, with Preface, by Rev. A. AINGER. Globe 8vo. 5s. (Golden Treasury Edition). 18mo. 4s. 6d. Globe Readings Edition for Schools, Globe 8vo, 2s.
THE VICTORIA SHAKESPEARE.

SHAKESPEARE.—The Works of WILLIAM SHAKESPEARE. In 3 vols., Crown 8vo, 6s. each. Vol. I., COMEDIES. Vol. II., HISTORIES. Vol. III., TRAGEDIES.
₊ This Edition, dedicated by permission to Her Majesty the Queen, is from the text of the GLOBE EDITION, and is printed by R. and R. Clark of Edinburgh. No pains have been spared to produce an edition at once convenient and beautiful. A new Glossary, more complete than in any other popular edition of Shakespeare, has been specially prepared by Mr. ALDIS WRIGHT. The Volumes may be obtained separately.

SHELLEY.—POEMS OF SHELLEY. Edited by STOPFORD A. BROOKE, (Golden Treasury Series.) 18mo. 4s. 6d. Also a fine Edition printed on hand-made paper. Crown 8vo. 12s. 6d.

SHORTHOUSE.—Works by J. H. SHORTHOUSE.
JOHN INGLESANT : A ROMANCE. Crown 8vo. 6s.
THE LITTLE SCHOOLMASTER MARK. A Spiritual Romance. In Two Parts. Crown 8vo. 2s. 6d. each ; or complete in one volume, 4s. 6d.
SIR PERCIVAL : a Story of the Past and of the Present. Crown 8vo. 6s.

SKRINE.—UNDER TWO QUEENS. Lyrics written for the Tercentenary Festival of the Founding of Uppingham School. By JOHN HUNTLEY SKRINE, Author of "Uppingham by the Sea, ' &c. Crown 8vo. 3s.

SLIP IN THE FENS, A.—New and Popular Edition. Globe 8vo. 2s.

SMITH.—POEMS. By CATHERINE BARNARD SMITH. Fcap. 8vo. 5s.

SMITH.—THREE ENGLISH STATESMEN. A Course of Lectures on the Political History of England. By GOLDWIN SMITH. New Edition. Crown 8vo. 5s.

SONG BOOK. WORDS AND TUNES FROM THE BEST POETS AND MUSICIANS. Selected and arranged by JOHN HULLAH. (Golden Treasury Series.) 18mo. 4s. 6d.

SOPHOCLES.—OEDIPUS THE KING. Translated from the Greek of Sophocles into English Verse by E. D. A. MORSHEAD, M.A., late Fellow of New College, Oxford, Assistant Master at Winchester College. Fcap. 8vo. 3s. 6d.

SPENSER.—COMPLETE WORKS OF. Edited by the Rev. R. MORRIS, M.A., LL.D., with a Memoir by J. W. HALES, M.A. (Globe Edition.) Globe 8vo. 3s. 6d.

STANLEY.—Addresses and Sermons delivered during a Visit to the United States and Canada in 1878. By ARTHUR PENRHYN STANLEY, D.D., late Dean of Westminster. Crown 8vo. 6s.

STEPHEN (C. E.).—THE SERVICE OF THE POOR; being an Inquiry into the Reasons for and against the Establishment of Religious Sister-hoods for Charitable Purposes. By CAROLINE EMILIA STEPHEN. Crown 8vo. 6s. 6d.

STEPHENS (J. B.).—CONVICT ONCE: and other Poems. By J. BRUNTON STEPHENS. New Edition. Crown 8vo. 7s. 6d.

STEWART.—THE TALE OF TROY. Done into English by AUBREY STEWART, M.A., late Fellow of Trinity College, Cambridge. Globe 8vo. 3s. 6d.

STRETTELL.—SPANISH AND ITALIAN FOLK SONGS. Trans-lated by ALMA STRETTELL. With Photogravures after Sketches by JOHN S. SARGENT, E. A. ABBEY, MORELLI, and W. PADGETT. Royal 16mo. 12s. 6d.

TANNER.—THE ABBOT'S FARM: or, PRACTICE WITH SCIENCE. By HENRY TANNER, M.R.A.C., F.C.S., late Professor of Principles of Agriculture in the Royal Agricultural College; Examiner in the Principles of Agriculture under the Government Department of Science. Author of "First Principles of Agriculture," &c. Extra fcap. 8vo. 3s. 6d.

TENNYSON.—Works by LORD TENNYSON, D.C.L., Poet Laureate.
COMPLETE WORKS. New and Revised Edition, with New Portrait. Crown 8vo. 7s. 6d.
COMPLETE WORKS. An Edition for Schools. In Four Parts. Crown 8vo. 2s. 6d. each.
COLLECTED WORKS. In Seven Volumes. Fcap. 8vo. 5s. each.
(A limited number of copies are printed on Hand-made Paper. This Edition is sold only in Sets, price £3 13s. 6d.)
    Vol. I. EARLY POEMS.
    Vol. II. LUCRETIUS: and other POEMS.
    Vol. III. IDYLLS OF THE KING.
    Vol. IV. THE PRINCESS: and MAUD.
    Vol. V. ENOCH ARDEN: and IN MEMORIAM.
    Vol. VI. QUEEN MARY: and HAROLD.
    Vol. VII. BALLADS: and other POEMS.
MINIATURE EDITION. A New Edition, printed by R. & R. Clark of Edinburgh.
    THE POETICAL WORKS. 10 Volumes. In a Box. 21s.
    THE DRAMATIC WORKS. 4 Volumes. In a Box. 10s. 6d.

TENNYSON.—Works by LORD TENNYSON, D.C.L., Poet Laureate—*continued.*

LYRICAL POEMS. Selected and Annotated by FRANCIS TURNER PALGRAVE. (Golden Treasury Series.) 18mo. 4s. 6d. Large Paper Edition. 8vo. 9s.
IN MEMORIAM. 18mo. 4s. 6d. Large Paper Edition. 8vo. 9s.
THE TENNYSON BIRTHDAY BOOK. Edited by EMILY SHAKESPEAR. In two sizes. (1) Extra Fcap. 8vo. Edition on Hand-made Paper with red lines. 5s. (2) 14mo. 2s. 6d.
THE BROOK. With 20 Illustrations in Colours, by A. WOODRUFF. Medium. 32mo. 2s. 6d.

THE ORIGINAL EDITIONS. Fcap. 8vo. :—

POEMS. 6s.
MAUD: and other POEMS. 3s. 6d.
THE PRINCESS. 3s. 6d.
IDYLLS OF THE KING. (Collected.) 6s.
ENOCH ARDEN: &c. 3s. 6d.
THE HOLY GRAIL: and other POEMS. 4s. 6d.
IN MEMORIAM. 4s.
BALLADS: and other POEMS. 5s.
HAROLD: a Drama. 6s.
QUEEN MARY: a Drama. 6s.
THE CUP: and the FALCON. 5s.
BECKET. 6s.
TIRESIAS: and other POEMS. 6s.
LOCKSLEY HALL, SIXTY YEARS AFTER, and other Poems. 6s.

TENNYSON (HON. HALLAM).—JACK AND THE BEAN-STALK. A Version in Hexameters by the Honourable HALLAM TENNYSON. With 40 Illustrations by RANDOLPH CALDECOTT. Small 4to. 3s. 6d.

TENNYSON'S "IN MEMORIAM": ITS PURPOSE AND ITS STRUCTURE. A Study. By JOHN F. GENUNG. Crown 8vo. 5s.

THIRTY YEARS.—BEING POEMS NEW AND OLD. By the Author of "John Halifax, Gentleman." New Edition. Crown 8vo. 6s.

THROUGH THE RANKS TO A COMMISSION.—*New and Cheaper Edition.* Crown 8vo. 2s. 6d.

TOM BROWN'S SCHOOL DAYS. By AN OLD BOY. With Seven Illustrations by A. HUGHES and SYDNEY HALL. Crown 8vo. 6s.; Golden Treasury Edition. 4s. 6d.; People's Edition. 2s. People's Sixpenny Illustrated Edition. Medium 4to. 6d. Illustrated Edition, printed on fine paper. Extra Crown 8vo. 10s. 6d.

TOM BROWN AT OXFORD. New Edition. With Illustrations. Crown 8vo. 6s.

TOURGÉNIEF.—VIRGIN SOIL. By I. TOURGÉNIEF. Translated by ASHTON W. DILKE. Cheaper Edition. Crown 8vo. 6s.

TREVELYAN.—CAWNPORE. By the Right Honourable Sir GEORGE O. TREVELYAN, Bart., M.P., Author of "The Competition Wallah." New Edition. Crown 8vo. 6s.

TURNER.—COLLECTED SONNETS, OLD AND NEW. By CHARLES TENNYSON TURNER. Extra fcap. 8vo. 7s. 6d.

TYRWHITT.—OUR SKETCHING CLUB. Letters and Studies on Landscape Art. By the Rev. R. ST. JOHN TYRWHITT, M.A. With an Authorised Reproduction of the Lessons and Woodcuts in Professor Ruskin's "Elements of Drawing." New Edition. Crown 8vo. 7s. 6d.

VELEY.—(Works by MARGARET VELEY, Author of "For· Percival.")
MITCHELHURST PLACE. New and Cheaper Edition. Crown 8vo. 6s.
A GARDEN OF MEMORIES; MRS. AUSTIN; LIZZIE'S BARGAIN.
Three Stories. 2 vols. Globe 8vo. 12s.

VIRGIL.—THE WORKS OF. Rendered into English Prose. By JAMES
LONSDALE, M.A., and SAMUEL LEE, M.A. (Globe Edition.) Globe 8vo. 3s. 6d.

VIRGIL.—THE AENEID. Translated into English Prose by J. W. MACKAIL.
M.A., Fellow of Balliol College, Oxford. Crown 8vo. 7s. 6d.

VOICES CRYING IN THE WILDERNESS. A Novel. Crown
8vo. 7s. 6d.

WARD.—ENGLISH POETS. Selections, with Critical Introduction by
various writers, and a general Introduction by MATTHEW ARNOLD. Edited by
T. H. WARD, M.A. Four Vols. Crown 8vo. 7s. 6d. each.
Vol. I. CHAUCER TO DONNE.
Vol. II BEN JONSON TO DRYDEN
Vol. III. ADDISON TO BLAKE.
Vol. IV. WORDSWORTH TO ROSSETTI.

WARD (SAMUEL).—LYRICAL RECREATIONS. By SAMUEL WARD.
Fcap. 8vo. 6s.

WARD (MRS. HUMPHRY).—Works by Mrs. HUMPHRY WARD:
MILLY AND OLLY; or, a Holiday among the Mountains. Illustrated by
Mrs. ALMA TADEMA. Globe 8vo. 2s. 6d.
MISS BRETHERTON. Crown 8vo. 6s.
THE JOURNAL INTIME OF HENRI-FREDERIC AMIEL. Translated,
with an Introduction and Notes, by Mrs. HUMPHRY WARD. In Two Vols.
Globe 8vo. 12s.

WEBSTER.—Works by AUGUSTA WEBSTER.
DRAMATIC STUDIES. Extra fcap. 8vo. 5s.
A WOMAN SOLD, AND OTHER POEMS. Crown 8vo. 7s. 6d.
PORTRAITS. Second Edition. Extra fcap. 8vo. 3s. 6d.
THE AUSPICIOUS DAY. A Dramatic Poem. Extra fcap. 8vo. 5s.
YU-PE-YA'S LUTE. A Chinese Tale in English Verse. Extra fcap. 8vo. 3s. 6d.
A HOUSEWIFE'S OPINIONS. Crown 8vo. 7s. 6d.
A BOOK OF RHYME. Crown 8vo. 3s. 6d.
DAFFODIL AND THE CROAXAXICANS. A Romance of History. Crown
8vo. 6s.

WESTBURY.—FREDERICK HAZZLEDEN. By HUGH WESTBURY.
3 vols. Crown 8vo. 31s. 6d.

WHEN I WAS A LITTLE GIRL. By the Author of "St Olaves."
Illustrated by L. FRÖLICH. Globe 8vo. 2s. 6d.

WHEN PAPA COMES HOME : The Story of Tip, Tap, Toe. By
the Author of "Nine Years Old," "Pansie's Flour Bin," &c. With Illustrations
by W. J. HENNESSY. Globe 8vo. 4s. 6d.

WHITTIER.—JOHN GREENLEAF WHITTIER'S POETICAL WORKS
Complete Edition, with Portrait engraved by C. H. JEENS. 18mo. 4s. 6d.

WILBRAHAM.—THE SERE AND YELLOW LEAF: Thoughts and' Recollections for Old and Young. By FRANCES W. WILBRAHAM, Author of "Streets and Lanes of a City." With a Preface by the Right Rev. W. WALS-HAM HOW, D.D., Bishop of Bedford, Suffragan of London. Globe 8vo. 3s. 6d.

WILLOUGHBY.—FAIRY GUARDIANS. A Book for the Young. By F. WILLOUGHBY. Illustrated. Crown 8vo, gilt. 5s.

WILLS.—MELCHOIR: A Poem. By W. G. WILLS, Author of "Charles I.," "Olivia," &c., Writer of "Claudian." Crown 8vo. 9s.

WOOD.—THE ISLES OF THE BLEST, and other POEMS. By ANDREW GOLDIE WOOD. Globe 8vo. 5s.

WOODS.—A FIRST SCHOOL POETRY. Compiled by M. A. WOODS, Head Mistress of the Clifton High School for Girls. Fcap. 8vo. 2s. 6d.
A SECOND SCHOOL POETRY BOOK. By the same. Fcap. 8vo. 4s. 6d.

WOOLNER.—Works by THOMAS WOOLNER, R.A.
MY BEAUTIFUL LADY. With a Vignette by A. HUGHES. Third Edition. Fcap. 8vo. 5s.
PYGMALION. A Poem. Crown 8vo. 7s. 6d.
SILENUS: a Poem. Crown 8vo. 6s.

WORDS FROM THE POETS. Selected by the Editor of "Rays of Sunlight." With a Vignette and Frontispiece. 18mo, limp. 1s.

WORDSWORTH.—SELECT POEMS OF. Chosen and Edited, with Preface, by MATTHEW ARNOLD. (Golden Treasury Series.) 18mo. 4s. 6d. Fine Edition. Crown 8vo, hand-made paper, with Portrait of Wordsworth engraved by C. H. JEENS, and Printed on India Paper. 9s.

YONGE (C. M.).—New Illustrated Edition of Novels and Tales by CHAR-LOTTE M. YONGE. In Twenty-six Volumes. Crown 8vo. 6s. each :—

Vol. I. THE HEIR OF REDCLYFFE. With Illustrations by KATE GREEN-AWAY.

II. HEARTSEASE. With Illustrations by KATE GREENAWAY.

III. HOPES AND FEARS. With Illustrations by HERBERT GANDY.

IV. DYNEVOR TERRACE. With Illustrations by ADRIAN STOKES.

V. THE DAISY CHAIN. Illustrated by J. P. ATKINSON.

VI. THE TRIAL. Illustrated by J. P. ATKINSON.

VII. & VIII. THE PILLARS OF THE HOUSE; or, UNDER WODE, UNDER RODE. Illustrated by HERBERT GANDY. Two Vols.

IX. THE YOUNG STEPMOTHER. New Edition. Illustrated by MARIAN HUXLEY.

X. CLEVER WOMAN OF THE FAMILY. New Edition. Illustrated by ADRIAN STOKES.

XI. THE THREE BRIDES. Illustrated by ADRIAN STOKES.

XII. MY YOUNG ALCIDES; or, A FADED PHOTOGRAPH. Illustrated by ADRIAN STOKES.

XIII. THE CAGED LION. Illustrated by W. J. HENNESSY.

XIV. THE DOVE IN THE EAGLE'S NEST. Illustrated by W. J. HENNESSY.

XV. THE CHAPLET OF PEARLS; or, THE WHITE AND BLACK RIBAUMONT. Illustrated by W. J. HENNESSY.

XVI. LADY HESTER: AND THE DANVERS PAPERS. Illustrated by JANE E. COOK.

YONGE (C.M.).—Works by CHARLOTTE M. YONGE—*continued*—

XVII. MAGNUM BONUM; or, MOTHER CAREY'S BROOD. Illustrated by W. J. HENNESSY.

XVIII. LOVE AND LIFE. Illustrated by W. J. HENNESSY.

XIX. UNKNOWN TO HISTORY. A Story of the Captivity of Mary of Scotland. Illustrated by W. J. HENNESSY.

XX. STRAY PEARLS: MEMOIRS OF MARGARET DE RIBAUMONT, VISCOUNTESS OF BELLAISE. Illustrated by W. J. HENNESSY.

XXI. THE ARMOURER'S PRENTICES. Illustrated by W. J. HENNESSY.

XXII.—THE TWO SIDES OF THE SHIELD. Illustrated by W. J. HENNESSY.

XXIII.—NUTTIE'S FATHER. Illustrated by W. J. HENNESSY.

XXIV.—SCENES AND CHARACTERS. Illustrated by W. J. HENNESSY.

XXV.—CHANTRY HOUSE. Illustrated by W. J. HENNESSY.

XXVI.—A MODERN TELEMACHUS. Illustrated by W. J. HENNESSY.

THE PRINCE AND THE PAGE. A Tale of the Last Crusade. Illustrated. New Edition. Globe 8vo. 4s. 6d.

THE LANCES OF LYNWOOD. New Edition. With Illustrations. Globe 8vo. 4s. 6d.

THE LITTLE DUKE: RICHARD THE FEARLESS. New Edition. Illustrated. Globe 8vo. 4s. 6d.

A BOOK OF GOLDEN DEEDS OF ALL TIMES AND ALL COUN-TRIES, Gathered and Narrated Anew. (Golden Treasury Series.) 4s. 6d. Globe Readings Edition for Schools, Globe 8vo, 2s. Cheap Edition. 1s.

LITTLE LUCY'S WONDERFUL GLOBE. Illustrated by L. FRÖLICH. Globe 8vo. 4s. 6d.

A BOOK OF WORTHIES. (Golden Treasury Series.) 18mo. 4s. 6d.

THE STORY OF THE CHRISTIANS AND MOORS IN SPAIN: (Golden Treasury Series.) 18mo. 4s. 6d.

CAMEOS FROM ENGLISH HISTORY, From ROLLO to EDWARD II. Third Edition, enlarged. Extra fcap. 8vo. 5s.

SECOND SERIES. THE WARS IN FRANCE. New Edition. Extra fcap. 8vo. 5s.

THIRD SERIES. THE WARS OF THE ROSES. Extra fcap. 8vo. 5s.

FOURTH SERIES. REFORMATION TIMES. Extra fcap. 8vo. 5s.

FIFTH SERIES. ENGLAND AND SPAIN. Extra fcap. 8vo. 5s.

SIXTH SERIES. FORTY YEARS OF STEWART RULE. 1603-1643. Extra Fcap. 8vo. 5s.

P'S AND Q'S; or, THE QUESTION OF PUTTING UPON. With Illustrations by C. O. MURRAY. New Edition. Globe 8vo, cloth gilt. 4s. 6d.

DYEWORDS: A COLLECTION OF TALES NEW AND OLD. Crown 8vo. 6s.

HISTORY OF CHRISTIAN NAMES. New Edition, revised. Crown 8vo. 7s. 6d.

THE HERB OF THE FIELD. Reprinted from "Chapters on Flowers" in *The Magazine for the Young.* A New Edition Revised and Corrected. Crown 8vo. 5s.

MACMILLAN AND CO., LONDON.

RICHARD CLAY AND SONS, LONDON AND BUNGAY.